*USA TODAY* BESTSELLING AUTHOR

# DALE MAYER

## A Psychic Visions Novel

# ENDGAME

ENDGAME
Beverly Dale Mayer
Valley Publishing Ltd.

Copyright © 2025



ISBN-13: 978-1-778866-80-7
Print Edition

## Books in This Series:

Tuesday's Child
Hide 'n Go Seek
Maddy's Floor
Garden of Sorrow
Knock Knock…
Rare Find
Eyes to the Soul
Now You See Her
Shattered
Into the Abyss
Seeds of Malice
Eye of the Falcon
Itsy-Bitsy Spider
Unmasked
Deep Beneath
From the Ashes
Stroke of Death
Ice Maiden
Snap, Crackle…
What If…
Talking Bones
String of Tears
Inked Forever

Insanity

Soul Legacy

Coveted

Endgame

A Mother's Love

Boxed Sets and Bundles

https://geni.us/Bundlepage

## About This Book

Tandy's every instinct told her to jump in and to take over the care of her two half siblings. They were twins, born to her mother later in life. Tandy hadn't been in a position to help her older siblings, a guilt that still ate at her. These twins, however, had special needs, and she wasn't sure she was up for the challenge. Nonverbal, they appeared to live in an alternate world, one she didn't know how to reach.

Keller worked alongside Grant in the FBI and was considering how his own growing psychic skills could be better utilized, when he was asked to help on a case that had very unusual elements. These were elements that Stefan and Dr. Maddy hadn't seen before—and that was saying something.

Not until he meets Tandy does Keller realize how unusual and potentially sinister this case truly is …

**Sign up to be notified of all Dale's releases here!**
https://geni.us/DaleNews

# CHAPTER 1

S TEFAN PICKED UP the phone, his tone warm and cheerful. "Dr. Maddy, it's always good to hear from you."

Her tone on the other end was stark and devoid of all humor. "We'll see how you feel when you hear what I'm calling about."

Immediately his good mood fled, and he nodded. "It's so often that way between us, isn't it?"

"It shouldn't be though," she grumbled, "and I wouldn't be calling about this if I had any solution."

"Which means you don't, so speak up. What's going on?" he asked.

"Twins, boys, five years old, nonverbal, both synesthetes."

"Seriously?" Stefan asked in astonishment. "Nonverbal? How do you know that they're synesthetes?"

"Well, I wouldn't, except for what appears to be an older sister, who brought them in to me as a special request. Honestly, she's been emailing and calling me for quite a while, looking for some assistance," she explained. "Normally I wouldn't take on anything like this, but this case? … As soon as she said they were both synesthetes and both nonverbal, it really piqued my interest."

"Naturally," Stefan confirmed. "So, what did you find?"

"Well, it's more about what I didn't find," she shared, "and it makes no sense, but, according to the older sister—"

"How much older is this sister?" he asked, immediately interrupting.

"Quite a bit from looking at her, but I don't really know. I would say, early thirties, as a rough guess."

"And they're siblings? That's an awful lot of years between them."

"According to the sister, the mother was a drug addict and took drugs quite freely throughout the pregnancies. This sister was the result of a teenage pregnancy, and then her mother lost several children in between, including a couple lost to the foster care system. This older sister spent time with her grandmother to avoid foster care, but the grandmother couldn't handle all the younger ones, and there was a lot of back-and-forth among all the children and the mother, the grandmother, and foster care.

"Once this elder sister was old enough to be out on her own, she worked hard to improve her circumstances and to build something better, trying to move on from such a chaotic childhood. Meanwhile, her mother kept making poor decisions and, at some point, became pregnant with these twins.

"This older sister had gone into early childhood development and, after her mother died of a drug overdose, ended up caring for these siblings, who were almost five at that point in time. So I think she's only had them for a few months. Her mother didn't tell her about any of the developmental issues, and this sister had been away from the family house long enough that the kids were strangers to her, and she didn't know what she was even looking at.

"She found a letter from her mother, explaining something about the twins, even adding that the mother herself also had the same abilities but never managed to learn or to make sense out of anything she saw in the world. Drugs provided a far easier way to handle it, so that's what she did. Of course the older sister is quite pissed, but she's also very worried about how best to care for these children."

"Well, that's wonderful of her," Stefan stated. "A lot of people wouldn't take on children like that."

"No, but I think she's in a quandary and not at all sure what she's supposed to do to help them."

"What is it you're supposed to do?" Stefan asked, letting the humor back into his tone. "People ask all kinds of things, but we don't always have answers."

"No, no we don't," Dr. Maddy agreed, "though I did sit down and do a full physical on the twins."

"And?"

"Physically I would say that they're fairly healthy," she shared. "I'm not sure of the reason they are nonverbal. I didn't see anything suggesting they had any kind of health condition that prompted that type of response. However …"

"Ah," Stefan noted, "here comes the famous however."

She groaned. "I definitely feel there's an issue between them that is not of this plane."

Stefan let that sink in, as the silence deepened between them. "And did you get any idea of just what is wrong on the other plane?"

"No," she admitted, "and I guess that is why I'm so stumped and kind of upset because I can't see what is happening."

"So, you want me to take a look?" he suggested.

"I know you're busy, but I was wondering if that was … possible."

"Are they in our children's hospital?"

"No, that's the other thing. I have found no medical condition that requires hospitalization for these two boys. Just because they're nonverbal doesn't mean they can't lead full, healthy, happy functioning lives."

"No, of course not," he murmured. "So, they're at home?"

"Temporarily I have them here at Dr. Maddy's floor," she said and then took a deep breath. "And I mean temporarily. It's certainly not a place for them, if that's not where they need to be, and, of course, all the beds here are at a premium."

"Of course," he agreed. "So I presume you had somebody moved out in time for them to come in."

"Yes," she said, "and the twins absolutely love being here, but it's not where they belong. I think the sister is relieved that we're at least looking at this, but she wants answers that I'm not sure we have."

"Of course not, and answers of this nature are never easy to give anybody anyway. Do you have any idea if she has abilities?"

"Oh," Dr. Maddy said, "I didn't even think to ask her that, and I don't think she would consider any of this in the realm of abilities. She doesn't know quite what synesthetes or synesthesia means, though she did look up the terms. So she has a basic clinical understanding but doesn't really understand what form the twins have. The mother said something about colors."

"Absolutely nothing wrong with that," Stefan declared, with a note of humor, "and in many ways that just enhances their daily existence."

"And potentially," Dr. Maddy murmured, "that's why

they want to stay where they are."

"That's also an interesting theory," he muttered. "I can take a look at them this afternoon, if you are okay with that."

"I would really like that," she said warmly, "particularly … No, I won't give you any heads-up. You let me know what you find."

"Is this something you haven't seen before?"

"Honestly," she replied, "I'm pretty sure it's something you haven't seen before either."

# CHAPTER 2

TANDY GOODMAN SLOUCHED into the chair and stared at her phone yet again. She hated being as attached to it as she was, but she kept waiting for answers from Dr. Maddy, from anybody. Tandy felt horribly guilty yet wasn't sure what she could even do up until now. Of course Tandy knew about the twins. Her mother had called several times over recent years, leaving voicemails looking for assistance with them, but Tandy had refused to answer or to respond to her mother's calls. Tandy had walked away from her mother years ago and had been more than happy to keep it that way. Her mother had always needed financial assistance, emotional support, and so much more besides that.

For the first time, Tandy cursed her mother for most likely committing suicide by willfully overdosing. Yet she also knew her mother had been in a bad mental state, and it wasn't fair to judge her, particularly when Tandy hadn't been around to step up to help. Then again, what do you do with a parent who hadn't been a parent and instead had fobbed off you and the rest of your siblings onto the foster care system or any other relative who would take in some-body, anybody? A mother who then continued to have children without a thought or care for what would happen to them—or what was happening to the others she had already had. Tandy still remained a little bitter, although she very much wanted to think she'd worked out all that, but obviously she hadn't.

When the phone rang, she jumped at it. "Hello," she answered. She frowned at the strange voice on the other end.

"My name is Stefan," he announced. "I've been asked by Dr. Maddy to take a look at your siblings and to see what I can make of the situation."

"Thank you." She sighed with relief. "Are you a doctor?"

"I'm a specialist," he clarified, with a note of humor.

"Okay, and what, if anything, did you find?"

"If anything?" he asked.

She frowned. "The note from my mother revealed they were nonverbal—and had been for years—but she didn't say from birth," Tandy pointed out. "I know it may sound very strange, but I don't know very much about them."

"You haven't had anything to do with them in all these years?" he asked.

As seemingly no judgment filled his tone, she relaxed a bit. "No, I didn't have a great relationship with my mother and left as soon as I could. Any actual parenting I had was mostly done by my grandmother, and that was on my father's side, and she didn't have any use for my mother either."

"I'm sorry," Stefan muttered. "That just makes it hard on everybody."

"It sure does," Tandy agreed, with a note of surprise, "and now I'm not sure what I can do for the twins."

"Your mother just gave you guardianship of these two?" he asked, his tone still calm and quiet.

Maybe it was the whole general atmosphere around him that made her answer him so readily. "Yes. I believe she took her own life and left the guardianship of these two with me, but why she would do that, I don't know. She didn't leave a letter explaining herself, just sharing her decision to appoint me as their guardian."

"Probably because she assumed that you would be a better parent than she was."

"And yet how could she possibly know that?" Tandy asked in frustration. "I haven't had anything to do with her, and now, all of a sudden, I have these twins in my care."

"Do you have any other children?"

"No. If my childhood had been anything close to normal, I might have had some of my own. Yet I felt I didn't need to add any more neglected children to this world. I've always thought enough abused children were out there."

Immediately Stefan picked up on the word *abused.*

She groaned. "Forget I mentioned that."

"I will for the moment," he conceded. "Do you know that these children were abused?"

"I don't know anything about them. I don't know who she lived with these past years. I don't know if anyone else may have harmed them. I don't know anything," she cried out. "I literally got a call from the police, saying my mother had died, likely of an overdose, and a note had been found, saying to call me if anything happened to her and that I would take care of the twins."

"But she did that without asking you beforehand, right?"

"Of course." Tandy groaned. "That was my mother. She did all kinds of crap that you wished she wouldn't do, yet it didn't matter because she was who she was."

"And just that alone," Stefan noted, "makes it doubly hard when you lose a parent. In these cases, you feel guilty because you didn't have more of a relationship and yet a sense of relief because all that craziness you've endured your whole life finally stops."

Tandy stared down at the phone and whispered, "It's almost as if you know."

"I do know," he confirmed in a gentle tone. "Not all of us have such messed-up lives, but many of us do. And, in your case, what I presume was a relatively calm life you've carved out for yourself away from your mother has now gone haywire, bringing back all those feelings of chaos and anger."

"Yes."

Silence came. Then in a solemn tone, he asked, "Are you looking to put them into foster care?"

"I don't know that I have a choice," she admitted. "I certainly don't feel equipped to handle two children I don't even know, who appear to have special needs that I don't know anything about or how to handle."

"Which is also why," he added, his tone turning brisk, "it's so interesting that your mother left them with you."

"I don't think it's interesting at all," she declared, with a snort. "I think it's typical of my mother to step away from her own responsibilities and to let somebody else handle the mess she created. She did it to my grandmother for years."

"And I understand you have other siblings."

"Apparently so," she muttered, "and you'll think even worse of me, but I haven't done anything to track them down either."

After a bit of silence on the other end, he added, "We're so good at trashing ourselves for not being a better person, aren't we?"

That brought tears to her eyes. "I don't know why you would say that," she whispered, "but, yeah, any normal person would have tried to find them and to bring the family together."

"With the foster care system and adoptions, it can be hard to trace these children, especially as a civilian, even as a relative. Yet we can also hope that the children have landed in good families where they are currently settled. As much as they might want to know that they have another sibling, it doesn't mean that they need you to step up and to take care of them."

"I so hope that could be true," she replied fervently. "God knows I have enough guilt in my world right now, and I can't really handle much more."

"Of course not," he agreed. "I understand there's also a massive age gap between the twins and you."

"Yes. They're only five, and I've just turned thirty," she shared, with a note of humor. "My mother was nothing if not prolific."

"Too bad she didn't think beyond the point of conception."

"Yeah, too bad for a lot of things. I just want to know what the twins need, so I can figure out whether I can handle this or even should consider taking them on."

"Is there an alternative?"

"I don't know," she admitted. "Nothing I know of besides foster care. At this point in time, I'm questioning everything."

"And do you work?"

"Yes, I work full-time just to support myself." She didn't go into any specifics.

Stefan asked, "Do you have any experience with children?"

"No, not really," she murmured. "My mother seemed to think I had gone into childcare, and, as far as she's concerned, that made me the best person to look after them."

"Ah, that would make sense." Then his tone sharpened. "I gather that's not what you did."

"No, it's not what I did," she muttered. "Though right about now I wish I did have some child-care experience. Instead, I went to school to become a nurse."

"That's also a great profession."

"It's certainly one I thought would put food on the table better than being in the daycare field or early childhood development," she muttered. "I didn't dare tell my mother."

"Your mother would have asked for money, I presume?"

"As she did constantly anyway, even after I broke all contact, yes," she confirmed. "Sometimes there's just nothing you can do to help people, especially if they aren't helping themselves. Then suddenly they're gone, and you wonder if you were supposed to do so much more."

"There's always more anybody can do, but, when addiction and drugs are involved," he explained, "there is a limit to what anybody else can do, especially if the addict doesn't choose to help themselves."

"And yet if we had given her a little more time, a little more of a chance," she stated, "maybe she would have beaten it."

"Maybe," he replied, "maybe she would have. But there's also a damn-good chance that things would have continued exactly as they were, and she could have had another half-dozen babies."

"God," Tandy muttered, as she rubbed her head. "I don't even want to think about that."

"I'm going in to see them tomorrow," he announced.

"Wait. I thought you already saw them."

"Briefly, yes, but I want to go in and run some tests."

"Go ahead. I know they can't stay there for long, and

Dr. Maddy is only doing this because I pushed so hard to get some help, but I'm really at my wit's end. I don't want to put the kids into foster care, and I don't have any money saved up for the level of care that they would need privately. So, if anybody can do anything, I would appreciate a heads-up as to the best direction to go."

"Will do," Stefan replied cheerfully. "I'll call you afterward." With that, he ended the call.

Tandy stared down at her phone, wondering just what the heck that was all about because surely he could have done whatever tests he wanted the first time around. Then she realized that maybe as the twins' guardian—or at least the guardian temporarily in place—Stefan probably needed permission from her to do anything with the twins.

She sat back, wondering how on earth she had gotten into this position. She knew exactly who to blame. It was so damn typical of her mother to set up this scenario, then just step out of life and leave the rest of them to deal with it. Isabella used to laugh at Tandy and tell her how she was too serious and that she needed to live a little. Only Isabella's version of *living a little* was having unprotected sex when she was completely drugged out of her mind.

Tandy didn't know if the drug scenario had something to do with the twins' current physical abilities, but Tandy wouldn't be at all surprised. The doctors so far hadn't given her any diagnoses or any suggestions on how to improve their mental states, and it's not as if Tandy even knew the right things to ask.

All she wanted to hear was if they could ever be—and she hated this word and the idea she was even using it—*normal.*

Was this something to strive toward? It sounded awful

when she asked it in that way, but she didn't know any other way to put it. How else was she supposed to look at her siblings, except to wonder if something normal was ahead of them in this world, or was their current existence in silence all they had? Was this the best they could look forward to? That didn't say much for the life they would have, and it signed up Tandy for a life of caregiving that she might not be able to handle either.

Feeling even more stressed and with her self-esteem sinking further, she picked up the note from her mother. The note basically shared nothing, except that Tandy would handle this now, and Isabella knew that Tandy had the full ability to do so. She stared down at the note once again, noting the backside was a receipt and partial at best. Wondering what possible belief her mother could have that Tandy was capable of handling whatever this was. As far as she was concerned, she wasn't capable of handling any of it. She didn't even know what *it* was. How was she supposed to raise two special needs kids? They weren't even her kids, and there was no money for the special help they might need for a lifetime. There was nothing.

Tandy groaned. Once again money had reared its ugly face in her world. She had worked so hard to position herself to make decent money, and it felt as if she had spent a lifetime trying to get off that poverty level so she could breathe. Now her mom had put her right back over the edge with the care of two of her siblings, children she didn't even know. And yet the siblings had looked at her with such joy that it had broken her heart. No matter what she thought of her mother—in the past or in the present—none of it changed the fact that Tandy was responsible for her twin brothers.

Dead or alive, her mother was still who she was and had acted consistently in this instance, and nothing would change that. It just made Tandy so sad because these kids deserved so much more. That was the real issue here because, as far as she was concerned, they deserved so much more than her, a half-interested and *completely out of touch with children* sister, who had suddenly found herself in the role of parent.

She went over to her kitchen and made herself yet another small pot of coffee before sinking onto her couch, tears coming to her eyes. It usually happened when Tandy considered her life with her mother, then foster care, then back to her mother's custody, with one chaotic mess after another, until finally Tandy's grandmother had removed Tandy at fifteen.

After that, things had calmed a little bit in Tandy's life, although she always felt the threat of being jerked back into the system or into her mother's ongoing horror. Tandy had never known what anything close to normal was, not until living with her grandmother. Now Tandy thought it must be some great big cosmic joke that her mother had put Tandy in this parental position after all this time. She could easily imagine her mother smirked, having played the last card on Tandy, having won some twisted game.

Isabella left two kids in need of a mother and other kids desperately in need of their own lives, in need of something of their own that could help them get through this chaos called life. And it just sucked that the person who had created this trauma for them was the very person supposed to do everything they could to make their world happen, but in a good way, not like this.

Never this.

STEFAN WALKED ONTO Dr. Maddy's floor and headed for her office, where he found her standing outside the door, waiting for him.

She handed him a cup of coffee as he approached. "I thought we would go visit with them first."

He nodded, accepted the cup, then followed her to one of her special rooms. These rooms could hold patients, if need be, for temporary treatments, or while they were waiting for beds, if there was a hold-up.

As he walked in, the children looked up and laughed. He smiled, seeing the joy and the sheer love and warmth in their faces. "Wow," he murmured to them and to Dr. Maddy. "This is a lovely surprise."

One little boy, his name was Matthew, got up and raced over, throwing himself into Stefan's arms. Careful to not spill his coffee, Stefan hurriedly put down the cup and swung the little boy up into his arms and held him close. The little boy babbled away in his own mind, in a serious conversation of some kind. Stefan laughed because, to a certain extent, he understood Matthew—maybe not all of it, but definitely part of it. It was Matthew's light language. Stefan glanced over at Dr. Maddy, smiling at the other little boy, Mark, who stared up at Stefan, a little bit more serious, a little bit more wary.

Still holding Matthew, Stefan squatted down beside Mark, where he sat on a little stool, and smiled. "Hi. I thought I would come back and see you today."

Mark nodded at Stefan but didn't say anything.

Then Stefan felt the buzz in the air, the communication between the two twins, and realized that they weren't nonverbal. They had just chosen to be nonvocal, and that was a whole different story.

Fascinated, he sat down crossed-legged, with Matthew in his lap and still in his arms. "How are you doing today?" he asked Mark.

Mark just nodded again, glancing at him warily, his gaze going to Dr. Maddy and then back to Stefan.

"I'm a friend of Dr. Maddy's," Stefan offered.

Mark nodded again, but his suspicious gaze never left Stefan's face.

Stefan recognized the signs, but he wasn't exactly sure what else was going on here.

Dr. Maddy sat down on the floor beside them all. "How are you doing today, Mark?" she asked.

Mark just looked at her, his eyes big and solemn, and, of course, he never spoke a word.

However, on the ethers, Stefan heard the twins chatting. He heard them laughing and talking. He couldn't quite hear the conversation yet, as their frequency was a bit fuzzy to pin down. Stefan wasn't sure exactly what they would do if he tuned into their conversation and answered them.

Dr. Maddy popped into his mind and suggested that they try it.

Stefan agreed. It would be better to know. He nodded slowly, and then, picking up on the conversation in the ethers, he fine-tuned the frequency, moving aside the chatter, and he spoke telepathically first to Mark. *It's really nice to meet you.*

Mark's eyes widened fearfully, and he bolted off the little stool that he had been sitting on and ran into Dr. Maddy's arms.

Dr. Maddy's arms closed around Mark and held him close. She hugged him warmly, letting him feel comfortable.

Then, in the same conversation on the ethers, she added, *We thought it might be easier to talk to you over here.*

Mark reared back and stared at her in astonishment.

Dr. Maddy smiled. *Yes, we can talk in this way as well.*

The child clearly didn't know what to say and frowned at his brother, who looked to be absolutely delighted. Still frowning, Mark glanced at Stefan and then back at Dr. Maddy. In the ethers, Mark whispered, *Nobody does this.*

*Oh yes,* Stefan countered, *some of us do, just not very many. Dr. Maddy is very special because she can do this.*

Mark just stared at Stefan and back at Dr. Maddy.

Dr. Maddy gave Mark a reassuring hug, her hands stroking his back. *Sometimes the patients I work with don't want to talk in the other world. Sometimes they feel safer here, so I come in here and work with them.*

Mark looked around, questioning. *Are others here?*

*There are,* Dr. Maddy answered, *but not necessarily right where you are. You have to be in a place where others can talk to you.*

Matthew laughed and added, *I want to talk to them. I want to talk to them.*

Mark shushed him. *Shh, we don't know if it's safe.*

Those words broke Stefan's heart. As much as he had seen the signs of child abuse, he also knew that children, when they needed to, would disappear inside. It was a coping mechanism, and these children hadn't had any reason to come back out of it. *You do know a whole world is out there?* he asked Mark.

He just nodded, his eyes huge as he stared at him, not fearfully, but definitely not with any trust.

Stefan knew it would take some time to get there.

Matthew laughed. *We don't have anybody to play with*

*sometimes. Maybe we could play with them.* He turned and looked at his twin brother hopefully.

Mark was obviously the leader, the one who kept them safe, and, when it came to relationships on this side, it was very often that way.

Mark was the leader, and Mark was also, by far, the most fearful, so he had taken on the role of keeping his little brother safe. Even though they were twins, in Mark's mind, he had deemed Matthew as the *little one*, the one who had to be protected, as if something Mark did could keep them both safe. Clearly in Mark's mind, keeping them safe was keeping them here on Dr. Maddy's floor.

Stefan faced Mark. *Nobody is trying to force you out of the ethers or out of Dr. Maddy's place.* Mark just stared back at him, with that solemn look that broke Stefan's heart. Stefan smiled and added, *I just thought maybe it would be okay if we came to visit every once in a while.*

Stefan didn't ask for Mark's permission because it was way too early, and, chances were, he would tell Stefan to disappear. Then, if he didn't, Mark would leave. Therefore, Stefan didn't give Mark that opportunity. Stefan looked over at Dr. Maddy. *It's lovely in here,* he began. *We should have brought some tea and snacks.*

Immediately Matthew pulled out of Stefan's hold, threw himself into Dr. Maddy's arms colliding with Mark, and added, *Can we have snacks? Snack, snacks, snacks,* he cried out joyously.

She laughed. *We'll see about that, but, yes, you guys aren't eating very much at all.* She looked back over at Mark and smiled. *Are you hungry? Would you like a snack?*

Mark nodded slowly, but his gaze never left Stefan.

Stefan knew he was the reason that Mark was struggling

to relax. *I can leave, if you like*, he offered. *I just wanted to confirm you were okay in here.*

*We're good*, little Matthew replied, as he ran around, screaming about snacks and looking at his brother, asking, *It's okay, isn't it?*

Mark was hard-pressed to answer his brother because everything inside Mark wanted to run.

Stefan saw it in the little boy's eyes and in Mark's every action, as Mark had learned to run in the past. Yet right now he didn't have any place to go. So, with Stefan here with Dr. Maddy, Mark wasn't sure whether the twins' special haven was safe or not.

Mark looked over at his brother, frowning, but Matthew was having none of it.

*Snacks, snacks, snacks*, he cried out joyfully.

Finally Mark relented, then looked over at Dr. Maddy and nodded. *Yes, please.*

Dr. Maddy laughed. *Fine. I'll go get some.*

*No wait*, Mark cried out. Dr. Maddy looked at him for further explanation, but the child just stared, Mark's gaze going nervously from Stefan to Dr. Maddy.

Stefan took note. *How about I go get them?* he offered. *That way Dr. Maddy can stay here with you.* Mark nodded, his gaze ever wary, not even trusting what Stefan said. Stefan looked over at Dr. Maddy and asked, "Where will I find the snacks?"

She smiled. "Have Alana get you some, and you can bring them back in here."

He nodded, then getting up very deliberately, his movements slow and careful, he stepped out of the world in which the twins lived and gave himself a physical shake, finding himself in the adjoining observation room. In his mind's eye, he saw Dr. Maddy, physically fine, just waiting on the other side of the ethers for him. Yet, here in the real world, Dr. Maddy was perched on a chair in the observation room, seemingly meditating.

He looked up when Alana appeared and explained, "We're supposed to bring snacks in."

She nodded at him, then looked back at Dr. Maddy in her frozen state. "That's a good thing, if they'll eat, but I don't know how that's supposed to work." She walked over to the closet and then handed him a picnic basket. When he looked at it, she shrugged. "Dr. Maddy had it prepped and ready. I don't know why."

He laughed, took the basket, then stepped back into the children's make-believe world.

Mark gave a sudden jolt when Stefan reappeared so quickly. He smiled at Mark and explained, *I just had to pick this up. Dr. Maddy had it all prepared for us.*

Mark eyed the basket curiously.

With another glance at the magic basket in his arms, he looked over at Dr. Maddy and clicked into their own special frequency and shared, *Cool trick.*

Dr. Maddy smiled. *Yeah, it is.*

Stefan had never seen a basket that could appear in one realm and then into the other.

*Of course you have*, Dr. Maddy corrected. *As always, all it is, is visualization.*

*I know*, he murmured. *But, when I open this, what will I find?*

She turned and looked at the kids, now speaking on their frequency. *What would you guys like for a snack?*

*I want whatever is in that basket*, Matthew exclaimed, crowding her and looking at the basket hopefully.

*You mean, like, milk?* Dr. Maddy asked, smiling.

*Milk would be good*, Matthew replied, but he kept staring at it.

*Oh, so you want something else?*

He nodded. *I want something else, if there is something else*, he replied, turning to her.

*Oh, there's something else*, she declared. *But it would help if you told me what you want. This basket holds all kinds of things.*

*Maybe you could just give me some of the things inside the basket, and I could go from there*, Matthew suggested, with the typical delight of a five-year-old not wanting to decide, in case it would limit his choices somehow.

She laughed, then looked over at Mark. *What about you, honey? What would you like?*

Mark stared at her and asked, *Do you have a cookie?*

*I do have cookies*, Dr. Maddy confirmed. *Is that what you would like?*

Mark nodded.

Dr. Maddy opened the basket without letting anybody else see inside, then pulled out a huge cookie for Mark. Mark's eyes lit up as he stared at the cookie, then at Dr. Maddy. *It's okay, honey. You can have it.* When he still hesitated, Dr. Maddy understood his hesitation. *No, you don't have to do anything for it. It's just a cookie for you to enjoy.*

Mark reached out hesitantly, and Stefan waited, his breath almost caught in the back of his throat, watching to see if the little boy would accept something so simple. Then, just when Stefan thought that Mark would, the world around them disappeared, and he was back in the office with Dr. Maddy.

# CHAPTER 3

TANDY STEPPED INTO the main area where the kids' room was, then walked toward Dr. Maddy's office. Tandy arrived in time to see Dr. Maddy and somebody else talking very animatedly about something. The conversation completely died when she showed up, and she gave the man a wry look. "If anything ever told me that your discussion was about the twins, you guys clamming up when I arrived is a pretty good indicator."

Dr. Maddy chuckled. "Not necessarily, but definitely a lot is going on with those kids."

"Of course there is." Tandy gave a headshake. "Isabella, our mother, never did anything easily. Anyway, I just finished work for the day and thought I would stop in and see how they're doing. How are they?"

"Do you want to see them?" Dr. Maddy offered, as she stood up.

"I don't think it would make a bit of difference, since they don't respond to me at all."

"That would be something to see," the man beside her noted. He smiled at Tandy. "I'm Stefan, by the way."

"Oh, right," she muttered, feeling foolish. "You were running some tests on them today."

"I ran a few, but it's still too early to say anything."

"Yes, of course," she murmured, feeling an age-old weariness, as with everything else that she'd dealt with where Isabella had been concerned. "I really hope there is some treatment."

He just nodded noncommittally.

Tandy wasn't sure whether that was good or bad. "I feel as if you guys already have some idea of what's going on, at least more than I do," she added.

"I don't know about that." Dr. Maddy smiled her way. "It's definitely too early."

"But you can't keep them here for long, as you told me," she pointed out. "And I'm sure I can't afford anything along the line of what's required to keep them in this place." Tandy glanced around nervously. "I'm finally doing okay moneywise, but it's taken a long time to get here, and I don't have a clue how I'll afford the proper care for the twins."

Dr. Maddy continued to smile. "Some funding assistance is available, particularly for a ward of the state."

"Sure, but then I would have to sign them over, wouldn't I?"

"Have you signed anything accepting guardianship yet?"

She shook her head. "No, the lawyer didn't seem to think I wanted to do that, and I think he's been busy prepping paperwork for just the opposite. Yet I haven't ..." She stopped, frowned, and relented awkwardly. "I haven't done anything to stop him."

"Of course," Stefan agreed.

"You guys are awfully amiable," Tandy murmured.

"I think you're judging yourself enough," Stefan shared. "You were thrust into a pretty difficult position right from the beginning, so I don't think anybody will judge you, except *you*."

She groaned. "And yet that seems to be the worst condemnation anyway."

"It absolutely is," he agreed, with a knowing smile, "but you're not alone in this."

"Yes, I am," she declared, "and anytime I try to contact someone about the twins' situation, I basically get more of the same. *It's my problem.* They make it very clear that I have to make some decisions."

"I'm sure you do," Stefan replied. "That's not what I meant. Just that other people out there can help."

"Maybe," Tandy conceded, "but I certainly don't know who they are yet. Until I have a grasp on how I'm supposed to keep these kids, I'm just not comfortable with this situation."

"Are you considering keeping them?" Dr. Maddy asked.

Tandy looked over at her and grimaced. "Every time, every damn time I think about *not* keeping them, it fills me with absolute dread and horror. If *anybody* would have helped me way back when, it would have done an awful lot for my life," she admitted, "and it is something I can possibly do for them. And it's not that I don't want to, but it's just the special needs aspect that worries me. They require so much more care, yet I have to work to make a living," she explained.

"Right," Dr. Maddy agreed, "so let's take you in, so you can visit with them for a little bit." With that, she led the way into another room, where the two kids were playing with some LEGO blocks, with a decidedly blank look on their faces. The twins looked up as Tandy came in.

Tandy squatted beside them and smiled. "Hi, guys. How are you enjoying being with Dr. Maddy?" There was just nothing, no answer, no response of any kind, and it broke her heart. Tandy sniffled back her tears, turned to face Stefan and Dr. Maddy. "How does anybody handle this?"

"If they were your children," Dr. Maddy began, as she squatted beside them, "the parents work hard to try and find ways to make their situations better. And I will admit that, in many cases, they're handed off to institutions where they live. But just because these twins are nonverbal doesn't mean intelligence isn't in there." She gave Stefan a look, as she added, "So don't make that mistake."

"Right," Tandy replied, turning to face her siblings. "And how do you know what they need? How am I to know what it is that they want or could use on a regular basis?"

"I think that comes with time and a little bit of practice," Dr. Maddy shared, as she stroked Matthew's shoulder. Matthew showed absolutely no sign of responding. "I'm not saying that only you should look after them," she clarified. "That is a massive responsibility for you to take on, but I do think we can do some things to improve their situation and to make it a little easier."

"Easier for me or easier for them?" Tandy asked.

Dr. Maddy smiled at her in approval. "That's a very good question because we want to ensure you and the twins get all the help and assistance we can muster for you three, so you all can live as normally as possible."

"Is there such a thing as *normal?*" Tandy asked, staring at her little siblings. She wanted to cry, but she also wanted to wrap them up in her arms and to tell them that it would all be okay. And yet how could she do that? Even when they looked at her, they didn't really seem to see her. "I feel as if they don't know anything about me."

"Do they?" Stefan asked, as he squatted beside her, smiling at the kids.

Mark stiffened ever-so-slightly at his approach.

Tandy instantly frowned. "Does Mark do that to you every time?" Tandy asked, noticing Mark's obvious reaction.

"In a way, yes," Stefan confirmed, with a casual wave, "but we can't judge Mark simply based on my being here."

A horrible thought came to Tandy, as she looked back and forth between Stefan and Dr. Maddy. "And does Mark do this every time when men are involved?"

Dr. Maddy hesitated for a moment, then nodded slowly. "Yes, at the moment it appears that all men make Mark feel threatened, at least to some degree."

Tandy winced, then nodded. "That would be because of my mother's boyfriends, most likely," she noted in a flat tone. "I know that two of my other siblings were sexually assaulted before they were removed to foster care as well."

Dr. Maddy winced, then nodded. "Unfortunately it is something we do see from time to time."

Tandy didn't say anything but felt Stefan studying her. She glared over at him.

He smiled. "You *were* a victim," he began. "You aren't anymore, and that is something you should be proud of."

"No," she argued, "there's no pride in that. If I had done something about it at the time, maybe there would be some pride. There's really just the horror of having endured." He stared at her with a calm compassion that made her uncomfortable.

He added, "You have come a long way in the healing."

"I have," she conceded. "And I guess that's why I'm so hesitant to step into something that would send my own healing backward."

"Of course," Stefan replied, "also not something you should feel guilty about."

She gave a broken laugh. "You can let me off the hook

all you want, but the only person whose opinion really counts is mine."

He gave her a beaming smile and nodded. "And that," he declared, "is exactly right and just goes to prove my point. You've come a long way, but is there more to go? Probably. Could it be a lifetime of learning and healing? Yes. Does it matter that you are not there yet? No," he stated, without giving her a chance to say more. "You won't be doing anything other than trying to live your life in the best manner anyway."

Astonished, she stared at him, then frowned. "I don't normally talk about any of this."

"Of course not," Stefan noted, "and I understand it well. In your mind you've come a long way."

"I have," she snapped.

He nodded. "You have, indeed, and wanting to help your siblings is where I can really see the healing."

She shook her head. "I don't know that there's any healing in that avenue because I still want to run every time I see them."

"And yet here you are," he pointed out.

"*Yeah.*" She frowned, as she glanced around. "But it's one thing to come here to visit and to see how they're doing, and it's another thing to take them home," she pointed out. "I don't know that I am equipped for that."

"I don't think you would need to take them home full-time," he shared. "I'm pretty sure some assistance is out there for you."

"Is there?" she asked, turning to him. "So far, nobody has spoken up about it."

"We can help with that," Dr. Maddy interjected. "We need to do a full assessment first to figure out just what they need for care, then take it from there."

Just then a noise was heard outside the door.

Dr. Maddy straightened, then looked at the kids and smiled. She nodded to Stefan. "Would you stay here for a few minutes?"

He nodded and added, "As long as Mark is okay with it."

Mark stared at him but didn't make a move either way.

Dr. Maddy quickly stepped out of the room. Stefan smiled at Tandy and added, "The twins really are doing well here."

"If you say so," she muttered doubtfully, as she stared down at them. "I want to communicate with them, but I feel they don't want to speak to me."

"That's because in many ways they're locked in their own world," Stefan explained. "They're locked in the safety of where they are."

She stared at him and winced. "So, you're thinking they were assaulted too?"

"I can't confirm that," he admitted. "At least not for sure. Do you know anything about their life with your mother?"

Tandy shook her head. "No, but I do know the cops were just brought in to deal with some material they found on the computers in Isabella's apartment, which was also where they found her body."

"In that case, let them do whatever investigation they need to, and we'll see what we can do from our end."

It was almost as if she were being dismissed, but then the door opened, and Dr. Maddy stepped back inside. She had a handsome man with her.

She smiled at Tandy. "This is Grant, a friend, who

works with my husband sometimes, and he's an FBI agent," Dr. Maddy explained. "When I mentioned that I had the kids here, he shared that he had seen something come across his desk."

Tandy frowned at him. "The FBI?" she asked nervously. "What does that mean?"

He hesitated, then crouched beside her, smiling at the two children, and asked Tandy, "Shall we go talk somewhere?"

She bit her bottom lip, slowly stood up, and then nodded. "I guess I need to know the worst of it, so yes."

"Take my office." Dr. Maddy offered. "We'll stay here with the kids."

Meanwhile, Grant nudged her into Dr. Maddy's office. As soon as she got inside, she stayed in the doorway and asked harshly, maybe even more so than she intended, "What?"

He hesitated, then replied, "Your mother left behind a lot of material, pornographic material, involving children."

"Meaning that she had this material for herself?"

His gaze narrowed as he studied her. "Does that sound like her?"

"No. I admit that she was a drunk, drugged out of her mind an awful lot of the time, but I don't think even she would stoop that low."

"I would be happy to hear that," Grant said. "Do you know who her boyfriend was or who else was in her life lately?"

She stared at him and replied, "I don't think you have that much paper."

The door opened, and another man stepped in. He had short cropped dark hair, with almost no smile to be seen. He looked over at Grant and nodded. "Dr. Maddy told me that you were in here."

Grant motioned toward Tandy and introduced them. "Keller, this is Tandy Goodman. Tandy Goodman, this is Keller Drummond. He's a local detective who acts as a liaison with the FBI as needed."

The stranger frowned at her, and she frowned right back.

"What has he got to do with this?" Tandy asked Grant, pointing at Keller, staring at the two men, now feeling more than nervous. The minute anybody mentioned porn—and seeing the reaction of Mark to Stefan—it was too much for Tandy. She'd already had enough heartbreak, and she didn't think she could handle too much more.

"The question is whether you had any idea what your mother was up to," Keller asked.

She stared at him in shock. "I don't know what Isabella was up to ten years ago, let alone this last little while," she declared. "She was many things, but a good parent, loving or even lukewarm, wasn't among them. She wasn't easy to get along with. I had to stay away from her to build a life for myself. If she was into any of this stuff, I didn't know about it, and I sure as hell wouldn't have condoned it."

"Of course not," Grant agreed, hurriedly sending a warning look to the newcomer. "Keller here just needs to ask some questions."

"Sure," she muttered, staring at him, but her mood rapidly declined. "Just so we know where we stand, I had nothing to do with my mother and her life before she up and killed herself with an overdose. I was not in her life in any way for many years."

Keller noted, "You're pretty adamant about that."

She snorted. "Yeah, you're not kidding. Isabella lived

one hell of a depraved, drug-fueled life," Tandy shared, "and the result in that room there is just part of it."

Keller looked back to where she was pointing, but he hadn't been in the room with the kids.

She groaned. "If you're in any way thinking I can help you with her recent associates or what she was doing, I can't. I don't know anything."

"So, what do you know?"

"Nothing. That's what I'm trying to tell you. You're free to go through her apartment, if there's even anything left. The landlord told me that Isabella was way behind on her rent, as in many months. So he was looking for me to take what I wanted right away, leaving anything he could sell to recoup the rent," she muttered.

Keller shook his head. "He's not allowed to touch anything at the moment. Your mother's death was classified as an unattended death, so, at the moment, we have stopped him from entering her premises."

Tandy gave a bitter laugh at that. "You better get in there quick because you sure can't trust him either."

Keller nodded. "Would you mind coming with me?"

She frowned at him. "What good would that do?"

"I don't know," he admitted, "but it would be helpful if you could."

She pinched the bridge of her nose, wondering when this nightmare would be over, and then slowly she turned to Grant. "You keep an eye on the kids' rights. I think Dr. Maddy cares, but I don't know how much she can do for them."

"If there's anything she can do, she'll do it," Grant declared. "Go with Keller and see if you can find anything of importance at your mother's house. Then we'll continue this conversation later."

"Great," she muttered. She hesitated because she hadn't had a chance to say goodbye to the kids, but then she hadn't even had a chance to say hello to them. It didn't seem they would miss her. Her shoulders sagging, she walked to the door and told Keller, "If we're going, let's go now."

KELLER DRUMMOND STEPPED outside and walked toward the parking lot. He turned to Tandy and asked, "Do you have your vehicle here?"

She nodded stiffly. "I do. I'll meet you there."

"Good enough." He watched as she headed toward her vehicle. He hadn't been told a whole lot about this case, only a bare-bones description, which was never enough to get complete impressions of the people involved. Still, what he saw was a touchy woman, maybe just plain prickly about life and not wanting anything to do with this, which was fine with him because he didn't either. But the fact of life was, sometimes, when the shit rolled, you had to step in and clean up the mess. And that's apparently what he would be doing on this one right now.

Plus, he had an inkling that childhood abuse was part of the equation with Tandy. He shook his head. He had escaped that nightmare in his own childhood, but other family members had not been so lucky. So he saw Tandy as a survivor.

He hopped into his vehicle, punched in the address to his GPS map, and more or less followed her out of the parking lot and onto the road. He kept an eye as to where she was going versus his GPS, and they both arrived together at the apartment. It was a rundown area in Seattle and had taken a good twenty minutes or more to get here. It was definitely more of a boarding house by the looks of it.

As he hopped out, he saw a drug exchange happening on the corner beside him. As soon as the street vendors and his customer saw Keller, they all shuffled away, picking up on the fact that Keller looked the part of some law enforcement agency. He just shook his head. He wasn't here to run anybody out of town, but the location and the activity just now told him a lot about Isabella Goodman. He joined Tandy, where she stood waiting for him. "Nice part of town," he commented.

She snorted. "It's better than the streets, which is where she was living the last time I saw her."

"Indeed," he noted, as he faced her. "How long has she been off the street?"

"No clue," Tandy replied. "Isabella comes and goes, depending on how her income is."

"And what was her source of income?"

She eyed him and shared, "Last I knew, … she was prostituting herself on the streets."

He winced. "That's got to be hard to handle."

She shrugged. "What was harder was when she decided I should be on the streets making money for her to spend."

He stared at her. "I presume that didn't go over well."

"It not only didn't go over very well but, because of that, I finally managed to get my grandmother to take me in. She'd been holding off, not wanting anything to do with Isabella. However, when Grandma realized how bad it was for me, she did step up," Tandy admitted. "And my life was forever changed because of it. So, I do know what a little bit of assistance can do for a person."

"Exactly," he agreed. "I bet you're grateful for your

grandmother."

"Yeah, no kidding. Gwen, my grandmother, was one hell of a lifeline for me." She shook her head. "She passed away about one year ago. Although she wasn't a warm and caring person, she was the answer to my prayers back then. I worked hard to ensure she knew what a huge difference she had made in my life and how grateful I was," she shared.

"Did you ever try to get her to take in any of the other kids?"

"We never really even knew how many Isabella had or where they even were," she noted. "And it was clear that my grandmother had tried her best to endure my mother, which was more than she could handle. I don't know what all went down between them, but I didn't push it. Her taking on an almost full-grown adult who was to the point of looking after herself was a whole different story than tracking down the smaller kids, who had most likely been lost to the system, not to mention the pair of twins who came along quite a bit later. And somewhere along the line, it became a question of who was taking care of whom."

"Right," Keller agreed, "and it's always so easy to judge." He caught the surprised look on her face, and he nodded. "We don't all come from nice happy childhoods," he shared, "so I'm certainly not judging where you came from either."

"That's good," she muttered, with a nod. "And, if Isabella was into porn, kiddie porn, I don't even know what to say." The dread in her tone said it best. She stared up at the apartment. "I wish to God that subject hadn't even come up."

"Would she have done it for drugs?"

"Yes," Tandy replied, "but then I've never met a drug addict who wouldn't do absolutely anything they could for their next fix. It's not as if it's a conscious choice anymore." She shook her head, as if shaking away the bad juju. "It's a drive for something they must have, and, when they don't get *it*, it doesn't matter what avenue is offered to get *it*, they'll take it. Would I have thought she would do something with the kids in that way? No, but, if she was in a desperate drug-induced or withdrawal haze, I don't know what she may have set up," she conceded. "Especially considering the state these children are in. I fear they've already been abused in their young lives, but I really don't know for sure."

Keller didn't say anything about that. "I understand she left you a note?"

Tandy snorted. "If you could call it that, yes. She left me a ripped piece of paper, telling me that the twins were my responsibility now, and I would do a better job than she could. Or something along that line."

He sighed. "A hell of a thing to do."

"It's a hell of a thing to do, but again, I think, once the drugs take over, common sense goes out the window, and nobody in that state cares about anybody else, focusing totally on themselves."

"She probably thought she was doing them a service," Keller suggested.

"Yeah," Tandy muttered. "If any of that porn crap was what she was into, her committing suicide definitely did them a service because now maybe we can get the twins the help they need. But I still don't think there's any replacement for a full-time clean and sober mother," she murmured. "Yet that seemed to be beyond the scope of what Isabella could do."

He led the way to the apartment, keeping a wary eye on

Tandy. He wasn't sure what to think of her, and she seemed to be fairly thrown by the sudden turn of events in her life. He couldn't imagine being tossed five-year-old twins like that without a care, particularly twins who needed serious extra help. Had their mother done it as a lifeline? Had she committed suicide, rather than taking an accidental overdose, because she knew she was causing so much pain for everyone, and this was her way out? He didn't know, and likely no easy answers were to be found at the moment either.

As they got up to the run-down apartment, he looked over at Tandy and asked, "Are you ready?"

She snorted. "Hell no. God damn, no, I'm not ready. But we're here, so let's just get in there and get it over with."

He unlocked the door and pushed it open. Immediately the stench of unwashed bodies, soiled furniture, musty clothing, and moldy food assailed their noses.

She took several deep breaths, shuddering from the onslaught. He watched her in concern, but she just waved him off. "I'm here," she snapped, "and I won't stay for long, so let's do this as quickly as we can."

Just getting started meant stepping in over pizza boxes, and he wasn't even sure where some of the curtains had come from, but they looked as if they had been here for a very long time. He just shook his head and kept walking forward.

She looked around and asked, "Were the twins found in here?" He nodded. She closed her eyes and whispered, "Jesus fucking Christ."

"I know," he agreed. "That makes it harder for everyone, even us."

She pinched her lips together as she stared around the

room. "And why are we here?"

"Looking for anything that looks suspicious, anything that looks as if it might help the kids, anything at all that would give us answers. By *answers*, I mean about the porn in particular."

The heat swept down her cheeks, up her cheeks, and then down again, before she bent over in a dry-heaving state. She took a moment and straightened up then stepped forward. "Not exactly what I thought I would be doing with my life," she muttered.

"And I'm sorry for that," Keller said. "Obviously we have some things to sort out, but, after we settle this matter, hopefully you can establish some normalcy." She just looked at him, and he realized how hard that must have sounded. "I don't mean it in a bad way, disregarding all you've done so far in your life to counteract all this. I would suspect this was your beginning too," he guessed. "Yet obviously we have an investigation to do. So, if other people are involved, then we need to get that cleared up fast."

"Of course," she stated, her tone thickening and turning almost formal.

Keller knew her shocked reaction was in relation to the stress of the situation. Still, he hoped to keep her moving forward, so she didn't focus on how bad this room was and how badly this whole mess could end up being—as it could end up particularly ugly, and she would be caught right in the middle of it.

He added, "Let's go through the place quickly. Then we can leave and get some fresh air."

"How does anybody even live like this?" she asked in wonder, as they stepped over the garbage strewn across the floor. "I blocked out most of the smells, but I'm still seeing a train wreck."

"I don't know how anyone lives like this," he replied. "It's definitely not something that I could do."

"I don't think anybody could," she murmured.

They made their way to the bathroom, which was even more disgusting. Her breath caught in the back of her throat, and she made a gagging sound, as she quickly backed out of the putrid room. The toilet didn't look as if it had been flushed in days, as evidenced by a full dump still in it. She just shook her head and kept retreating.

He reached out a hand and said, "Okay, I can search the bathroom, but I need you to go check out the bedroom."

She stared at him, wide-eyed, took a moment, and then headed to the bedroom.

He followed, hoping it wasn't as bad as the bathroom had been.

A filthy mattress seemed to be under a pile of clothing, but it was pretty hard to tell even what was what. She wearily scrubbed her face. "I don't even know what I'm supposed to be looking for."

"Anything," he said, "absolutely anything."

"And you'll come in here with me, I presume?"

"Yeah, as soon as I do a quick check on the bathroom," he shared, glancing back at the room he had absolutely no interest in returning to, but he knew it was part of the job.

She snorted. "At least that's off my plate." She walked through, stepping on the clothing, on the mattress. "I see children's clothes in here and adult clothes." She reached down, but then looked at him and asked, "I know it sounds petty, but do you have any gloves?"

He pulled gloves from his pocket and handed her a pair, then put some on himself. "It's not petty," he stated. "In this situation, it could be life-saving."

She nodded, then stooped to pick up what appeared to be small clothing. She frowned as she looked at it, then shook her head. "This is the wrong size."

"What do you mean, the wrong size?"

"The twins are about five," she shared, gingerly lifting the shirt, frowning at it. "This is smaller. I would say, maybe for a two-year-old. What does that mean?" she asked.

"I don't know what it means," Keller replied, "but I hope it doesn't mean what I'm thinking it means."

She turned to face him. "What do you mean by that?"

"I'm hoping Isabella didn't have another child, one we don't know about."

Tandy blanched. "I hadn't considered that."

"I don't think any of us did, and, given the condition of this place, I don't know if it's even possible. Could she have gone through another pregnancy and given birth without you knowing?"

"Oh, God, yes," Tandy declared, "very possible. I meant it when I said that I've had as little contact with her as I could for a long time, but that seems to be something you guys just don't get."

"It's not that we don't get it," Keller clarified. "As I look around a room, I understand it more and more, but could she have hidden a child?"

"I guess maybe the question is, was she pregnant two or three years ago?" she asked, turning to him. "She was never one to use birth control, and I know she had multiple miscarriages."

"I'll ask the coroner."

"That would explain the baby clothes though," she muttered, as she stared at them, her heart sinking. "She always had this attitude that life would get better sometime. Yet, no matter how many times she got help for a time, her life just never got better."

"Do you have a theory why?"

"The drugs," she stated. "Isabella could never get off them, and, if you can't get off them, it's pretty-damn hard for anything to improve, not with all her attention focused on getting more." Tandy went silent for a bit and added, "I'll go through this, but please find out if she was recently pregnant."

"Will do," he replied. Keller didn't bother telling Tandy that he didn't have any high hopes of proving another birth, even a more recent one, especially if Isabella had had a home birth.

He watched Tandy for a long moment as she picked through some of the clothes. It was interesting what she was picking through, not so much for memories' sake, but almost as if to figure out something about her mother that Tandy didn't understand. When she walked over to the closet, he headed back to the bathroom and did as professional and as fast a search as he could.

He found all kinds of needles, some drugs—illegal and legal—hair products, skin cream products, and a whole lot of nothing, including no toilet paper, which definitely made him pause. But given everything else he'd seen, it wasn't exactly a surprise. He walked back into the bedroom to see Tandy pulling down boxes of stuff from the top shelf of the closet.

He stepped over and offered, "Let me help." Together, they lowered the boxes to the ground, and, when she looked at him, he caught the expression on her face. "You really don't want to open them."

She glanced at him and asked, "Would you?"

He smiled and shared, "In this case, I'm happy to even see boxes. So far, nothing here tells us anything we didn't already know."

"Right, ... well, fly at it," she muttered. "I can't imagine anything good is in there."

"Maybe not, but I hope it won't be that bad." He quickly flipped off the lid on the first box, and she sucked in her breath. It held an assortment of baby stuff, and it seemed to be memories, keepsakes. With a small cry, she bent down and picked up a photo. It was of Isabella and the twins sitting happily, still not quite to the sitting-up stage, so maybe six months old, maybe less than that. Nobody else was in the picture.

"It looks as if she really did enjoy having the babies," he murmured.

Tandy didn't say anything for a long moment without saying a word. He wasn't sure if he should push it or not and was trying to decide, when she took it out of his hands.

"She had a lot of issues, but the one thing she wanted was a family."

"She had one," he noted, "lots of kids apparently."

She winced, then nodded. "Yes, lots of family, just not necessarily in a good way."

"And yet ..."

"I know," she snapped, "and I'm not judging her. I can't. God knows her life wasn't easy, and I didn't make it any easier."

He frowned at her. "Surely you can't hold yourself to blame for any of it."

She stared at him. "Can't I?"

"No," he snapped right back. "Not when you have a drug addict who can't get off the drugs, yet keeps having babies and not taking care of them." He shook his head. "I presume she had opportunities to get help?"

"She had a lot of opportunities," Tandy stated bitterly. "But none of them was enough to keep her off that stuff. She just went from one substance to another, depending on her boyfriend of the moment."

"Of course," he noted, recognizing the anger and yet also the guilt. "You cannot blame yourself for this." She just nodded, and he saw that she wasn't quite convinced, yet was desperate to be convinced. He reached out a hand and squeezed hers. "I mean it. Let's not go there right now. You still have an awful lot of adjustments to go through, not to mention two five-year-olds who need you," he pointed out.

She choked up at that, which was hard to see.

"So, if you have any wish to do something right or wrong in this instance, let's focus on getting them the care they need, so they won't be suffering the consequences of your mother's actions for the rest of their lives."

"They already are suffering," Tandy whispered, choking up again, tears in her eyes. "Years ago I started thinking of her as Isabella, not as my mother. As a way to get distance, I suppose. How messed up is that?"

"It's a coping thing, I would guess," he suggested. He bent down and popped open the second box, and it was more of the same.

She rummaged through both boxes, finding more photographs, which was odd because that meant somebody had taken them, which was not that common in this digital age of cell phones and selfies.

"Why did she keep photos, when she didn't keep the kids?" he asked, staring down at them, an ugly feeling in his stomach.

Tandy shrugged. "I don't know. I didn't have any contact with her, and it shows in times like this. What else would she do with the pictures though?" she asked, staring at him. "These look to be keepsakes, which isn't something I would have expected of her. Her existence has been too transient for keepsakes."

Keller nodded. "Yet you're not seeing that as quite right yourself, and I'm not seeing it either. I just want to confirm that we have answers to all the questions."

"That's probably not possible," she muttered. "My mother was an enigma, but so much of it was hidden by the drugs that had a hold of her, drugs that she couldn't let go of."

He didn't say anything, still staring down at the photos.

Tandy asked him, "What are you thinking?"

Not answering, he reached into the third box and found more photos, most of them babies. Nude, happy, and running around on the floor in various positions. Innocent pictures, unless … He held them up for her to see.

She stared at him, looked at the photos, and moaned. "Please tell me these weren't used for what I'm thinking they were used for."

He switched his gaze to meet hers and asked, "And what are you thinking?"

She whispered, "From the look on your face, it's not good. It can't be good at all."

"And here I thought I had a perfected my no-comment smile."

She shook her head. "It doesn't take much to put two and two together here," she muttered, as she sank down beside him. "As bad as this could be, I'm really hoping it's just mementoes."

"Me too," he muttered. He snagged up the boxes, looked around, and asked, "Do you see anything else that might be helpful?"

"No, not yet, but I haven't gone through everything."

"Let's get that finished," he replied. "I'll be taking these with me."

She clearly wanted to say something and then closed her mouth and carried on, which was really smart because she wouldn't like any of the answers he had to give her. These photos needed to go to the international sex crimes division to see if they were posted all over the usual creepy websites.

The real question remained to be answered. How old were the kids at the point in time that these photos stopped, or had they never stopped? Or maybe the request for a whole lot more than just photos had taken a toll on Isabella Goodman, to the point of suicide. At the moment, Keller really hoped so. He really hoped that Isabella had some touch of humanity still left in her at the very end.

He hoped that she had had a decent bone in her body and had finally recognized the poisonous lifestyle she was luring her kids into, then decided to make a change for the better, even if it meant killing herself to stop the pain for her kids. She should have been able to give them up to foster care, to hand them over to an orphanage, or to do something to save them, but instead she had continued on this sick pathway.

That was the part he had trouble forgiving Isabella for.

# CHAPTER 4

TANDY WAS NUMB when she walked into her apartment. While with Keller, it had been all she could do not to scream and to rail at her depraved mother and everything she had done wrong in her life. But now, as Tandy walked into her empty apartment, she felt some of the numbness wearing off, with a greater need to scream out loud at the top of her lungs, howling insults at this woman who had caused so much pain for so many people. Especially her own children.

But Tandy couldn't afford to let loose. She couldn't afford to lose control, and she sure as hell couldn't afford to let any of her neighbors know how much pain Tandy was really in. It didn't matter that screaming would probably help, but Tandy could allow no outward shouting when it came to living privately, keeping things under wraps, and staying in control. And, for now, that's what was important. She knew the shrinks would have a field day with her, and no way would she give them that chance, not then, not now, maybe never.

Instead, she broke into deep heart-wrenching but quiet sobs and cried until her heart ached, full of so much pain and sorrow that she had no idea how to even progress. She was on her couch, the tears drying on her cheeks as she stared out at the world. It had been many years since she'd had any suicidal thoughts herself, and, for the first time in a very long time, she wondered if she could even keep going this way.

The more she found out about Isabella, the more Tandy hated her. Blocking it off for years had helped, but not now, not when she realized everything else Isabella had been into. And yet … it was too late for blaming Isabella. Too late for anything really. Tandy had no way to do what she wanted to do. Scream at Isabella, scold her, be a bitch to her face.

Once again her mother had gotten away with doing whatever the hell she wanted, with no punishment or consequences. Once again the consequences for her actions were to be borne by her children. When Tandy had been younger, she'd often told Isabella that she needed to do something to get thrown in jail, so she would get clean and sober. Yet Isabella had a pat, albeit sarcastic, response, saying that wouldn't happen. The authorities would simply prescribe a maintenance level of drugs, just not good ones, until she got out. Then she would be right back at it again.

At one point in time, Isabella had cried in her arms, wailing how she wanted to get off the drugs, that she didn't want to be controlled by them. Yet, as soon as she had woken up the next morning, she'd scoffed at that and had declared, "No way in hell I'm getting off drugs, and you can complain all you want, but this is my life."

Many times Tandy told her mother to get it together, and many times Tandy was told that, if she didn't like it, she could fucking move somewhere else.

It hadn't been very long afterward that Tandy had pleaded with her grandmother to take her in before Tandy was forced into prostitution herself. That being the final straw, Tandy finally walked away from Isabella, courtesy of Gwen Lance Goodman, with Isabella screaming *Good riddance* at Tandy as she walked away. Their relationship hadn't improved at any time since, but the fact that Isabella had left the twins with Tandy now was something she couldn't begin to understand.

What possible reason could Isabella have for doing that? It's not as if Tandy had any experience with having kids, raising kids, or even being in the general vicinity of them. Hell, she'd barely been raised herself. Anything positive in her life had been self-taught, based on whatever she'd learned in this life.

She could almost hear Isabella laughing at her, saying, *You still did a better job than me, so now they're your problem.* If her mother absolutely loved to do one thing, it was to dump her own responsibilities onto other people, and it looked as if she had managed to do that yet again. Still so angry it was hard to even see straight, Tandy managed to get up on her feet and to head in for a hot shower. Her face was blotchy and caked with the salt from her tears, and the rest of her just hurt, a pain that would take a long time to subside.

She'd had these breakdowns before. Thoughts of her mother would send Tandy into spirals, until she'd finally learned to handle some of it. But how did you handle knowing that absolutely nothing in your life was considered worthwhile by the people who were supposedly there to help you? And now Tandy was in the same position that Isabella had been in because of Tandy's siblings. And yet, if she was to help these siblings, what was Tandy supposed to do about all the other siblings Tandy could have who had gone into the system?

At one point in time, she had tried to find information about them, but nobody would let her have access, and now she just had to wait for them to show up—if they cared enough to find her and then to show up on her doorstep. She couldn't imagine anybody else wanting to. If, by the grace of God, the other siblings had ended up in decent homes, Tandy couldn't imagine them wanting to reach out and to touch base with anybody connected with their previous life. And, if they didn't remember their previous lives, well, that was probably a blessing too.

Tandy stepped out of the shower—feeling sixty instead of thirty—wrapped in a towel around her torso, with her hair in another, as she headed toward the kitchen and the coffeepot. She was pretty sure that coffee was the last thing she needed at this point, but there were just times when nothing else would make a difference. At least coffee would be a jolt to her system that potentially would improve her viewpoint, at least for the moment.

With the coffee dripping, she quickly dressed in leggings and a T-shirt, skipping a bra because she was at home and who the hell cared anyway. She gave a hoarse laugh. She was so damaged and broken just from all the years with her own mother. Yet, as much as she hated to say it, it was a bloody gift to the twins that Isabella was gone right now, though saying it made Tandy feel even worse. It's as if she couldn't do anything right, and it was all just terrible.

She sat on the couch with a cup of coffee and stared out the window, wondering what her next move should be. Could she even care for the kids? She did a lot of shift work, and a lot of that was so she could avoid the worst parts of life, and maybe that was enough for now. It just seemed all so far beyond what she thought she could do or would be doing at this stage. But she wasn't sure if it was even worthwhile to consider keeping the twins. That they were her siblings was one thing, but the reality was that they were complete strangers and that other people might be in a better position to help them.

When her phone rang, she stared at it, not wanting to talk to anybody. When it finally stopped, she sighed with relief, only for it to start up again. She frowned and eventually answered it.

Keller greeted her by saying, "I won't go away."

"That's too damn bad," she muttered, "because I want you to."

"Look," he muttered. "I get it. Your life with her sucked, and now you're torn between keeping the kids or not keeping the kids, and who would be a better parent, and of course you're certain you'll be a terrible parent because your life is completely screwed up because of what Isabella did to you," he suggested. "I'm not a shrink, and I can't tell you how to handle any of this," he stated, "but what I called to tell you is that some of those photos were definitely used on kiddie porn sites."

Immediately the bile rose in Tandy's throat, and the coffee that had recently gone into her stomach rose up and came flying out, as she threw up on her living room floor. She ended the call, racing to the bathroom, where she vomited again and again.

When she finally staggered to her feet, she went back out to the living room to clean up the mess. She couldn't even imagine the depravity facing her and facing them. When the phone rang again, she stared at it, not wanting anything to do with it, but knew that he would just hound her over and over again. When she finally answered, her tone was dry and croaky. "What?" she barked. "Haven't you passed on enough bad news for the day?"

He hesitated and then muttered, "I'm sorry. I delivered

that news a little rough."

"There's no good way to deliver that news," she declared, staring down at her phone. "You would probably make millions if you ever found a way."

A note of humor slid through his tone as he added, "I guess I hadn't considered what your reaction to this might be. I'm sorry."

"Neither did I," she snapped, "or I would have taken the call in the bathroom."

"Are you okay?"

"No, I'm not fucking okay," she muttered, as she sat down on the floor, "but I'll survive."

"Good, that's what I needed to hear."

"Whatever," she muttered, fatigue building in her tone. "What am I supposed to do now? The kids, ... they'll need even more counseling than I thought."

"I know it's not a good thing," he added, "but at least the children were so young, you know, in the photos ... that maybe they won't remember them."

"But those pictures are on the internet ... forever," she pointed out. "*Forever.* When they're teenagers, when they're adults, those photos will still be there."

"We can't ever take anything down, even if we wanted to," he admitted. "We take it down in one place, and it pops back up somewhere else. But we can try at least and can take down the ones that we can. I get it," he said, hearing her scoff, "there's no justice in this. It does explain some of what we were seeing though."

"Sure," she muttered, "but that's not anything I want to acknowledge."

"Part of the reason I called you back was to see if you knew any of the men in her life."

"Knew, knew?" She gasped in horror.

"No," he snapped, his tone sharp as he cut through her immediate horror.

"I'm not saying that you knew them. I just wondered how we would contact anyone or even find out who she hung out with."

"Oh Christ," she muttered, rubbing her head. "I don't know. Years ago, yes, but now I have no idea."

"When did you last speak with her?"

"Months and months and months ago," she replied, staring off into the distance. "I don't even remember when. I guess it might be on my phone though. Just a second." She brought up the text messages, while he waited. "The last text I have is January of last year," she noted. "I think she might have called since then though. She was always looking for money. As soon as I got a job, she thought I should support her and the kids."

"Of course she did. It was an easy out for her."

"Maybe," Tandy muttered. "I didn't honor that."

"And again, not your fault," he snapped.

She didn't say anything, staring off in the distance, trying to figure out what she could do right now, something for the twins and for herself.

"What I need to know," Keller repeated, a bit impatiently, "is who she hung out with."

"I guess you should probably start with her landlord," she replied. "I know, when she had no money for rent, she used to do him, … let's say, *favors.*"

"Favors?"

"Yes, favors," she stated, taking a deep breath. "Whenever Isabella ran out of money, she would sell herself on the streets to get her next fix. I don't know whether the landlord would consider himself a client or not. I would say probably not," she added, "but there were times Isabella would say things, like, she would have to talk to him and see if she could trade in favors."

"So, trade in favors for another month's rent?"

"Something like that," she agreed. "I don't know."

"Fine, I'll talk to him. Any old-time friends?"

"Yes. His name's Danny. They've been friends, and I say that loosely, but they go back forever."

"Okay, that's good," he replied. "Do you know how I can get a hold of him?"

"On her phone, I would guess."

"But she had no phone with her body," he shared. "It's one of the reasons I'm asking you. We don't have her cell."

"Oh, that's weird." She thought about that for a moment. It was out of character. "In all the chaos of her world, the one thing that she always seemed to keep up was that phone. So that makes no sense to me."

"We need to find it because all her contacts will be on it."

"If anybody wanted to get rid of her and wanted to keep themselves out of trouble, getting rid of that phone would do it," she pointed out.

"Do you think anybody out there would want her dead?"

She snorted. "At various times in my life, me for one."

"Let's rule you out for now. Anybody else?" he asked.

"I'm sure there are plenty more," she stated. "I just don't know who they are. So, you need to find her associates."

"I'll get to work on that." He hesitated and then added, "I'm really sorry about all this."

"Yeah, me too," she muttered, "but sorry doesn't fix anything, does it?"

"No, maybe it doesn't fix anything," he conceded, "but at least maybe you can see that you're not alone and that there is some help for you."

"And what about the kids?" she asked. "Is there any help for them?"

"Yeah. As long as Stefan and Dr. Maddy and even her husband or other law enforcement are working on this," he explained, "the kids are getting the best care possible. Honest to God," he stated, "more than the best care." And, with that strange comment, he ended the call.

Tandy looked around the room, then shouted at Isabella, "How could you do that?" And when the response came almost immediately, Tandy stared at the ghostly image in her living room.

*Because this way at least you would take care of them,* the ghost said to her. *Whether you like it or not, whether you think that you're better than the rest of us or not, this is your next step in life.*

"They're your kids," Tandy snapped, staring at the pearly white mist. "How could you choose to leave them?"

*I left long before they were born,* the ghost stated sadly. *Unfortunately this is the one thing I could do for them.*

And, with that, the image faded away.

# CHAPTER 5

"SOMETHING IS STRANGE—*PSYCHICALLY* strange— about the twins," Dr. Maddy shared with Stefan, their tones rumbling through the din of the hospital.

He nodded. "I definitely got that too, but they're content in their ethereal world, and that already puts them pretty high up in the psychic realm. They've created an entire place, a social structure within their minds for themselves," he noted, "and they appear to be quite happy."

"I don't know that *happy* is the right word," Dr. Maddy clarified. "I think it's more a case of *protected*, and that's what Mark is after."

"Of course, and we can't fault him for that."

"No, of course not," Dr. Maddy murmured, "but it breaks my heart to see such guardedness and pain already in a five-year-old."

Stefan nodded. "Mark has already learned some very painful lessons, and we need to confirm that he's safe now."

Dr. Maddy sighed. "Apparently the authorities found photos in the mother's place that may have been used for internet kiddy porn sites."

Stefan went quiet for a moment. "I guess that's not a surprise, is it?"

"No, not a surprise, but it's just so ugly. We don't know whether the twins were abused or if they were just sitting for these photographs to be taken. The pictures go from infancy onward," she added, her tone catching.

Stefan softened his tone. "Anything to do with children is so hard. … If we can convince the twins to come out of their fantasy world, we could show them that the real world around them isn't so bad. That might be enough to bring them back to the reality of life, to speaking, to living a fuller life."

"But they need a safe place for that," Dr. Maddy pointed out, "and a permanent safe place. Since they cannot stay here forever, we need to find something for the twins and must get it ready for them. And get them ready for it too."

"I agree," Stefan replied. "I feel as if Mark will do everything he can to keep his brother in the ethers with him, and he may feel that Matthew is more scared than he is. Thus, Matthew follows Mark's lead blindly."

"Wouldn't you be scared?" Dr. Maddy muttered. "Just thinking about what they saw and maybe experienced is enough to make all of us understand Mark's need to keep him and his brother safe and to potentially keep everybody else away from them."

"I certainly understand that," Stefan acknowledged. "That doesn't mean that whoever was exposing the twins to this nastiness even gives a crap though."

"Do you think the twins are in danger now?" she asked.

"Oh, I wasn't thinking along those lines," he stated. However, as the thought rumbled through his brain, he grimaced. "I'm not sure that's an easy answer either. The only reason they would be in danger," he began, "was if somebody needed them for something. I don't even want to guess what that *something* would be."

"What are you thinking it could be?"

"We don't have any way to know, since their psyches are all over the place. But it could be anything from them being sold, and a financial deal to be completed, to their being a good source of income from their photos shown online," he suggested, "so I don't know. They are safe here, but, other than that, I don't know."

"I would say that Mark definitely believes that they still aren't safe and that he's determined to keep Matthew in there for as long as possible. We also know that the longer they live in this fantasy world, the harder it will be for them to come back out," she pointed out.

"Very true, but there's a valid reason for why they're hiding, and I would suggest that, as long as we can solve that problem for them, they would come out on their own."

"I wonder," she murmured.

"What about their sister, Tandy?" Stefan asked.

"I heard her screaming earlier," Dr. Maddy shared, almost absentmindedly. "It's hard to hear everybody's pain all the time."

"So why do you allow yourself to be open to it?" he asked.

She sighed. "Because I'm still trying to figure out what's going on with the children, and I thought, if I opened up to Tandy, maybe I could figure out more of what's been going on in their lives. Yet she's got so much pain in her own world that I'm not sure it was a smart thing to do."

"So, she probably hasn't dealt with her own childhood either."

"I think she's dealt with what she could deal with at the time, but, as with so many of us, we have layers. So, as you deal with one, then a million more come back," she muttered.

"Right. … I heard her as well," he admitted.

"I'm surprised you didn't reach out."

"I'm not sure she's ready for that."

"And yet I definitely get the feeling that Tandy has walls in place to keep us out."

He thought about that and then nodded. "You're right, and I guess that's not surprising."

Dr. Maddy asked, "Do you think she has abilities?"

"We all do."

"I know. I know," she replied impatiently. "But, just like the kids are very adept at creating this world on the ethers, where they feel safe, do you think Tandy can do that?"

"Yes, I do. I think she created a world where she got away from her mother, and now we've brought her back from that world, and I don't think she appreciates it at all," he stated.

"I didn't talk to Keller yet," Dr. Maddy began, "but I heard something about his being a little disturbed. I guess Keller told Tandy the news about the photographs on the internet, and she had a very strong physical reaction."

"Honest to God, that makes her more normal," Stefan noted. "Anybody who isn't affected by any of this is someone I would be looking at rather strongly."

"Right," she agreed, with a tiredness that made him frown.

"These kids are really getting to you, *huh*?"

"I don't know that it's these kids in particular," she explained, "as much as it's the fact that the world is such a messed-up place."

"We need to focus on the parts of it that aren't messed up," he noted, "knowing that we can do what we can do, and that's it."

"Now if only you took your own advice."

He smiled. Dr. Maddy was always very good at keeping him grounded too. "I think I'll see the kids tomorrow on the ethers. I was just wondering about something."

"What are you wondering about?"

"I wonder if Tandy has any idea what the twins can do or what they *are* doing."

"You could always ask her."

"I could, but I'm not sure she's ready for that just yet."

"Maybe not," she murmured. "On the other hand, no time like the present to ask."

He snorted. "That depends on whether she wants anything to do with me or not. I'm still a male and, in her eyes, a possible enemy."

"We need all the history we can get in order to help all three of them come out of this intact, happy, and adjusted. So feel free to question her. You may start to grow on her."

"Now you're asking for the moon," he quipped.

"No, not just the moon," she corrected, "the sun, the stars, *and* the moon." And, with that, she waved goodbye and returned to her office.

# CHAPTER 6

TANDY WOKE THE next morning, tired and fatigued. She still had a few days off and planned to finalize the funeral arrangements for Isabella. People around her kept talking about her *mother*, but Tandy hadn't thought of Isabella as a mother for a very long time. Over the years, she'd become just *Isabella* to her. Tandy had chosen cremation for Isabella, so her body would go from the morgue to the mortuary, and eventually the ashes would be released to Tandy. At least she thought so but maybe not. She sent Keller a message, asking about that. He'd given her his contact information last night, and, in spite of herself, she'd written it down.

He responded to her text with a text. **Let me check.**

That was good, since, as long as he was checking, she didn't have to, and that gave her a little bit of distance between everything going wrong in her world right now. When he responded almost immediately, she smiled in spite of herself.

"Thanks," she whispered out loud, relieved that the body would be released. **I'll arrange for her to be picked up for cremation.**

His response was yet again almost immediate. **Is that what you want to do?**

**Yes**, she replied. **Why wouldn't I?** She experienced a

moment of confusion, as she considered what else she was supposed to do. Isabella had always said she wanted to be cremated, so here Tandy was, taking care of her so-called mother's wishes yet again. "Damn it, I've got to stop doing that," she muttered to herself. "She is who she is, and she's gone. Let's just give it a rest."

She was talking to the empty room because her mother, although she had visited last night, was now long gone. It made no sense that Isabella had even been here last night. Ghosts generally don't have that kind of control so quickly after death. Tandy should know, as she'd seen more than her fair share of them. That was something else that Isabella had tried to monetize in Tandy's life.

Unsuccessfully so because Tandy failed to perform like the trick pony Isabella had tried to make out her daughter to be. That had been another huge fight because her mother didn't understand why Tandy didn't want to demonstrate that she could talk to ghosts.

Tandy just shook her head because Isabella never gave a shit about anybody else. However, if it made money, then she was all for exploiting other people's pain. That was the basis of yet another of those big mother-daughter fights, and, because of that, her grandmother had taken in Tandy. Isabella trying to make Tandy work on the streets, turning tricks and selling sexual favors, was the final straw for Tandy's grandmother, and she'd finally stepped up and had allowed Tandy to stay with her. As much as Tandy was damn grateful, it had also not been the easiest upbringing with her grandmother. Plus, Isabella constantly tried to make Tandy feel guilty about abandoning ship, which had been rather horrific too.

She dressed quickly, phoned the crematorium to make

arrangements for the body to be transferred and to notify her when the ashes were ready to be picked up, even though she had no clue what she was supposed to do with them.

That's when her mother responded, *Bury them somewhere nice, a place with roses.*

Tandy stiffened and ignored her.

*You can't just talk to me when you want to talk to me*, Isabella declared, almost vindictively. *I'm here, and I'm not going away.*

Tandy turned, eyed the same pearly mist, and declared, *Yes, you are.*

*See? I made you talk to me already*, she replied gleefully, *so why would I leave? This is fun.*

As Tandy looked back, the mist gathered around, taking a form, Isabella's form. She actually had a cigarette hanging out of her mouth. *Good God, same old, same old. Why the hell are you even smoking?*

Isabella looked at her in surprise and then laughed. *Why the hell not? It's not as if it will kill me. Where I'm at, fire is all about, but not so much drugs or alcohol. What a shame.* And, with that, she went off in peals of laughter.

*Did you commit suicide?* Tandy asked Isabella, point-blank.

Isabella stared at her and immediately zapped out of view.

She'd been like that in life too. If there was a way to get out of anything difficult or painful, she took it.

As a child, Tandy had pleaded with her mother to get off the drugs, and her mom kept telling her that it wasn't a problem, but of course it was a horrific problem. Isabella was just like every other drug addict out there, happy to give you every excuse they possibly could, until they're finally ready to do something productive about it.

Yet Isabella had never shown up to any of her rehab dates, had never appeared anywhere to get professional help, even though funding had been established for her and appointments had been made. Tandy herself, as a young teen, had gone looking for that funding for Isabella. Tandy had approached the courts and every rehab center that she could find. One had finally given in to her persistent demands, only to have her mother never bother to show up. Many people had told Tandy how that was the problem with a drug addict. It had to be their choice to get better, and you could bend over backward doing what you could, but, if they chose not to show up, that was their decision. It was ultimately up to Isabella.

It had broken Tandy's heart again and again. After that, she only wanted to walk away and to stay away. After she'd moved in with her grandmother, she had had essentially no contact with Isabella—until Tandy got a job. Somehow her mother found out about that, and then thought Tandy should pay for Isabella's everything. Her grandmother had stepped in finally, stating, if Tandy gave Isabella *any* money, Tandy would be out on the street herself. Her grandmother made it clear that nothing she did to help Tandy would go to Isabella, and Tandy could deal with those terms or could move out. She'd immediately agreed because the last thing she wanted was to end up on the streets herself.

She'd quickly finished school, had done the best that she could at the time, and, even after college, remained in her grandmother's house. She helped Gwen when she could, and Gwen continued to help Tandy.

Meanwhile, Isabella had never let Tandy forget how she had *abandoned her mother*, but it's not as if Tandy lived with

Isabella any longer or that sending money to Isabella would have changed anything. Any resource would literally have just gone to drugs, more and more drugs. As far as Isabella was concerned, this was just the way it was with addicts.

So Isabella had resumed asking Tandy for money since the twins were born. Isabella had apparently had a home birth, and, while Tandy knew about the twins, she'd had no contact with them. And now she had to wonder if she should have. Those damned *should-haves* were killing her.

Tandy winced at that, knowing how hard her grandmother had fought against Tandy having any contact with her mother. The relationship between Gwen and Isabella had definitely been a no-love-lost kind and for a lot of good reasons, as far as Tandy could tell. But her grandmother had nothing but disgust for Isabella the entire time, and Gwen had never forgiven nor forgotten what Isabella had done. Tandy never knew exactly what happened, but she could imagine all sorts of bad things.

When Tandy's phone rang, she stared down at it, not sure who was calling and hesitant to answer it. But just like with Keller, she knew this caller wouldn't go away either. She answered it finally, and, when the caller identified himself as Stefan, she asked, "Why are you calling?"

With a note of humor in his tone, he replied, "For one thing, I wanted to give you an update on the twins."

"And for another?"

"I wanted to see if you were okay," he added. "Some of this has got to be pretty traumatic for you."

"Some of it?" she repeated, with a groan. "How does any of this become *some of it*? ... And how did you even think to call me?" she asked suspiciously.

And that brought a chuckle from him. "I'm very good

friends with Dr. Maddy and her husband, Drew, the FBI agent."

"Right, so that just means you also know Keller and Grant then."

"Yep, although they are local law enforcement not FBI," he agreed cheerfully. "And when these types of cases come up, we're all involved. There are no easy answers for anybody, so we always take care to confirm that everybody is handling it okay."

"If I say I'm not dealing with things okay," she snapped, "what will you do about it?"

"You might be surprised," he said. "If you need counseling or therapy, that is available too."

"Not for free," she grumbled. "Medical care in this part of the world is pretty rough."

"But you're a nurse, and you have medical coverage, do you not?"

"I do," she confirmed.

"And then there are other kinds of therapy," he suggested.

"Yeah, and what therapy is that?"

He laughed. "I was about to question you on your psychic abilities."

She gasped in shock, and she almost heard Stefan's smile again.

Stefan asked, "Do you talk to ghosts? Do you have premonitions, or just what is your field?" he asked curiously.

Stunned, she stared at her phone.

He continued. "Or are you just not comfortable talking about it?"

"Good God," she cried out, "who the hell is?"

"I am, but then it's something that I deal with on a regular basis."

"What do you mean, you deal with it on a regular basis?" she asked.

"Now that you ask, I'm fairly well-known for it," he replied, "and I work with the police a lot too."

"Yeah, the police are not very helpful in many ways," she murmured. "And if you don't have any background that they feel they can trust, believe me that they don't want anything to do with you."

"I hadn't really considered that, but you're probably right. Yet, because I do have a background that they're quite happy to deal with," he added, "that's never been an issue for me."

"Aah, lucky you," she said, with a snort.

"So, you admit to having abilities?"

She stared down at the phone and shook her head. But that wasn't an answer, not an audible one. "No, of course I'm not admitting to something like that," she declared.

"We think the twins have abilities."

She stared at the phone, shocked. "Like what?" she asked cautiously, wanting to twist her mother's neck yet again.

"I am inclined to tell you, but the question really is, do *you* have abilities? If you do, then we have some idea of what the twins can do."

"That's not how abilities work," she declared, "which you should know. What kind of abilities do they have?"

"I suggest you come down and visit with them today."

"I can do that," she said. "I took some time off work."

"Good. How about …"

She could almost hear him checking his calendar.

"How about in an hour?"

"Great," she muttered. "I'll be there."

"Good," he said and ended the call.

She frowned, noting that she hadn't told him no and that she hadn't told him yes either, when it came to her having abilities at least not in the way that he would likely believe. And what kind of abilities did he have?

She quickly sat down to search Google for him and sat back, shocked at everything she found. When he shared that he was fairly-well-known, he wasn't kidding. What would it have been like to have had him in her life when she was younger?

Dear God, that didn't bear thinking about. And it's not as if she had any abilities that she would even talk about, and she sure as hell didn't want anybody else to know anyway.

Isabella knew, just because she had been there as Tandy grew up. So, while Tandy had been talking to the dead people around them, Isabella had been so delighted, thinking she could charge people for this, and she often did—until Tandy grew up and was able to fake the outcome.

As soon as Tandy started getting poor results, Isabella would turn on her and would ask her why. Puberty worked as an answer for a long time, much to the disgust of her mother. Tandy's need to find a way out of the rat race her mother had built up for Tandy had involved getting her to lie, since her abilities had actually grown stronger. But even still, she wasn't comfortable talking about them and sure as hell didn't know anyone with whom she could trust to share this information.

"Maybe Stefan though," she pondered, as she got dressed and headed over to Dr. Maddy's floor, where the twins were staying. But, if they had abilities, what did that mean for Tandy? Maybe it meant that Tandy was the person who should be looking after the twins. But how the hell would she do that, when she had to work for a living?

As she walked inside the building, Dr. Maddy headed down the hallway, talking to Stefan.

They both looked up and smiled at her.

Tandy frowned.

Stefan laughed. "Good, keep that chip on your shoulder. It will hold you in good stead."

"Really?" she asked, staring at him. "I can't say it's done anything for me so far."

He smiled. "And sometimes life is that way. Sometimes life is good, and sometimes it's just something you don't trust."

"I've got the *don't trust* part down pat," she murmured. "So, what's this about the twins having abilities?"

"Oh, did he tell you?" Dr. Maddy exclaimed in delight. "It's really quite something."

"I don't know about any of this being *quite something*," Tandy declared, staring at her. "Why would anybody be happy about it?"

"Why would you *not* be happy about it?" Dr. Maddy asked, studying Tandy. "To have any abilities makes it so much easier to navigate this life."

"No," Tandy countered, staring at Dr. Maddy. "It doesn't help at all. All it does is confuse everything."

Dr. Maddy stopped to face her. "We really do need to talk about those abilities. There are people out there who can help you."

"Help me?" Tandy repeated, frowning at them, shaking her head. "I'm pretty sure there isn't any help for this."

Dr. Maddy smiled. "I have abilities, and so does Stefan," she shared, "so, if you ever want to talk, I will always be ready to listen. Let's go see the kids."

Such eagerness filled her tone that Tandy stared at her.

"Have you found a way to interact with them?"

Dr. Maddy turned to her, her face filled with a huge beaming smile. "That's one of the reasons we wanted to bring you here," she replied. "Come on." Dr. Maddy led her into a small room, where the twins were playing. They both looked up, but outside of that movement, absolutely nothing in their faces showed any progress, any understanding, any recognition, anything.

Tandy stared at them, her heart sinking. "I thought you said—"

At that, Stefan reached out and touched her hand, and the room morphed into something else completely. There were the twins, chattering away at each other as they built some sort of … what? Tandy didn't even know what they were building with, but the twins were assembling some magnetic tiles, and they were quite happily erecting this big tower in front of them.

Stefan was here, and so was Dr. Maddy.

Tandy looked around in amazement because, although it was the same room, it wasn't the same room at all. When the children spotted her, Mark's jaw dropped, and he looked at Tandy in delight, and the little boy, Matthew, got up and raced toward her, throwing his arms around her. She didn't know what else to do but open her arms, close them around him, and hug him tight.

"You came," Matthew cried out in joy.

"I did," she murmured. "I didn't know this is where you were."

"Mom told us that she would tell you," Mark stated, his gaze intent, as if looking for deceit.

"Did she?" Tandy asked. "Maybe she didn't get a chance to."

At that, her brother studied her for a moment. Then the clouds cleared, and he smiled at Tandy suddenly. "You're here now," he said, making room beside him. "Sit down, and we can play."

Stunned, and moving almost as if she were automated, Tandy sat beside her siblings and played with the building blocks in whatever world this was. Stefan and Dr. Maddy were also here the whole time.

When the kids started to show signs of fatigue, Dr. Maddy stepped in. "Now I would say it's time for a nap."

Both twins nodded, but they reached out their arms toward Tandy and asked her, "Will you come back?"

"Yes, of course," she declared. "Of course I'll come back."

And, with beams of smiles that brought tears to Tandy's eyes, the twins looked over at Dr. Maddy. "Okay, we'll go to sleep now." And they headed to the twin beds, set side by side. Hands connected, they rolled against the wall, and the entire room morphed into something yet again. Tandy looked around to see the two children sound asleep in their beds. Stefan and Dr. Maddy stood here too, staring at Tandy, as she slowly stood up. Yet there were no magnet tiles, no play area, just two children sleeping in the beds.

She turned to face the two of them and, in complete confusion, asked, "What the hell just happened?"

STUDYING THE INTERACTIONS via the special window in the next-door observation room, Keller heaved out a sigh. "I'm not sure what I just saw," he murmured to Grant. Drew nodded, and Grant did the same. Keller had learned today that physical contact with a psychic ground wasn't necessary to see inside this crazy world Keller had just witnessed. He shook his head. Did everybody get gifts when hanging around Dr. Maddy and Stefan? If so, it sure made it that much easier on Keller to see these psychic visions.

Drew gave a short laugh. "This stuff is still so foreign to me. Even after all the years I have been married to and have worked with Maddy, I learn new things about her world," he murmured. "Yet apparently being around her has helped my own intuitive abilities to develop, but I'm not gifted at all, and I still don't know what I'm looking at." He turned to Keller and added, "Yet when you touched my shoulder, for as long as your hand rested there, I saw what you probably saw. Amazing." He shook his head. "Amazing and scary."

Grant nodded. "I agree. I still have no psychic abilities either. I leave all that to the professionals."

"Don't be so quick to say that," Drew replied, with a knowing smile.

Keller studied Grant. "So did you see what I saw?"

When Grant just shrugged, Drew smiled at Keller. "The fact that you're even developing these gifts with Dr. Maddy around is huge."

Keller grumbled. "Not really. I prefer black-and-white evidence to this stuff."

Drew shook his head and smiled. "What did you see?" he asked Keller curiously. "I always wonder if you see the same thing as we do, when we get this special access."

Grant again nodded.

Keller began, "I'm not sure that I can even describe it, but it seemed as if the kids were playing. Tandy was sitting with them, and they appeared to be quite happy to see her. Everything *seemed* to be normal," he admitted. "Then, all of a sudden, the room shifted, with the two kids sound asleep in that room right there." Keller pointed at the view from the observation window, shaking his head.

"And the cameras in that room confirm the twins were sound asleep the entire time we've been watching from this room," Grant confirmed. "When we arrived, we were also told that they were asleep."

"I know, but that's not how I saw them," Keller clarified. Just then the light over the window blinked.

Grant nodded toward it and shared, "That's Dr. Maddy telling us we can go back to her office."

"*Great*," Keller muttered. "I feel completely useless here." Keller turned to Drew. "She has quite the place, doesn't she?"

Drew nodded. "You have no idea. She works miracles here, and a lot of people would do anything they could to keep this place open."

"Has she had any problems keeping it open?"

"Not really. Every once in a while we get some bad press, but she seems to stop it pretty quickly. She comes from the heart, and people get fantastic results here, and that's all anybody with a sick child really cares about. Results are what matters. Nobody really cares about how it happens." And, with that, Drew left them.

"I don't even think I want to ask how," Keller muttered, as he stared at the rooms they walked past.

"You now know," Grant teased, with a chuckle. "But nobody, including Dr. Maddy, can really explain it. *Energy work*," he noted, with a shrug of his shoulder, "is not the easiest thing to describe."

"Nope, it sure isn't."

Grant added, "The fact that you're even talking about it is pretty amazing."

"Not really," Keller snorted, followed by a laugh, "though I'm not exactly sure where I fit in all this."

"You're looking into the possible murder of Isabella, and that's pretty much what you're supposed to be doing," Grant confirmed, "and I'm looking into the pornography issue, plus if Isabella had been targeted by somebody across state lines."

"I don't understand how her death falls into your jurisdiction though."

"We do have the kiddy porn, which is something I don't normally handle, but, because it involves a possible murder and the possible abuse of these kids, and now the Dr. Maddy connection," Grant explained, "I pretty well put myself into it."

"That must come with a certain amount of seniority," Keller replied.

Grant laughed and nodded. "Yep, it sure does. I could work for Dr. Maddy full-time, just trying to troubleshoot cases that she pulls up in her world, and it's definitely something I've considered."

"Seriously?" Keller frowned at him.

Grant shrugged. "Yes, Dr. Maddy's patients end up with peculiar circumstances sometimes, and I always thought I would probably make a full-time career of investigating those cases."

"That's pretty sad too, though," Keller murmured. As he thought about it, he added, "I guess if you find more cases than this one, that would make some sense."

"Sadly, we find lots more like this one," he shared, "and unfortunately sometimes only people like Dr. Maddy and Stefan can handle these kinds of cases. ... Yet nobody really understands what these kinds of cases even are, which is precisely why it's their purview," Grant noted, with a laugh. He pointed to the door coming up and added, "That's Dr. Maddy's office. We'll go in there."

Grant led the way and walked inside, as Dr. Maddy looked up at her husband's good friend with a bright smile. Grant gave her a gentle hug, then turned to nod at Stefan. And then he caught sight of Tandy and smiled.

Keller nodded a greeting to Tandy, who just frowned in return. He wasn't sure how he felt about her yet. His instincts were usually pretty solid most of the time, but, at the moment, he wasn't sure he could trust them. Some pretty bizarre things had gone on in that observation room. Keller turned to Dr. Maddy. "I would love an explanation of what went on in there."

She looked at him with interest. "What did you see?"

He explained a little bit about the kids playing, and then, all of a sudden, that shifted to them being asleep.

"So, when you saw them the first time, they were playing?" Tandy asked.

He faced her and nodded. "We came in a few minutes late. We were in the observation room."

She nodded, then glanced over at Dr. Maddy and Stefan. "They were just about to give me an explanation of what I saw. Maybe you're a part of that too."

"Not sure I am," Keller shared, turning to look at the two experts. "Can somebody explain what's going on?"

Stefan smiled. "It's a little hard to explain," he began, "because we're not exactly sure ourselves, but these kids are strong enough in their abilities to design a make-believe world where everything else disappears around them."

"You can only be in their world if you're invited into their world," Dr. Maddy quickly added.

"You were invited? By the twins?" Keller looked at Dr. Maddy, and she nodded.

Stefan confirmed, "That's correct. We were both invited in. Well, it was more that we barged in the first time, but then we stayed with the twins' permission. Being their sister, Tandy was also included," Stefan noted, turning to her.

She frowned at him. "Was I though?" she challenged.

Stefan grinned. "I distinctly remember them asking you to come play with them."

She thought about it, then nodded. "I guess so, if you want to look at it from that perspective."

"Is there any other way to look at it?" Keller asked her curiously, "especially from a child's viewpoint?"

She shrugged, and he saw what may have been confusion—or maybe irritation, he wasn't sure. But something was definitely going on in her space, but then again she'd gone through a lot recently.

Tandy frowned at Stefan. "But how is it that I ended up in that same world?"

"Because you were invited in," he replied.

"And what does that have to do with their being synesthetes?"

Stefan smiled at her. "Did you know that about them?"

"I'm not even sure I know what that means," she exclaimed, raising both hands. "All of this feels very much out of my depths."

"I'm not at all surprised. Although synesthesia is not uncommon, it is only found in about 17 percent of the population, per the surveys," Stefan pointed out. "However, in the case of your siblings, they seem to have the ability to take it to the extreme."

"Since when does that have anything to do with creating

a make-believe world?" she asked.

"That's the fun part," Dr. Maddy exclaimed, "because it really doesn't. A Synesthete is someone who mixes, combines, switches senses—or to give one hypothetical example, some can see colors around numbers, so sight yet experienced via mathematics, a thought calculation, a different medium. When some hear music, they see colors. So they're mixing hearing and sight together in that circumstance. Some people could touch someone and then either get music or potentially colors. There are all different kinds of variations, but the most common is seeing numbers in color."

Tandy just frowned blankly at Dr. Maddy, and Keller had to admit he was struggling with the concept himself.

"If that percentage is correct," Keller noted, "I'm surprised it's not something I'm familiar with. After all, I've been a detective for years."

Dr. Maddy smiled at him. "It's not something that most people talk about, and a lot of people probably don't even know they have it or even a variation of it," she murmured.

"But none of that has anything to do with them creating what I just saw," Tandy pointed out.

"That is quite true," Dr. Maddy admitted, with a smile. "But children, particularly children who have experienced trauma"—she paused, her gaze going from one to the other—"will often check out. It's too painful to be where they are, so they find a way to literally leave the world they're currently living in."

"And you're saying that's what they're doing?" Tandy asked. "Because they looked very ..." She frowned and added, "I want to say they looked very *active* in the world they were in."

"They were very active, but it's the safe world they created, not the world we all live in."

"So, you're saying that they were so traumatized by something in their lives that they created this make-believe world?" Keller asked. When Dr. Maddy nodded in agreement, Keller sighed. "Okay, I get that. So they've created this world where they're elsewhere, they're happy, they're doing their own thing, but do they stay in that world?"

"That's the way it seems. That's where they feel safe and comfortable, and that's where they are staying. It appears that Mark is the ringleader."

"Ringleader?" Tandy asked. "Is there such a thing?"

Dr. Maddy replied, "In this case, yes, as he appears to be very protective of Matthew."

Keller watched the sorrow and the pain in Tandy's expression as she heard that, and, for the first time, he realized just how hard this was hitting her, even if she didn't want to care—or, whether she was aware of it or not, she already cared about these children very much. He patted her shoulder. "Maybe it's a good thing."

"To me, it just means that it's a *necessary* thing," she clarified, staring at him. "It means that there's a *reason* for it."

"And we already know some of the reasons," he pointed out. "If Mark's doing this to protect Matthew, maybe he's been able to keep him safe from some of what's happened." He turned to look at Dr. Maddy. "Is that why they're nonverbal, if that's the proper term?"

"I would suspect that's why," she agreed, nodding her head. "Yet I feel there is another layer involved, so we obviously have more studying to do."

"And what will it take for them to come out of this little world they've created?" Tandy asked. "After all, they've chosen this make-believe world. So, if it's a choice for them to stay, it should be a choice for them to come back out."

Dr. Maddy smiled at her and nodded. "You are quite correct. It is a choice, and, if we can make Mark feel comfortable and safe, I think there's a good chance we can convince them to leave their make-believe world."

"*Good chance*," Tandy repeated, her gaze narrowing. "I don't like that it's a *chance* and not a certainty."

"There are no guarantees in this," Dr. Maddy stated. "We have an awful lot of psychological issues here that need some time to heal."

Keller watched Tandy's shoulders sag. "Are you the same as them?" he asked her.

She frowned at him. "I don't even know that term, and I wouldn't have thought so. I have nothing in common with them, but I'm pretty sure Dr. Maddy will dispute that."

Dr. Maddy laughed. "Now why would I do that?"

She snorted. "Because I was in there playing with them, and I'm sure you'll say something about the fact that, if I could play with them in that space, then I had some affinity to whatever they were doing."

"But then you do have abilities, even if you don't want to share that with other people," Stefan noted. Tandy turned to glare at him. He just smiled and nodded. "Most of us here do, and even those who didn't before are slowly developing them," he said, with a crooked smile in Keller's and Grant's direction.

Tandy asked Keller, "You too?"

"Oh, not like these people," he declared, with a big smile. "I'm very much the standard black-and-white detective type, with some good instincts."

At that, Dr. Maddy burst into laughter. "You were," she clarified, "but you certainly aren't now."

"Maybe not, but sometimes I do think it would be a whole lot easier if I could go back to the old way of doing investigations."

"Of course it would be easier," Tandy agreed, "but once you open that doorway …"

"What doorway did you open?" Grant asked her, almost in a challenging note.

Keller was surprised at that. Normally Grant was extremely moderate, but something about Tandy was pushing Grant's buttons.

Tandy shrugged. "I'm sure if you've dug into my history at all, you would already know."

"And maybe we haven't dug deep enough."

At that, she paled.

Dr. Maddy suggested to Tandy in a gentler tone, "If you would just tell them, law enforcement wouldn't have to dig, but I can assure you—now that you've even mentioned that much—they'll have to, if you don't explain it."

Tandy glared at them all, her gaze going from one to the other. "It's not something I'm particularly proud of nor want people to know about."

"Of course not," Grant agreed. "I swear to God that probably applies to us all."

"Maybe, but you probably weren't paraded around as a psychic by your mother, trying to make money and to cheat people."

Grant frowned at her. "Did she do that?"

Tandy snorted. "When I was young, before I realized what I was doing, I was talking to dead people," she admitted, with a dismissive wave of her hand. "Dead people. … Like who the hell does that?" she muttered, staring at Dr. Maddy.

Dr. Maddy just smiled and didn't say anything.

Tandy continued. "But, as soon as Isabella thought that I might be a ticket to a better world for her, her personal cash cow, she was all about taking advantage of it. And, for quite a while, my life was pretty horrible. Not only did I have the dead people to contend with, and I wasn't at all sure how that was supposed to work, but I also had Isabella out there drumming up more attention to it. She was trying to pawn off information on kidnap victims and missing persons and deaths. She would read the papers and then contact people, saying that I was psychic. She would insist on my contacting or doing what I could to find these missing or dead people, and, when I couldn't, she would just make shit up. Of course I got the blame when things went wrong, and she always had a fast tale or a convenient lie, something to keep people on the line, bringing in more money," she muttered.

"What happened then?"

"I deliberately started lying to her, telling her that I couldn't see things, probably because I didn't have enough food or I didn't have God-only-knows what. Hitting puberty was a godsend because I could use that too," she added, "but it didn't matter. It didn't matter at all. Isabella just kept using me as a way to make money, one way or another. Until we got broken into one night by a rather desperate father looking for his daughter, and we were both held at gunpoint, tied to a chair, while I was supposed to contact this girl. Unfortunately I had no problem contacting the girl, and she told me in no uncertain terms that her father had killed her in a drunken rage but couldn't come to terms with what he'd done."

At that, silence fell over the room. "That's a bit of a ham

scramble, isn't it?" Dr. Maddy muttered. "You're damned if you do, and you're damned if you don't."

Tandy gave her half a smile. "Exactly, and, after that episode, I stopped telling Isabella anything. Believe me, it was a miracle that we got out of that, and, to this day, I still don't know what happened. I was pretty rattled by it, but to my mother it just seemed to be some lark. When it was over, she took off right away, had a hit of drugs, and it never seemed to bother her again."

"Did you ever do drugs?" Keller asked, trying to phrase it nicely, but knowing that there wasn't any real way to be nice about it. She immediately shook her head, and he felt a sense of relief inside at her answer.

"No," she stated. "I'd already seen way too much of the side effects, way too much of the negativity in that lifestyle."

"And she didn't force you?"

"She tried a couple times." Tandy didn't elaborate.

"So, the psychic stuff just went away as a business at that point?" Keller asked her.

"After that guy broke into our home, I told Isabella that I couldn't talk to dead people after that, that I couldn't see anything anymore, so she finally had to stop. She was pretty disgusted, and she tried email cons for a while, tried website scams, trying to con people into giving her money for answers, but I wouldn't give her anything else. She just started making shit up, but it didn't really fly. Either people didn't really believe her or had done some research, I don't know," she added. "She went back to prostitution to get her drug money, and then had the bright idea to send me out there too. Between that and the guy breaking into our house, I finally managed to get my grandmother to take me in."

Keller frowned. "So, she hadn't been involved in your life up until then?"

"No, she had no love for my mother and refused to help her in any way."

"What about for you?" Keller asked, studying her features, wondering at a grandmother who wouldn't take in a child.

"Before that, she thought that I was a psychic, and she didn't want anything to do with me, being *the devil's work* and all."

"And yet she did take you in after all?"

"I told her it was all fake. I told her it was all a lie and shared what my mother had been doing," Tandy explained. "As a teen I was rather desperate to get out of any situation involving Isabella, and that seemed to be the only avenue, so I was all for the lying to Isabella and to my grandmother," she admitted bitterly. "I know I have a lot to make up for in life, but I don't see that I should be punished for trying to get out of a bad situation, which was not of my own making."

"Of course not, there is no judgment for doing what you needed to do to survive," Dr. Maddy declared, studying her. "There's no reason for you to think along that line."

Tandy gave her a haunted look. "There have definitely been plenty of times that it comes across loud and clear in my head. Because of Isabella, we scammed people out of money, out of hope. Those people were desperate for answers, and my mother just jumped right in there. Anything to milk them for a few more bucks, completely ignoring their pain," Tandy shared. "I don't use my abilities because of that."

"And yet you have them," Stefan stated.

She looked at him, then shrugged. "If you want to call them that, yes."

"It feels very much as if you need to say something else

in all that," Dr. Maddy noted, "but we're not here to push you."

Keller couldn't help but notice the relief that washed over Tandy. Definitely more was in there, but he wasn't sure what it would take for her to open up, particularly in the circumstances they were in.

"None of this …" Tandy began, "nothing helps us in terms of my siblings. As for Mark and Matthew, I have no idea about them."

"No, but it might explain why they had no problem with your playing with them," Keller noted. "I'm not sure I would be offered the same opportunity."

"If they saw your gifts, … maybe," Tandy suggested, "but I don't even know what your gifts are."

"I'm not sure I know either," he stated cheerfully. "It's not exactly something I've ever worked to develop. I swear to God it's only because of working alongside Dr. Maddy that I would consider I even have any."

"Of course," Tandy agreed, "and being with gifted people like this just helps you to increase your abilities."

"That's not why I'm here," he stated, his tone curt.

"Not why I'm here either," Tandy declared, "but it doesn't change the fact that being in proximity to other psychics builds energy."

"Have you worked with any other psychics?" Stefan asked curiously.

Tandy faced him, frowning at him for a long moment, then shook her head.

Again Keller felt as if something was there that she wasn't sharing, and, while he couldn't blame her, it was still frustrating. He wanted answers, and she just wasn't up for providing any.

# CHAPTER 7

T ANDY LET HERSELF into her apartment. It took her all her energy to get inside and to lock the door before she collapsed onto the couch. Her energy was at an all-time low, and she needed to do something about it before she collapsed again, which was not something she was prepared to do. Yet the ghost of her mother was around, and her mother had always been a negative influence on her.

With that thought came the snap of a rebuke from Isabella. *No, I'm not. I never was. You just always saw me as the enemy.*

Tandy gave a bitter laugh and ignored her mother. The fact that Isabella could read her mind half the time and seemed to be in her own thoughts the other half really terrified Tandy. She was terrified that Isabella had found some strange way to stay alive, well past her expiration date. Tandy threw up as many mental blocks as she could handle right now, with her low energy, then stretched out and closed her eyes.

She hoped she would crash into a power nap, so she could get up and function afterward. But instead of Tandy sleeping peacefully, the thoughts just kept running around and around in her head. That the twins were psychic shouldn't have come as a surprise. That they were hiding out from the reality of the harsh and cruel world that they had lived in was something else again. It made Tandy feel absolutely horrible to think that they had suffered while she was in a position to do something, even if she didn't have any real understanding of what she could have done. Yet the fear that she could have done something to save them from so much pain refused to let go.

Isabella still droned on in the background, not leaving Tandy alone until she talked to her mother. But Tandy had no intention of talking to Isabella, not right now, not when she was in this space, not when she was so exhausted from everything else going on. Especially not after seeing the twins living as they were, hiding away together in this make-believe world because it was safer that way. Tandy had never had anyone to keep her safe, not that she was jealous of the fact that the twins had each other, but it just reminded her that, if she could have done something for them, maybe she could have saved them from this pain.

She remained here on the couch, dry-eyed, not sure what to do or even how to navigate past this, when her doorbell rang. She groaned and mentally willed them to go away, but instead she heard Keller call out. She yelled back, "I'm too tired for this. Go away."

First came silence, and then he asked, "Are you tired from someone yapping at you, or are you just tired?" he called out.

She frowned at that, then slowly got up and made her way to open the front door to glare at him.

His gaze narrowed as he studied her features.

"Don't tell me that you're worried about me," she stated in a mocking tone.

"Would it be so surprising?" he asked, as he stared at her curiously.

"Of course it would be," she declared, with a wave of her hand. "That's not what people do."

He stepped inside and closed the door, almost as if he cared about keeping her world private from the curiosity of the neighbors. "And yet," he added, "you're clearly exhausted to the point that something isn't quite right."

"Sure, lots of things aren't quite right," she muttered, "and it doesn't change a damn thing."

"Do you want to explain that?"

"No, if I wanted to explain that, I would have," she said in exasperation. "Why are you here?" He hesitated to respond, and she glared at him. "This better be good."

"Okay, I was worried about you," he admitted.

And the truth, so simple and so honestly delivered, shook her to the core. She stared at him, tilted her head, and asked, "Why?"

"Because you didn't look so good when you left, and you kind of bolted out of Dr. Maddy's office."

"Of course I did," she declared. "In case you hadn't noticed, it was a pretty startling afternoon."

"You got to play with the kids though," he pointed out.

"Sure, kids I don't really know. Kids I don't really have a connection to, yet are blood kin and damaged in such a way that this imaginary life is a preferable life for them," she summarized, staring at him. "How is knowing that making anything better in my life or in theirs?"

"Back to the guilt again?"

She shrugged. "I'm not sure how I'm supposed to *not* feel guilty, yet I don't know what I was supposed to do," she shared. "I didn't even know about them. Or maybe I did, but I just didn't want to know."

*That is so like you*, snapped her mother.

Tandy turned and glared around the room. When she

caught herself reacting, she swung back to find Keller staring at her. She waved her hand. "Don't worry about me."

"I am worried about you," he repeated, "and it seems as if maybe today was a bit much."

"It's always a bit much," she snapped, as she walked into the kitchen and put on coffee.

"Have you eaten anything?"

She shook her head. "I'm not hungry, and I doubt anything would stay down."

"We can't have that," he murmured. "Let's at least get some real food into you." He opened the fridge and sighed. "I guess we're ordering in then, aren't we?"

"If you want food, you better," she stated, as she made coffee. "It's not as if I have anything here."

"I see that," he replied, frowning at her, "and you're a nurse."

"Yes, I'm a nurse," she confirmed.

"And where do you work?"

"I work in the cancer unit." When he frowned at her again, she shrugged. "Why? Am I not allowed to?"

"Sure, you're allowed to," he said. "I'm just surprised that you would work in such a place."

She laughed. "Is there any better place? It's not as if any good place to work exists for me."

"Maybe not," he conceded, "and I'm sorry if this all seems very intrusive. I'm not trying to be so difficult."

"Yes, you are," she declared, with a look in his direction. "I think it goes along with *your* job."

"Maybe," he noted. "And maybe I want to go back to your comment about … *is there any good place to work for you.* I do enjoy my work, but we see an awful lot in life that isn't easy."

She stopped and then nodded slowly. "I would agree

with that, and that's also part of what I do at my job."

"And yet," he added, "you see ghosts."

"Most of the people I work with haven't died yet."

His eyebrows shot up at that. Then he nodded. "That's a really valid point. I hadn't really considered that—working on healing the dead."

"Everybody thinks that because you've got cancer, you're at death's door, and sometimes it is true. Sometimes you are right there, and nobody can do anything about it, but a lot of times the survival rates are excellent, and people in active treatment are the ones I prefer to work with."

"Why?"

"Because they're positive," she said, looking at him. "I'm not just dealing with families losing a mother, a sister, a daughter. I'm dealing with people who are pursuing treatment with a positive mind-set, and it's just easier to heal and to work with them as well."

"And the ones who don't make it?" He hesitated, then added, "Do you talk to them afterward?"

She shook her head. "No, ... at least not usually. Most of the time they have moved on. So, if they won't make it, and I know they won't make it, I try hard to help them find peace with their passing," she explained. "If there's one thing I can do for them, it's that."

He raised a brow. "That's huge."

"It is and it isn't," she muttered. "It's still a failure, and, for so many people, it shouldn't be. It's closing a door and opening another one."

"And do you really believe that?"

"Of course I believe that," she stated crossly. "I see dead people. What is it you want me to say?" He just smiled and shrugged, giving her a nod. She groaned. "I feel as if I just said something that was a test."

"Not at all," he replied, "but we all have such different takes on death to begin with, and, if you work in a cancer unit, you'll see death on a regular basis."

"But I don't see the deaths," she pointed out. "That's the difference. I'm not there actively in a hospice environment helping them."

"And have you considered doing that?"

She shrugged. "Sure, I've considered it, but it's just not a stage of life I want to work on yet." He just nodded. She groaned. "Maybe eventually."

"*Maybe eventually* is good enough for me," Keller replied. "Nobody has to do the same thing forever, and it would put a ton of pressure on you to do what you could do to help them cross over."

"But I don't want to help them cross over, that's the problem," she stated. "I want to be on this side, where they're still fighting."

"Of course. That makes sense too."

"I don't know," she muttered, her shoulders slumping as she poured a cup of coffee. Then she stepped back and looked at him. "Sometimes it just seems so useless, when we all end up in the same damn place anyway." He let out a bark of laughter at that, tugging a smile to her face. "Sorry, that was just my morbid sense of humor."

"No apologies necessary," he said. "I appreciate it. I also sometimes need respite from all the darkness I work with too."

"*Right,*" she noted, with a roll of her eyes. "Anybody dealing with sex trafficking, online porn, and sexual abuse of children?" She shook her head. "I don't think I could do that."

"Which is probably why you've avoided the twins."

"Back in that room, I wondered why I hadn't done anything for them."

"Up until now you were ignorant of it."

"Are you saying, if I'm *not* ignorant of it now, it's up to me to do the right thing, correct?"

"You were always going to do the right thing," he stated, with a smile in her direction. "You just hadn't come around to accepting it yet." And, with that, he walked into her living room and sat down on the couch. "What is your mother saying that's scaring you?" When she stared at him, he waved his hand. "Don't bother lying. I can already tell you've been talking to her."

"I shouldn't be talking to her. She's recently dead, and she should have crossed over." Her gaze darted around to a chair discreetly.

His eyebrows shot up. "But she didn't, right?"

"No, she didn't."

"And why is that?"

"Because I think she was murdered."

KELLER'S BREATH SUCKED in, and he stared at Tandy for a long moment. "And when were you going to tell us that?"

"I don't know," she admitted. "Maybe when I had some proof of it, and maybe when I cared."

He gave her a smirk. "I can see that you're trying to be tough, sweetheart, but I can also see that you're trying to figure out how to bring the twins home, how to help them, and how to help yourself as well. You can't do everything, and, believe me, being confused about your feelings for your mother is very understandable."

"Why would I be confused, God forbid? Isabella, my mother, ran in a bad crowd, and she made my life hell."

"But, if she was murdered—and I'm just saying *if* because you don't have any proof—it's understandable that you wouldn't have brought it to us. Yet now that we do know that you can talk to her, maybe you could give me a little bit more information. Then I can see about finding her killer."

"Why?" Tandy asked. "Chances are it will be one of the same assholes involved in the sexual assaults of my siblings."

"Even more of a reason," he snapped, his tone hardening. "Those are the assholes I want to get off the streets."

He was right. She knew that he was right, but when was doing the right thing ever easy? She nodded grimly and asked, "Do you want coffee?"

"Thank you. I would love some coffee." She groaned at the very polite way he had replied. So he smiled, hopped up, and offered, "I'll get myself a cup, thanks."

"Yeah, you do that," she muttered, as she curled up on the end of the couch and watched from her position.

He came back with a cup of coffee and sat on the other end of the same couch. "Now, why don't you tell me what Isabella told you?"

"The thing is, it doesn't matter what she says because I can't trust or believe anything out of her mouth. She's no different now than she was before. She was a liar then, and she's a liar now."

He looked at her closely for a long moment. "That's interesting too, isn't it? We tend to think that, as soon as people are dead, they suddenly become this really good person."

"I think people are the same on this side as on that side, at least until they make peace, heal, or whatever," she shared, "and I'm not sure there is a *whatever* in some of these cases. Obviously I have an awful lot of anger against Isabella, and it's building right now because of the twins," she admitted. "So this probably isn't the best time for that conversation."

"No, but it's not a bad time," he pointed out. "If you think about it, the sooner we can do something about the twins and whoever may have murdered your mother, the sooner it can all go away."

"But will it? Or will you want me to testify in court too?"

"Only because of your conversations with your mother can we get something moving on this matter. However, that's not something I can put you on a witness stand for."

"Oh," she said, brightening, "that's a really good point."

"Yes, so do you want to share a little bit more, please?"

She shrugged. "Isabella gives me shit all the time. She wants me to take the twins, wants me to do a better job than she did, *blah, blah, blah*. She gives me hell in general because I live alone and don't have a man. What else do you want from me?" Tandy lifted both hands in frustration. "It's not as if she's sitting here saying, *Hey, go after so-and-so. He's the one who killed me.*"

"So, how do you know she was murdered then?"

"She told me so," Tandy answered in the same offhand way. "She told me that I needed to look after the twins, although there was more urgency about it, as if she finally understood at least some of the shit she had been up to."

"Do you think she understands the drug issues?"

"Oh, sure she does, and I'm sure a part of her even now wishes she could get a fix."

"That doesn't bear thinking about," he murmured. "Ghosts on drugs, good God." He watched the corner of her mouth twitch at the thought, and he smiled to himself. Tandy needed to lighten up. She'd had a rough few days, weeks, months, or maybe a lifetime for all he could tell, and the sooner she came around to not being quite so prickly, it would help in the case.

He'd probably come across too strong in the beginning, but it was hard to understand what her hesitation was when two helpless kids were looking to her for assistance. But considering what she'd been through, it was no wonder she was wary. Now he just had to confirm that she didn't stay wary of him at least, so they could get a little further down this pathway.

Tandy eventually spoke up. "She told me that somebody did this to her, that she didn't do it to herself. When I asked her who, she just shrugged and said she didn't know, she didn't remember. My guess is that she was probably in a drugged-out haze anyway."

"Right, I hadn't considered that."

"Which is part of the problem. Just because she may have been killed doesn't mean she was aware enough at the time to recognize what was happening or who was doing it," she muttered.

"And again not things we particularly want to see."

"No, of course not," Tandy agreed, "and you're looking for somebody to point a finger at, and it just won't be that easy."

"Stefan is always telling me how it's not that easy," Keller shared, with a smile, "but having some abilities helps a lot when I'm on a case."

"How?" she asked. "You still have to find the physical proof to present in court."

"Sure, but sometimes the psychic element gives me a direction to go looking for that proof. Not always, but every once in a while, we can come up with something that gives us a way to move the case forward," he explained, "though I never get enough psychic answers to solve a case."

"Right. I think ghosts are just that way too," she noted. "Instead of telling you something directly, they give you more of a tongue-in-cheek response."

"And what about the ghosts you talk to? Are they the same?"

"I think they're all the same," she declared, with more feeling than he expected.

"You are talking to just good ghosts, right?" he asked. She stared at him, and he watched as the wheels went around in her brain. "Not all ghosts are like your mother."

"I didn't say my mother was good or bad," she pointed out.

"No, but neither are you saying anything else."

"There are a lot of good ghosts. There are a lot of funny ghosts. There are ghosts that don't want to cross over because they're pretty happy in the situation they're in. There are ghosts that can't wait to cross over, and there are those that are so lost they don't even realize they need to."

"Why is your mother here?" Keller asked.

"I think because of the twins," she guessed.

"That makes a lot of sense. Often family members keep the ghosts here."

"Sure, but she's still what she always was in life, which is very irritating. I don't want her here, still slamming me and the twins the whole time. And she has other kids too, but that doesn't seem to matter to her."

"Of course not," Keller stated. "It's bad enough to have a bad *adoptive* parent, but to have the failed parent be by blood, yet still hanging around and haunting you, that would be tough."

She laughed. "Yes."

"Can't you banish her or something?" She frowned at him, and he saw a light come into her eyes as if it had never occurred to her, but then it was doused almost immediately. "Maybe once you settle up what's happening with the twins, and you make a decision regarding them," he suggested, with a shrug, "you can tell Isabella to butt out and maybe find a way to keep her out."

"Maybe," Tandy mumbled, staring off in the distance.

"And, yes, it's fair." Her gaze zipped back to him, and she frowned. "No, I'm not reading your mind, but it's pretty easy to see that you have to work your way through such a concept."

"I have to work through some things anyway," she murmured, "and this is just one more."

"Of course," he agreed, with a smile. "But remember she only comes into your life if you let her in."

"And that's easier said than done. I feel as if she's always had a way into my life, and, if I didn't move a long way away, she was just there, always a permanent part."

"And when you did move away, what happened?"

She frowned and considered it. "She never really bothered me, although she would call me, looking for money all the time. My grandmother used to tell her to go make some more money on the streets, if she needed to feed her drug habit, but to leave us alone."

"I'm sure that didn't go over well."

"No, it didn't, but neither did breaking into my grandmother's house and stealing her TV and her treasured personal items from my grandfather. When you have a druggie in your life who will do those things," she shared, "there's really no talking to them."

"Did you ever ask your mother about it?"

"Yeah, I did." Tandy laughed. "You know what she said? *It felt good because she'd wanted to hurt the old biddy for a long time.*"

# CHAPTER 8

TANDY PRESSED AGAINST her temples. "Look. I've got a really shitty headache, and I don't need any more of this right now. Would you mind just leaving and giving me a break?"

"The headache came since you got home?"

"Yes. We moved a lot of energy doing whatever the hell that was today at Dr. Maddy's place. I didn't even know you saw us."

"I was in the observation room," he shared, with a smile. "But again, I only got there when you were already playing with them, so I didn't see the beginning."

"Which just means you bought into the same vision." She stared at him, almost confused.

"I know. I'm already trying to work through that in my head."

She sighed. "I think the twins are quite talented, and whoever they choose to let in doesn't really have a choice."

"That could be true," he conceded, "which means that they need a strong hand to help guide them."

She stared at him. "And now you're back to that whole *me* thing."

"No, I'm not back to that whole *you* thing. Maybe you aren't the best person to raise them," he stated, waving his hand in dismissal, "but maybe we should be asking Stefan and Dr. Maddy."

Tandy nodded in agreement, but her mind was already screaming, *No, they're mine.* And seeing Keller's lips twitch made her think he heard her. She groaned and asked, "Are you sure you can't read my mind?"

"I'm positive I can't read your mind," he stated. He stood up, walked into the kitchen, rinsed out his coffee cup, and brought her a glass of water. She stared at it. He explained, "Often when we get headaches, particularly in energy work, it's due to a lack of water."

She frowned but accepted it, took a sip, and realized she really did want it and quickly downed the entire glass. "Thank you. … I hadn't realized how thirsty I was."

He nodded and walked to the front door. She felt a sense of relief that he would leave her to her own demons.

But then he looked back at her and asked, "How about I bring in pizza?" When she frowned at him, he frowned right back and laughed. "I have to eat too."

"Maybe, but you can go home and eat."

"I could, but I could also order a pizza and share it, so you would get food too."

"I eat," she protested, although her fridge was empty, and she sure wasn't up for going shopping tonight. Honestly, pizza sounded damn good, but she would be the last one to say it to him.

He pulled out his phone, and, while she remained open-mouthed, he ordered two large pizzas. When he ended the call, she complained, "You didn't even ask what I liked."

"Ham and pineapple," he stated.

She frowned at him. "How could anybody like ham and pineapple?"

He burst into laughter and asked, "Have you ever tried it?"

"No, of course I haven't tried it. Why would anybody put those two things on the same pizza?"

"Ah, and that is why you'll love it." She shook her head, but he just nodded and smiled.

"Meaning that you've already ordered one of those."

"Yeah, and one with everything."

"What if I'm a vegetarian?"

"Are you?" he asked, looking at her in consternation.

"No," she snapped. "That doesn't mean I like high-handed men either."

His lips twitched at that, and he nodded. "I'll try to remember that."

She sighed. "Why are you doing this?"

"I'm hungry, and so are you. It'll make you less hungry if you eat."

She rolled her eyes at that phrase. "I am a nurse, you know?"

"And I also know that the shoemaker's children often end up going barefoot."

"What does that mean?"

"It means that you have to do what you have to do for everybody else," he shared, "but you don't often do what you need to do for you and yours."

"I won't suffer. I've just not had a chance to go shopping. This has all kind of hit me a little hard."

"That's also why I'm happy to help make this next hour or so a whole lot easier on you," he pointed out. "So just say *thank you* instead of arguing." When she glared at him, he went, "*Uh-uh.*"

Finally she muttered, "Thank you."

He grinned. "Now, may I have another cup of coffee?"

She waved him into the kitchen, and, as she sat here, her

mother appeared. Tandy glared at her and said, "No."

*No what?* Isabella snapped.

"I don't want to talk to you. Go away."

*You need me to tell you some things. Otherwise you won't look after the twins.*

"I didn't say I was looking after the damn twins," she muttered, glaring at her.

At that, Keller poked his head out of the kitchen, looking around the living room.

She glared at him too. "I told her to leave."

*No, you didn't,* Isabella argued, with a complacent tone, *but look at that. You have a man in your home. I do like to see that. Maybe you're a chip off the old block after all.*

"No, I'm not," she snapped between clenched teeth, "and you can disappear anytime now."

*Don't want to,* Isabella said, with a chuckle. *I kind of like this. I get to sit here and check up on you.*

"You won't check up on me for long," Tandy declared. "I'll banish you to hell and back before I let that happen."

Isabella stared at her. *I'm dead. How can you be so mean to me? You should at least grieve the fact that I'm gone.*

"Or I should cheer," she snapped but immediately felt terrible. Her mother blinked out of existence, and Tandy groaned as she sat back, staring at where Isabella had been.

Keller stepped out of the kitchen and walked toward her. "Was that your mother?"

"Yes, that was my mother," she snapped. "She brings out the worst in me."

"Even dead, *huh*?"

"Are you kidding? I think she specializes in pissing me off and ruining my life. *Especially* since she died."

"Any idea why that is?"

"She wants me to look after the twins, for one."

"And she already named you the guardian. Why come to you now?"

"I don't know. Maybe she's jealous that I'm alive, and she's not."

"Or she's looking for a connection to you that she didn't have before."

"She won't get it now either," Tandy declared, "and don't go all pious on me about how I should love my mother."

"I won't," he agreed, raising one hand. "Some parents deserve love, and some deliberately do so many things wrong to hurt people that there's no way to find your way back to love. You can silently forgive them, but it's damn hard to forget."

She stared at him and then slowly nodded her head. "Exactly. I might eventually forgive her but forgetting? That's a different story."

"Have you considered therapy?"

"Yeah, twice a week for quite a few years now. I stopped it for a while and thought I was doing great, and then Isabella died and dumped all this on me, so I put in an SOS call to get a little bit of help to straighten out my world again," she shared. "And I never felt that I wasn't capable, until my mother found out about my therapist. And, since then, she won't leave me alone. She considers any mental assistance to be for weak people, so that's what I must be, right?"

KELLER WATCHED TANDY struggle to get the words out, but he let her speak her mind. No matter how much reassurance he tried to give her, he saw that she didn't really believe him. Such was the damage her mother had done to her child, even though the child was now an adult, still struggling to deal, but Keller saw that happening over and over again.

Only later after they ate, as he got up to leave, was he struck by one of the things that had really bothered him. "That's why you're not worried about her having been murdered."

She frowned at him. "What are you talking about?"

"I wondered about it because it's not as if you're asking anybody to solve Isabella's murder."

She eyed him warily. "You probably just think that I'm happy she's dead and that I would rather celebrate with a bottle of champagne instead, *huh*?"

She was so used to having people think the worst of her, that it was always the first thing that came to mind. He immediately shook his head. "No, but I get the feeling that you don't believe her because she has lied so much of her life. So you think she's lying now."

Tandy's dark eyes stilled, and she slowly nodded. "Yes, that is more of a concern for me. Every time I trusted anything she told me, it turned out that she'd lied. So I don't know why she wouldn't lie about this, when it keeps all the attention firmly on her."

"And is that all she's about?"

"It's all she's ever been about," Tandy stated. "Even when I had a boyfriend in high school," her tone dripping with mockery, "she seduced him. I should have told the authorities then because he was only seventeen and a minor."

He winced. "I suppose she told you about it, right?"

"Of course she did. She told me how he was no good for me, and any guy who would pick up with her had to be bad."

"And did you ever ask him about it?"

"I did, and it took a bit, but he did admit to it," she replied. "That was something I had a hard time forgiving her for."

"Again, it's not so much about forgiving. It's never being able to forget."

"Exactly. She always wanted me to bring home boyfriends, and I just laughed at her. I would say, like hell, and she would come back, knocking me for not having any self-confidence saying if the males were so great, she shouldn't be able to take them away from me."

"She had a point."

"Sure, she had a point, but, then again, I don't know if she didn't drug them. But that one boyfriend in particular was also young and was looking to be sexually active, yet I was holding back. Another lesson my mother harped on is to *never hold back or you'll lose him*," she quipped, with more self-mockery.

He winced and nodded. "If you run into trouble overnight, give me a shout." When she looked at him in surprise, he shrugged. "Just a hunch."

"A hunch of what?" she asked, bolting off the chair and looking around. "Why would anybody want to hurt me?"

He hesitated and then replied, "I'm not sure anybody would want to hurt you, but I'm afraid that, if Isabella *was* murdered, there's a good chance somebody might suspect that you know something."

"I don't know shit."

"But *they* don't know that," he pointed out, with a serious expression on his face.

"Why would anyone even care?"

"Any chance your mother had anything of value?"

"Only whatever drugs she would have had on her at the time," she stated. "Other than that, I have no clue."

"Okay." As he went to pull the door closed, he added, "Lock it behind me." When he shut it firmly, he waited until he heard her lock the door, before he walked out to his vehicle.

As he looked up, she stared out the window at him. He quickly waved, but she slammed the curtain closed in front of him. He had to laugh at that. She was prickly through and through, but something was fascinating about it.

Maybe it was the whole injured-bird thing. He didn't generally go for damsels who needed rescuing, but, in this case, Tandy was something completely different, at least as far as he could tell.

Dr. Maddy contacted him just then, as he got into his vehicle.

"Where are you?" she asked curiously.

"I've just left Tandy's place," he replied. "Why?"

"I was concerned about her and the kids," she said. "What is your take on her now?"

"I think she's confused, twisted up with guilt, and doesn't want the responsibility of the kids. Yet, more than that, I think she's afraid she'll fail, just like her mother failed. I think an awful lot of issues are going around in Tandy's brain, which makes it hard for her to do anything at the moment."

"Oh, that's an interesting point too," Dr. Maddy noted thoughtfully, her tone sounding far away.

"Why? What are you worried about?"

"The twins accepted her immediately, as if they already knew her."

"Oh." He thought about the ramifications of that. "Do

you think she's lying about how that worked out today?"

"No, but I'm not sure she understood it to be anything different than before, except for the fact that we were in this clinical setting that may have made it look somewhat different."

"Whoa, whoa, whoa. What are you talking about?"

"I think she's played with them lots of times, but I think she's done it in their world without necessarily understanding."

"How would that work?" he asked, frowning.

"I'm not sure, but it could be from her dream state."

"Oh. Do you know that her mother is still around and bugging her?" He relayed a little bit of the conversation that he'd had with Tandy about her mother.

"Interesting, and yet she doesn't believe that her mother was murdered?"

"That would be my guess, but I don't know for sure. She can't tell fact from fiction when her mother gets into the conversation," he said, "and she's pretty twisted up over a whole lot of things that her mother has done to her over the years." And he mentioned seducing the boyfriend as an example.

"Jesus, Isabella must have been an incredibly insecure woman to go after her daughter's boyfriend, just to prove that she still had it."

"Right, but it messed up her daughter pretty well too."

"Tandy's stronger than she looks or thinks she is, though."

"Maybe, but it will take her quite a while to believe you."

"Maybe," she murmured. "I do think she has skills that the twins need in a big way."

"Why? Because she can go in the ethers and play with them? But that still leaves them in an institution like yours because the rest of the world won't accept that they're off having a normal life in a fantasy world."

"I know," she grumbled. "And, for that reason, I need to get them back into this world, where we can give them a different kind of help."

"And how far gone do you think they are now?"

"Not at all," she stated. "They're extremely cognizant and aware in that world, but *wary* is the dominant feeling. They're safe there, and they have no wish to come out. So, until we can make it safe on this side, and we can convince them that it's safe, then it won't help them to leave their make-believe world."

"I think Tandy wants to keep them, but I don't think she sees a way forward to make it happen safely. I think she's worried about being a failure, like her mother, not wanting to repeat the same mistakes, not wanting any of that history to overlap into the world she's in now."

"Isn't that so sad?" Dr. Maddy muttered. "She's anything but her mother."

"I also noticed," he added, "that there's never been any mention of her father—or the father of the twins."

Maddy sighed. "More about him would be very helpful to know, but I'm pretty sure Grant checked the birth certificate for the twins, and no father was registered. But where is he, does he have any idea what's going on with his twins, assuming he even knows about them?"

"Unless," Keller pointed out, "he's one of the abusers."

"Right," she replied, her tone turning brisk. "All things that would come to pass in time, but right now we don't have the information we need to make those kinds of guesses. I'll definitely keep them here for a few more days."

"Days?" he repeated, with a knowing smile. "You know this won't be settled in days."

"No, not days, but hopefully we can do something in that time period to help them shift. It would really help if they were back in reality, instead of hiding in their own private world. If we can at least get them to come back part-time, we can get some better funding and set them up in another place."

"Really?" he asked. "And where would you let them go to?"

She laughed. "Right, I'm not sure yet," she admitted. "It will be very difficult to let them go and to not have people who understand how special they are."

"Are you sure you haven't set up a place just for people like them?" he asked, a note of affection in his question. "I mean, it is what you do."

"It is what I do, and I have to check around to see. I have been looking, but we're so damn busy all the time that it's hard to find an empty bed."

"I have faith in you," he declared, smiling down at his phone. "If nothing else they have you as a champion, and that is worth a lot."

"Maybe worth a lot in theory, but it's just not a permanent answer," she muttered. "Even though I think they're quite happy with us."

"And yet you wouldn't need to be there, would you?"

There was a moment of laughter before she admitted, "Very good, and you're right. I certainly don't, but sometimes it does make it easier."

"Might make it easier," he pointed out, "but, if you don't need to be there, you can help them transition from wherever you are."

"And again, more truth," she noted, a smile in her tone. "I'm glad to see you're picking up so much of this."

"I'm not sure I am," he countered, "as I'm coming from a very different point of view."

"And yet it's also fascinating that you saw what was happening in the room."

"I know, but I'm not sure whether I joined the mass-hysteria, or I was afflicted on my own," he said humorously.

Her laughter rolled through the phone, making him smile. "That is something I'll leave up to you to figure out."

He groaned and said, "That's cheating."

"No, this is all about being who you need to be," she stated, with a smile. "And, in this case, never more so. Anyway, if you are coming by later tomorrow, I might have a little bit of news."

"Can you just tell me about it now?"

"No, not right now," she said. "I need to go in and do some body scans on them."

"I would absolutely love for you to tell me that they weren't abused."

"I'm really hoping I can tell you that tomorrow," she added, "but, at the moment, it's just too early. The fact that they have gone to such extremes to stay safe says an awful lot."

"And yet one thing I don't understand. How is it the kids think this fantasy world would make a difference? They're there, and a guardian spirit doesn't mean that they are safe physically."

And, with that, she sighed. "That is very, very true. Unfortunately, right now, we can't prove it one way or the other. I'll talk to you tomorrow." She ended the call.

# CHAPTER 9

W HEN TANDY WALKED into the hospital to start her first shift after several days off, several of her coworkers greeted her with smiles. Although she generally stayed to herself, she was happy to have coworkers who seemed content to be friends at work and to not bug her about being friends outside of work, something she couldn't really handle right now. Hell, she didn't handle socializing ever, but those were just the facts of life when you had a messed-up childhood. You were always looking for problems that didn't exist, and, even though you did your best, it seemed as if it just came out of nowhere and kicked your ass.

Still, she quickly settled into the routine of the day. It was busy, but she knew several of the patients, and she was always happy to see progress. A couple of them weren't doing very well, and that was just plain hard. However, several of them were doing better, and that made her smile. As it was, by the end of the day, she felt the toll on her.

Not even questioning her decision, and although tired, she drove to Dr. Maddy's floor, looking to check in with the twins. That they were family was one thing, but that they were psychic just cemented a bond she hadn't expected would even exist. She still couldn't let go of the feeling that she could be doing so much more for them. She didn't know that she had any skills, not like everybody else did. Talking to ghosts didn't seem to qualify as a skill to her. In fact, it seemed to be more of a negative in many ways. But, if she could do something else, she was definitely open to it.

As she walked onto Dr. Maddy's floor, one of the other nurses who saw her the other day waved at her.

Tandy asked, "Any chance I can see the twins?"

She frowned. "I have to check with Dr. Maddy."

Tandy nodded and took a seat in the waiting room. Almost immediately Dr. Maddy stepped out of her office, looked at her in surprise, and then smiled. "Hey, good to see you."

"It was kind of hard to stay away," she murmured. "I was hoping maybe I could see them?"

"Sure, you can. I haven't checked on them in the last few hours since their lunch time, so let's go see them together."

"What about the tests and things? Have you gotten anywhere on that?"

"We've started to run quite a few," she admitted, "but that doesn't mean that we're seeing any results yet."

"What kind of tests?" Tandy asked curiously. "There's not anything you can do psychically, is there?"

She laughed. "You would be surprised what we can do psychically, but it's still never really enough in many ways, and the results have to be something that traditional medicine can handle."

"And yet none of this is something traditional medicine can handle," Tandy declared, "and the minute there's any talk about something weird and wonderful, you and I both know that they'll run, particularly when it comes to funding."

She smiled. "I gather you haven't had a great experience in that way."

"No, I sure haven't. But then I'm not sure what I expected after my mom tried to rip off everybody."

"Let's hope that was a long time ago and that you won't meet some of the same people."

"And yet you and I both know," Tandy stated, "that karma can turn around to bite you in the ass as soon as you try to hide something like that."

"So, we don't hide it," Dr. Maddy declared. "We allow it to be where it needs to be, and we just carry on."

Tandy wasn't sure it was all that easy, but, for Dr. Maddy, it seemed to be, and that was an interesting possibility.

As they neared the twins' room, Dr. Maddy cocked her head.

"Are they sleeping?" Tandy asked.

Dr. Maddy smiled at her. "They're always sleeping."

"Right, just not always sleeping on all levels."

"Exactly, and, yes, physically they're sleeping, but spiritually they are up and apparently bouncing on the bed," Dr. Maddy shared, with amusement.

Tandy stared at her. "That would be lovely to see."

"Lovely?"

"Yes, to see something so, I don't know, *normal.*"

"Oh, the twins are very normal, just that they're keeping a parallel existence," she murmured.

"So, how do we get them to come back to this existence? Otherwise they'll spend their entire lives in an institution, basically in a vegetative state."

"I don't know about *vegetative,*" she clarified, still with that knowing smile.

"You know what I mean though," Tandy said impatiently. "If they can't function on a physical level, they'll end up in an institution."

"Yes, that part is true," she murmured. "Anyway, let's go have a talk with them."

As they headed into the room, Tandy asked, "Where is the observation room that Keller was in?"

Dr. Maddy turned to her and nodded. "We can go there first, if you want." She opened up a small door and let her in.

One wall was definitely almost all glass, where they could see into the room that Tandy had been in before. "Don't you think that's an invasion of privacy?" she asked.

"It's pretty necessary when we have cases like this," Dr. Maddy replied.

"And you don't think it's exacerbating their need to avoid coming out?"

"I hadn't considered that," Dr. Maddy admitted, looking at Tandy, "but it's something to take into account now, though." As they stared down at the two kids, both were curled up in bed, once again with their hands joined.

Tandy sighed. "Just seeing them holding hands kills me."

"I know," Dr. Maddy muttered. "There's a certain poignancy to it, isn't there?"

"They just look so lost in a way."

"I don't know about *lost,* maybe *found,* if you look at it another way. Mark, as the eldest, has done incredibly well by them."

Looking at her, Tandy nodded. "If that was the goal."

"Safety was the goal," Dr. Maddy confirmed, "and we can't ever forget that the human body is amazing when it comes to self-preservation."

"I guess. I just wish there hadn't been a need for it."

"As we all do, but right now we can't live in a fantasy realm just because the twins want to. Now let's go in and see them." She opened the door and they stepped inside the same room, as before.

There, the kids were climbing something, almost like a jungle gym on a kids' playground. Yet Tandy knew it didn't exist in the actual room itself. Especially as she could see them on her own—unlike Keller, who seemed to need Stefan's touch.

The twins saw them, and both came running, arms outstretched for hugs. It was automatic to open her arms to accept the hugs, even picking up Matthew and swinging him around, laughing as she did so. This world was so real, so unbelievably real that she wanted to question Mark about how he'd made it, but knew that would likely start something which Dr. Maddy wouldn't be happy about. Currently Dr. Maddy was busy hugging Mark, who seemed to be quite taken with her.

When the kids calmed down from the excitement of having company, Matthew asked for food. Tandy wondered how food worked in this make-believe world where they seemed to exist full-time.

Yet Dr. Maddy replied, "Yes, of course." She turned to Mark and asked, "What would you like?"

Mark shrugged. "I'm not very hungry."

"Maybe not, but to have something would be good," she replied in a wheedling tone.

Mark smiled. "Okay."

With that, Dr. Maddy seemed to create something out of thin air and produced it for Matthew, who immediately snagged it, laughing and taking off with it.

Tandy watched him go, seeing the joy, the happiness, and the fun-loving spirit that Matthew had. Then her heart ached for everything they had been through that made this the existence they preferred. Almost immediately with that thought came the reminder that Matthew himself may not even know that anything existed other than this. This was the world his brother chose to keep them in, and that was even more painful to Tandy. She didn't know how Mark would handle a separation from his brother, particularly if his brother didn't have the same trauma. Tandy figured Mark would not take the separation very well at all.

They stayed with the kids for a good hour, and then Mark himself stopped the visit, saying that they were tired and that it was nap time. Completely oblivious to any of the other signs going on, Matthew nodded and agreed, saying he was tired. He got up, walked over to the bed, and the two of them curled up, until they resumed the hand-holding position on the bed, exactly like what they looked like through the mirror.

Tandy and Dr. Maddy left the room, quietly closing the door behind them. Still wondering at everything going on, Tandy stepped into the observation room and studied the kids, but it looked as if absolutely nothing had changed. "That's just amazing," she murmured.

"Amazing and scary."

"Yes, I'm all about the scary part now," Tandy admitted. "I don't understand how Mark can create that world and can be so aware of what he's doing and working so hard at it, while Matthew potentially has no idea."

"He has no idea because he's into the same alternate program that Mark is, and Matthew has much less awareness of what could happen out in the real world or what might have happened to keep them there."

"But you think Mark's aware?"

Dr. Maddy looked at Tandy, her lips twitching and

asked, "What do you think?"

She thought back to the little five-year-old boy who seemed to be way too mature for the way he acted and nodded. "Yes, absolutely. I think he knows."

"Good," Dr. Maddy stated. "That's one layer of deception he won't be able to pull on you."

"Good God," Tandy muttered. "I don't even want to think about that. … The thought of raising a child is one thing, but raising two is on another level. Yet raising two who aren't even my own and who are psychics with this incredible gift to live in an alternate world and to never even step out of it?" she began. "That's …" She stopped, completely bereft of words.

"Amazing, challenging, and completely defying all logic," Dr. Maddy offered. "I get it. Believe me that I do. They are quite the pair."

"Yes, that's definitely something I would say, but, along with that joy and—I don't want to say cohesiveness—but almost cohesiveness, I have to wonder how much of it is manipulation on Mark's part."

"All of it," Dr. Maddy declared. "And his brother loves him and trusts him, so, for Matthew, there's absolutely no challenge to it."

"Why would there be? Mark's always been there to keep Matthew safe and is doing so now." It was so sad and yet so incredible that Tandy couldn't even begin to feel sad for them. "Mark's truly amazing."

"And that's one of the things that we need to remember," Dr. Maddy said. "Mark is amazing. He's done something amazing, and we have to give him credit for that."

"But how do we get him to understand that it's safe to come back to reality?"

"I'm not sure, and that is the question we're all trying to figure out," she replied. "We all want them to come back intact, and that's an entirely different story as well."

Tandy frowned at that. "Meaning that the trauma of the real world could be too much for Mark? That he might choose *not* to come back? Or he might come back but need an incredible amount of help in order to understand where he's been and what he's been doing?"

Dr. Maddy grimaced, followed by a nod. "Something like that. Plus, the shock of what could have happened to him—or what may have happened to him—will always be there and can be potentially damaging, regardless of whether we get him back or not. He's keeping it well and truly away from the world they live in."

"But for how long?" Tandy asked, turning to face Dr. Maddy. "How long can Mark keep this up?"

"Unfortunately," Dr. Maddy began, "I would say indefinitely. If we don't do something to prod Mark into *wanting* to come back out, this will be their life. They will be the children in the bed, comatose, and yet free spirits in a fantasy world they've created themselves."

Tandy muttered, "They will be trapped, living like empty ghosts."

KELLER WALKED UP to Tandy's apartment. He hadn't given her any warning that he was coming. He just happened to be in the neighborhood and felt compelled to stop in. He'd long ago given up the need to find an excuse for such compulsions. As he walked closer, he felt a sense of urgency. He picked up the pace, and, instead of taking the elevator to her third-floor apartment, he raced up the stairs. And even then, he was too late. As he got there, the door was open ever-so-slightly. He swung it wider, his weapon already out and ready, as he called for her. He got no answer, so he called again. Pushing open the door fully, he barged in.

Her place was empty, and, although he would say it was trashed, it appeared to be more randomly searched. He looked around, frowning as he tried to understand what had happened. Realizing that he'd probably just missed the intruder by minutes, he raced outside of her apartment to the far end windows of the hallway to see if any vehicles were pulling out, but he saw nothing obvious.

Walking back to her apartment, one of the neighbors opened their door and stared at him suspiciously. He held up his badge, but, instead of making her feel better, the woman tried to slam her door. He called out, "Wait, wait, please. Did you see anybody here at Tandy's apartment?"

She frowned at him. "Who's Tandy?" He pointed to the open door several down from hers, and she shrugged. "I didn't hear anything, but some guy was here not very long ago, and he looked beyond odd."

"Beyond odd in what way?"

"Pure white hair," she replied. "You don't see that very often. Yet he was young but not so young."

"So, his hair was maybe bleached or something?" Keller asked. "How old, twenty, thirty?"

She stared at him. "I have no idea. He could have been fifty for all I know. I just was struck by the white hair and very pale features."

"Did he have any makeup on?"

She shrugged. "How would I know?"

"You saw his face?"

"Again … I don't know. I just caught a glimpse, and all

I saw was white hair."

He nodded his thanks and asked, "About how long ago?"

"I just wanted to take out the garbage, but, when I saw him, I didn't," she shared. "So maybe five, ten minutes ago."

He nodded his thanks and headed back to Tandy's apartment. As soon as he got inside, he picked up his phone and called her. She answered with a slight note of irritation, but then he was used to that. "Where are you?" he asked.

"On my way home, why?"

"Because I'm at your apartment, and it was broken into."

"What?" she gasped. "Why the hell would anybody do that?"

"I don't know. I just came up here, found your front door open, and, unless you have decided to redecorate since I was here last, it looks as if the place has been tossed."

"I don't have anything for anybody to toss," she stated crossly. "And unless they took things to pawn them, I don't know why they would have done that either."

"No, neither do I," he said, his tone calm as he looked around, "which makes me even more interested."

"What interests you about that? The fact that my mother claims she was murdered still doesn't mean that anybody would give a crap about me."

"I don't know about that," he countered, his tone gentling. "I think you are very quick to write yourself out of this."

"I'm hoping to," she snapped. "Believe me that I'm hoping to. I'll be there in five." And, with that, she ended the call.

He walked carefully around the small apartment, looking

to see if anything gave him any answers. In the bedroom, some of the drawers had been dumped, as well as boxes from the closet too. Yet it almost looked as if it was a quick job but not necessarily a thorough one. Somebody seemed to be looking for something, but they didn't seem to look all that hard. Maybe they felt as if they didn't have much time. Seeing that not a whole lot was here to begin with, maybe they didn't give it their best efforts.

Frowning, Keller made sure not to touch anything.

As Tandy walked into her place five minutes later, she stopped and gasped. "My God."

He saw the fatigue on her face and realized that she probably just got off work. "I'm sorry. This is not exactly what you need when you come home from work."

"It's not what I need at any time," she muttered, glaring at him. "I stopped by Dr. Maddy's floor to see the kids."

"How are they?" he asked.

Her face softened, as she shrugged. "They're amazing."

"That they are," he agreed, with a gentle smile. "And were you welcomed into their world?"

"Yes, I was." She smiled at the thought.

Such a note of wonder filled her tone that Keller had to stop himself from commenting on it, which would have just set her off even more. But she really didn't appear to have any concept of how relationships worked or how she would be welcomed in lots of situations. "I'm glad," he replied. "Were they playful?"

"Very," she confirmed, laughing. "And in that world …" She just shook her head. "Who would have thought?"

"I wouldn't have," he admitted. "The fact that I saw what I did just continues to blow me away."

"Of course," she noted. "Believe me that I feel the same way."

"Were they any different today?"

"No, except that Mark seemed to call the shots a little bit more strictly today, as if he didn't want everybody getting too comfortable."

"Which would make sense if he were the appointed security guard."

"Of course." She sighed. "It's just so depressing to think that a child of five years old has such a need for it."

"I know, but he seems to be doing a pretty amazing job in there."

"Yes," she admitted. "He is. Mark's obviously very talented." Keller just smiled.

With that, she wandered around her apartment, shaking her head and surveying the mess. "Outside of causing me added stress and a headache for an hour or two while I straighten up all this again, what would be the point?" she asked, staring around her apartment at the mess.

"I don't know. Do you know for sure that you locked it?"

"I would have said yes without even thinking about it," she began, "but, now that you've questioned me on that, it's possible I left without locking it, but that would not be my normal habit." She began picking up living room cushions to straighten up the room. "It's just so depressing. You come home from work after a long day, and you find this," she muttered, as she continued to clean up around him.

He helped straighten up the big pieces of furniture where the cushions had been tossed, and within a very short time her living room was back together again.

She asked, "Do I even want to go look in my bedroom?"

He smiled and shared, "I thought the mess was less in there than out here."

She walked into the bedroom and nodded. "And that makes no sense either. If I were to hide something, it would be in here. Or at least I would have thought that's where people would have expected me to hide stuff."

It was a curious comment on her part. Keller studied her carefully. "Have you hidden things before?"

"Sure," she replied, completely open. "From my mother all the time. Anytime I made five bucks, if it wasn't hidden, she stole it, and it was gone."

He winced at that. "I'm sorry. That is a pretty rough way to live."

"It is," she murmured. "And now I'm trying to figure out what possible reason somebody could have for doing this." She kept straightening up and muttering to herself, as she put away the last few things.

He had to admit that it didn't take very long. "So, was this deliberate? Was it an interrupted thing, or was it a ruse on the surface to make it seem to be breaking and entering? And do you have no idea why anybody would care?"

"No, I sure don't," she said, as she stared at him. "And if you're thinking this is connected to Isabella, I have absolutely no idea why it would be."

"It will be a question I need to ask, even though I'm sure you'll say no, but is there any way your mother would have had anything valuable?"

"I don't think so. Wait. Let me rephrase that. If she had something valuable, she didn't know about it because, if she had, she would have sold it."

And that made total sense to him. He smiled and nodded. "In that case we'll just keep an eye on what's going on here. Sounds to me as if you could use some food."

She plunked down onto the couch, blowing wisps of her

hair off her face as she stared back at him. "Don't tell me you'll feed me again."

"It wasn't in my plans, but I'm certainly up for it."

She waved her hand. "Not pizza again though, please."

He didn't waste any time and took advantage of the fact that she appeared to be fairly open to the possibility today, and he quickly ordered Chinese. She smiled when she listened to the order. So, when he ended the call, he asked, "So, what about that order was wrong?"

"Nothing was wrong," she replied. "I probably would have ordered something very similar."

"Good," he noted, with a bright smile. "At least that way I know you'll eat it." She glared at him, and he laughed. "Any comment like that seems to get your goat immediately."

"Of course it does," she snapped. "I do eat, you know?"

"Good, I'm glad to hear it."

She frowned and added, "And you don't need to be looking after me."

"Oh, that's even better then," he stated, with the same cheerful smile. He didn't know whether he was happy to deliberately antagonize her or just the fact that she seemed so woebegone and lost right now had his protective instincts kicking in. "Besides, food is on the way, and we can finish cleaning up the kitchen in the meantime. You'll have a clean house again, before you know it."

She sighed, then got to it, which didn't take very long to put the rest of the apartment to rights. She shook her head as she sat down again. "I really have no idea why anybody would do this."

"I was about to ask, but I figured you were already prepping your answer."

"Which makes it sound as if you think I'm lying."

"No, I don't think you're lying at all. I don't understand why anybody would want to do this either, but the simplest answer is that they think your mother had something. Did you get anything from her?"

"Just that strange note," she muttered.

"May I see it?"

She frowned at him, then got up, went to her bedroom, and stopped.

"What?" he asked.

"It's not here," she said.

He nodded. "If it was the only thing from your mother that you had, would you have put it somewhere else?" He kept a close eye on her as she went through various places that, in her mind, were where she might have put it.

Then she stopped, turned back to him, and declared, "It's not here."

"Interesting," he muttered.

"No reason for anybody to want that note," she stated, staring at him. "Absolutely no reason at all."

"We don't know the reasons why anybody does anything," he murmured in response. "Remember that."

She snorted. "I don't want to remember any of this, thanks."

He had to laugh. She had such a prickly exterior that nearly everything she said had an almost humorous slant to it.

She groaned as she stared at him. "I don't know why anybody would have wanted it."

"I didn't see it, and I would have liked to."

"Oh, that's easy." She brought up her phone and pointed. "It's right there." Then she handed her phone to him.

"You took a photo of it?" he asked.

She nodded. "That's an old habit with Isabella. Everything in her world was lies and threats and cheats, so, if I didn't have proof of what she'd told me, she would gaslight me, saying I had lied or I had misunderstood or had twisted the truth somehow." Tandy took a moment and sighed. "So, yeah, my mother was the best reason for keeping documentation."

"I'm sorry," he muttered. "That's a horrible way to live out your childhood."

"I'm not a child anymore," she pointed out, her tone cooling. "So, it doesn't really matter."

He read the note and frowned. "This is a very strange note."

"Right."

Then he read a section from the note out loud. "*It's your turn. It's my time. Now it's your turn. Best now you get your own chance to raise kids and to see how good a job you do.* There's almost a spitefulness to it," he murmured.

"Yeah, that would be my mother," Tandy confirmed, followed by a hysterical laugh. "If she could upset somebody or could do something in a way that would make life better for her and worse for somebody else, Isabella was all for it. But, toward the end, she didn't have the energy for that. She was all about getting her drugs, and that took so much out of her that there wasn't really much left for anything else. There wasn't any energy for spitefulness."

"Maybe that's a good thing," he noted.

"I don't know. It just brings back all those feelings that I don't even want to examine."

"And you have no clue why this note would matter to anybody?"

"Why *would* it matter to anybody? Even if she had a lover or somebody who she was close to, that's not exactly a love letter."

"Right," he agreed, "and that's why I'm confused."

"And maybe they didn't pick it up. Maybe it's still caught up in this mess somewhere," she suggested. "I've put things away, but that doesn't mean it wasn't mixed up somewhere. Maybe he didn't take it as a lark but to throw it out."

Keller pondered that and then shrugged. "Yeah, we may find it eventually, but still, this note doesn't really say anything."

"No, it doesn't really say anything, but it doesn't *not* say something either. So maybe they were afraid that somebody would read between the lines."

"What was it written on?"

"A piece of scrap paper, with some bill on the other side."

He frowned at her and nodded. "So, maybe *that* part was important."

She stared at him, then shrugged. "If it was, it's gone. I don't remember anything more about the other side. If it's here still, maybe I'll find it. If it isn't, maybe I won't." She stared at him. "It didn't occur to me to save the back side."

"So, you didn't take a picture of the back side?"

"No, of course not." She waved her hand about. "Would you?"

"No, probably not," he admitted, "but if it was on a bill or something curious like that, the other side could be the reason it was picked up."

"Maybe, or it could just be nothing."

He smiled. "And maybe it is nothing." He laughed. "I

guess we'll have to wait and see."

"Yep, we absolutely will," she muttered. "I don't have a clue, and, at this point in time, I'm not too worried about it."

"What about the cremation?" Keller asked her.

"I still have to deal with them too. They charged my credit card, so presumably she was cremated today."

"Do you want to go down there and get the ashes?"

"Hell no, I don't want to go down there and get the ashes," she snapped, "but obviously I have to. Why I have to, … I don't really know when I think about it." He just smiled, and she nodded. "See? Everybody's got all these lovely answers but me."

"Nobody's got any answers," he replied. "We're all just hoping to find you an easy pathway forward."

"Yeah, me too," she muttered. "How long before dinner?"

He checked the tracking and smiled. "About five minutes."

"Damn."

"Why?" he looked at her curiously.

"I wanted to have a shower. It might make me a little more human."

"Anything that makes you more human is an absolute yes in my department," he teased, "so go for it. It can sit here on the counter for a few minutes until you're done."

She looked at him, as if pondering whether it was a good idea or not.

"Go," he repeated. "I don't care if you have a shower. Obviously it'll make you feel better, so go." She still hesitated. "And if you're worried about me being in the apartment, I can go wait outside, if it's that big a deal to you."

That had the desired effect, as she snorted at the suggestion. "Yeah, you won't be a problem." And, with her pride now firmly back in place, she got up and headed into the bedroom.

"And if you do find that note, let me know," he called out.

She just slammed the bedroom door behind her, which was what he expected in the first place. Now that she'd mentioned it was written on a piece of scrap paper, he really wanted to know what the hell was on the other side. She hadn't taken a photo of that side, and he probably wouldn't have either, unless there had been reason to be suspicious of it.

But now that he knew Isabella was involved in all kinds of drug dealings and maybe was, indeed, murdered, then maybe the contents of that bill or scrap paper were important. He sat down on the couch and texted Grant on what had just happened to her place and about the note being missing at this point.

Grant called him not long afterward. "Any reason why anybody would take that?"

"I didn't fully explain that in the text," Keller began, "but apparently it was written on the back of some scrap paper, maybe a bill or something. Tandy didn't really take a close look at it and didn't take a picture of the back."

"What about the note itself?"

"I do have a picture of the note itself. I'll send that over." Within seconds that had landed in Grant's in-box as well.

"Fascinating," Grant muttered, "the note doesn't really say anything."

"True, and I'm not even sure that it really was intended for Tandy. It's not addressed to anyone. Plus, if you think about it, it doesn't say, *Hey, I'm killing myself. I can't do this anymore.* So, it's not a suicide note. It's just a bitchy note. And yet that's something Isabella was known for as well."

"True. That's very true. But I might run this by forensics, as I see something on the back was bleeding through. Like when you get a letter in the mail and can read through the envelope. Let's see if forensics can work some magic on this. Give me a day or two on this."

"I ordered in some food after helping her clean up her place. I want to confirm she eats," Keller shared, knowing that Grant would say something smart, but surprisingly he didn't.

Grant noted, "Apparently she also went to see the kids today."

"Yes, she told me. She got a really good reception."

"And that's good, though I still don't know that she's ready for any of this."

"I don't think anybody is," Keller said, with a laugh. "It's one thing to become a parent of your own kids—"

"And another to suddenly become a parent of somebody else's, let alone two kids, plus kids who are psychic and obviously have issues. I guess it's probably a little late for this, but I'll say it anyway. Take care of yourself when it comes to that." With that, Grant rang off.

Not sure what he meant, Keller really wanted to text him and ask him about it but figured that probably wouldn't go over too well. Frowning as he contemplated Grant's words, he started making notes on everything Tandy had shared with him today, adding it to a file he had started on his phone. It wasn't very long before he didn't hear the shower. He hemmed and hawed, then finally got up and walked to the bedroom door and knocked.

She opened the door and glared at him.

"Just checking," he explained. "I didn't hear the shower."

"That's because I haven't got there yet," she snapped.

He looked at her, noted the tears on her face, and nodded. "You don't have to be strong all the time, you know?"

"I sure as hell do," she declared, glaring at him. "That's what happens when you're alone. Nobody else steps in to help you, and, sure as hell, nobody has your back."

He finally realized she wasn't even speaking about herself but about the kids. And yet it *was* all about her. "You want to help them," he said, "and that's great. And maybe you're the right person to help them, and maybe you're not. It's too early for that yet. Just give it a little time and see how you feel about it."

"If they don't come out of their little play area, it doesn't matter how any of us feel about it because that's where they'll stay. That will be the level of care that they need," she wailed, rubbing her face. "Now go away. I'll be out in a few minutes." And, with that, she slammed the door in his face.

He burst out laughing for some reason, having absolutely no problem with her prickly personality. He understood why it was there—as a mechanism to keep him away and to keep herself safe. He just didn't think she understood what she was doing, and that, in its own way, was kind of fun. Clearly she had her own elements of safety that she'd put in place, and, whether she realized it or not, she was doing the same damn thing as her twin brothers.

And, in some ways, Mark might be doing it a little bit better.

OVER THE NEXT several days Tandy returned to her apartment to find Keller waiting there. Again. It had become his daily pattern ever since the break-in. She shook her head and declared, "I'm okay, you know? You don't have to hang around to confirm that I'm *not* getting broken into."

He just nodded and didn't say anything, yet not moving either.

She glared at him. "*Seriously?*"

"Good, glad to hear that."

"So, why are you still hanging around?"

He gave her a lopsided smile. "Maybe I just want to."

She stared at him, then shook her head. "Nope, that's not happening."

He had to admit for a moment that the rejection hit him hard, and he wasn't even sure what to say.

She added, "No way you're the kind of guy to hang around for that reason."

He stared at her and realized that it wasn't a rejection of him but of her, of her own ability to attract a partner, to have a partner, or to have anybody even seriously interested in her.

"What? You don't think it can happen?" he asked curiously, pulling back on his own negativity and emotions.

"I just don't know why it would," she declared, staring at him.

He smiled. "I don't think you have any idea just how attractive you are."

She snorted at that. "It doesn't matter if I am or not. I can't imagine anybody signing up for this headache in my world, and you know about the headaches. So no way. Something else must be going on."

"Wow," he muttered, "you seriously have trust issues."

He looked to the left and to the right of this hallway to see if anybody lingered nearby, overhearing this conversation.

"No, I don't," she argued. "I have no issues and no problems with people because I just don't trust anybody."

He burst out laughing, and she glared at him. It was all he could do to pull back some of the laughter.

"I don't understand why, when I say truthful and honest shit, you find it so hilarious," she grumbled.

"I'm not laughing at you and your problems, sweetheart. I'm just glad that you are okay."

She groaned, shot a look at his empty hands, and then asked him, "You didn't bring dinner today?"

He controlled the burst of laughter wanting to come out. "I thought we would cook today."

"We should probably *not* cook," she replied. "I cook because I have to, but it's not because it's good enough to eat." And that set him off laughing again. Finally she snapped, "Great, apparently I'm a never-ending source of amusement to you." She waved her arms. "You might as well come in." She quickly unlocked the door, stepped inside, and froze.

She froze so fast that he bumped into her as he was coming in behind her. Immediately he grabbed her shoulders and asked, "What?" He looked around but couldn't see any threat. "Are you okay?" He turned her to face him. Her eyes were open but unfocused. She had gone into some trance state. Knowing that neighbors could be around and that anybody could see them standing half in and half out of the doorway, he gently nudged her forward and quickly closed the door behind them.

He walked her to the couch and sat her down. She moved completely normally and sat normally, and yet it was obvious she wasn't here. He didn't know what to do and was afraid that doing anything more would disturb something else altogether.

He called Dr. Maddy. When she didn't answer, Keller called Stefan. When Stefan answered, Keller quickly explained what was going on.

"Interesting," Stefan replied. "Don't touch her further. Just stay by her side and see if she's interested in coming back at all."

"How am I supposed to know that?" Keller asked in bewilderment, as he stared down at this woman, who even now seemed to have taken a breath and just froze that way. For his own satisfaction as much as anything, he studied her wrist, feeling for a pulse. Of course it was there, and it was crazy of him to even question that, yet he knew it wasn't so crazy. He wasn't crazy, but this whole mess was getting crazier by the minute.

Stefan asked a few more questions and then added, "Just leave her be, and, if she doesn't come back out of it in a few minutes, maybe ten or so, give me a shout."

And, with that, he ended the call, leaving Keller to stare down at Tandy, frozen in time.

# CHAPTER 10

THE HAND SHAKING Tandy was urgent, strong, forceful, giving her no quarter. Tandy groaned several times, trying to fend it all off, and then finally managed to get enough energy to come up with a fist and start really fighting back. The urgent tone changed, now calm and soft.

"It's okay. It's all right. You're safe. I just needed you back here with me."

Finally she opened her eyes to find herself on the couch, her hands and feet up, as if defending herself. And there was Keller, staring at her with evident worry on his face. She blinked at him several times.

Then he nodded. "As much as I'm glad to have you back," he began, "it would be absolutely wonderful if you *never* did that again."

"Do what?" she whispered, but her throat was hoarse and dry.

"You went into a trance and didn't come back out," he exclaimed. "As soon as we got to the door, you opened it, and you just … froze."

She frowned, trying to process what he said, then winced, stared at the door, and looked around her apartment. "Are you sure?" she asked.

"Yes, I'm sure." He half-laughed, half-groaned. "I'm definitely sure."

She swallowed several more times, and he got up and brought her back a glass of water. "Thank you," she whispered, as she accepted a sip.

"How are you now?" he asked.

"A little bit better, I think," she replied, with a wry note in her tone. "I have no recollection of what just happened, but, according to you, I was out of it, at least for a bit."

"Yeah, you absolutely were," he snapped, staring at her with that same intensity.

She waved him off. "I'm fine now."

"Maybe, but you literally went from one moment to another into a deep trance."

She nodded. "Yeah, and I think I got thrown into some pretty weird nightmares too." She didn't want to tell him about the strangeness she had seen or about the weird images, but the fear choking her throat bothered her the most. She massaged her throat gently and whispered, "It feels really rough."

He went to refill the water glass again. When he came back, he muttered, "See if you can get some more of this down."

She took another sip and then another, each one going down a little smoother. When she finally could, she got up, still holding the glass of water, and wandered around her living room, stretching and loosening up her muscles. Everything was sore, as if she'd been in a major fight. She looked over at him. "How long was I out?"

He shrugged. "Twenty minutes, thirty maybe. I don't know," he wailed. "If you're asking from the beginning, I would say closer to forty-five. I was just about to call Stefan back and to ask what I should do, when I saw some movement from you, and I just yelled at you to get your ass back here again," he admitted, with a sly smile. "I was telling you in my mind to come back, but I wasn't exactly seeing any response."

She frowned. "I did hear somebody telling me to come back, saying that it was okay, but I couldn't really see or figure out where I was or who was speaking to me. ... I wasn't really looking," she said, by way of apology, "as I was stuck somewhere."

"Yeah, it's the *somewhere* that bothers me."

She didn't say anything because most people weren't accustomed to somebody going off in a strange trance, and she wasn't exactly sure what it had been either.

He asked, "Do you do this often?"

She stared at him and shook her head. "I'm not sure what I'm supposed to say to that," she replied. "Has it happened before? Yes. Has it happened recently? No."

He nodded and asked, "When was the last time?"

She gave him a long look and sighed. "A very long time ago." He hesitated, but absolutely no way she would go into what had happened before. "Let's just say it was completely unrelated to this." He didn't push it, but she could tell he was not impressed with her answer. *Too bad.* He'd come a long way in getting past her defenses, but absolutely no way she would explain about that. She got up and headed to the bathroom, used the facilities.

When she came back out again, she saw him still standing there, but now he looked more pissed than anything. "Sorry," she muttered. "I'm a trial, I know."

He shook his head. "I'm not pissed at you. I'm pissed that I didn't know what to do. I'm pissed that *this* could just happen, and what if nobody was here?"

"I would have just collapsed on the floor, and that would

have been the end of it, until I woke up again," she explained. "So really it's not anything you should worry about."

"And what if it happened while you were outside or … driving?"

She winced. "Let's hope it doesn't happen just for those reasons." She had to keep her composure. No way she would let him blow this up into something that would need even more of an explanation. "This is just another example of why I'm apparently a lot of work and why you should reconsider being friends with me."

He glared at her. "And that's enough of that shit."

She looked at him in surprise. "What? I'm just being honest."

"No, you're not being honest," he argued, getting red in the face. "You're being as honest as you understand that to be, but that's *not real* honesty." She blinked at that. He threw up his hands. "Never mind. I won't sit here and yell at you. I'm too damn glad that you're back."

And with that, she realized he really was worried about her, as in seriously worried. She just nodded, not sure how to even respond. She wasn't used to people who cared, wasn't used to people who gave a shit in any way. It was a weird feeling.

He grimaced. "I get it. You're not used to anybody even being in your space, let alone in your life, much less your heart, but that trance shit was pretty scary." Just then his phone rang, and he answered it, without even looking at the number, and muttered, "She's come out of it."

"Good."

Tandy heard Stefan's response in a weird echo.

"Keep an eye on her."

"Yeah, I will," Keller muttered, "but she's trying to pass it off as being nothing."

"Let me talk to her."

"I'll put you on Speakerphone." And, with that, he glared at her. "Stefan wants to talk to you."

She rolled her eyes at that. "I'm fine, Stefan. Thanks for helping Keller."

Stefan chuckled and replied, "I'm glad that you're fine, but I highly suspect this isn't the first time, is it?"

She winced, avoiding Keller's glare. "Nope, but it's been a very long time."

"Then maybe you need to examine the stressors of the last time and see if something similar has come back into your world now."

"That," she declared crisply, "is something I will *not* be doing."

There was a note of surprise on the other end. Then Stefan immediately agreed. "Okay, if it brings up that kind of a reaction, then obviously you need to take some time to work on those issues."

"That's not happening either," she snapped.

"Got it," Stefan replied. "However, if it happens again, you can bet that the stressor, whatever it is, is back in your life. While you might want to ignore it, that won't be so easy to do now."

"Why not? Last time I managed to just block it out."

"Yes, but now it's returned, gotten through your block. And whether you tell me the details or not, the fact appears to be that you've had problems with this for a long time. Your solution to block it has now failed, meaning that, as much as you've fought to keep it away all this time, it has continued to fight to stay in your life. You need to keep that in mind." And, with that, Stefan ended the call.

Tandy frowned, as she realized that Stefan sounded legitimately worried.

Keller turned and looked at her. "What the hell does all that mean?"

She blinked at him, then shrugged. "It's not as if he gave me step-by-step instructions on how to keep safe from this."

"Agreed," he spat, staring at her. "It's also not something that you seem to be completely oblivious about."

She avoided his gaze, then shrugged. "I'm not exactly clear on that either," she muttered.

He groaned. "I have no idea, for sure, but whatever it is, can we just maybe not do it again?"

She snorted. "Wouldn't that be nice?" She tried to keep her tone steady, but it was a little hard.

Just then his phone beeped with a text.

**Forensics got something. Meet me at Endgame.** Grant added an address and a link.

Keller clicked the link and frowned. Some hocus-pocus shop. He turned to Tandy. "I have to leave." Yet he didn't move away.

She smiled at him and nodded. "Good. I'm just fine, honest."

"And why is it good?"

"Because then you won't be here to hassle me," she declared, dropping her smile. He stiffened and glared at her, and she snorted. "I should be fine now."

"Yeah, you say that, but you can't stop it by yourself, and now I don't think it's safe to leave you."

"It is definitely safe to leave me," she stated.

He shook his head. "I don't think so." And he went to make a phone call.

She grabbed his hand. "Stop it. I'm telling you it's okay."

He let his breath out slowly, all the while glaring at her.

She glared right back. "Look. I know you don't like hearing that, and you don't like to even consider that something that you don't understand just happened before your very eyes. You want to know more, but I'm not prepared to give you more."

And that really pissed him off.

SHE ADDED, "SO go, go off and be you. Do whatever it is that you need to do. I'm fine." And, with that said, Keller left with no other option but to accept her at her word, she managed to get him out of her apartment. As soon as the door closed behind him, and she heeded his words of warning to lock the door, she collapsed back down on the couch.

Almost immediately her mother appeared. *I told you it wouldn't work*, she snapped.

Tandy glared at her. "You never told me that at any time," she declared, looking at the *mother* who had never been a *mother* in any of the ways that mattered. "You never helped at all. All you ever did …" Tandy stopped because there was no point arguing with a damn self-centered ghost. All it would do was upset everything, including herself again.

*No, I told you back then*, her mother began, then frowned and shrugged. *At least I tried to.*

"You didn't tell me shit," Tandy snapped, glaring at her mother. "And each time I passed out, you just thought it was a game. A game you thought I was making up to get out of making money for you."

Isabella visibly winced, as much as a ghost was able to. *I am sorry. ... Apparently I owe you an apology.*

Tandy stared at the ghost, nonplused for a minute. "What did you say?"

Isabella flushed. *You could be nice.*

"Wow," she muttered. "I could be, but, after all the shit you've put me through, I'm still trying to figure out who you are right now."

*I'm the same person I've always been.*

"If you are," Tandy stated, "then fuck off. I want absolutely nothing to do with you." And, with that, she waved her hand and put up a shield, slamming her mother onto the other side of her front door, using the same method she'd always done to get her to stop being in her face. It seemed to work for a moment, as the ghost shimmered outside.

But then Isabella snapped back inside again and roared at her. *You can't do that to me.*

"Yes, I fucking can," Tandy snapped, slamming her door shut again, this time knocking her mother outside with the physical force of it. Tandy sat back down. For the first time in ages, she brought up memories that she thought she had buried long ago. Not only had they *not* been buried, they'd merely been stomped on, waiting to come back.

Stefan was right.

If this was happening again, Tandy's life was about to change—and not in a good way. This time, she knew that, if this was happening again, she definitely needed help in a big way, but it couldn't be just anybody.

And that would be the problem. She needed help, and it might require somebody like Stefan, somebody who understood energy, somebody who understood these crazy, stupid abilities. But she really, really didn't want to explain anything. Not now, not ever. Some things were just too painful to bring up.

STEFAN CONTACTED DR. Maddy.

"I know," she answered, without even giving him a greeting. "But I don't have any answers yet."

He chuckled. "And I wasn't asking necessarily for answers."

"Yes, you were," she claimed, with a smile in her tone. "You're just as curious about these two kids as everybody else is."

"They are pretty fascinating," he admitted. "But curiosity is never a reason to forget why they're there."

"Exactly," she agreed.

He hesitated and then asked, "What's your take on Tandy?"

"Another fascinating person," she murmured, "with some pretty major issues of her own."

"As do the rest of us."

"Exactly, just like the rest of us." Dr. Maddy sighed. "You would think that, after all this time, it would be easier, and we would have more answers, but instead it seems as if all we ever do is get more questions."

"Tandy also appears to have quite a bit more going on than she's telling us."

"And you can't blame her for that."

"I don't know if you've talked to Keller yet," Stefan noted, "but you do need to ask him about what happened in her apartment today. I can give you an overview but not the details. I think he's still trying to figure his way through it himself."

"I wouldn't be at all surprised, since he's relatively new to a lot of this. Although he's been dealing with much of it all his life, he just didn't realize why he was different in so many ways," she shared, with a note of humor. "It seems as if people with abilities either don't know that they're different or don't want anybody to know that they can do things because they just keep getting into crap over it all."

"Of course," Stefan agreed. "In this case, apparently Tandy got home, touched her wall, and went into an incredibly deep trance."

"Oh, that's fascinating," Dr. Maddy muttered. "And did she have an explanation for it or say where she went?"

"None that Keller could get out of her, but she was pretty disturbed at the end of it. He didn't want to leave her alone, but she more or less kicked him out."

"Right," she murmured. "I think that's her MO. She's adamant about blocking everybody out and trying to carry on her own, hoping she can control this."

"But we also know that's not likely to happen," Stefan added. "You and I do at least."

"I know. I know." Dr. Maddy groaned. "I'm not at all surprised that she has abilities, considering she's related to the twins."

"And do we know anything about that relationship, other than what she's told us?"

"Meaning?"

"I just feel as if something is there."

"And it's possible, but I'm not sure anybody will tell us at this point. If she's going into trances now, that could be a problem in itself."

"It could be," he agreed. "Keller seems to think it's quite a big problem, and yet she was quick to brush him off."

"Of course, a big problem to her is having anybody know that this is actually happening. She can't control the outcome if everybody knows about it. I could speak to her."

"I was thinking about doing that myself," Stefan shared.

"And you're probably a better person in this instance. I'm not sure where the trances are coming from or whether she's potentially got other skills that she's not recognizing. However, if you can help her sort out what those are, that might be a good thing."

"Possibly," he conceded. "Keller did say that she's a little bit aggressive at the moment."

"Sure, she is."

"He also told me"—and he chose his words carefully—"that it appeared to be something from her history, or maybe not even a history. I don't know how to explain it, but he noted that she appeared to be quite terrified."

"*Terrified*," Dr. Maddy repeated, then groaned. "I wonder how much of this is all related to the mother's lifestyle and the fact that we already have two damaged kids here."

"It wouldn't be a stretch," Stefan replied. "Tandy mentioned that, once she got out of Isabella's house, she never really had much of a relationship with her mother."

"And yet she is now talking to her mother, or at least the ghostly version of her mother. Any chance that it really isn't her mother?" she asked suddenly.

*Silence.* "There's always a chance, but it's nothing we've seen before," Stefan replied cautiously. "Interesting that you would ask that."

"I don't know. I just don't know," Dr. Maddy admitted. "Once again we have a weird case where nothing really makes a whole lot of sense."

"We have seen those before," Stefan noted, "and we do

end up with answers eventually, but they often aren't the answers we expected. I'll talk to Tandy, and I'll let you know what she says."

"Be careful with her," Dr. Maddy pointed out. "She's incredibly stressed, and, if something is upsetting or terrifying her right now, she's in a tough position."

"A tougher position than you know, if she's that terrified," he pointed out, "because, as far as her mother is concerned, Isabella was murdered, but Tandy herself doesn't necessarily believe it. She believes her mother is nothing but a compulsive liar, even in death."

"And she still thinks that way, after the break-in and the trance?"

"I think it's more that she doesn't believe a tiger changes its stripes just because it dies."

"She has a point. We have seen a lot of people who didn't end up being any better in spirit form, especially when they haven't crossed over."

"The question is, why hasn't Isabella?"

"You might have to contact her yourself and see," Dr. Maddy suggested, chuckling.

"Thanks," he muttered. "Not exactly a job I want to do."

"And not one you have to do either," she claimed. "Just remember that there is only so much of Stefan to go around."

"I know," he conceded, "but I do feel that, whatever *this* is, it's connected to the twins."

She groaned and whispered, "I'm afraid you're right there. So, if you find out anything, please let me know."

After he ended the call, he sat here for a long moment, wondering about the best course of action. His wife walked in and sat down beside him, with a gentle smile on her face. He asked Celina, "When you see the music going on around you, you can see the colors, right?"

She looked at him curiously and nodded. "What about it?"

"Do you sense anything else differently?"

"Oh, I'm not sure what you mean by that," she replied cautiously. "I don't get any other sensations outside of joy. Joy in the music, joy in whatever is happening," she shared. "So I don't think that quite answers your question."

"The trouble is, I'm not really sure *what* question to ask."

"Generally you would just start asking," she noted, with a smile. "The fact that you haven't means that you're concerned about the response to your questions."

He chuckled. "As always, you're very astute."

She smiled at him. "Just reach out to her. She's probably too scared or too unaware that she could even contact you. Plus, considering that you come with a *grand* reputation, a lot of people don't feel they could approach you."

"Likewise, a lot of people want to because they think that I can help."

"And often you can," she pointed out. "The trick is figuring out which ones you can and which ones you can't."

"You are right, as always," he agreed. He hesitated, looked at his phone, then pulled it out. Immediately his wife got up and walked out. "I can do it later," he suggested, stopping in the midst of dialing.

She turned to him and shook her head. "No, you can't. This one is important." And, with that, she walked out.

He frowned at that. She was getting more and more sensitive to his cases as time went on. He wasn't sure whether that was a good thing or not. It was always hard to keep work and home separated, but, when you have a wife as intuitive as his, it became impossible. Still, he chose to dial, and, when Tandy's sleepy tone answered, he winced, wondering if he'd woken her. "Are you all right?" he asked, not sure where to go from here.

After a moment of disoriented silence, she whispered, "Is this Stefan?"

"Yes, it is."

"Of course it is," she muttered, with a sigh. "I was wondering about calling you, but I decided I shouldn't bother you."

That confirmed his guess right there. "Why did you want to call?" he asked.

"As you know, something happened today, something that I had hoped would never happen again, but now that it has, I don't know how to make it go away again."

"A little clarity would help."

"Yeah, it would help me too," she declared in a rough tone. "I don't even know that I have an explanation."

"You don't need to explain, but, if you could give me a more detailed retelling, it would help me to clarify some of the issues."

"I touched something on the wall when I came home. It felt like something I hadn't felt in a very long time, and I hate to say it, but I pretty well passed out from it."

"Passed out or went into a trance?" When she hesitated, he continued. "There's a big difference, and I assume you already know that, but it's obviously easier for you to acknowledge that you passed out, rather than the alternative."

"I don't think I want it to be a trance," she admitted painfully.

"Was that something your mother would request of you?"

"Sometimes," she muttered. "More than that, it was something ..." When she hesitated this time, Stefan waited and let her speak when she was comfortable, so the silence stretched on and on. Then she sighed. "I know this will sound awful, and I sure as hell don't have any proof of it, but I felt she used to do something to me in order to get whatever reaction she wanted."

"Do *to you?*" he asked.

"Yes," she whispered. "The problem is, now that she's gone, ... it shouldn't be happening. So, if it was always *her* doing it before ..."

"Just say it without thinking. I'm listening here."

"I just want to know that, if Isabella's really gone, who is doing this now?"

# CHAPTER 11

---

ANDY WAITED FOR Stefan to respond, and, when he didn't, she added, "Or is that a little bit too much heebie-jeebies stuff—or maybe just plain old conspiracy theories?" She couldn't stop the self-deprecating laugh as she said, "I'm fine. Whatever it is, I'll be okay."

"Stop it," Stefan snapped.

She stared down at the phone. "Sorry." She wasn't sure how to respond to his change in demeanor.

"Stop trying to pass this off as something that's not important. Listen to me, Tandy. If it sent you into a trance, I need you to understand that it is important."

"Is it though? Isabella used to send me into a trance all the time."

"I know this will sound really stupid, and we sure as hell should have asked sooner, but, because Isabella wasn't alive anymore, I don't think we gave it any thought. So here goes. Did your mother have abilities?"

"She did. I don't know exactly what kind, and honest to God most of the time she was so drugged out that, even if she did have abilities, she wouldn't have been able to make much sense out of them." There was silence on the other end. She sighed. "I don't understand what difference that makes."

"Considering that we have the twins struggling to adapt

to a normal life, and we have you going into a trance for whatever reason," he replied, "the question in my mind is, what connection does your mother have to any of it?"

"I hope to God it's none," Tandy noted. "I know that most people wouldn't understand, but I very much want that woman out of my life."

"I do understand," he stated. "And, no, I do not blame you, not after all that your mother has done," he pointed out, "and you need to stop blaming yourself. It's not serving you very well."

She snorted. "The world blames anybody who's got problems with their mother. And, just because she's dead, I can't suddenly decide that she is a good person at heart and that I should just get over her."

"No, you aren't supposed to do that at all," he shared. "And, in this instance, it seems as if your mother had an awful lot to answer for."

"Sure, she probably did, but she has somehow escaped punishment, if death is an escape," she said mockingly. "And the bottom line is, it doesn't matter. It's not as if I can get answers from her."

"Are you sure?" he asked.

"I'm sure. You think that it's easy to talk to ghosts? Still, talking to ghosts or having them talk to me doesn't mean that they give you the answers you want."

"Now that, I do know, as I talk to ghosts a lot myself."

It took her a moment, before she finally responded. "You do?"

"Yes, I sure do. I've spent a lifetime helping souls cross over."

"Well then, help mine cross over and get her out of my life," she snapped aggressively. Then she groaned. "I don't even know why I'm so distraught," she muttered. "It's not as if this is anything new."

"And yet it seems you're feeling it anew."

"I am feeling it's new to me," she conceded, "and I think it's just because it hasn't happened in quite a while. That and I thought I was finally in the clear."

"And you weren't expecting it to happen again?"

"No. Abso-*fucking*-lutely *not*."

"Did your mother know how much you hated this?"

"Eventually, but not at the beginning, or, if she did, she didn't care." At the silence on the other end, she added, "Look. It's not that I have a hate-on for my mother, though I'm sure it sounds that way. But really I'm still adapting to the fact that one, she's gone, that two, she left me such a mess, which is so typical of her, and that three, I don't know how to handle what just happened in terms of whatever that vision was."

"Did you see something?" he asked, his tone turning sharp.

She frowned, startled by his change of tone. "No, I don't think so."

"You don't think so?" he asked cautiously. "You hadn't used the word *vision* before. Take a moment and think about it."

"I don't think I saw anything. Is that what you were expecting? That I would have gone into a trance and had a vision or something?"

"It certainly happens that way for a lot of people, so if you did have something happen, understand that it's a completely different scenario, and one that would potentially have a different kind of outcome."

"That makes no sense either." She groaned. "I really just

want all this to go away."

He laughed, but it was a gentle laugh. "Just because you want it to go away doesn't mean it will, particularly if you are strong with abilities."

"I don't have abilities, except talking to ghosts."

Stefan snorted. "I don't believe that for a minute. However, I'm sorry that nobody has any empathy for what you're going through."

"I don't need that," she muttered. "I just want it all to stop."

"What is it you want to stop, exactly?" When she hesitated, he explained, "I can't help you if you don't tell me."

"Yeah, and if I tell you," she began, once again in that hard mocking tone, "you'll probably hang up the phone and have me committed."

"That I won't do," he declared, his tone sharp. "I get that you don't know me and that you think that the world out there is a very unwelcoming place, but I've been there myself. Dr. Maddy has also been there. That's one of the reasons we do what we do, to help people like us, like you—like the twins."

"Oh God, the twins," she muttered. "I can't believe what they've created. If I had any idea that I could do something like that, I would have done it myself," she declared. "Life with my mother was hellish, but life with her boyfriends was beyond hellish, and escaping that torment would have been worth any cost."

"Were you sexually abused?" he asked, point-blank. So much so that it completely surprised her.

"You could say that," she murmured, "and it's one of the reasons why some of my other siblings were removed from the home."

"And yet none of the others were. Why is that?"

"I don't know why that is," she said. "Apparently Isabella redeemed herself somewhere along the line."

"But you don't believe that."

"God, how could anybody believe it? Look at the child porn material found with the twins," she wailed. "She didn't change a bit, and she is just as messed up now as she was then." Almost immediately Tandy felt something in the room around her. She glanced around and muttered, "And I swear to God that woman is haunting me."

"Haunting you or trying to tell you something?"

"I don't know, and believe me that I really don't want to find out."

"And that's fine. You don't have to," Stefan replied. "She might have a problem, and she might be hoping she can explain something to you. You do get a choice in this."

"If I had a choice in this, I wouldn't be in the position I'm in right now. I'm here because of that damn woman. And the fact that she's still in my living room half the time, ruining my life, is devastating, and I want nothing to do with it."

"Can you tell her to go away?" he asked cautiously.

"I've tried, and then I talk to her because of something she says that's completely outlandish and outrageous, and I realize that, even though she is dead, I still can't just walk away."

"And why is that?"

"Because there's something I still have to know from her. Every time I try to walk away, it keeps coming back, and I realize that I'll never be free until I find out what that is."

"And what is it that you want to know?"

She hesitated. "I can't tell you. Some things are just too

awful to speak of."

"Maybe, but I've seen a lot of it, and I've heard pretty-well everything the world has to throw at us. So, if you need somebody to help you, to talk to, I'm that person."

"Are you though?" she muttered, starting to cry. "And how do you feel about murder?"

And, with that, she burst into tears and disconnected the call.

KELLER HAD MET with Grant and had uncovered another prong to this investigation, which Grant took on. More information wasn't necessarily a good thing at times. Keller shook his head and entered his apartment and sank down at his desk, feeling a little numb. His phone rang, rattling him out of his confusion. He stared at his cell, still perplexed and admittedly disturbed by Tandy's trance and by this latest lead to the voodoo shop. When he saw Stefan was calling, he asked, "What's up?"

"Tell me exactly what you saw when Tandy had her episode."

"I already told you. She just froze. I nudged her inside and helped her sit on the couch, just to relax and to help her get out of whatever she was caught up in, but she didn't talk. She didn't do anything."

"Did you—and I know this will sound a little weird—but did you sense anybody else around you?"

Keller frowned. "I'm not sure that I would have, even if somebody was there," he replied cautiously. "It's not as if I'm like you guys. Nor am I as strong in my gift."

Stefan laughed. "You're a whole lot more like us than you think. And you'll see it more now, particularly if you start caring for somebody, and weird stuff happens around them."

"This was pretty damn weird. I won't lie. Everything I saw there was very weird."

"Of course, and that's why I'm asking for a few more details."

"I don't really have details to give you, and she gave me the brush-off right away."

"Are there any histories of old cases connected to her mother?"

"What do you mean?" Keller asked, confused.

"Tandy mentioned something about murder."

"Right, her mother believes she was murdered. But that's according to her mother," he noted, with a sigh, "and Tandy doesn't believe anything her mother says."

"I saw that too," Stefan shared, "and I can't really blame Tandy, not after a lifetime of pain and listening to her mother's lies."

"I was hoping when people died that they cleaned up their act and learned right from wrong," Keller shared. "But, so far, from what I have seen, Isabella hasn't done that."

"She's caught on this side still," Stefan pointed out. "And sometimes people learn, and sometimes they don't. They just hang on to that same anger and nastiness that they had when they were alive and had a body."

"God, when you say it like that, it all just sounds kind of creepy."

Stefan nodded, forgetting that Keller couldn't see him. "It is creepy," he confirmed. "It's very creepy, but that doesn't change the fact that, in many of these instances, they are either waiting to see justice done or they're after re-venge."

"Meaning that Isabella could be after revenge because she was potentially murdered?"

"It's possible, although I am not sure she has the, … don't take this the wrong way, but the wherewithal."

"Oh, I get you," Keller said. "I'm not so sure she does either. But what's this about murder then, if that's not what you're talking about?"

"I didn't say it's *not* what I'm talking about, but could you search the history on Isabella Goodman and go way back, like twenty years, make that thirty, and see if she's connected to any other murder cases, unexplained deaths, or anything like that?"

"Sure," Keller replied cautiously, wondering what the hell Stefan was up to.

"I know it's an odd request, and, if you are not comfortable, I can certainly ask Grant to do it."

"Oh no, I'll do it," Keller stated, "but you've certainly got my interest piqued."

"And it could all be for nothing. I'm not saying anything is there."

"I hope not," he muttered, "because that would mean something completely other than what we thought was going on here."

"I really need any information you can find."

"Fine. … I can probably do some of that tonight." Keller hoped the local cops had ample probable cause to do a search of the premises at the Endgame shop.

"That would be great, and let me know soon, please." And, with that, Stefan rang off.

For Stefan to ask for deaths tied to Isabella was bizarre and unusual in itself. Yet it made sense to do a deep dive into the history on the mother, since she appeared to be a pivotal figure in this whole case. Hell, Isabella was possibly psychic as well. It could certainly stir up more issues, but it depended on whether she was one of the good guys or one of the bad guys.

"Who are you kidding?" he muttered to himself. "There is no good guy in Isabella."

It seemed as if everybody involved in this case was a bad guy. Keller shook his head at that and quickly brought up his laptop and sat down to do some research. It didn't take long to see that several deaths had happened in Isabella's life.

"No wonder she's such a basket case," he muttered, as he stared at some of the case files. Seven deaths surrounded Isabella. Three of those had no solutions, were unexplained and yet were not accidental. So, he had no answers. When he called Stefan back, Stefan answered the phone immediately.

"Seven," he greeted Stefan. "Seven deaths were associated with Isabella or involved her. Now, I have a caveat. You wanted this fast, and this information is what I found to date, based on just the cities we currently know that Isabella lived in, provided by Tandy. So I could find more theoretically, especially if Isabella used another name. Anyway, based on that, of the seven found so far, three had sketchy circumstances with no answers, which includes Gwen's death. The other four were closed, pending further evidence to proceed on these cases, which includes Gwen's son, Isabella's partner. They never married."

"I was afraid of that," Stefan muttered. "I don't suppose I can get the details of the cases from you."

"I can do that," he agreed, scratching his chin. "I really want to know what this is about, though."

"I'm sure you would," Stefan stated. "Then again, so would I."

He groaned. "Is everything always so cryptic?"

"Yes. In these cases, everything is always cryptic, but not by choice. I just don't want to dish out any more hurt to somebody who's already been hurt so badly," he explained.

At that, Keller thought about the twins and Tandy. "Are you thinking that Isabella is a serial killer or something?" he asked in astonishment. "If that were the case, I could really only see any killings as drug-fueled hazes."

"But are those the kind of killings that you're seeing in these cases?"

"No," he noted. "One shooting, one stabbing," he began, as he went through the files, "and another one appears to be a drug overdose. That death I could see Isabella doing, not necessarily even on purpose. That could have been an accident. You already know about Gwen's death and her son's. These other three could all be drug-related but not necessarily murder."

"Send me the files, send me whatever you can, and maybe hook Grant into this, will you?"

"Got it," Keller replied.

"And as soon as you have a little more information for me, I would sure appreciate it."

"Yeah, I do have something else." Then he shared with Stefan what little Keller and Grant had uncovered about the voodoo shop called Endgame, with the albino shop owner who may have been Tandy's intruder. Plus, the Be Part of the Eternity Coven literature all around the shop had been a red flag too.

Stefan sighed. "It just gets worse, doesn't it?"

"And when you mentioned that you didn't want to increase the hurt," Keller said, with a sinking feeling, "I presume you were talking about Tandy." When Stefan hesitated, Keller knew the answer. "God damn it, that girl's already got so much trouble, and the last thing she needs on her back is more."

"She's got more trouble than she knows," Stefan declared, "and somehow I have to figure out who and what's behind it, then see if there's any way to stop it." And, with that terrifying statement, Stefan ended the call.

# CHAPTER 12

TANDY HAD A hot shower, dragged herself to bed, and somehow managed to fall asleep. Exhausted and worried, and yet not finished thinking about her conversation with Stefan, Tandy worried about the trance she had fallen into. Finally she fell asleep.

The next morning, she got up and headed to work. The day went smoothly and pretty much was business as usual. After work, she felt a humming sensation. She noted nothing else but that, and it tugged at her and automatically took her to Dr. Maddy's floor to see her siblings. As she walked into the hospital, she didn't even ask anybody and headed straight for their room. It was almost as if her feet were preordained on a certain mission.

By the time she walked into their room, they were out cold on the bed. She frowned, not accustomed to seeing them like that, and a message came to her.

*Close your eyes.*

When she opened her eyes again, there they were.

Mark smiled at her and spoke in a very gentle way. "Thank you for coming."

She narrowed her gaze at him and asked, "Did I have a choice?"

Mark shrugged. "Maybe, but then maybe not," he replied.

She sat down cross-legged beside Mark, with Matthew running into her arms. She looked over at Mark. "You can't always have everything the way you want it."

Mark gave her an inscrutable smile and just remained quiet.

At that moment, she realized that her little brother *was* getting everything he wanted so far. "I'm not sure it's a good idea for me to keep playing with you here."

"It needs to be here," Mark stated. "We're not going out there."

That was the first time Mark had acknowledged that there was an *out there*, and Tandy didn't quite know what to say but just nodded. "That could change."

"It could, but it won't."

"And why not?" she challenged.

Mark stared at her. "Because out there, … all kinds of bad things happen." And, if it wasn't bad enough that Mark understood what evil was out there, he went on. "As you know."

Mark acted so much older than a five-year-old. Tandy frowned as she looked closer, trying to sort out what was going on here.

Then Matthew came around to give her another big hug and said, "I'm glad you came."

"I'm glad I came too," she murmured. "It would be nice if you could visit my house too."

"Yes," Matthew agreed, as he looked over at his brother. Then his smile fell away almost instantly. "But Mark won't come."

"Maybe he will," Tandy shared. "We just need to give him a little bit of time."

"It won't happen," Matthew stated, with a headshake.

"He doesn't like leaving."

"But you have to leave in order to know if you like it at my home," she pointed out.

He giggled, and she glanced over at Mark, not necessarily comprehending and not necessarily upset. It was almost a vacant look, and she called out, "Earth to Mark, Earth to Mark."

Matthew giggled uproariously at that, as Mark snapped back and glared at her.

She smiled and nodded. "At least if I'm here, let's communicate." Then she worried that Mark would tell her to get up and leave if she wanted to play those kind of games. She couldn't quite understand what was going on, but then Matthew went over and gave Mark a hug.

"It's fine," Matthew said, wrapping his arms around Mark.

Mark wrapped up Matthew and held him close.

That image almost broke her heart. Once she realized that it literally was just a little five-year-old boy trying to protect everybody, she added, "Other people can help too."

Mark just looked at Tandy with both a weariness and a wariness to his expression.

"Not everybody will hurt you," she said.

Mark didn't say anything, and Tandy didn't know if he even understood.

When the door to this room opened, Dr. Maddy came in. Instead of just coming into the room, Dr. Maddy literally came into the playroom, as if the transfer from reality to this world was incredibly easy for her. Dr. Maddy smiled at Tandy. "I'm glad to see you came by again today."

"I wanted to see my siblings," Tandy shared.

Matthew laughed, ran over, and gave Dr. Maddy a big

hug. Dr. Maddy squatted on the floor, now sitting cross-legged, and hugged him back. He turned and sat in the circle of her arms and generally just played with her hair. The foursome continued to enjoy a sweet visit. Tandy didn't broach anything else with her brothers, and she watched as Dr. Maddy played with them.

Then Mark stood up and announced, "It's time for us to go."

Immediately Matthew nodded, acknowledging it was naptime, then raced over to his bed, where he hopped in.

Tandy watched him do that, blinking back tears in her eyes as she realized how accustomed he was to this movement. To this motion of needing to go to bed in this fake world. It was all too real for him. She stood up and nodded. "I need to go too."

Mark stood as well, a little bit standoffish. Still friendly but wary.

She smiled at him. "I'll come back again." Mark just nodded. "I want you to know that I *will* come, so you don't have to call."

Mark narrowed his gaze, almost the beginning of another spark of temper.

Tandy smiled and added, "And it's okay to call for me. It's okay that you called." And, with that, she walked over, gave Mark a gentle hug, walked to the bed, and bent to hug Matthew carefully, then stepped back and followed Dr. Maddy out of the room.

As soon as she got out into the hallway, Dr. Maddy turned to her. "We really don't want to push them at this stage."

"I understand." Tandy wiped at her eyes. "I'm sorry about that. I'm a little frustrated at the moment."

"And that might be, but we never take it out on the kids."

"Did I take it out on them?" she asked in astonishment.

"No, but we can't push their recovery or try to force them to come back into the world that they have willfully left behind."

"I feel bad about that, but …" She winced and added, "I'm pretty-damn sure that Mark compelled me to come here today, right now, whether I wanted to or not."

Dr. Maddy stared at her. "What do you mean?"

"I feel as if I got orders to show up," she replied, with a small smile, "*Mark's* orders. As soon as I got to work today, I kept getting hit with these messages. … *You need to go visit them*, over and over. So, I was trying to explain to Mark that he could come visit me too and that I would come visit them regardless, and he didn't need to send me those messages."

Dr. Maddy looked at her thoughtfully. "That would be interesting if he was doing that."

"Sure, it would be interesting, but it's also difficult to stand by and to just let him get into my head like that. I don't want to slam the door and lock him out."

"No, please don't do that," Dr. Maddy muttered. "I understand the wish to do it sometimes," she admitted, her lips twisting in a smile, "because I deal with people who have a lot of demands and who want things in their own world, but we do need to keep the door open."

"Which is why I was trying to gently tell Mark that I would come without the urging."

"Do you think he believed you?"

Tandy shook her head. "I feel as if he was testing me."

"Testing you?"

"Yes, testing me." And then she stopped and looked at

Dr. Maddy intently. "Did it ever occur to you that he's awfully adult in his communications?"

Dr. Maddy eyed her and slowly frowned. "I hadn't considered that, but I will now."

"Please do," Tandy muttered.

"You're thinking something is wrong there too?"

"God, that just makes me out to be a complete asshole," she muttered. "It's not that I'm thinking something is wrong, and yet maybe I am. Could it be a possession thing? I don't know. Could it be our horrid mother influencing Mark? Definitely. … Apparently I have a whole lot of issues—and conspiracy theories. I don't know what is right and what is wrong. I don't even know what the truth is anymore," she murmured.

"And you shouldn't be too worried about it either. There are a lot of things in life we don't understand, and, if we can get through some of it here, it will make life a lot easier."

"Sure, but then you want to ask questions because you need to know what's happening, and you want to confirm that what you're doing is your own free will." She went quiet for a moment, then took a deep breath. "I want to make sure I'm not being manipulated by another master manipulator."

"Ah," Dr. Maddy noted, with a smile. "So that upsets you the most, doesn't it? Your mother?"

"Oh God, you have no idea what life with my mother was like," she said, "and, even though it's been years, suddenly I feel as if I've been sucked right back into it, and I can't get out."

"You can get out," Dr. Maddy declared, "any time you want."

Tandy stared at her hopefully. "You say that with so

much confidence, but everybody doesn't have the same abilities you have."

"Oh, but you absolutely do," Dr. Maddy corrected her, "and I know that for a fact."

"How could you?" Tandy asked, staring at her. "I don't know anything at the moment, so I don't know how you possibly could."

Dr. Maddy chuckled. "It may be difficult but not impossible. You may feel it is, but I've seen an awful lot. You're very talented in energy work, and I have seen it. So I can say with confidence that you've got this."

"No, that's my brothers' gift, apparently."

"Maybe," she agreed, "but I'm talking about you and your own skills."

She looked at Dr. Maddy and whispered, "I can't go back to what was going on in my life. You have no idea. I went through periods of complete blackouts, not knowing where I was or *what* I was, day to day," she shared, "and it was endless torment."

Dr. Maddy's gaze narrowed, and she nodded in understanding. "No, we don't want that to come back," she agreed. "That sounds awful."

"And it was my mother," Tandy clarified, "always my mother, finagling and working the system. I can't go back to that. I just can't."

"Your mother is dead, Tandy. Isabella is dead. You need to remember that."

Tandy burst into uncontrollable laughter. "You have no idea what my mother in life was capable of and how tormented my whole world was. I know that nobody is supposed to be grateful when their parent dies, but I was, dear God, I was. And now she's still haunting me in death."

"And you can tell her to buzz off," Dr. Maddy suggested. "That is within your power."

"Is it?" she asked hysterically. "Because so far she's not listening."

"And that's because she's desperate to tell you something. She's desperate for you to understand. Listen to that and then let her go. I'm asking you to give it a chance because I know that it would bring peace for both of you."

Tandy stared at Dr. Maddy and shook her head. "I don't know about that. I was suicidal when I was a teenager. I just couldn't handle waking up every day, not knowing what I did or who I did it with. And not knowing if it was my free will or my mother and her drugs," she explained. "It was the most godawful feeling, and I can't go back to that. I won't."

"And you don't need to. Isabella is not here anymore. You control what contact you have with her. Answers may come if you leave the door open, but, if you don't, that's your choice."

Tandy groaned. "I know I should just say, *Fuck off*, and she should be gone, but somehow it doesn't happen, and whether that's because I have allowed her that kind of power or what, I don't know," she whispered. "But I need it to stop."

Dr. Maddy studied her curiously. "Why do you think you haven't been able to make it happen?"

"I guess I'm afraid that she needs to tell me something, and this is the last chance, but I really want to know. Yet the things I want to know I will only doubt them now she's dead. So why couldn't I get the answers while she was alive? She has systematically and deliberately destroyed everything in my world," she stated, "and I can't afford to let her back in again."

"Even though she's dead?" she asked.

"Yes, especially now that she's dead."

At that, Dr. Maddy's eyebrows shot up. "Do you think she has even more power now that she's dead?"

"Yes," she exclaimed, staring at her. "Absolutely, yes."

"And why is that?" she asked in confusion. "She has no body, no way to move around this world."

"No, maybe not move around this world, but she was incredibly powerful before. And the problem with that was, back then, the drugs kept her more or less contained, or maybe *useless* is a better word," she noted. "But now that she doesn't have the influence of the drugs, she's even more dangerous than ever."

Dr. Maddy just stared at her, wordless.

"I know you don't believe me," Tandy muttered, raising both hands. "God, I sound stupid even to myself."

"You're not stupid," Dr. Maddy declared, "though it concerns me that this woman has this much power over you when she's gone. That should never be something you have to deal with."

"Maybe not," Tandy muttered, "but this is my crazy world now, and it doesn't matter what anybody says. While Isabella's here, she has the power."

"No," Dr. Maddy corrected. "*You* do. You just need to take it back."

AFTER THE CALL from Stefan, Keller stood up from his desk in his small apartment, tossed his wallet and keys into the small bowl on the side table, and then headed into the kitchen. He opened the fridge, pulled out a cold beer, popped the top, and took a long slug.

Moving to the living room, he stared out into the coldish evening. The sun had started to settle, bringing a chill to the air. And yet the chill filled his soul, as he realized that this was one strange case that would end up being a whole lot worse before it was done. When a snicker came from behind him, he stiffened and slowly turned, only to glare at the ghostly form in front of him. "What do you want?" he asked, his tone hard. "Nobody comes in here without permission."

*I did,* the woman declared, with mocking laughter.

He tried to sort out some understanding as to who had barged into his space, but he wasn't used to ghosts coming in where they weren't wanted.

*Because I'm no ordinary ghost,* she announced, with a laugh.

"Maybe not," he replied, "but that doesn't make you welcome here."

*Too bad. If you don't want me here, kick me out.*

He wasted no time and, with as much effort as was required, he booted her completely free of his space.

A surprised yelp came, as she disappeared into the ethers.

"And don't come back," he yelled.

When only silence came, he sagged onto his couch. But unable to just rest easy, he hopped up, opened the glass door, stepped out onto the small patio, and flung himself onto his big lounge chair. It's not as if he ever got much chance to sit out here, but the theory was nice. He was happy to have time off when he got it, but he had a fairly steady stream of cases to work on. He had more than his fair share of weird and wonderful woo-woo stuff going on in his world too, but not as if he had anybody he ever talked to about it. Grant seemed to understand that, and Keller knew that Dr. Maddy certainly did, but that part didn't endear him to this work.

Keller pondered the woman who had just been here, wondering who the hell she was and why. It had happened a time or two before, but usually he had a little more control over it, and he wondered at his defenses having sagged enough to let her through in the first place. When his phone rang, he looked down to see it was Stefan.

"Did you recognize her?"

"No, did you?" He frowned down at his phone, wondering why he was on Stefan's radar all of a sudden.

"I felt it, not because I'm tracking you but because I'm keeping an eye on anything to do with Tandy."

"What has *this* got to do with Tandy?" Keller asked in astonishment.

At that, Stefan chuckled. "That was a question I hoped you could answer."

"God no," he murmured. "I have no clue. I was hoping that it was just a random ghost, trying to get into my space."

"Has that happened before?"

"I hate to say it, but yes," he admitted. "Sometimes they're just pushy as hell. Everybody talks about ghosts needing to go to the light and all the rest of that *blah, blah, blah*," he noted sarcastically, "but I tend to find the cranky ghosts."

Stefan laughed. "And that is only because you let them in."

"Exactly why I booted her out hard," he declared in a more jovial tone.

"I heard it too, and she was a very unhappy ghost at having her abilities getting trimmed."

At the mention of *abilities* and *trimmed*, he frowned again at his phone and asked, "So, does this mean something more than I thought it would?"

"I don't know," Stefan conceded, "but what I can tell you is that Tandy's mother, the one who was supposedly murdered, had abilities, and now that she's dead, Tandy appears to be even more terrified of her."

"But she's dead."

"Exactly, and, according to Tandy, that's made her even more powerful."

"Jesus," he muttered, as he sat out in the cold breeze. "Is that even possible?"

"I don't know," Stefan replied, but a cautious note had entered his tone. "Every time I think I can't be surprised anymore, something happens that surprises me all over again."

"Christ, for Tandy to believe that though—"

"Helps to make it a reality. The fact that Tandy believes it so deeply," Stefan pointed out, "also helps bring it into fact. Any time we have a belief system, it allows the other person an increased power in our world, so it makes sense that Isabella is more powerful in a way. What we don't want is for Isabella to take advantage of whatever is going on for her own purposes and to gain more power. It's bad enough that Tandy believes Isabella is all-powerful, and we can't have Isabella thinking that too." Then Stefan disconnected.

Keller shook his head, after the call ended. It made no sense to him, but then he hadn't come across anybody who was that determined to make his life miserable. Yet Tandy seemed to have spent her lifetime with such a person.

As he sat here, he felt an odd presence again. He got up, stormed back inside, and, sure enough, there was the same spirit in his living room. "Don't bother getting comfy," he snapped. "You're not sticking around." And, with that, he gave her a mental boot to kick her back out again. Oddly enough, it was that much harder this time to evict her. He frowned and gave her a harder boot yet again.

She laughed. *Oh, you can do that for the moment, but I'm getting stronger. I've got your number. So, as long as I've got that, believe me that I've got you.*

# CHAPTER 13

TANDY CAME HOME the next day, tired and worn out. Work had been steady all day, with no chance for breaks in any way, and it had exhausted her. As she made her way back to her apartment, she found Keller sitting there, waiting just outside her door. She glared at him. "I'm too tired for this shit."

"Good because I'm too tired for *any* shit."

Her eyebrows shot up. "Problems?"

"Of course there are problems," he snapped bitterly.

More bitterly than she had expected.

"So, this mother of yours," he began.

Tandy winced. "Yeah. What about her?"

"Is she always this inconsiderate?"

She froze, and then slowly turned from the act of putting the key into her lock. "What do you mean?"

"I think you know what I mean."

"How the hell could I know what you mean?" she asked in exasperation. "My mother is dead, remember?"

"Yeah, I know, but I want to know why she's trying to haunt me."

"Oh Christ," she muttered, staring at him in shock. "Seriously?"

"Yeah, seriously."

Then she frowned and asked, "So you can ... Can you see her?"

"Yes, I can see her," he snapped, "and I don't like it. Every time I kick her out, it seems as if she goes away, then comes back stronger."

"Yeah, that's her," Tandy said grimly. "So, you have to stop kicking her out because she feeds off it somehow, and she gains strength from it." He stared at her, wordless, and she shrugged. "I don't know what to say. I know it's all BS. I know that everybody thinks it's because I believe it. I don't even know what to say." She opened the door finally, her fingers trembling with effort as she realized that her mother really was once again causing chaos in her world. "Look," she told him. "I'm sorry. I don't know what I'm supposed to say to you. You have contacts in your world with far better skills than I do." She shuddered, as if shaking off a bad vibe. "Believe me that my mother is not somebody you want to trifle with."

"Somehow I get the feeling that she's glad to be dead."

Tandy hesitated, then looked at him as she walked over to the coffeepot. "I hadn't considered it that way, and you could be right. I don't really know."

"But she's free of the drugs this way, right?"

"Yes. … Maybe. I did see her ghost smoking that first time she appeared," Tandy shared. At Keller's shocked expression, she just shook her head. "Who knows? Still, I think you could be right about her being happy to be dead."

"How powerful was she when she was alive?"

She winced. "Very. She was powerful, but you've got to understand that was why she stayed pretty-well drugged up."

"No, I don't understand that at all."

"The drugs kept her abilities in control."

"Sure, I get *that* part," he stated, "but then *why* would she take the drugs just to numb her abilities?"

Tandy stared at him for a long moment and muttered, "She didn't always take the drugs willfully."

He sucked in his breath and groaned. "Okay, now you need to explain that."

"Not sure I can," she said, "but she hung out with a lot of less-than-savory characters, and some of those characters would give her the drugs so they could have sex or whatever."

"Do you remember an albino character?"

Tandy flinched. "You gotta remember that I was kid, a young teen, before my grandmother got me out of there."

"So did you see an albino with Isabella, or did you not?" Keller pushed.

"Is it important?"

"Hell, yes."

"I thought he was just someone out of my nightmares."

"Someone she shared drugs with and had sex with?"

Tandy frowned. "Possibly."

Keller sighed. "And yet she didn't appear to argue with that much."

"I don't know about that," Tandy clarified. "Remember that all my information is old. I haven't had any willful contact with her in a very long time."

"Willful contact? Did she ever come to you in spirit form, when she wasn't dead?"

"Yes, but usually when she was hospitalized and unconscious. Her spirit was free to roam at that point," she explained. "I never really knew what to do with her."

"Of course not. Jesus, what the hell are you supposed to do with a parent who's obviously irresponsible and who's not looking after who she should be looking after, and then she runs free and causes chaos whenever she can?"

"Exactly," Tandy said, with a wry smile. "And I'm sorry that you appear to be somebody she has latched onto."

"The question is why?"

"I don't know, although, if I had to hazard a guess, I would say it's because of me." She hesitated then added, "I didn't realize that you saw ghosts."

"I generally don't *see* them," he noted. "I tend to get rid of them before they have a chance to materialize, but Isabella's not taking no for an answer."

"No, she wouldn't," Tandy said, with a broken laugh. "That's my mother. There's something poisonous about her, and I know we're not supposed to speak ill of the dead, but I'm really not sure what else I'm supposed to say about her."

"I think I need to know more about her history."

"You mean, the fact that other dead people were in her life? Sure," she agreed, "and other dead people were in her associates' lives too."

"I get that," Keller said cautiously. "The names that you gave us that we could run down didn't have much in the way of histories. Mostly drugs, drug dealing, breaking-and-entering charges, that kind of thing."

"Yeah," she agreed, "anything that would buy them drugs, but they weren't all like that."

"Is there anybody in particular you want to mention?"

"I don't know their names," she wailed. "You've got to remember this was a long time ago, before I was fifteen." She felt his gaze on her, assessing, trying to see if she was telling the truth. She finished with the pot of coffee, then turned and glared at him. "I can only tell you what I know, what I remember," she added, "and what I don't know, I just don't know."

"And I get that," Keller said, "plus we've got the kiddy porn as well."

"Exactly," she muttered. "Did you look at anybody there?"

"Our cyber division is looking at it, along with the FBI," he shared. "So, it's not so much that we're *not* looking at that, but we're looking at *all of it*, and it's taking time."

"Of course it does," she muttered. "All this stuff does."

"What I also really don't understand," Keller began, "is how does any of this come back to you, and what has that got to do with your mother, who's out there trying to survive as a ghost?"

"I think she's been trying to survive for so long that she doesn't know anything else."

"And yet I got a definite malevolence off her."

She stared at him and nodded. "Of course. She's a very mean and complicated person."

"If she were a true junkie, she would be all about the drugs."

"She was definitely a stereotypical junkie, living in squalor most of the time. But who knows? Maybe her abilities turned her that way in the first place. Scared of them maybe? I don't know. When she was lucid, she was still crazy, but, on drugs, she was crazier."

"But was it because of her own abilities that she looked for them in you?"

"Maybe," Tandy guessed, "but, as I told you already, I also had a few run-ins with a couple of her friends, and that just set her on that path."

"I wonder if she was put in a similar position herself, being exploited for money."

"Maybe. I don't know, but you would think that if she had been exploited herself, she wouldn't have done that to her own daughter."

"And yet she ended up using you as just another meal ticket."

She winced and nodded. "Can't say I appreciate the way you put that, but it's true, yes."

"And I'm not trying to hurt you by putting it that way," he explained, "but I really would prefer to call a spade a spade."

"Sure," she noted, "but realize that this particular spade is somebody who didn't have very much in the way of morals or ethics to begin with. I don't know what she was like as a teenager. I don't know anything about that. I don't know if there are other grandparents out in the world, other than my grandmother, but she was from my father's side. So I have no clue about Isabella's immediate family. For that matter, I don't know squat about Gwen's immediate family either— other than her son was my father. While she never talked about her son, my birth father, she expressed nothing but sheer disgust for my mother all these years."

"And your grandmother now?"

"She's dead." Tandy winced as she told him. "I always felt bad that I wasn't here to help her when she really needed it."

"That would have been nice," he agreed, "assuming you could do anything."

Tandy snorted. "With my hospice nursing training, I could have helped her a lot. As for all these special abilities? To me, they really don't mean jack shit. They haven't done me any good, not that I can see."

"I'm not sure they have done me any good either," Keller replied, with half a smile. "But it does make me curious about what your mother did with her gifts and what she may have been responsible for."

Tandy stared at him. "I'm not sure I like the way you said that last part."

He gave a solemn nod. "I'm not sure what I'm even thinking about, but it is something I need to look into."

"Well then, look into it," she said carefully, "and maybe keep me out of it while you are at it."

He smiled. "If it's possible, I'll try."

"Good enough," she muttered. She turned to him and asked, "Do you want coffee?"

"Yes," he murmured, as he watched her. "I would love a cup."

She quickly poured two cups, handed him one, and then added, "I do need a shower, and I need food."

At that, the doorbell rang.

She groaned. "God, I really can't deal with anybody else right now."

"How about food?" Keller asked in a laughing tone. She stared at him, and he nodded. "I haven't eaten either, so the least we can do is share some dinner."

"Is that the least we can do?" she asked, with a groan. "It sounds to me as if that's you still wanting to get more answers."

"If you don't have any answers to give me, you don't have any answers to give." But his gaze was watchful as he waited for her reply.

The doorbell rang again. They both ignored it.

"Even just saying that," she snapped, glaring at him, "seems that you're testing me."

"I'm not testing you at all," he said. "If I thought you had more answers, believe me that I would be on your case a whole lot more. But I'm not."

"That's good," she grumbled, "because I need to get

food, and I need a chance to de-stress before tomorrow. It was a tough day at work."

"Do you have any healing abilities?"

The doorbell rang yet again.

She froze, turned to him, and in a wary tone asked, "Why? Why would you ask?"

His eyebrows shot up. "It's a simple-enough question."

"No," she said, "it's not a simple-enough question. No question with you is simple."

He half smiled. "Okay, I can see your point on that one, but I didn't mean it in a bad way."

"Maybe not, but I'm still not sure what I'm supposed to do with the question."

"How about answer it?" he suggested, his gaze narrowing as he walked to the door and opened it up to accept a food delivery. He came back in with the bag and put it on the kitchen table. "It's really not that hard of a question."

"So, my answer is, *I don't know.*" When he turned to face her, she shrugged. "How would I even know about that?"

"For Dr. Maddy, it's easy. She works with healing all the time."

"Maybe for her," Tandy replied, "but she's also truly gifted and probably can see the results of her work. I work with cancer patients, and I don't know that I've ever seen any healing come from my gifts. I don't know that I would ever see those results."

"I hadn't considered that," he said, with a nod. "I guess that makes some sense too. Still, you're awfully cagey about it."

"I think I'm cagey about anything that you ask," she noted, "because it seems as if something else is always involved."

"No, absolutely nothing else is involved," he told her. "I was just asking a question."

She sent a wry look in his direction. "Yeah, just asking a question means that you're curious about something, and I'm not sure I want to know what that is, especially if it relates to me." Giving him one more odd look, she headed to the bag and opened the top, smiling when the smells erupted. "I don't know what this is," she muttered, closing her eyes and savoring the delicious aromas, "but, wow, it sure smells good."

"It's Indian."

"I got that much," she said. "That curry smell is pretty hard to miss. It's truly wonderful."

"Good." He smiled at her. "It's one of my favorite places and is just around the corner from here."

"Really?" she asked, frowning at him. "I need to find more places close by, particularly if they're reasonably priced." She stared down at it. "I don't eat enough sometimes," she confessed, "and, if I bought prepared food, then I might eat enough to get me through my days."

"That makes perfect sense because you really should be eating more."

"Sure, I should be eating more," she agreed, with a roll of her eyes. "With my job, it's just not all that easy to get bathroom breaks much less food breaks."

He laughed as he picked out a few plates and utensils from the drawer and brought them over. "Now, let's sit down and eat a proper meal, and then I'll leave you to have a hot shower and to get an early night."

"That would be lovely," she murmured.

He looked at her and added, "And yet you seem totally surprised that I'm even okay with leaving early."

She shrugged. "When you're here, there's always something else on your mind, as if you want something from me," she muttered, her gaze super watchful.

He smiled and shook his head. "I'm not looking for anything. I'm not asking any more questions. You're in the clear tonight."

"Maybe," she muttered. "It still feels weird."

He burst out laughing. "It's all good." He pointed to the food on the table and said, "Now eat." And, with that, he sat down across from her, waiting for Tandy to join him.

She sat down cautiously, not sure even sharing a meal was something she could trust him with, and yet it felt as if she *should* trust him. She groaned as she settled.

"What's the matter?" he asked.

"I'm just … I know it sounds insulting, and I don't mean it to be that way."

He put down his fork and focused on her.

She continued cautiously. "It just seems that I don't really know which way is up with you. I don't know what you want from me, and I don't really understand why you're here."

"I'm here because I *don't* want something from you," he replied, taking a moment for that to sink in. "I am concerned about you. You don't eat, and you had a recent break-in, and your mother is a ghost who haunts you, and you are worried about the safety of your twin brothers. And now Isabella haunts me. So, after figuring out that your mother was the ghost in my living room, making my life miserable, it seemed a natural thing to come and find out from you how much of an irritant she could be as a ghost."

"She was a huge irritant as a living breathing human," Tandy declared, with a twitch of her lips. "So I can't imagine it will be any different now that she's a ghost."

"*Great*," he muttered, "because she did tell me that the harder I tried to get rid of her, the stronger she will become."

"That was always one of the things that she used against us. When she learned what made us tick, just as soon as she figured that out, she used it against us. And that wasn't about just us—as in me and my grandmother or anybody else in the family," she explained, catching his watchful expression. "She did that to everybody. She was always looking to play the angles, always looking to figure out how to improve her own life."

"She sounds like such a lovely woman," he quipped.

"She was a desperate woman in many ways," Tandy clarified. "But, even at that, I don't have any reason to excuse her. She was a mean son of a bitch, and she cared only for herself. So, if I'm not the most welcoming or the most open about all your questions, you should know why."

"Of course. I don't really expect anything other than that."

"Which is sad too," she noted, "because, if you think about it, there should be something out there that would make sense of Isabella's actions, but that something really doesn't exist. I'm not sure even psychology can explain the way she was. On a strictly physical level, she was obviously a drug addict, who caused a lot of pain for a lot of people, but it's more than that. I don't think she had feelings like the rest of us. She cared about nothing and no one—other than herself. That's just one more of those bits of pain that I have to live with, knowing that she ruined a lot of other lives too."

"But that's not your fault," he pointed out. "And, because it's not your fault, you can't take on that guilt."

"Are you sure?" she asked with a broken laugh, even as

she stabbed her fork impatiently into the container and served herself some food. "I swear to God that woman has me upside down and backward."

"And I know you've heard it before, but it really is because you let her."

And that was the last straw. She tossed her fork onto the table and glared at him. "You didn't live with that woman for the first fifteen years of your life. You didn't get all her phone calls over the years afterward. You've only been visited by her ghost one time."

He held up a hand. "I know you don't want to hear this, and I wish I could go back in time and could save you from that life with her. I get it, and believe me that I understand. I'm not making light of all she put you through. I'm certainly not dismissing all the harm she caused you and others, harm that you and the twins and all the people she scammed are still dealing with today, and even tomorrow, again and again. However, we need to deal with Isabella *now*—that means you and me. That means even Stefan and Dr. Maddy need you and me to join up and to battle your mother, to beat her down, to kick her out of this realm. We need you. You can't act all meek and weak. You have major skills. Act like it." He raised his hand. "Sorry to be the bearer of bad news, but somebody has to point it out to you."

Tandy growled. "I already just had Dr. Maddy tell me that the only reason Isabella is so all-powerful in my mind is because I have given her that power," Tandy snapped. "And honest to God, that's pretty rough to hear at the best of times, but when you're worn out, tired, sick, and worried about the twins, it's really not helpful."

"Of course it's not helpful," he agreed, "but the end result is very helpful because it allows you to see that all the manipulative things Isabella used to do to you as a kid are still present in your mind. She still does this to you even as an adult because …"

"*Because I let her*," she snarled, cutting him off. "I heard you the first time, but stopping her isn't easy."

"Of course not," he said, as his tone became more soothing, "and I'm not saying it is. I'm just saying that somehow we must find a way to break you free of her control—even if it takes all four of us together, to bolster your self-esteem and to beat down Isabella's."

She stared at him, then down at the food, and back at him. She sighed, even feeling a sense of rightness settling inside her. "That's what it is, isn't it?" she asked. "Even now, even from the grave, she's controlling me."

"Yes," he confirmed. "Somewhere along the line you have fallen back into the mind-set of that child she can manipulate. Even though you worked so hard to get away, to get free, and to make your own way in life, the minute you slipped back into that victim role, that daughter role, Isabella had free rein over your emotions again."

Tandy stared off into the distance, tears gathering in the corner of her eyes. "That just makes me angrier."

"Good," he declared. "Be angry, be *really* angry, and don't let her get to you like that. I can understand why she was doing it, and maybe even how she was doing it, but she can't continue if you don't fight her," he explained, as he patted her hand. "Pull back into your own energy and don't let her take control of you. I think you'll find your life being very different if you can just do that."

She picked up her fork and then industriously busied herself by serving up food on the two plates. By the time she had two heaping platefuls, with more still in the to-go containers, she frowned. "You really did buy a lot, didn't you?"

"Hey, I wanted to ensure you wouldn't starve." He studied her, trying to keep his facial expression in check.

She nodded. "I won't say no to that either," she said, giving him a small smile. "I am hungry, and it was a very long day."

"So don't take this as pressure or anything, but I'm just interested in finding out more. I feel awkward just asking, but I'll do it anyway. Have you ever tried to help heal somebody?"

She looked over at him and shrugged. "Have I sent out good wishes and things like that? Yes. ... But I don't necessarily always see the same patients again and again. The ones who I do see again are in treatment, so, even if they have improved, I never would have thought it was because of me," she explained, with a shrug.

"But it doesn't seem as if you think *anything* is because of you."

"What do you mean?" She frowned. "Oh, we're back to that *lack of self-esteem* again, aren't we?"

"We certainly are back to some of it," he stated, with a wry smile. "Let's just keep the conversation moving smoothly ahead, and maybe we'll come up with a way to stop your mother from taking over."

"Is she taking over or is this just mental?"

"Of course it's mental," he stated, "but it also involves energy. The more you give in to who she was, the more she is that same person. She doesn't have the right to do this to you now that she's gone. She didn't have the right to do it when she was alive, but as the drug-addled adult in charge of you and your siblings, it just happened that way. The fact that she's still doing it just shows the bond that she has with you."

"Bond?" she repeated, staring at him.

"Yes," he declared pointedly, "*bond*. She couldn't do it without *you* having a strong bond with *her*."

"I don't know about any bonding, but I know very well that she used to manipulate me. I know that one way or another she somehow put me out—in a trance or hypnotized or drugged or whatever—so either I didn't know or didn't care what was happening at the time. I don't know all of what she has done to me, and I think that's been one of the scariest things for me, you know? Not knowing what I might have done when she had me under her control is a horrible feeling," she whispered.

He leaned forward. "And are you thinking something bad happened?"

"Maybe," she whispered, "maybe something *really* bad."

# CHAPTER 14

TANDY DIDN'T SAY anything more on the subject after that. Mostly fear had stopped her, but even now, the next morning, as she lay in bed contemplating what was going on in her world, she realized she needed help to do something constructive about her mother's influence—over her and the twins.

Were Dr. Maddy and Keller right?

Was it just a simple case of Tandy giving away her power, and her mother once again taking advantage? It seemed bizarre that she should be in this power struggle when Tandy was the one alive and Isabella was dead, but then it probably went back to fear about the power Isabella still might have.

Tandy had all these images in her brain, with bits and pieces of memories that sat in the background of her mind, never really letting her understand what had gone on, but fearing the truth because her mother was just that kind of a person. And even that didn't make sense.

Was Tandy afraid she'd been raped?

Was she afraid she'd murdered somebody?

Was she afraid of … what was she afraid of?

The answer was literally all of it. She had zero control of these memories and hadn't told anybody that and didn't have any idea what to do about ridding herself of them. Who was she supposed to tell after all these years? She didn't know. Her grandmother hadn't been much help.

Gwen had been the type where you sucked it up, and you buried whatever was too painful to let out in the world, and, if you didn't do that, it was bound to come back, only to bite you in the ass. Gwen was all about keeping the world close enough that you could stay hidden, if need be. Tandy's efforts to tell her grandmother what had gone on had proven fruitless when the old woman just basically shook her head, saying she couldn't handle it, and, for both of their sakes, Tandy needed to just forget about it.

And, in a way, as Tandy was a child back then, maybe that was probably exactly what she'd needed to hear at the time. Just to recognize it was there, but that she would deal with at some point in the future, when she had the resources to do so. Her grandmother not being able to deal with it and stomping it down had given Tandy permission to do the same. She could hardly blame Gwen for this reaction. Her grandmother had had a tough-enough time as it was.

As Tandy had looked at all the kiddie porn photos in Isabella's closet and had seen the depravity of the world that Isabella had lived in, Tandy had to wonder and to worry if she herself had been abused in the same way. It was too much to think about, and yet she couldn't stop doing just that because the thought had reared its ugly head.

Swearing, she got up and took a shower, wishing it would cleanse her soul and her body at the same time. Afterward she went to her kitchen and put on coffee, with the hope that it would give her some peace, some clarity. But, until then, she did the same damn thing she'd always done with these troublesome memories, which was stuff them right back down in the dark, where they belonged, and not give them the chance to breathe again.

And none of that made any sense now, not knowing what had happened to the twins. So what was Tandy supposed to do with them? They were obviously extremely special, and she didn't want anything bad to happen to them, but they were also her siblings. Was she the right person to take them in?

She didn't see how it was even possible though. Maybe if they had help, but how was she supposed to look after somebody else if she didn't have any way to look after herself?

Groaning, she poured a cup of coffee and sat back down in the living room, staring out at the crazy world around her. Her mother would be having a heyday if she knew just how twisted up this was making Tandy. When she heard a laugh beside her, she stiffened but refused to look.

*Still the same old Tandy, aren't you?* the ghost said in a mocking tone beside her. *Still can't get your shit together.*

Tandy glared out the window, refusing to engage. It was the only way she'd ever been able to handle Isabella. If she got violent, that was a different story, but generally her mother hated being ignored and would eventually leave.

I *don't have to leave now, do I?* she declared in that same mocking tone. *This is the perfect life for me.*

"Except for the drugs. How can you function without the drugs that kept you alive all that time?"

Her mother's ghost glared at her. *I had an ailment,* she stated stiffly. *The fact that you can't understand that just makes you that much more pathetic.*

Of course that's what her mother would do, turn everything around so it was Tandy's fault. Once again she just shut up.

Her mother's ghost laughed. *As if you have any ability to*

*stop me*, she muttered. *That's a joke. You couldn't even deal with me when I was alive.*

"Nobody could," Tandy noted, not even looking back. "You were just one drugged-out mess on a daily basis. Outside of feeling pity because you were such a hot mess, nobody gave you another thought." She could almost hear her mother's hiss. Tandy continued to taunt her mother. "You still have to make yourself the center of attention, don't you? Even though your boyfriends didn't give a crap whether you were comatose or not, as long as they got laid on a regular basis."

Her mother's hiss got louder, and, for whatever reason, it made Tandy feel better.

Tandy continued. "Yeah, you don't like it when I dish it right back to you, do you? You don't like being talked to that way or facing the reality that the rest of us saw. Right? And yet that was the reality of your life. You're pathetic now, and you always have been," Tandy snapped.

Her mother's ghost blinked herself out of existence and disappeared into the ethers.

Tandy looked around, then started to laugh. "Good riddance," she called out. "You don't need to come back anymore. There's no welcome for you here."

She shook her head but felt remarkably better. The only problem was that it would likely be a false sense of bravado, maybe even short-lived. Her mother's ghost still carried that semblance of the horrific life that she used to have, and Tandy didn't know how to deal with this version of her. And how sad was that?

"Christ," she muttered, as she stared around her living room. "There has to be a way to keep you out of here."

Almost immediately her mother's ghost popped into her

living room again. *Don't bother even trying to boot me out of here*, she said, with a sneer. *I like this. I like it just the way it is, and I won't let you change it.*"

"Yeah, and I just did boot you out. So how will you stop me from doing it again?" Tandy asked, mocking her mother. The fact that she ever thought her dead mother had power was preposterous now, and, for the first time, Tandy saw how silly this was. "You're not alive, Isabella. You're dead. You ruined the one chance you had at a life and at being a good person," she declared, staring at the faded ghost of her mother. "And even now you're just a shell of a weak, pitiful person, struggling to regain something, but you're not that strong," Tandy snapped. "And no way in hell you're strong enough to do what you want to do now."

Her mother glared at her and then, in a tone full of deadly promise, she whispered, *I will be. Just watch me, bitch.*

STEFAN HEARD THE word *bitch* in his mind. It held a strong reverberation of negative energy running through his feed. Frowning, he lay in bed as he sorted out just who and what was happening. His wife reached out a hand and stroked his arm. He squeezed her fingers and murmured, "I'm fine."

"You're fine," she agreed, staring at him intently, "but somebody … somewhere is not."

He chuckled. "Unfortunately, that is the state of the world."

"I know," she murmured. "It's just so sad that this is what it always comes down to."

He didn't argue with that because she was right, and it was damn sad that this happened every time. Somewhere, somehow, somebody was in pain and was suffering. And with that came the message as to who it was. "Ah, in this case, it's Tandy." Celina looked at him and frowned. He nodded. "The sister to the twins who Dr. Maddy is working with."

"Ah." She nodded. "She's got quite a lot of issues to deal with, doesn't she?"

"I think we all do," he added, "but, in this case, I think the issues Tandy has to deal with are things she's not even expecting."

Celina chuckled. "I think that's the same for all of us in many ways. We end up dealing with issues we didn't anticipate instead of those we may have expected or even planned for." She paused, smiling. "When I couldn't see anybody, I thought I was blind. Yet the blindness wasn't even the issue. Is it something like that for Tandy?"

"Something like that, yeah," Stefan said. "I'll need to contact her."

"I'm heading off for a shower," Celina shared cheerfully, "so you don't even have to get out of bed."

He laughed. "You sure I can't convince you to stay in bed with me?"

"Nope, not happening," she teased, chuckling as she darted toward the shower. "At least not this morning. I'll take a raincheck though."

He smiled as he watched her turn on the water and get into the shower. His wife was incredibly special. ... Just the fact that she could tolerate the craziness of his life said a whole lot more. He closed his eyes and settled in to see just what was going on in Tandy's world. Almost immediately he got bits and pieces of visions and realized that Isabella Goodman was running amok again.

*Not just amok,* came a voice in his head. *She's making*

*threats that I don't know if she has the power to make, but I need her to go away.*

He opened his eyes in surprise to see Tandy in spirit form, glaring at him. He stared at her in amazement and muttered out loud, "This is an interesting twist."

*What?* she asked, with a wave of her hand. *You were peeking into my life, so I thought it would be easier if I just brought you straight in.*

He burst out laughing and nodded. "That works too."

She looked around and frowned. *I'm in your bedroom now, aren't I? That seems awkward. If you want to meet somewhere else, you'll have to tell me how to do this correctly. I just followed your signature back.*

He listened in amazement at her explanation for how she found him. It was incredible. A little daunting but incredible. He shook his head in amazement. "For somebody who says you have no clue what you're doing, you are doing some really impressive things."

*I don't know what I'm doing,* she snapped back at him, still glaring.

He saw her ghostly frame, this light-teal-blue shimmer that gave an irritated shrug. He grinned. "The color is lovely, by the way."

She frowned at him, not understanding.

Stefan realized that she honestly didn't realize just how magical what she had just done was.

*I don't know anything about colors,* she replied stiffly, *but I need help, and I didn't know who else to ask, and, since you stepped in, I figured you would be it.*

"Did you see me?" Stefan asked.

*No. I want to say that I felt you, but I don't really know what that means.*

He laughed out loud. "Good enough. So what do you need help with?"

*My mother.*

"Wow, a lot of people need help with their mothers."

*Ha, ha, very funny.* Tandy snorted. *Mine is a ghost, and she's making some pretty serious threats.*

His eyebrows shot up. "I did hear a voice and something about *bitch*, and then it disappeared."

*Yeah, that was Isabella, calling me a bitch and basically telling me that she would take care of me, one way or another.*

"Take care of you?" Stefan repeated.

*Yes. I wasn't very accommodating at being the good daughter,* she explained, *and I guess I antagonized her.*

"Antagonizing ghosts isn't necessarily a smart thing to do, but, in your case, I can see that it was much better than being meek and mild."

*Exactly,* Tandy agreed. *Something in me snapped, and I told her that I wouldn't take this anymore.*

"That's a good thing."

*Is it though? I said some things, and that's when she started threatening me, and I've got to tell you ...* Tandy took a breath, her form shimmering in front of him. *Her threat sounded pretty damn real.*

"Interesting," he noted.

*Yeah, well,* interesting *doesn't really work for me,* she declared, staring in his direction, before glancing around and frowning. *You're not alone, are you?*

"No," he replied in a mild tone, "my wife is here."

*Oh dang,* Tandy whispered. *I guess that makes sense. I'm sorry. I should have asked first.*

"That would have been interesting in its own right if you had," he noted, "but this is pretty damn good as it is."

*Why?* she asked, turning to look at him.

"You really have no idea what you've just done, do you?" he asked, and again he sensed the confusion in her expression. "Never mind, we'll go back to that later. What is it you think your mother can do?"

*I don't know.* Tandy raised both hands in frustration.

At least that's what he thought she did. Her form was moving in and out of clarity, as the emotions took hold of her. "When she threatened you, did you get any idea what she had in mind?"

*No, I didn't. I didn't at all, but … she would probably go after whatever my worst fear would be, if she had a way to figure it out.*

"If she knows you well, as she probably does, she already knows that. So, what would your worst fear be?"

Reluctantly she answered, *My worst fear is that somehow she gets to the twins.*

He stared at her in shock, his heart suddenly slamming against his chest. "Good God."

*Right, I know it's probably far-fetched.*

"No," he countered, "it's not far-fetched at all. When they live so much in their dream world as they do right now, … it makes them more vulnerable in some ways."

*But they're doing it so they're not vulnerable, right?*

"I know, but, if certain people knew that, and if certain people got in there, they could make the twins' lives literally hell. Good Christ." He threw back the bedcovers, hopped up, and rushed out. "I'll meet you at the twins' room on Dr. Maddy's floor in thirty minutes."

And, with that, he gave a wave of his hand and basically snuffed out the connection.

DR. MADDY HEARD the roar in her ears. When Stefan roared, it meant *Move.* She was already up on her feet and thundering down the hallway, not even sure of her destination. She hit the ground running and found herself racing toward the twins. She was even more panicked as she realized the younger more vulnerable generation was in trouble right now. She ran as fast as she could, several nurses stopping in their tracks to get out of her way, and others coming in behind her.

As soon as she got to where the twins were, she drew in a deep breath, stepped into the observation room, and took a quick look. Both were sound asleep, but, of course, that's all they ever were. Sound asleep or comatose sleeping, one or the other. With that, she moved into the room itself and stopped because they were also sleeping in their fantasy world. And that was unusual, except for designated naptimes and such.

Dr. Maddy also noted a weird sensation in the room. She frowned, sifting through as many different visions as she could, looking for what was causing all the disruption and found another entity in the room, yet not necessarily something she could put her finger on.

Frowning, she immediately started clearing the energy of the room, getting rid of anything and everyone that didn't belong. She'd never had to do that in a situation like this, but she also trusted that Mark had a good reason for hiding, which meant that he probably knew who this was. So, that wasn't good. And, for the first time ever, Dr. Maddy felt fear, and it was coming off the kids. She turned, looked around at the energy in the room, and immediately continued to purge as much as she could.

When she came upon a little resistance, she used a ton of

energy and blasted it out. By the time Stefan walked into the room, short of breath, he turned around, studying the room, and then looked back at her. She shook her head and motioned him into the adjoining room. As soon as they were in the observation room, Tandy barreled inside too. She was winded and bent over as she took several deep breaths.

"I gather you guys ran all the way," Dr. Maddy noted.

Stefan just nodded.

"Most of the way, yes." Tandy asked, "Are the twins okay?"

"They are," Dr. Maddy noted cautiously, "but they are hiding."

Tandy nodded. "Yes, and that is what I would expect."

"And why would you expect that?" Dr. Maddy asked her, eyeing her closely. "What is it that's just gone on?"

"Isabella, my mother," Tandy said. "She made some pretty big threats."

"You mean, your mother's spirit," Dr. Maddy stated for clarity.

"Yes, exactly."

Dr. Maddy frowned as she looked over at Stefan.

He just nodded at Tandy and added, "I asked her, when she came to visit me—on the ethers."

At that, Dr. Maddy's eyebrows rose.

Stefan carried on quickly, telling her all he knew. Then he told her about asking Tandy what she feared as the worst thing Isabella could do, and Tandy shared it was Isabella hurting the twins.

Tandy asked Dr. Maddy, "When you got here, was there any disturbance?"

"Yes," Dr. Maddy confirmed, "but I'm not exactly sure what it was. But definitely an energy was here that I didn't like, and I've been working at cleaning it out since I got here."

Stefan nodded. "Considering that the twins aren't out and playing—"

"Exactly," Dr. Maddy said, "they clearly got the message that there is danger."

Tandy turned, looked at Dr. Maddy, whose hand was against her chest as she stared through the window at the twins, still sound asleep. "It looks as if they're in the same world, in our reality now," Tandy noted, her tone a little convoluted as she tried to explain her thoughts.

"That's because this is their defense mechanism. They know that, when they're in danger, this is what they do."

"Are you sure that they're safe in there?" Tandy asked. "Because my mother, if she thinks she can get in there after them, I'm certain she will try. Regardless I have no idea what she would do."

"Isabella may be trying, and I did chase an energy out of here. It did give me some resistance, but this is my space," Dr. Maddy declared. "And nobody is allowed in here uninvited."

Stefan smiled at her. "Yet, with all the safeguards in place, how did her ghost even get that far?"

"Believe me, I need to figure that out," Dr. Maddy snapped, with a nod in his direction, "because, if she took down my security barriers, it would show a level of energy control we have yet to see."

"Or she ignored it," Tandy interjected. "I know that I haven't really spoken very much about Isabella, but you have to understand that nobody is more conniving or more duplicitous than she is. Just when you think you know who she is, she changes. She was very much a chameleon."

"And do you think that ability is something that she still has now?"

"I don't know," she muttered, clearly frustrated. "I'm so green to all this energy stuff, and I think a lot of that has been all about her."

"In what way?" Stefan asked.

"Her keeping me down in a way, or my being so afraid of what I might have done when she had control of me. So I've refused to allow any of my skills to develop, and then somehow now, with the twins, everything has just gone wild, and I feel very much out of control."

"And yet, in a way, you are controlling yourself and your energy very smoothly," Stefan pointed out.

She looked at him blankly and shrugged. "If you say so. I don't have anything to compare it to."

"So, are you thinking," Dr. Maddy began, "that Isabella has some abilities she has managed to keep, even while she's over on the other side?"

At that, Tandy turned to her. "Are they supposed to lose the ability when they go to the other side?" she asked.

Dr. Maddy looked at Stefan, and Stefan at her. Both of them shrugged.

Stefan explained to Tandy, "Every time we think we have it all figured out, we run across something that doesn't apply to what we know to date. Somebody comes along who breaks that rule or it doesn't apply to them at all."

Tandy nodded. "Isabella would be somebody it wouldn't apply to."

"And yet your mother spent a lot of her life drugged, is that correct?" Dr. Maddy asked.

"Yes, yes, and whether that was … I thought it was because she was a drug addict, and, when you're an addict," she shared, with a wave of her hand, "it's particularly hard to get off the drugs."

"Yes," Stefan agreed, with a nod, "that is very true. On the other hand, some people use the drugs to blind themselves to things going on around them or *within them*."

"And maybe that's true of Isabella. Maybe she couldn't deal with her gifts, so she wanted the drugs to quell them. I don't really know." Tandy shook her head. "I can't express to you how much I avoided having anything to do with her after I realized that I was …" She hesitated and shrugged. "I felt as if I was being preyed upon while she had control of me."

"In what way?" Dr. Maddy asked.

Tandy winced. "I don't know, and that's half the problem." She looked over at Dr. Maddy.

Dr. Maddy nodded. "Anything you tell us is helpful."

"Is it though?" She turned to Stefan. "There's a fear in me, while I was living with my mother, of what was going on with me when she had me in whatever state she had me in—trances, comas, whether hypnotized or drugged, since she used to control my states pretty well. I also know that she used to give me drugs, even though I didn't ask for or want them. I would actively fight her, … but she had this weird ability to stop me from doing anything. She would wave her hands, and I would just freeze."

Tandy groaned and closed her eyes, trying to get a grip on herself. "I know I sound like a complete moron, and, yes, I'm absolutely terrified of my mother, but you have to understand what my life was like with her. I'm afraid that, while I was in this state, I was potentially raped, and that maybe … it was more than once, … actually many times," she shared, trying to stiffen her tone and to take the warble out of it. "And I worry. … I'm afraid I did some terrible things while I was in that state—terrible things to other people."

Stefan stared at her in shock, and she nodded.

"The worst thing is, I'm afraid that I may have killed somebody."

# CHAPTER 15

TANDY SAT IN Dr. Maddy's office, a hot cup of herbal tea warming her hands, knowing that some heavy explanations were required, and yet not sure she had any answers for them.

"You need to tell us exactly what you remember," Stefan said.

"I don't remember much," she replied, looking over at him, "and believe me, I have spent a lifetime trying to forget everything in my world. Some of these memories are incredibly painful. Some of them are beyond anything in terms of comprehension."

Stefan nodded, patted her hand. "Tell us what you know. Start wherever and whenever you want to."

She cradled the cup in her hands, sipping the warmness, trying to gather her thoughts. "Before I start, remember that most of this occurred before I was able to get away from her and to live with my grandmother, so my memories are through the eyes of a child or a young teen. I was afraid of Isabella and the people around her. At times I even wondered if she was into something really strange, like human sacrifices and stuff," she added, with a hysterical laugh.

"She hung out with a lot of very strange men, got into a lot of very strange rituals, and did a lot of crazy things. All the while, this was my mother, and she was this drugged-out nightmare who couldn't put food on the table. When she was conscious or slightly aware, she was incredibly erratic and difficult to talk to. She would move from normal and calm to absolutely insane with rage in a split second, and the rage was almost always if I interrupted her."

"Do you know what she was doing when you were interrupting her?" Stefan asked, frowning.

"Not necessarily, but I remember how she had these altars set up everywhere. Whether she was doing something good or bad, I couldn't tell you." She studied Stefan's expression, which had grown graver the more she talked. "So, all I'm really doing is giving you a wide-open idea of things she could have been doing," she explained, "but I don't have any proof that she was doing any of it."

"Did she have any interests in the afterlife?" Stefan asked.

"I don't know about that in particular," she admitted, "but I do know that she used to gather with others to worship this ... religion or whatever. They all seemed to be like her."

"What does that mean, *like her*?" Stefan asked.

"Mean?" she repeated. "Other drug addicts, other streetwalkers, other people who worshiped altars in their homes."

Dr. Maddy nodded. "We're getting the picture."

"I'm glad you are." Tandy shook her head. "I really don't have any explanations. I am worried about the twins though."

"Yes, and with good reason," Dr. Maddy confirmed. "I wouldn't have known to come if Stefan hadn't warned me."

"And I wouldn't have known if Tandy didn't contact me about it first," Stefan shared absentmindedly, as he studied her.

"That's a good thing," Dr. Maddy agreed, with a big smirk, "even if her methodology was unorthodox."

He snorted at that. "Let's just say it was a dose of my own medicine."

Dr. Maddy chuckled. "I'm not sure that's a bad thing either."

He rolled his eyes. "No, it never is, but it was definitely an interesting feeling though."

Tandy looked from one to the other and muttered, "I have no clue what you're talking about."

"I know," Stefan admitted, "and that's what makes it even more fascinating."

After a long pause, Tandy muttered, "I don't know what I'm supposed to do from here."

"We'll have to add some more security for the twins," Dr. Maddy stated.

"Security?" Tandy snapped, with an outrage that came from nowhere. "You do realize this is in ghostly form, right?"

Dr. Maddy chuckled. "Yes, I do realize that." She nodded and then sighed. "We do have some defenses for that."

Tandy's eyes widened, her gaze going from Dr. Maddy to Stefan and back.

Dr. Maddy added, "We do have some experience with this kind of predator."

Tandy stared at her. "Please don't tell me this is a thing."

"Then I won't tell you," she said, "but some, who don't cross over immediately, may not yet determine that they did things that were wrong and then want to make them right. While a lot of people are good, the others? ... They weren't great in life, and they aren't great in death either."

"Christ," Tandy muttered, staring at her.

Dr. Maddy nodded. "I know. It's a shock. You always

think about death as *your life passing before your eyes* and the pearly gates and being gathered into heaven with the angels and all that stuff."

Tandy shook her head. "I don't understand what my mother was into, but I wouldn't have thought that living forever was something on her wish list."

"And nobody said it was," Stefan noted, "unless that's what you're thinking she was doing with all those altars."

"I don't know," Tandy muttered. "I did ask her about it, but she just laughed, and I remember her telling me that I was too stupid to figure it out."

"Oh, that's lovely," Dr. Maddy muttered, with a grimace. "I guess I need to see what's on her autopsy."

"Why?" Tandy asked cautiously. "I don't think they did one. It was an unexplained death, but she was a well-known drug addict and had been in and out of hospitals several times because of close calls."

Stefan turned to her. "And how many of those close calls were more of her experimenting with her altars and such than anything?"

Tandy stared at him, hating the way his words made her skin crawl. "I don't know," she whispered. "Maybe if somebody could talk to her entourage of male friends, we might get a better idea, but that isn't something I'm willing to do."

"No, that's fine," Stefan replied, raising a hand to stop that thought. "You don't need to talk to them again."

Dr. Maddy frowned. "Are any of them trying to stay in touch with you?"

"I don't know that I would recognize any of them from my childhood. Well, except for the albino, but I thought he was just a monster from my nightmares," she shared. "So it seemed as if a few tried after I moved out. Isabella kept trying to get my location and my phone number, but, when she realized I was with Gwen, Isabella got really angry. Yet she never came close to my grandmother."

"So, your grandmother is gone, correct?"

Tandy nodded. "Last year."

"And your mother has recently died, yet now she is once again reaching out to you, right?"

"Something like that, yeah," she said, frowning. "You make it sound as if my grandmother was involved."

"It's quite possible that your grandmother kept you safe all those years."

"She really hated my mother."

Dr. Maddy nodded. "And it sounds as if she may well have had a good reason for that. I presume she blamed Isabella for the death of her son. When did your father pass?"

Tandy shrugged. "You would have to check the police file to be sure, but, in my child's mind, I was about eight years old when I heard he was gone."

Dr. Maddy asked, "Do *you* think your mother had anything to do with your father's death?"

Tandy stared at her in shock. "God, I hope not. ... That would be one more burden I wouldn't want to bear."

"You seem to take a lot on yourself. Why would it be your burden?" Dr. Maddy asked.

She shrugged. "Because, in my mother's world, everybody else bore the burden."

Stefan shook his head. "And yet there's no burden. If your father's dead, he's dead. So he hasn't come around to bother you in any way?" Stefan pointed out, turning to her with a questioning expression.

She shook her head. "No, I haven't had any contact with

him. None, even though I lived with his own mother for years. Remember that my biological father wasn't in my life at all."

"Good, then presumably … either he didn't have abilities or, if he did, he wanted to move on and crossed over nicely."

"I would have thought so, but I don't know that," Tandy replied. "All I can tell you is that my grandmother hated everything to do with my mother. If Gwen could have done something to make Isabella's life miserable, Gwen would have, except that she wouldn't have wanted any contact with Isabella in the first place."

"Interesting," Stefan noted. "Sounds as if we need more history here."

"I don't know what history you'll find, but, according to my mother, my father was a drug addict. So maybe one took the other down that pathway. I don't know."

"That would certainly explain your grandmother's hatred—if she thought that your mother led her son down a life path that ended up killing him."

"Maybe, I don't know." Tandy raised her hands in frustration. "It all happened a long time ago."

"Meaning, you had no contact whatsoever with him?" Dr. Maddy asked.

"Meaning, I had no understanding or even any idea of who he was … *ever*. It was one of the hardships for me to even contact my grandmother because I didn't know her either. I think it took her a while to sort out whether she wanted any contact with me or not."

"But she did eventually come around," Stefan noted.

"Yeah, she did, but reluctantly. When she finally realized that I was in grave danger, and powerless to stop it, she stepped up in a way that I was … I am extremely grateful for."

Dr. Maddy agreed, "That's one thing we can all be grateful for."

"Yes," Tandy murmured. "I just know that somewhere along the line something caused such an intense hatred that the two women wouldn't have anything to do with each other."

"And with Isabella's loss of a husband and Gwen's loss of a son, if there was blame on either side, that would definitely foster that kind of hate," Stefan pointed out. "It's hard to forgive somebody who let you down, or who believes that they led her son down the wrong path that resulted in his death." Stefan looked over at Tandy and added, "I'll get Keller on it, if he isn't already."

She stared at him in surprise. "You will get Keller on it?"

His lips twitched. "Yes, and, if I need to go above Keller to get more help, I'm pretty sure I can do that too."

Tandy wasn't sure what to think about that.

Stefan smiled at her. "Just relax. You're not alone anymore."

"Are you sure?" Tandy asked, looking around nervously, "because that's one of the things that my mother excels at. She isolates people, and then they become hers."

Stefan shook his head. "You're not hers anymore, so remember that. I know I keep saying that she's dead and that you should be free, but you're only free if you claim that freedom for yourself."

"Yet, according to what I'm hearing, I should never have let it go in the first place."

His smile was the gentlest she had ever seen. "We can trash ourselves until we're blue in the face, and it doesn't make a damn bit of difference. Just start now, decide, and go forward with it. You need to realize that she does not have that hold over you, and whatever it is that she's doing or thinks she will do, she's not. We do have a lot of tricks on our side, and we *will* protect the twins," he declared. "Isabella will not get to them. In your case, you need to help yourself, and we will help you do it as well." He took a moment to pat her hand. "We have to confirm that your mother understands that her grip here ended when she lost her life. She does not get to come back in to create havoc just because she wants to."

"Are you going to tell her that?" Tandy asked, staring at him. "If so, she will tell you where to go, and she isn't one to mince words."

He chuckled. "She already tried. I get it. She has abilities we may not have seen, but we have abilities that we haven't yet developed. It takes something brand-new like this to make us sit down, sort it out, and put protections in place. So, I get it that she terrifies you, and you're worried about what may have happened in the past, but right now we need to focus on the twins and you in the present."

Tandy took a deep breath. "*You* need to focus on the twins. They're innocent of anything that might have been done, and they deserve a life free of all this torment."

He nodded, but his gaze was intense as he stared her down. "And the thing that you need to remember is that *you* deserve that too."

KELLER ANSWERED THE call absentmindedly, as he searched through the files in front of him. When he heard Stefan's voice, he stiffened. "Is everything okay?" he asked, all his senses coming fully alive and alert.

"Yes, but … a couple things just happened, and I need you to listen."

He sat back as Stefan went over the events of the day. "You've had a busy morning," he replied when he could.

"We have, and so have the twins."

"Have they come out again?"

"No. As far as they're concerned, it's still not safe."

"And apparently it isn't safe at all, so good on them for understanding that."

"It's kept them in this relative safety so far," Stefan noted. "It's just damn sad that it has to be this way."

"That is very true," he murmured. "What do you need from me?"

"I need a deeper background history run on the mother and on anybody around her. Isabella Goodman has become a mystery, and we need to get her sorted out as soon as we can."

"I'm looking at a file right now," Keller shared. "On one of her cronies she hung out with all the time. And it involves lots of assaults, lots of petty thefts, domestic violence—that kind of a thing—but drugs seemed to be the dominant issue between them."

"What do you think the drugs are all about?"

"I'm not sure yet if she was trying to escape the life she was in and even her gifts or if she was using the drugs to enhance something in her mind, including her gifts, that she thought she could do. I realize all that sounds pretty nebulous as usual."

"Sometimes there just are no answers," Stefan pointed out, "at least until we get into it further. I also need to know what happened to Tandy's father."

"Right, he's not even listed on her birth certificate."

"And yet she knew to contact her grandmother."

"And her grandmother is dead now too, right? Leave that with me, and I'll get back to you on some of this stuff."

"Good. Also watch your back."

"My back?" Keller repeated. "Why in the hell would you be worried about my back?"

"Yes, you need to watch your back. If I were you, I would be worried. This Isabella woman has already contacted you, and it was pretty nasty as I recall."

"Yes, and yes. Has she made any contact with you?"

"Not so much me, but"—Stefan's tone turned humorous—"I have to tell you what Tandy did this morning."

While Stefan explained, Keller sat back and stared at the phone. "She walked into your bedroom, and you didn't know she was coming?"

"Yeah, thanks for that reminder," Stefan muttered wryly. "But, yes, she showed up in my bedroom, as I do to many other people. It gave me an ... let's just call it *an insight* into why sometimes people are not terribly happy when I show up."

Keller burst out laughing. "Oh my God, that's perfect. But to think that Tandy could do that? It's pretty amazing."

"Not just that. She doesn't really realize that what she did was anything unusual."

"So, we'll find out she's mega-talented?"

"Either she's mega-talented, and her mother likely kept it squashed, or because of the twins and what's happening here and now, all these talents of Tandy's are bubbling up, after having been locked down for way too long," he theorized. "I'm not sure what's going on, but Tandy was completely nonplussed and didn't seem to realize that what she had just done was rare and unique."

"I like her even more now," Keller admitted, chuckling. "Anybody who can get the jump on you, that says something."

"Yeah, it tells me that I need to beef up my guards," Stefan admitted, only partially joking. "And that's why I'm warning you. That mother of hers is fairly dominant."

"No, she's very dominant. I had her in my apartment, and I wouldn't give her the time of day, but it wasn't that easy to throw her out the second time either."

"Do your best to keep her out completely. The more avenues that get shut off, the better."

Keller cut him off, "But that'll just send her to Tandy and the twins."

"Yes, maybe," Stefan conceded. "However, we can't give Isabella access to anybody else. And we'll have to fight this with Tandy's help on the inside, not the outside."

"Do you think she's capable?"

"Oh, … I think she's very capable. I just don't think she realizes what she can do and what she can't do. And what she is doing is so unconscious that it's amazing to see."

"I would love to have seen her crashing appearance into your bedroom," Keller shared, chuckling.

"I wouldn't say that too loud because, chances are, she will walk into your bedroom one day, should you ignore her or not respond in time."

"Interesting," Keller noted. "So far it's only ever been you who could do that."

"Dr. Maddy can as well," Stefan added, with that same note of humor. "And, if three of us can, you know perfectly well that a lot of us out there can. They just don't know it yet."

"Tandy probably doesn't do it because she likely considers it an invasion of privacy."

"I can definitely tell you that Tandy *wasn't* considering my privacy at all this morning." Stefan chuckled again. "It was rather interesting to be the recipient of this."

"Good," Keller said, still smiling. "And I'll get you the rest of that information as soon as I can."

"Sooner," Stefan replied. "I need it sooner rather than that. And I may need your help *inside* as well." And, with that, Stefan ended the call.

Those surprising last words left Keller swearing. He started pulling as many files as he could. When his phone rang again, he was ready to swear once more, until he realized it was Tandy. He answered it cautiously. "Hey, I wasn't expecting a call from you."

"Of course not," she stated crossly. "I can't say I've been openly friendly or even encouraged you to contact me."

He smiled. "Luckily that didn't stop me. Now, what can I do for you?"

She hesitated and then asked, "Is there any way to get information on my father's death?"

His eyebrows shot up. "Stefan asked me that earlier."

"Oh good," she said in relief. "I know he mentioned that he was, but I'm finding, … I'm lacking patience right now."

He nodded. "What I don't know is if there will be much of a file. Do you have your father's name?"

"No."

"Okay, what was your grandmother's name?"

When she gave it to him, he frowned. "I think I know that name." When Tandy didn't respond, he continued in a rush. "Okay, spill whatever you're thinking. Why do I know that name?"

"Her death was suspicious. Maybe she was murdered," she whispered.

"Oh, Christ."

"Yeah, I don't know if it's been solved or not," Tandy noted. "I don't think so, since nobody's contacted me in the last year."

He pinched the bridge of his nose. "Are you a suspect?"

"I don't know," she muttered, "but I would be shocked if I wasn't. I'm the person who benefited the most."

"In what way?" he asked, his tone turning brisk.

"She left me the house, so I have a home in my name that didn't include my mother."

"That's a good thing," he said. Then he frowned and noted, "Yet you're renting an apartment to live in."

"I know," she muttered.

"You want to explain why?"

"No," she snapped, "I don't."

He sighed. "One of these days you'll have to open up and talk to me."

"Maybe, but not today."

For the first time he heard a *maybe* instead of a *hell no.* "Any reason not today?"

"I'll go back and see the twins, ... to see if I can ... coerce them out."

"Aren't you there now?"

"I was. I left to get a bite to eat, but it's not as if I can go home. I need to get back to the twins."

"Then go back. If you feel a nudge to follow your instincts on this, then you follow your gut. It's the one thing that will keep us alive, when everything else fails."

"It seems as if everything already has failed," she muttered.

"Give me at least some idea of why you aren't living in your grandmother's house."

"Because I'm looking at selling it," she shared, "and, if so, I didn't want to get too attached."

"And why would you sell it?"

"Memories," she stated succinctly. "Too many memories." And, with that, she ended the call on him.

He frowned and quickly sent Stefan a text. Then dug further into Tandy's grandmother's and Tandy's father's backgrounds, starting with a search of police records.

Just then Grant contacted him. "Hey, did you just ping to pull the Peter Wallace Goodman file?"

"Yeah, I did. Why?"

"It's one of the FBI's cases," he replied. "Who is this guy?"

"Apparently, at least from the little I've found while researching right now, it looks to be Tandy's father."

Grant whistled at that.

Keller asked, "Why are you asking?"

"He was killed in a ritualistic killing quite a few years ago. He was found pinned to a tree and suffered a long and terrible death."

"Jesus, I thought it was a drug overdose."

"I think that's eventually what killed him, yes, but he was injected with drugs while he was hanging there. Whether making the experience worse or better, I don't know," Grant interjected. "But it's a case we've kept on our radar for some time."

"And yet that doesn't seem to be a typical FBI case to me."

"No, except that there are a couple of them."

"Ah, crap. Please tell me they weren't in any of these

towns." Then he mentioned the three locations where he knew Tandy had lived.

"And that's exactly where they were," Grant confirmed, his tone excited. "Why? Why would you know those locations?"

"Because those are places that Tandy remembered living with her mother."

"Ah, crap."

"Yeah, so it looks as if we have an awful lot going on in this case. Stefan has asked for any information on Tandy's father and on her grandmother."

"The grandmother?" he asked. "Why her?"

"She's dead too. Possibly murdered."

First came silence, then Grant asked, "Do we have any idea how?"

"I'm still trying to pull the file," Keller shared. "I'm really hoping it's not a ritualistic killing."

"I hope not too," Grant muttered. "I've got to tell you, it's pretty easy to understand why Tandy's grandmother absolutely hated her mother, if this is how her son died."

"I hear you, but we don't have any reason to understand how this comes back to Isabella."

"No, we don't, except that Isabella's the only one who survived."

"But not for long," he pointed out. "Remember that she's dead now too."

"Send me the files too," Grant ordered, his tone curt. "And we need to keep an eye on Tandy."

"Why is that?" Keller asked, his stomach sinking.

"Because she's the common denominator in all this."

"She already fears she is a suspect in her grandmother's death because she's the one who inherited."

"Which always makes for a good suspect," Grant noted. "What did she inherit?"

"She told me about the house, but she's not living in it, something about wanting to sell it, not wanting to get too attached, memories, et cetera."

"Interesting," he muttered. "Either way it merits further looking into, so keep your heart separate when you're considering her too." And, with that, Grant ended the call.

Keller stared down at the phone, wanting to say out loud that it was too damn late for that. His heart was already involved, but he didn't know in what way that would be true because it shouldn't be. He hardly knew the woman, yet wondered where she was, what she was up to, if she'd eaten, stopping by with food to confirm she was okay. Whatever excuse he had to make, he was up for using it.

He didn't feel as if she was against his efforts to ensure she was okay either. It almost felt as if they shared a certain camaraderie at this point, and Grant might agree with that camaraderie, but maybe not in a good friend-zone way. Not good either if she was heavily involved in all these cases. Then chances were, she was also heavily involved in another way as well, and Keller wouldn't like anything he found out about that.

Just because she acted completely innocent and terrified didn't mean she really was. She could be very involved in all this mess in a way Keller didn't even want to think about. And he certainly wasn't above having the wool pulled over his eyes just because she was a pretty woman. In fact, she was stunning, but he didn't think she saw that. And that was yet another issue. Just because she didn't see it didn't mean it didn't exist. Maybe she just acted as if she didn't see it, and yet truly she did.

He wasn't sure of anything at this point, and none of this made sense. Yet the one thing he did recognize was that it all needed to be looked into. And, with that, he got back to work.

# CHAPTER 16

THERE WAS NOTHING good about today, even though Tandy had a couple days off. She remained in bed and stared up, realizing she was finally getting a day to herself, if there was such a thing. She didn't have to work, and she had desperately needed some downtime for a while now, so had scheduled a few days off a couple weeks ago—before Isabella died and had bequeathed her twins to Tandy's care. So here Tandy was, with all this time on her hands, and probably at the worst time, considering everything else going on. At least if she was at work, she was busy. Without the work, she was left to just sit here in a fog, all on her own.

When the doorbell rang, she frowned, stared at the clock, and realized it was nine. Then her phone buzzed. She looked at her phone and groaned. Right there in front of her was a text from Keller.

**Let me in.**

She grabbed a robe and stumbled her way to the front door. She opened it without looking, and he glared at her.

"Did you even check the peephole to see if it was really me?"

"No. Who else would send a text saying, *Let me in*, then not be the one at the door?" she snapped back.

"At least you saw the text," he mumbled.

As he stepped inside, she glared at him. "You know,

some of us get a day off every now and then, so we can sleep in."

"You were already awake," he muttered, with a wave of his hand.

"Yeah, I was awake, but that didn't mean I was ready to get out of bed."

"Go back to bed then. A little bit of sleep might make you easier to deal with."

"What do you mean by that?"

He stared at her. "I have some questions."

"That's nice. What makes you think I have any answers?"

"Maybe you do in this instance. I don't know. But we need to do a whole lot more investigating into your family."

"Christ." She moaned, pushing back her tousled hair. "You know I don't have anything to do with them, right?"

"You may or may not have very much to do with them," he noted, "but these are questions that you're the only part of the family left to ask."

"Great, so my mother leaves a trail of BS behind her, and I'm the only one left to answer all the questions? I'm the one who gets to be involved?"

"Yeah, that's pretty much it," he said, smiling. "Go get changed and I'll put on the coffee."

"What if I don't want to get changed?" she asked mutinously.

"Fine, don't then." He smirked, again waving his hand but at her chest. "Trust me that I have no objection to the view."

When she looked down and saw the bulk of her left breast was no longer inside her robe, she glared at him and stormed out of the room. She heard sounds of him making coffee as she quickly got dressed, ran a brush through her hair, then deftly swung the length of her curls upward into a high ponytail, before she walked back into the kitchen.

He looked up with a smile and quipped, "Such a shame to ruin the view."

"*Right*," she grumbled, "but, if you had shown up at a decent hour, I wouldn't be in this awkward position."

"It is a decent hour," he argued, staring at her in astonishment. "Everybody else is at work."

"Yeah, except me. Therefore, it's *not* a decent hour because I wanted to sleep in for a change."

"But you weren't asleep," he pointed out.

She groaned, knowing there was no way to win this argument. "Whatever," she muttered, "and I don't have anything to tell you about my family."

"Maybe not," he agreed, "but I have to ask, and best to go through it with me at least once, before somebody else gets here."

"Who's that?" she asked, frowning at him.

"Grant, who works a lot with Dr. Maddy's husband, Drew."

"I've met him. What does he want with me?" she asked.

"Unfortunately he's got questions too, and all about your family."

"*Great*," she muttered. "And again I don't know very much about my family, and I've already told you that."

"Do you have any ideas about your grandmother?"

"No, I have nothing."

"How did she die?"

"I told you that it was a suspicious death and is still under consideration."

He nodded. "Not sure you told me or somebody else

did," he shared thoughtfully.

"I don't remember who I told, but I told somebody. What difference does it make anyway? That's a matter for the police."

"Oh, yeah, let's not forget, that's what I am."

"No, you're some special investigator who works for Stefan."

He stopped, looked at her, and then burst out laughing. "I'm really not, but I'm sure Stefan would enjoy that description very much."

"Then why do you do so much for him, if you don't work for him?"

"I'm a liaison," he replied, with half a smile, "but I do like your description better."

"Whatever." She glared at him. "God, I'm tired of people making fun of me."

"Nobody's making fun of you," he declared. "And that's not how I intended this to come off, so I apologize for that."

She walked over, poured herself a cup of coffee, and muttered, "I don't care. Ask your questions so we can be done with that, and then you can go. I guess the question I really have is, what the hell does any of this have to do with me?"

"A lot of it has to do with you, by way of blood."

"Blood only," she snapped. "Remember that."

"I do, but, from the bits and pieces of conversations you've had with everyone, nobody has the whole picture, and that is what I want."

She glared at him. "I'm not sure anybody has the whole picture—including me."

"And that is something for me to keep in mind," he admitted. "So, I apologize in advance if it sounds as if I'm being heartless, but I'm really not."

"You really are," she countered, rolling her eyes. "You just don't want it to be taken that way."

He laughed. "I can work with that too."

She looked at him warily as he made himself comfortable, opening up the fridge and checking for food. Looking back at her, he asked, "Eggs?"

"Will you cook them?" she asked in a muted tone, wondering what he was up to.

"Absolutely," he stated, as he quickly went about making breakfast sandwiches.

When he put the plate in front of her, she groaned and asked, "Why are you looking after me if you're here just to ask all these questions?" She felt herself tensing up as he quickly worked his way through his eggs and then shoved everything aside. She'd only picked at hers, so far.

He glared at her. "Eat up."

"I am eating," she snapped, "but the way you're acting makes me extremely nervous."

His eyebrows shot up. "Why would that be?"

She stared at him and then gave a broken laugh. "Because it sounds as if you're about to accuse me of something."

He shook his head. "No, I just need you to be prepared to give me answers, and you haven't been terribly forthcoming in that regard so far."

Her jaw dropped. "What are you talking about?" she asked, putting down her fork. "In my book I've been very forthcoming. Do you know how few people I've explained *any* of this stuff to?"

"I don't think you've explained anything to me as it is," he clarified, with a wry look in her direction. "So, I'm not exactly sure how many people you would be telling anyway."

"What do you mean?"

He tapped the file that suddenly appeared on the table in front of him. "I need to double-check some things."

"Like what?" And now she felt everything tensing up inside.

He began, "You moved to Chattanooga at one time."

"Yes."

"And at some point in time you lived in various other cities, including Joplin and Tuscaloosa."

"Yes. I told you that already. Why are you asking me again?"

"That's good. I just needed you to confirm that those were cities you had also lived in with your mother."

"We were in several other places too," she added. "Not that I really remember the names of the towns, since I was pretty young at the time." She frowned. "What difference does it make?" she asked. "It's not as if I had any say over where I lived at the time."

"Right, and I've got that noted as well," he said. "There are definitely some other cases that have come up in connection with your mother, and those cases happened in those cities. I know it's a long shot, but it's something. Now do you have any idea how your father died?"

"A drug overdose," she shared. "That's what I was told, and I told you that."

"I pulled his file."

"I thought you couldn't find it."

"It was in a different state," he noted.

"I guess that makes sense," she muttered. "We moved a lot, but I don't imagine that I would have mentioned that earlier."

"I got there eventually," he said, "and I have to tell you it's partly because of your father's death that Grant needs to talk to you."

"Why?" she asked. "I don't know anything about it. I was a child when he died."

"And I get that," he told her. "Grant aligned the similarities of your father's death to some other cases of people whose deaths could possibly be linked to his."

"It was a drug overdose. Surely that happens all over the world. Why do just these *possibly linked* deaths concern the FBI? It's not as if that connects to anything here."

"Oh, that's Grant's business, being an FBI matter," Keller noted, with a wave of his hand. "All I can tell you right now is that I have a few other questions."

"*Right.*" She stared at him in bewilderment. "None of this is making any sense."

"And that's okay. We're trying to get to the answers. Just answer as honestly as you can."

"I have been," she snapped, glaring at him. "I just don't remember a whole lot of this stuff." Then she sighed. "But if I say I don't remember, a lot of people will think I'm lying."

He faced her. "Maybe a lot of people *won't* think you're lying."

She snorted. "My experience tells me that people *will* think I'm lying."

"Let's just keep answering questions, and I'm sure we can get some of it sorted. Do you know any specific details about how your father died?"

"No, just that it was an overdose."

"Okay, so, yes, it's true that your father did technically die of a drug overdose," he began. "But the police report describes it as a ritualistic killing. He was pinned to a tree and administered certain drugs while he was in this crazy position," he shared, "then expired in the same way."

She stared at him. "Expired?"

"Died," he stated bluntly. "He was upside down when he died. The autopsy was inconclusive, but his death was put down as a drug overdose. Murder."

"Murdered via drug overdose?" she repeated. "As part of a ritualistic killing? Jesus."

"Yes," he confirmed, staring at her intently.

"I suppose that's possible, knowing my mother. That would be something she possibly would have had something to do with."

"And when you say *possibly*?"

Tandy groaned. "I remember seeing images of … Jesus on the cross and things like that on her bedroom wall. And, as I told you before, she had altars and was into some pretty weird stuff, depending on the boyfriend at the time."

"And yet *this guy* was your father."

"I know," she snapped. "I understand he was my biological father. And I can't imagine what she would have been into, but, if any of it caused his death, then that would explain why my grandmother was so against Isabella and wasn't in a big hurry to take me in."

"Can we talk about your grandmother's death?" he asked.

She frowned. "My grandmother was found collapsed on the ground by the garage. The autopsy indicated multiple organ failure, yet there was no medical explanation for it, so her death was listed as suspicious. It happened when I wasn't home. That's one of the reasons I don't want to keep the house. I'm leaning toward selling it," she said. "The house wasn't exactly an easy place for me, yet compared to the other places I had spent my childhood, it was a place of retreat, a place of salvation. So, it's still hard for me to let it go. It's been a safety zone for me. Except now it is where she died so unexpectedly."

"Right," he agreed. "So did she spend a lot of time outside, gardening or whatever?"

"Not really. She was becoming more reclusive with age. Plus, I was there to run errands. She didn't even sit outside on the porch as she was quite the introvert and didn't want to talk to the neighbors."

He studied her for a long moment, then picked up a pen and started writing.

Tandy added, "Maybe she took out the trash. Isn't that possible?"

"Sure, it's possible," he said. "But who usually took out the trash?"

Tandy grimaced.

"*Right*," Keller stated. "So the report doesn't show a forensic visit of the house."

"They asked," she muttered, "but I can't say I was very positive about it."

"What do you mean? You didn't give them permission to enter the house?"

"She was found outside her garage, at the back of the property, so no real reason for them to have anything to do with the inside of the house."

"And is that where she normally parked?"

Tandy frowned, then slowly shook her head. "No, never. She never parked back there."

He let out his breath in a big *whoosh*. "And did you ever consider the fact that the police may have needed to know that?"

"They didn't ask," she said, raising her hands. "They asked damn little actually. I was a complete basket case, blubbering my eyes out over the whole thing. God, I've just blanked it all out of my mind because it was so damn painful to lose my grandmother. She was the only one on my side."

"I get that, but I would really appreciate it if you would bring back some of those memories." She glared at him and he grimaced, nodding. "I know. It's not what you want to do."

"No, I really don't want to revisit losing my grandmother, which just means that I'm still the number one suspect, just as I was back then, since I was the beneficiary."

KELLER SIGHED. HE began again, "I don't know if it makes you feel any better, but I don't have any notes on the case file here that points to you being a possible suspect. Remember that her death was suspicious but not necessarily murder, per the autopsy report anyway." He watched her shoulders sag in relief, and he realized just how much that had been weighing on her.

"You know how people force stuff down?" she asked. "I'm such a pro at doing that, but the trouble with this deal is that you never really get off the hook because it's not been solved. Thus, I've still got to keep that contained."

"Sometimes we don't get answers. This case is inclusive and suspicious. And will probably remain that way, barring any further updates or information. So I'm not telling you anything conclusive at all," he clarified. "I'm just saying that, on the books, it doesn't ever pinpoint you as being a suspect."

"I'm not sure I can trust in that either," she muttered,

with a wry look in his direction, "because anybody investigating this would automatically suggest that I was the number one suspect."

"But it's not been deemed a murder to begin with. Keep that in mind. And you weren't even there at the time, were you?"

"No, I was on shift."

"So, you have an alibi."

"But I could have hired somebody," she pointed out.

He smiled and asked, "You could have hired someone to kill your grandmother without leaving a physical mark on her or forcing her to ingest poison or whatever?"

Tandy shrugged.

Keller continued. "And what is your motive for this supposed murder?"

"I didn't do it, so I don't have a motive."

He laughed. "Exactly, but, if it makes you feel better, I can leave you on the suspect list."

"No," she cried out in shock. "Confirm I'm not on that damn list."

Obediently he made a point of erasing what he'd just put down on the paper.

She snatched the paper out of his hands and read it, then groaned. "You're making fun of me, aren't you?"

"No, but I'm serious when I say I don't believe that you were in any way responsible for this."

"That's a good thing," she snapped. "However, it always felt as if everybody looked at me differently, as if I'd committed some horrific crime against the only family member to ever help me," she shared, tears coming to her eyes. "And nobody ever gives a crap about what I have to say."

"Did you still feel that way, after you talked to the police?"

"Yes," she confirmed. "All they were concerned about was that I would get the house."

"Did you go through a process and get the house?"

"Yes, it was willed to me," she said, looking at him. "I didn't know that at the time, but it was."

"And was there money to go with it?"

"Some. My grandmother wasn't wealthy, but she had a little something, and all of it was left to me."

"No other family in her life are still living?"

"No," she whispered, with tears in her eyes. "My father was her only child."

"Ah, and that would have been very tough to lose him like that."

"It was terrible for her, I'm sure. Oh." She stopped and looked at him, slowly putting down her coffee cup. "Grandma didn't speak of her son to me, even though he was my biological father and I was living with her for over a decade. However, later in her life, she did share with me how she kept a box with all the articles and stuff on his death. I never looked at any of it because it was all just too painful for her to deal with," she muttered. "But that might still be at the house, if you're interested."

"Yes, I'm interested. I am very much interested to see it all. I should send someone over to make sure it is still there."

She frowned. "You don't have to sound quite so excited about it."

"I figure not much was leaked to the press, considering the gruesome details that I found in the official police report. So thankfully your grandmother should have been spared all that. However, as to our investigations, we should check it out. Your grandmother may have made notes that nobody saw." He grabbed his phone and sent a text to somebody.

When Tandy frowned as him, he added, "I just sent one of the locals over to see if the box is still there. And, hey, whether it relates to your grandmother's suspicious death or your father's murder—or your mother's possible murder for that matter—something important could be there. You have to realize that it's all related."

She stared at him. "When you say that"—she swallowed hard—"it doesn't sound very good."

KELLER STUDIED HER and slowly shook his head. "I'm sorry, but it's not good at all. You've had three family members die under suspicious circumstances, all within the last two decades or so." He took her hand in his and added, "Although that's a long span, just the fact that there were three in your own family means, in some way, they have to be connected."

She sat back with tears in her eyes and shook her head. "I don't want them to be connected," she muttered. "My grandmother hated and feared my mother, so much so that Gwen left me there with my mother for a long time because Gwen couldn't bear the thought of dealing with Isabella. Only once Gwen realized my childhood and early teens were far worse than she ever imagined, did she do everything she could to get me out of there and to keep me away from Isabella. I don't want to think that my father and my grandmother paid the price because it involved me, or that it is connected to my mother."

"And yet you're absolutely terrified that your mother had something to do with your grandmother's death, aren't you? I can feel it from here."

She closed her eyes and then slowly opened them and

nodded. "Yes, I'm so afraid Isabella might have. My mother has always carried around a lot of hate for people, and she had no compassion for anyone but herself."

"Which is why we're doing this," he stated. "If your grandmother was a good person, don't you want to see who did this to her get caught?"

"Of course, but, if you'll tell me that it was my own mother, can you imagine what that will be like? You know, the guilt? And, if not for my living with my grandmother, ... would Gwen likely still be alive?"

"How do you figure that?" he asked.

"Because I had cut off all contact with Isabella, staying as far away from my mother as I could. But maybe if I had helped her, maybe if I had gone over there sometimes and helped in some way, maybe Isabella wouldn't have done that. Maybe she wouldn't have killed my grandmother."

"And yet you told me how your grandmother was pretty tough in her own way and carried a huge hate for Isabella, which was returned in spades, so nothing you could have done would have fixed that."

"That's true," she admitted. "My grandmother was positive Isabella had something to do with my father's death. I had no idea of the details—until you just told me now—because Gwen would never talk more about it."

"Right, and you can see why now," he noted, "and what I told you is only part of what happened. So you can imagine the full details are pretty horrific."

Tears came to her eyes, and she nodded. "And that's another reason for me to feel eternally upset," she muttered, "because my father, according to my grandmother, was insane. And the fact that he fell for my mother was just terrible."

"What was your mother like after your father died?"

She stared at him for a long moment, before replying. "Dangerous as hell. She slid mentally, physically, and went into drugs in a bad way," she murmured. "It seemed that his death unhinged her. I'm not sure why, maybe because she loved him or maybe because he provided some structure in her life that she badly needed."

Keller snorted. "I beg to differ. Your mother didn't love anybody. She's incapable of it."

Tandy sighed and nodded.

"And why the hell was he hanging around your mother when you never even met the guy?"

"Who knows now? However, Isabella hated a lot of people, including Gwen, and Isabella found great delight in targeting those people with her wrath. Maybe my father kept Isabella more grounded, less filled with hate. If so, then losing him would have set free something inside of her. Something bad. From then on, she was just plain awful."

"How old were you when he died?"

She shrugged. "Maybe eight at the most, probably less. I don't remember. He was never in my life," she muttered. "I'm thirty. My grandmother's only been dead this last year, and my father died however long ago your paperwork says," she noted. "My mother has just passed away. So, in the past twenty-two years, I have lost my father, my grandmother, and now my mother."

She looked around the room. "I've got half a mind to call back that witch and have her answer some of these questions," she muttered, "because I sure as hell can't answer them myself."

"Do you want to try calling your mother?"

She laughed. "If there was ever a reason for my mother

*not* to show up, this would be it. She didn't do confrontations, but you can bet the next time I talk to her that I'll want answers, a lot of them." Without warning, she started to cry, not calm quiet tears, but deep gut-wrenching sobs that just tore at Keller's heart.

Getting up, he walked over, pulled her into his arms, and just held her close. She tried to pull away several times, but he wouldn't let her. He just tucked her up against him, waiting until the storm had passed.

As she dried her eyes, she looked up at him. "Are you sure your colleagues haven't warned you about me?"

"And why would they?" he asked, staring at her but knowing exactly what she would say.

"About how tears are the way to get out of everything," she replied, "and, if you think my mother didn't teach me that, you're wrong. She used tears as a weapon, and I hated it. I hated everything to do with her, and here she is, even now, ruining my life from the grave."

"I don't know that she's ruining your life," he clarified, "but it's obvious that you're struggling."

"An astute observation," she quipped, stepping out of his arms, "but not exactly rocket science."

"No, it isn't, and frankly you're still a long way from regaining control."

She stepped back more and glared at him. "Considering where I started, I've come a really long way, and I don't intend to go back to being the person I was."

"Maybe, but what brought this on?" he asked.

"The fear that she is going after the twins," she wailed. "Just knowing that Isabella's there, waiting for somebody to mess up and to give her an inch, just makes me hypervigilant for their sake."

"And that is a good thing," he noted, "but all of us are very confused as to what you think she can do from the other side."

"I don't know what she can do," she cried out, "but I know that, if you ever underestimate Isabella, it leads to trouble and can be catastrophic."

There wasn't a whole lot he could say to that, so he just held her as she burst into tears again. He did a quick mental search of her apartment but found no sign of her mother. There didn't seem to be a sign of anything, and oddly enough, as he thought about it, it was almost as if it was devoid of all personality. That was very strange in itself, and he didn't like it. Something was going on. "Have you seen her today?"

She shook her head against his chest. "No," she murmured. "I think she knows better than to come now. I wouldn't be kind if she went after the twins."

"And yet that's what you're afraid she will do, isn't it?"

"Yes, that's definitely what I'm afraid of. The twins don't deserve that. They deserve a chance to live without fear, not locking every door and window at night, afraid somebody will come in. And not to wake up the next morning, wondering why you're sore, tired, and exhausted, feeling nauseated because you don't know what happened to you," she whispered. "The twins deserve a chance to live a normal childhood. Not the one that I had."

"You haven't given me very many details about what your daily life was really like with Isabella."

She looked at him with a mocking smile. "The problem is, I really don't know all of it myself. I have memories of my life with her, of course, and everybody has a history they remember. However, in my case there is more. I have confusing images, feelings, smells, and sounds, but nothing that comes together in a way that I can call a *memory*, and it's not something I can easily create."

"Understood," he replied. "Maybe with hypnosis or some other techniques, we may be able to access those memories—if you want to."

He felt the shudder to his core as she tried to struggle free of his arms. "You don't understand what you're asking," she cried out.

"No, I don't understand most of that," he admitted, "but I can see the unknown terrifies you. So, one thing I really want to do is free you from the uncertainty of what *could have happened.* Confronting those awful snippets in your brain could at least free enough in your body that you can have a life without all these terrors."

She looked back at him, tears in her eyes. "And what if I find out I did something horrible?"

"Do you remember what you did?"

"No, of course I don't remember what I did. I was drugged or in a trance or comatose. I don't even know if I did anything. Still, my mother used to threaten me with these taunts, manipulating me."

"I really hate your mother," he muttered.

"Not as much as I do," she whispered. "You have no idea what it was like. I don't really think I can go through reliving any of that again."

"Again?" he repeated, picking up on her wording.

She shuddered. "I tried to get therapy at one point in time, knowing that I couldn't continue the way I was. But my mother contacted my therapist and *explained* so many things to her," she shared, rolling her eyes and once again reverting to that mocking tone, "that the psychologist wanted to lock me up. Wanted me to go get some *real* help," she explained.

"Define *real help*."

"The *pump me full of drugs* kind of help, and I just couldn't do it. There were no drugs I could possibly handle while my mother ran free, laughing her fool head off because I would finally get drugged up again."

"Yeah, I definitely don't like your mother," he confirmed.

"Many people didn't," she stated, "though a lot of people loved her. She had that power about her. There was this sense that she could do anything, and you sure as hell better be on her side because, when she did it, she would pull off some fucking miracle, and either you go along with her or you pay the price of *betrayal*. And I've got to tell you there were always people dying in her world. I just didn't know how or why—or if it had anything to do with her. She was with people who … I don't want to say were the worst of the worst, but that's what it seemed like to me. Remember that I was a child or a young teenager back then. Still, for all I know, it was just an occupational hazard, you know, part of being homeless and living on the streets and drugged-up half the time. And, if it wasn't that, it was the influence of the drugs."

She took a deep breath and continued. "Isabella would show up at home and just shake her head and say, *So-and-so died today.* I sometimes felt her pain, and other times she seemed to have no pain or compassion at all."

"Do you think she killed them?"

"No, in this instance I don't. Sometimes she was just so blasé about it, as if it was just life, and you had to make your mark before life stepped up and beat you down," she suggested, with a shrug. "I don't think she was a psycho-path, … but I'm sure a specialist would not agree with me."

"Probably not, in my opinion," Keller clarified, "because it sounds as if she's definitely in that category."

"Maybe she was, and I didn't see it. I don't know. I don't have any solid answers for you," she muttered. "I don't think I ever will."

"That's the problem with these cases. Sometimes we never get the answers," Keller grumbled. Then his phone buzzed. "Forensics," he said to her, standing up to the take the call in the next room. He was gone for about fifteen minutes.

When he returned, he lifted his cell phone. "Well, that call just proved me wrong."

"Proved you wrong on what?" Tandy asked.

"We got an answer on something. Well, as much as you can trust a drugged-out albino Eternity Cult member."

Tandy frowned. "Albino?" she repeated.

Keller nodded. "Yeah, I wasn't gonna say anything until I had some facts. The investigative team got enough evidence to get a warrant to search Endgame."

Tandy gasped. "Isabella talked about her *endgame* all the time.

Keller smirked. "I imagine she would, and this one is a voodoo shop."

"And you found an albino? So he's not just in my nightmares?"

"Sorry," Keller muttered. "Seems the albino owns the voodoo shop named Endgame, which promotes member-ships in their Eternity Cult."

"Oh my God," Tandy whispered.

"And," Keller added, "he had your mother's cell phone

at his shop, along with the note you are missing. So the cops busted him for the B&E at your mother's apartment, and the owner spilled his guts. Remember that he's a druggie too, but he said your mother was working on an eternity spell, and her husband offered his blood to assist her in this ritual. Except it all went wrong and your father died." Keller checked on Tandy to see how she took the news. She seemed shocked, which was a normal response, but at least she wasn't in a trance again.

He continued. "According to the Endgame owner, your father appeared to be in love with your mother, always hoping to get back into her life on a more permanent basis. However, as we all know, Isabella didn't love anybody, even your father."

DR. MADDY RACED out of her office once again, heading toward the twins. She didn't even bother with the observation room and headed right into their room. And, once again, they were still sound asleep in both worlds. She frowned and immediately felt another energy, maybe Isabella's ghost, but Dr. Maddy wasn't certain. Instantly she cleansed the room and snapped to whoever was here, "Get lost. They're not yours."

In confirmation, she heard a mocking laughter and a whisper, *Yes, they are.*

Dr. Maddy shuddered. "No," she snapped, glaring around the room. "They aren't. Not anymore."

*They will always be mine* declared the ghostly vision. *And nothing you can do about it.*

"Try me," Dr. Maddy boldly claimed, for the first time feeling every instinct within her rising up to protect these children.

*I don't have to*, the ghostly woman stated, with an oddly satisfied note. *I can find your weak spots any time, and I just did.*

"Doesn't matter," Dr. Maddy countered. "I'm not alone."

*Neither am I*, the ghost whispered, and then, with a mocking laugh, she disappeared.

Dr. Maddy leaned against the wall and stared down at the children, wondering what the hell was going on.

Almost instantly Stefan blasted into her mind. *Are you okay?* She winced at the volume, and he modulated it down. *Sorry.* Then he asked, *What the hell was that?*

*I was hoping you could tell me*, she replied, the fatigue evident in her tone. It felt as if every bone in her body was weak and trembling, as if she'd just battled to the end and had won this time, yet with no guarantee she would prevail in a second fight.

*Yes, you will*, Stefan stated. *We have no other option in these cases.*

*I know. … But what is her endgame?*

*Funny you should mention that. Keller found a link to Isabella at a voodoo shop, called Endgame, specializing in some Eternal Life cult or some such thing, along with blood sacrifices and whatever else. Did she really think she could escape death, could work her cons from the afterlife? We must find out what her true endgame could be. If she had eternal life, what would she do with it? But how was any endgame even possible after death?*

*That's really the issue, isn't it?* she murmured.

*How is it even feasible that she's acting as if she's somehow considering a return from the dead? Also remember what Keller told us too, about Tandy's father's death. Maybe that was a dress rehearsal to see if her father would live after death, before Isabella attempted it. But who knows? We are dealing with a deeply disturbed person, a drug addict, full of hate, yet gifted. … She doesn't even acknowledge her death*, he added, calmness returning to the atmosphere.

*And yet she does know, and she's made no bones about that.*

*But there's also that attitude that she has some control or some knowledge that nobody else does. But that doesn't mean she has the psychic strength or any ability to pull it off.*

*Maybe not.* Dr. Maddy lifted her hand, not surprised to see it still trembling madly. *Jesus, I don't know what that energy was, but I really don't want it back again. The thing is, I think it is Isabella. And she's gotten past all our defenses, and I don't know why.* Dr. Maddy considered that for a bit, and then added, *The only way it's coming in… and it sounds so wrong at so many levels, but it's as if she's riding in.*

*As if latching on to someone?*

*Yes, it's either you, me, nurses, or …*

*Tandy*, Stefan declared.

*Yes*, Dr. Maddy agreed. *And, if that is the case, I don't think Tandy would know.*

*No, she obviously doesn't know. It seems as if her mother has quite a death grip on her as it is.*

*And how is that even possible?* Dr. Maddy asked.

*I did hear she was groomed for it from a very early age.*

*Sure, up until she left home, but what happened after that?* Dr. Maddy asked. *It's one thing to get hooks into somebody, but it's another thing to have that level of power through those hooks.*

*And yet we have seen something like that before*, he muttered. *We'll have to do a scan of her system.*

*Good luck with that. You'll have to ask her for permission.* Dr. Maddy held back a chuckle. *Tandy is incredibly sensitive.*

Stefan added, *Tandy's also incredibly strong.*

*Yeah, I still can't believe she popped right into your world when she needed to talk to you.* Dr. Maddy couldn't help but laugh at this. *I don't know anybody else who has ever done that.*

*Only you,* Stefan replied, with a note of humor. *But it seems with every passing year that we find something new to amaze us in this craziness.*

*That's true too,* she muttered.

Stefan added, *I just want to know that Tandy herself is safe and that she's safe with the twins.*

She heard the questioning in his tone. *Do you have any doubts about that?* Dr. Maddy asked.

*It's not that I have doubts about Tandy's intent. I just don't know who has their hooks in her and what's going on here,* Stefan clarified.

Dr. Maddy groaned. *If Tandy's being targeted, then she's bringing in that same threat to the twins, in which case I can't have her close by.*

*No, of course not,* he muttered thoughtfully. *None of us can, that would be one danger too many.*

*Exactly, and in order for Tandy to get free of whatever this nightmare is in her world, she must get free of her mother.*

*Which she is working on, and she is making progress.*

*If Tandy can get into your world without you even knowing, then she is definitely strong in her gift. She's stronger than she knows, and maybe, with a little bit of help from us, she can get there.*

*The question is, how much is a little bit? What is our investment in this, and who is it we're trying to help?*

*Both the twins and Tandy,* Dr. Maddy stated instantly.

*And, if something in particular keeps Tandy wide open for this type of threat, you know we have to shut it off. It's not just her mother out there causing all this chaos, as she seems to be part of a cult now. So, if anybody else can come in via her mother, you know some of them have a lot more experience than Tandy does.*

*She has a hell of a lot of skills for somebody her age though,* he argued, *and I just don't get that.*

*No, I don't either, unless both her birth parents were gifted. Regardless, the fact that we haven't seen these skills before—from both Tandy and the twins—just makes me even more wary.*

*Of Tandy?*

*No.* Dr. Maddy reconsidered that and shook her head. *Not of her or the twins, but of who can use Tandy and the twins.*

*And yet she and the twins have been used all their lives, which is why we know it can happen again and again and again. We have to shut off that source. We must get Tandy to realize the confidence in herself and her gifts to get out of this. … And we must get the twins out of danger. I wonder if we could get all three to work in tandem against Isabella?*

*As you said, Tandy needs self-confidence first. Mark is already working from that mind-set, but then we have Matthew, who is more a follower than a stand-alone leader. For all those reasons, I don't want the twins out yet,* she replied, *not until the danger has passed.*

*That could be a long time,* he pointed out.

*I hope not,* she said, *because the longer they're in their own little world, the harder it will be to get them back out. Somewhere along the line the twins have to believe that they're safe, and, right now, no way I can convince them of that. Something has happened that they recognize as a threat, and they've gone into hiding,* she explained, *so there isn't anything you or I can say or do right now to change their minds.*

*And, for the moment, that's as it should be,* he conceded soberly. *Just thinking about them, believing in us, and their having something bad happen to them in the meantime is terrifying.*

*Terrifying and all too possible,* she muttered. *So, will you speak to Tandy, or will I?*

*I will. Definitely I will.*

*Good,* she muttered, *then get at it, and I'll see if I can set aside a few hours and come in with you.*

*It might take both of us,* he agreed, *particularly after Tandy's show of psychic strength.*

*Maybe,* Dr. Maddy replied. *I'm less concerned about that than I am about finding out what or who's inside her—maybe both.*

*So you're thinking a possession? You really think somebody is in there?*

She paused, before replying. *I don't know how there can't be. The trouble is, I don't know who it is and whether they're a permanent resident or just a casual visitor, hopping in and out whenever they want to.*

*Damn,* he muttered. *You make me so want to step in now and get this done.*

*Exactly,* she confirmed. *Everybody is in danger until it's settled, especially Tandy.*

# CHAPTER 17

TANDY SAT IN the same room as the twins, but they were curled up in bed in both worlds. She switched from one boy to the other, trying to coerce them out to play, but she got zero response. She felt a twitch from Matthew, as if he wanted to, and then he would still immediately, as Mark put a hold on him. The fact that Mark was so powerful and could do that was pretty amazing. Yet it was obvious that Mark had no intention of talking to Tandy, and that just made her very sad.

"I'm sorry," she muttered out loud. "I really don't want anything to happen to you two, and you have such a lovely place to stay and to play. However, if you can't find a way to come back out or to find the security and the safety to come back out here in my world, I don't know what will happen."

Still Mark ignored her.

"I don't have the ability to control a lot of what goes on out here," she admitted. "I'm not talking about the energy stuff, but it's all about the adults and managing your care."

She kept talking as Mark watched her passively. "You can stay in here forever probably," she shared, "but then you'll miss out on your entire lives. I don't think that's what either of you want, and yet you may not even realize what all you would be missing out on, what that would mean. Since our mother has passed on, I'm still realizing just what any of this means for me too. You have so much more of your life ahead of you, and I hate to see it not come to a point where you can step out into my world and fully enjoy it."

She continued to talk, hoping that, as they heard her tone, they would decide at least some comfort was here and would come out and see her. Yet it didn't happen. She stepped out of the room, depressed, heartsore, as she realized just how far the twins had to go. It wasn't much of a surprise that Dr. Maddy waited for her.

Dr. Maddy raised one eyebrow.

"They remain in their own world," Tandy muttered. "It's heartbreaking to see them that way, particularly after having seen into both worlds, where they were so full of life in the make-believe world. I had such high hopes that they could be free to be playful and happy and safe and secure in both worlds, not shut down in both." Tears started to form in her eyes, even as she spoke. She scrubbed them away impatiently, only to find Stefan behind Dr. Maddy, and behind him was Keller.

Tandy frowned at them all. "What's going on? Did something happen?" She immediately spun, looking at the children.

Dr. Maddy reached out reassuringly. "No, it's nothing to do with the children."

"Oh, thank heavens for that," she muttered. Then faced them, again frowning. "But obviously something is going on, or you all wouldn't be here."

"Why wouldn't we be?" Keller asked. "You're here."

At that, she shrugged irritably, wishing she didn't have that prickly reaction whenever he was around. "Maybe, but it feels as if there is more to it than that." She stopped, her gaze suspicious.

"It's fine," Stefan began, "but we do need to talk to you."

"Talking is one thing," she replied, "but ganging up on me? That's something altogether different."

Stefan shook his head. "You're among friends here."

"And yet this feels like … an intervention."

Keller's eyebrows shot up at that, and he asked, "Is there anything you need an intervention from?"

She glared at him, her gaze going from one to the other to the next. "Somebody explain, please," she snapped, "because you're making me extremely uneasy."

Keller patted her shoulder. "We're not here to do an intervention. We're not ganging up on you either, but we all do need to talk to you."

"Fine, then let me out of here because you're making me feel very claustrophobic."

He stepped back, and so did Stefan. And with that, the passageway widened enough for her to slip by both of them into the hallway, and she walked to the elevator. "Just stay back."

"Would you please let us talk to you?" Keller asked.

She shook her head. "No, because it still feels as if you're pinning me in place." She couldn't help that sense of being cornered. "You should understand that I don't do well with that."

"I can understand," he said, "and that's part of the reason we want to talk to you."

She stiffened and spun around to stare at him. "What's this all about?"

"Can we go into my office?" Dr. Maddy asked, as she motioned at nurses and other patients milling around. Everyone was staring at them.

Tandy frowned, thinking about Dr. Maddy's office, and realized that it was right here, and in theory she could leave there without any problems from them. "As long as I get to leave when I want to," she snapped, her tone hard.

"Absolutely," Dr. Maddy confirmed, with a knowing smile.

With one last look toward the twins, Tandy strolled into Dr. Maddy's office first and took up a position where she sat nearest to the door and had easy access. She saw the smile on Keller's face as he sat down beside her.

"You don't always have to be so wary, you know?" he murmured.

"Yes, I do," she argued, "particularly when you do things like this."

He looked at her in astonishment. "Do what? We came here hoping to deal with the twins, saw you here, and thought maybe we should talk to you about it."

At that, she calmed a bit, since his explanation seemed at least somewhat reasonable. She just nodded, her gaze going to the other two. "Okay, now what is this about?" she asked, with no give in her tone.

Stefan sat down beside her and began, "Thinking about your mother's abilities, did she have anybody in her world who believed in life after death?"

"Everybody did," Tandy declared, "the whole weird group of them."

He nodded. "And did anybody act as if they had found an answer?"

"Oh, good God, I have no idea. How would I even know that?" she muttered. "They were all pretty crazy, you know?"

"We don't know that," Keller corrected. "We really

don't know if they found some afterlife answers either."

She looked at him in astonishment and then started to laugh. "Seriously? You're the last person I would think would consider that to be an option."

"It's nothing that I've seen before," he admitted.

Stefan interjected, "Me neither, but I am not so quick to judge."

Feeling a rebuke, she groaned. "Look. I don't know what you're doing here. I came to visit with the twins, and unfortunately their condition hasn't improved as I had thought it would."

"Why did you think that?" Stefan asked.

"Because I had hoped that, over time, they would understand that the danger had passed."

"What danger?" Stefan asked.

She tilted her head, considering that thought. "That's the question, isn't it? I guess in my mind, I was thinking the danger was Isabella."

"And it still could be," Stefan replied, "but in what way do you think she's a danger?"

She stared at him and shook her head. "I don't understand."

"I know," he said, "but could you just humor us a little bit more?"

She let out her breath in a slow deep exhale and sighed. "Fine, I think my mother always had designs on some way of living forever, but I don't know whether that was her idea or some of the druggie men she hung out with. She used to talk about it all the time, but I didn't think there was any serious drive on her part."

"Did you ever see her attempt such things?"

Tandy snorted. "I did my best to avoid seeing anything

she did. Whether it was her banging some guy on the couch when I got home from school or something completely different," she shared. "Believe me that I tried to ignore what my mother was doing. So, I'm not sure what else you think she would be doing."

"We aren't either," Stefan conceded. "It's just come to our attention that your mother potentially thinks that she can control you from the other side."

"She's been doing a bang-up job of it, but I'm doing my best to not let her have that kind of control," Tandy replied, turning to look at Keller. She frowned at him. "Did you tell them everything?"

"There wasn't anything to tell," he said, looking at her. "Think about it. Your mother came to visit me, so that is my story. You went to see Stefan in his bedroom via the ethers, and that's your story. So really the best thing we can do is to share each other's stories and all be on the same page."

"I don't have a problem with being on the same page," she stated. "I just don't want this to be a case of where I'm always in the wrong."

"Whoa," Stefan interjected. "You can stop that thought immediately. You're not in the wrong on anything. We're trying to figure out to what extent Isabella may have had some contact, perhaps with another spirit on the other side, maybe one who was landlocked and has no intention of crossing over into heaven."

She stared at him, speechless. "Is that a thing?"

"She's contacting you right now, isn't she?" Stefan asked.

"Yes, of course," Tandy confirmed, waving her hand, "and making me miserable at the same time."

"And she's doing that for whatever reason she has in her mind, and we suspect it's because she thinks that she can control whatever is going on in this life right now from the other side," Stefan suggested.

"Which," Keller jumped in and added, "she appears to be doing."

"Yes, she does appear to be doing that," Tandy agreed. "I'm not sure what any of us can do about it though."

"You keep saying things like that, as if she's got some superpowers," Keller pointed out.

"I don't know whether she does or not," Tandy snapped. "All I can tell you is that she's made my life miserable because of the stuff that she told me that she would eventually get."

"What stuff is that?"

"She talked about how she would end up, not so much about living forever but to be the queen bee at the end of the day. As if she had some... I don't know..." She hesitated, looking for a word.

"Endgame," Keller shared.

Tandy nodded. "Exactly. She always talked about having an endgame."

"And did she dabble in any ritualistic things?"

"Yes, ... all the time. And apparently, according to her, ... so did my father."

At that news, Stefan stared at her.

She nodded. "That's what she told me, but I don't know if it's something we can trust."

"And that's a good point too," Stefan noted, studying her. "Did you ever see them doing the rituals?"

"Isabella and her strange men? Sure, but not my father. He wasn't in my life, remember? But those other men scared the crap out of me."

"Why?" Keller asked.

"Why do you think?" she snapped, frowning at him. "She used to get blood—from God-only-knows where. She never appeared to kill anything, not that I ever saw anyway. That would have freaked me out completely, and, if I'd known she was killing animals, I probably couldn't have held back from telling people about it."

"Which is why she probably didn't do it while you were around, if she did it at all," Dr. Maddy suggested.

"Possibly, I don't know. Isabella was devious, and I don't really understand what she was all about. Even now, all I feel is fear every time the conversation turns to her. If you want to talk about anything else, I'm totally okay, but the minute you bring her up, I just feel this cold clamminess taking over, and I want to puke," she muttered. "I would really rather have any conversation but that."

Stefan smiled at her. "But you're handling it so well."

"BS," she spat, staring at him. "I'm not handling any-thing. I'm terrified that I'm at fault for whatever it is that you're looking for some explanation on," she shared, "and I've already told one, two, or maybe all three of you that I'm afraid that, while I was drugged out, I did things, and I have no idea what."

"When you mentioned that you were sore when you would wake up, what does that mean?"

"I was sore, physically uncomfortable, with sore muscles and bruises. I used to have cuts as well," she explained, staring down at her wrists. "At one point in time a teacher thought I was suicidal. When I told my mother that, instead of getting upset, Isabella just laughed. *Good observation* is what she said, followed by *We'll have to change it then.* Afterward I found little cuts on my ankles." She held out her wrist, and very faint slash marks were still evident. She stared down at them.

"I never really got the impression that they did this to me, but I'm not sure that they didn't. I guess I'm too afraid to even go in that direction. It never really stopped until I left, and, even then, it seemed as if it may not have stopped at all."

"What do you mean by that?" Keller asked, as all three of them leaned forward, listening intently to every word.

She shrugged. "I don't know how I got them after I moved out."

"Did you go back and visit your mother?"

"No, not if I could avoid it. Every now and then I had to because of paperwork or some bullshit thing that had to be dealt with, but, for the most part, I cut her off and had nothing to do with her. One time I woke up and felt as if I had scratched my ankle, and the cut was in a new place. So I was always a little worried about it because I didn't really understand why or how it happened."

"Yeah, that's to be expected," Dr. Maddy murmured, studying her. "And you had no explanation?"

"No. My grandmother looked at it and told me that it wasn't really a cut, more of a scrape. She suggested that maybe something was in my bed or maybe I had scraped it when I was out working in the garden the night before."

"And that is also a reasonable explanation," Keller noted. "So you had no other reason to go looking for answers."

"Exactly," Tandy said.

"And was that the only time it happened?"

She looked over at them and slowly shook her head. "No, it happened more times, but … you're really scaring me right now."

"How often did it happen?" Stefan asked, his tone implacable.

When she bit her lip, Keller reached out and grabbed her hand. "Look, Tandy. We're doing this for your sake and for the twins. Just tell Stefan what he needs to know, and hopefully we can come up with answers for all this."

She swallowed.

"Just ballpark it, so we have some idea. What was it, once a year, twice, more?"

She winced and nodded. "Yeah, once a year and … always on my birthday."

They all sat back and stared at her in shock.

She raised both hands. "I don't know what your expressions mean. Believe me that I already put that part together, and it made no sense to me either."

"Good God," Keller muttered. "Had it been only on your birthday when you were with your mother?"

"No," Tandy clarified, "definitely not. It was much more often. I don't want to say weekly but kind of weekly." He winced at that, and she nodded. "That's why I'm not really too fond of anybody getting too close for too long," she muttered. "I know it makes me sound paranoid."

"You *should* be paranoid," Keller declared, his fingers clasping hers. "You had a pretty strange and stressful childhood, where unexpected things were happening to you, and you didn't know why."

"Exactly."

Dr. Maddy asked her, her tone firm, "I have another question for you, and you won't like it."

"I already know what you'll ask." She took a deep breath. "You want to know if I was raped. The answer is, I don't know." As Dr. Maddy stared at her, Tandy shrugged. "Was there pain? Yes, there was pain. Was there pain down there? Yes, there was pain down there. Do I understand why?

God no," she muttered.

The three people in the room just stared at her.

"I did ask Isabella about it, and she just laughed. She told me it was just my body getting ready for sex. It made me so disgusted that I never brought it up again because she had also told me several times that she had offered to sell me to some of her men to make an extra bit of money," she muttered. "I remember running out of the house and puking my guts out on the sidewalk. Have I had sexual relations since? Yes. Did it tell me anything? No."

Dr. Maddy let out her breath with a soft, gentle *whoosh*. "And that has to be hard."

"No, not hard, not hard. It was *fucking brutal.*" Tandy's gaze was watchful as she studied them. "I don't let anybody close to me. I don't trust anybody when I'm sleeping because I don't—I don't know what happens when I'm asleep," she shared. "And that terrifies me more than anything."

"Are you thinking something happens to you while you're asleep now?" Stefan asked.

She turned to him and slowly nodded. "Something definitely happens now. I thought all that shit would be done and gone with Isabella's death, but it's not. I don't know what it is. I don't know who it is, and, for all I know, it's me somehow," she suggested, shifting in her seat. "I just don't know."

"I have a proposal," Dr. Maddy stated.

Tandy stared skeptically from Dr. Maddy to Stefan and Keller and back around again.

Dr. Maddy continued. "Why don't you stay here on the ward for a few nights. We'll monitor what happens while you're sleeping and see if we can come up with answers for you."

She looked at her. "Like a prisoner?"

"No, no. Not a prisoner, definitely not a prisoner." Dr. Maddy shook her head. "That is not how I want you to look at this at all."

"Maybe not," Tandy conceded, "but that's the way it's coming across."

"That may be, but it's not my intention. I would prefer to use cameras, and I would probably stay here myself."

"Why?"

"Because I can see things that go bump in the night, and so can Stefan," she noted. "So, if something is happening to you that you don't know about or … Let me rephrase that. If something happens while you sleep that you are not consciously aware of, then it would be very good for us to figure it out."

Tandy stood up, already in flight or fight mode. "No, I don't feel safe here. Isabella can get in here, as she has already proved to all of us," she stated.

"You don't feel safe here or you don't feel safe being watched?" Keller asked.

"I don't feel safe in any of those circumstances," she replied, staring at him. "All of that is just too much. You'll sit there, watching me? … That's just wrong. I don't know what I'll do. I don't think I'll even be able to sleep."

"Okay," Keller murmured, "if that is the case, what if you had somebody you trust by your side?"

"And who the hell would that be?" she asked, staring at him. "You seem to think I have this vast network of friends, but I don't. I don't have any friends, and part of the reason is the fact that I could never really trust anybody. Not after my mother. I don't know what happened to me at any point in time in the first fifteen years of my life, and, at this stage, I'm not sure it's a good idea to find out."

"I would stay with you."

THE LOOK ON her face was shock first, then turned to misery, followed by outrage. It took a bit more persuading before he managed to convince her that he would stand guard.

"And yet," she muttered later that evening as they went back to collect an overnight bag, "your standing guard isn't any guarantee that Isabella won't show up."

"Correct, but I seem to be the closest thing to someone you trust so far."

She thought about it and then nodded. "Yes, but, if things go wrong, I won't trust you ever again."

He gave her a smile. "I have to hope that you will."

"Why do you care?" she asked, suddenly looking at him sideways.

"Because I do. I care about you, more and more."

"Why do *you* care?" She glared at him, and he shrugged. "I'm much more of a straight shooter myself."

"Sure, but that's not exactly straight shooting either."

He chuckled. "And yet it should be. So many problems in this world would be eradicated if people just talked."

"Sure," she agreed. "Yet conflicts drive economies, conflicts drive inventions, conflicts drive people to do more than they expected."

"And is that your belief, or are those your mother's words?"

She frowned at him and shook her head. "God, I have no idea. I do believe it though. You only have to look at how wars spurred change and the industrial revolution," she muttered. "So there's got to be something to it."

"Oh, I'm sure there is," he said. "I happen to agree with it. I was just hoping that it wasn't your mother's words."

"I don't imagine it would be. However, I had a professor who used to say things like that." She stared at him, once she finally had her bag packed. "I don't know what good this will do," she muttered.

"If nothing else, maybe it'll help you to trust a little more."

"I should trust Dr. Maddy, shouldn't I?" she asked, with a sigh. "It seems as if she does everything for everybody else."

"I'm just happy that you allowed me to come in and to sleep there—or rather *not* sleep there," he corrected at her startled look.

"You will sleep, won't you?" she asked, then frowned. "Never mind. I'm not doing it."

"I won't sleep. I promise. It was just a slip of the tongue."

She frowned, staring at him, unwilling to believe him.

He groaned, then walked over, wrapped her up in his arms and held her. "Maybe it was a Freudian slip," he suggested with a wry smirk.

She snorted, totally disbelieving this angle.

Keller added, "Regardless, we're doing this for your sake and for the twins. Let's find out if anything is going on and just what it is. How come you never told me before that you weren't sleeping?"

"I'm used to *not* sleeping, and I'm *not* used to sharing things." She glared at him.

He smiled because he knew her glare was just her way of chasing off anybody who might get too close. He was already too close. He just hadn't admitted it to himself, nor had she.

He nodded. "It will be fine."

"Yeah, being in a facility like that, it should be fine," she muttered. "But then you hear all these horror stories of what happens to some people who are incapacitated."

He winced because there was no shortage of scary stories out there. "I will make damn sure that nothing happens to you. And Stefan and Dr. Maddy will keep watch on the twins, so all three of you are guarded by the best people possible, people who you know already. So there won't be any interference."

She winced at that. "I'm not sure that's supposed to make me feel any better."

"Not sure it's supposed to make me feel any better either," he admitted, with a loud chuckle.

She stared at him. "How can you be so calm about this?"

"Because it's just for one night," he explained. "We'll just see if anything happens while you're sleeping."

She nodded. "What if something does?" she asked, staring at the buttons on her shirt, her fingers toying with them.

He saw how she'd wrapped herself up in all kinds of horrific possibilities that would drive sleep from her mind forever. "It's fine," he murmured. "I will be there. Stefan will be on call, and Dr. Maddy will sleep at the center as well."

Tandy lifted her head at that. "I think, in a way, that's partly why I agreed."

"What, not because I'll be there?" he asked, with mock injury.

She smiled. "Yes, partly because you'll be there," she admitted. "I don't think I should trust people too far, but, if you guys are both there, then maybe it will be okay."

He sighed at that, knowing there was no point in pushing her too hard. He wasn't sure, given the same set of circumstances, that he wouldn't be just as wary. He asked her, "Did you pack a toothbrush?"

She nodded. "I did." She looked around and sighed. "I guess there's nothing else to be done, so we might as well just go."

It sounded as if she were heading to a funeral, and that was not how he wanted her to think of this. But he could also see that the stress was getting to her again. "We can go now, and we'll pick up some dinner on the way."

"What? You mean dinner is not included?" she quipped, with mock surprise.

"It probably is, but I don't want to push Dr. Maddy's assistance any more than we have to."

Tandy stared and then nodded. "I hadn't really considered that, but this is probably putting her in an awkward spot, isn't it?"

"I don't think very much puts Dr. Maddy in an awkward spot. She runs the center, and, if this is what she thinks would be the thing to do, then it's the thing to do." Keller could tell that Tandy still really struggled with the concept, but he had her in the vehicle before she had a chance to really understand what was happening.

She put on her seat belt and groaned. "I feel as if I'm being very foolish, yet everything inside me is screaming at me to run."

He turned on the engine and frowned. "Why is it telling you to run?"

"Danger, there's danger."

"Okay, and what if it's something other than *you* telling you to run?"

She stared at him. "Okay, that's not something I really want to think about."

"But, if it was somebody else, other than you, telling you to run, that make senses because their very existence and hold on you could be what's in danger?"

She swallowed and nodded. "Again, not really something I want to think about," she muttered.

"Maybe not, but you also know that I am right."

"I know. I know. I do know that," she grumbled. "Just drive and don't give me a chance to overthink this. Otherwise I'm not going to Dr. Maddy's."

Not taking any chances, he pulled the vehicle out of the parking spot and onto the road.

"It's so weird to think that everything in my life that is wrong involves people who have died."

"Not everything," he countered, with a smile. "There's still a lot in your world that you haven't come to terms with that maybe you could use a helping hand with, but there's no pressure to deal with it all at one time. You've just lost your mother, and it's got to be a real mind bender, with conflicting feelings about her and with her still around as a ghost. Yet, in some ways, it's a relief to be rid of her and all the conflict and pain she caused."

Tandy nodded. "I do feel as if I'm already going around the bend on that one. I want to hate her for everything she did to me and the twins, everything that was so wrong in my life, and yet how do you hate somebody who gave birth to you?"

"You take a look at the whole picture and go with the stronger of the emotions. Then just leave the rest because so much else in your world has been so wrong for so long that you don't even have to justify why or how. You are not wrong for feeling the way you do."

"Yes, I am, because she's my mother. I may call her Isabella, but she's still my mother."

"No, she was the woman who gave birth to you," he stated flat-out. "That does not make her a *mother*, any more than she is a *mother* to Mark and Matthew. Did you ever see her when she was pregnant?"

"No—at least I don't think so. Wait. … I may have." Then she frowned. "I don't know *what* pregnancy. Not the twins because I was avoiding her on purpose after leaving home."

He looked at her. "Do you have any idea how many children your mother has had?"

"No, God, no. There could be lots of them out there. I don't know if they all lived. It's hard to imagine they all survived, what with all the drugs she used. Christ, just the thought of there being more out there freaks me out. I did try to look into the foster homes, trying to find some contacts for the others, but I didn't get anywhere. I don't have any idea what happened to them," she noted, her tone breaking. "I guess you can't find out either, can you?"

"Not unless … I'm not sure. I would have to ask Grant about that."

"Do that, if you can," she muttered, glancing over at him while he drove.

"Do you think they would have abilities?"

"I don't know," she said, with a shrug. "For all I know they've been a part of her life all this time, and she just never told me."

He glanced at her and then slowly nodded. "She would do that, wouldn't she?"

"Yes, knowing her, … she absolutely would. That's the basis of my problem. I've been kept in the dark and feel as if I've been used and abused for years. I don't know where the truth starts or stops, and I'm just now coming to terms with the fact that a lot of what I hated, of what I knew, isn't necessarily what I thought, and I'm probably hating for the wrong reasons," she explained, with a broken half-laugh, half-sob.

"We all know your mother was a liar. You can only deal with what's in front of you, so focus on that for now and don't go around the bend on other issues."

"Too late," she muttered, with a mocking smile in his direction.

"No, it's not. It's never too late," he declared. "Remember that. This is way too important. Your mental health is way too important to not see this through, but we need to take it one step at a time."

"You do know that anybody else would consider this whole *staying at Dr. Maddy's place* tonight a bit of a trap."

"What do you mean by a trap?" he asked, startled.

"If it was a psych ward, I would definitely not be staying because I would be afraid nobody would let me out."

"Did you say something about your mother trying to get you committed at one time?"

"Yes, but I passed all their tests, and Isabella didn't have any money. If she had had the money, I wouldn't have gotten out," she said. "How is that for a contradiction? Is it wrong that a part of me wanted to stay there instead of going home with her?"

"Let me guess. You got three meals, and you could sleep at night." He pulled into a drive-through and, as usual, ordered them food, without asking her what she wanted.

"When you're hungry all the time, three meals are a lot and becomes almost a driving force that you don't really understand. Yet I also have to remember that it was a very long time ago."

"Not for the child inside you," he pointed out. "Apparently … it's not been very long at all."

"And that's just foolish. I'm thirty years old," she muttered. She stared at him, as he drove. "None of this should even be coming up. I've worked really hard to keep it all shut down."

"Of course you did, and yet by doing that," he murmured, "maybe all you did was let it fester inside, and now that it's out, and you know that something more has been going on, it should be better if you don't stay locked up anymore."

"And yet it should be better," she argued. "All this should have stayed buried where it was."

"What if the same thing was happening to the twins? What then?"

She frowned. "That can't happen," she whispered. "Nobody else should have to go through that."

"But go through what? How do we know what they're potentially going through, if we don't know what you've been going through?"

She gave an irritable shrug. "It still feels like this isn't a good thing."

He smiled, as they pulled into the parking lot of Dr. Maddy's place. Tandy stared up at the huge center. "She's created quite a place here, hasn't she?"

"She has, indeed, and I don't know if you know anything about her, but, in many ways, she creates miracles here. People bring their children and get incredible results in terms of healing, and that's why the twins are here, I suppose."

"Yes, though I don't even know how they got here. Maybe that's a question I should be asking her," she muttered.

"Yeah, and maybe it would help you find some more of your own answers."

As they walked up the stairs, they were greeted by one of the nurses.

The nurse smiled and greeted them. "Hey, Dr. Maddy told me to take you to your room when you arrived." And with that, she led them down the hall, past the room where the twins were, and into what looked to be a gorgeous guest bedroom that anyone would have been more than happy to have in their home.

"Wow," Tandy muttered, "this is beautiful."

The nurse laughed. "It is, indeed. We do have parents staying here overnight sometimes, so it's a good thing to have a spare room. Every house has one, so why not every institution?"

"That makes sense," Tandy noted. "I just didn't realize it was a thing."

"And it's not a thing for everyone," the nurse noted, looking a bit apologetic. "We can't accommodate everybody, only in special circumstances." And she gave them another smile and started to the door. "I'll leave you to it." And, with that, she stepped outside.

"What does that mean?" Tandy asked. "What is, *leave me to it?*"

"It means you can get ready for bed, if you want to now, or we can go talk to Dr. Maddy."

"I want to go talk to Dr. Maddy," she stated, staring around the room hesitantly.

Keller nodded. "Sure, we can do that. But first, tell me. How does the room feel?"

She looked at him, surprised, and then shrugged. "Almost too good."

He stared at her for a moment. "So, we're supposed to have a terrible room for you because you feel so guilty about everything you haven't done in your life?" She frowned uneasily, and he nodded. "You're entitled to have a beautiful room too, you know?"

"Maybe," she conceded uncomfortably. "You're starting to bring up all kinds of bits and pieces that I'm not comfortable with."

"I understand," he said, "and I'm not trying to push it, but it's hard to hear you say that it's a beautiful room, but almost too beautiful, as if you don't deserve it."

"I don't feel that I do deserve it," she admitted, staring at him. "I know that just makes me sound more messed up than anybody else."

"No. You're not more messed up at all. You're in need of a good support system. You're in need of friends who believe in you and of people who are like you."

"Like me?" she asked. "I don't think that's even possible."

"If not me or Dr. Maddy or Stefan, how about siblings who are like you?"

Her face softened, and she nodded. "Maybe. I'm hardly in any position to take them on though, am I?"

"Maybe, maybe not. It's something you'll have to decide at some point. Or maybe they'll need to stay in a place like this forever."

"It's pretty here," she noted, as she glanced around, taking in the lighting and the soft gentle air of the place.

"It is, but if this isn't where the twins need to be, if this isn't where they should be, it still won't make them happy to be locked up, will it?"

"No. Being locked up is the worst."

And suddenly such vehemence filled her tone that he stared at her.

She looked back and shrugged. "Yeah, I don't know where that's coming from either."

"I suggest it's time we find out," he said.

She frowned and shrugged, clearly irritated. "I told you. I'm just messed up. You should just go find somebody else."

It was the first time she'd directly broached the reality that something was happening between them, and he smiled at her. "That's not so easy, is it?"

"Sure, it is," she muttered, with a wave of her hand. "The world is full of beautiful, talented women who would absolutely love for you to look at them the same way you look at me."

He chuckled. "I'm glad you see how I look at you. The thing is, you can't always pick and choose where you want to look and how you see people."

"Yeah, you might want to try changing that though," she muttered. "You have no idea how screwed up I am."

"Doesn't matter," he declared cheerfully. "In for a penny, in for a pound."

KELLER LED TANDY down the hallway to Dr. Maddy's office. There he found Stefan and Dr. Maddy, both waiting for them.

Tandy nodded her head, obviously not sure of what was going on or the least bit comfortable with the idea of any of this.

"She's here," Keller announced, with a genial smile as he placed a hand on her back and nudged her forward.

"Yeah, I'm here," she grumbled, staring at them, "but

I'm not really sure that I should be."

"Nothing bad will happen," Stefan shared. "We just want to do a few scans and confirm that nobody is influencing your system in any way."

She shook her head, staring at them. "That sounds like too much woo-woo stuff."

"*All* of it sounds like woo-woo stuff," he admitted, with a bright smile. "Then again, you know exactly how freaky that stuff can be."

"Yes," she snapped, and then she groaned. "I agreed to do it, and I'm here, okay? I'm just worried that I won't be able to sleep."

Dr. Maddy nodded. "I don't want to give you any sleeping pills because that will affect how you sleep," she shared, "and we're hoping that you put on a movie, talk to Keller here, and just drift off into a normal sleep."

She snorted. "That would be the ideal, though I highly doubt it will happen. I'll still give it a shot though."

It was obvious that she was trying hard, but it was an uncomfortable situation. "Any time you're ready for bed, feel free," Stefan suggested.

"Are you both staying here tonight?" Tandy asked him, her gaze going from one to the other.

"Quite possibly," Stefan murmured. "Depends on how long it takes you to go to sleep."

She laughed. "I can't really say, but, if it means that you'll be sitting here until I do, you might want to grab a nap. I've never been a very good sleeper, so it wouldn't surprise me if I go down and then come back up again."

"What happens when you do wake up?"

"Nothing much. I check that the house is secure." She gave them a mocking laugh. "I've never really been able to sleep well, and sometimes I get up and confirm that the stoves are off and that the doors and windows are locked, the typical paranoid behavior."

Stefan nodded. "And, if that's the case, and you feel the need to do that here, or you need to open the door and confirm we're here, you do that. We're not here to scare you. We're here to help."

And such a firm commitment filled his tone that she studied him for a long moment and then seemed to relax. "Thank you. … That does help."

"Good." Stefan faced Dr. Maddy and said, "I'll go grab some food because I haven't eaten yet. What about you?"

"Sure," she agreed. "We'll head to the cafeteria downstairs. Do you two want to come with us?"

When Keller looked over at Tandy, she shrugged and replied, "We bought sandwiches."

"Good," Dr. Maddy said. "Then head to your room, and we'll see how you do. Remember that I'm here if you need me." And, with that, the two of them got up and walked out of the office.

Tandy looked over at Keller.

He smiled and nodded. "That wasn't so hard, was it?"

"Depends on what the rest of the night is like," she muttered, "but I could use a sandwich."

They went back to her room, and he quickly unpacked the sandwiches. When they were done eating, he asked, "How about a cup of tea?"

"Tea would be wonderful," she murmured, then groaned. "While you're out making tea, maybe I'll get ready for bed."

He nodded, and she stepped into the bathroom and quickly changed. As soon as she was changed, and she stepped back out, she felt a weird energy around her. She shivered, and, climbing onto the bed, she whispered, "I don't know what the hell you're playing at, but tonight you just might get more than you bargained for."

And damn if there wasn't a ghostly laughter up and down Tandy's spine.

And damn if she didn't scream.

# CHAPTER 18

"WHAT HAPPENED?" KELLER asked, rushing into the room.

She glared at him. "How do you know anything happened?"

"Because I heard a scream in my head."

"Yeah, well, I just came out of the bathroom, and it got scary. I felt something in the room, and I said something about whoever it was might be in for a surprise tonight, and they just laughed, making me feel like I was the one who would get the surprise," she explained, shivering in the bed. "So, I scrambled into bed, looking to avoid whatever the hell is coming."

"Interesting," he muttered, as he handed her the tea. When she automatically went to take a sip, he added, "Be careful. It's still too hot." Then he took it from her hands and tucked it up on the night table for her.

"I really don't think this is a great idea," she muttered.

"And yet you weren't too worried, until I left."

"Yeah, and then you left," she pointed out, staring at him, "and it felt like …"

"Felt like what?" he asked. "Tell me exactly what it felt like."

"I felt something moving into my room, moving into my space, moving into …" she whispered, wincing visibly, "moving into me."

He let out his breath and studied her for a long moment. "That would be exactly the information we're looking for tonight."

"That's just fan-*fucking*-tastic. How about you guys do this ghost-hunting thing when I'm not around?"

He smiled at her. "I think Dr. Maddy would be totally okay with that, except for the fact that I don't think it's possible."

"Of course not," she muttered. Then they just sat and talked for the next little bit, until she started to yawn. "Did you put something into my tea?"

"Nope, I sure didn't," he replied cheerfully, "But it is the Sleepytime brand of tea."

She looked down at it and frowned. "Oh, I often have one of those."

"Exactly, so nothing out of the ordinary. It's been a stressful day, and you're tired. I would just go with that."

"Maybe," she muttered. "It's definitely been a stressful evening. I'm really worried about the twins."

"I think we all are," he admitted. "And we're hoping that whatever we find out tonight will go a long way toward helping them."

"I just don't understand that, if this facility has safeguards in place, how is it that the twins don't feel safe?"

"The same way you don't."

"How is that like me?"

"Like you, the twins don't believe anybody else can keep them safe. Maybe they've listened to people's lies before, saying they would keep them safe, when they didn't."

"I suppose so," she muttered, as she stared at him, frowning. They continued to talk until she started to drift off, and then she muttered, "I'll just rest my eyes for a bit."

"You do that," he said, with a gentle smile. "Nighty-night."

With that, she closed her eyes.

KELLER SAT IN the guest chair just off to the side of Tandy's bed. He had no doubt that he would stay awake all night because definitely some weird energy was in here. He quickly texted Stefan with an update, saying that she had drifted off to sleep, but it definitely felt as if they had company. At that, Stefan responded that they would be checking in momentarily. Keller sat back and waited. Not sure what he would see, if anything, or if whatever they did would be done quietly, on the ethers, without any noticeable activity in this realm.

On the other hand, he hoped that he saw something. Some fight for life or a fight for something. He didn't know what that meant. He didn't know what it would look like, and right now it was an unknown in his world. And Stefan was a huge unknown as well, in terms of his abilities. Keller had heard a lot of rumors but had never seen any of it in action.

Settling in, it wasn't long before the room darkened and deepened into almost a ghostly atmosphere.

Keller's nerves went on full alert, and everything inside him wanted to get up and run. This was not what he'd expected. He thought that Stefan and Dr. Maddy would provide a calm and soothing presence, so he wasn't sure what the hell this was.

Just then Stefan's voice came in Keller's mind, soft and soothing, telling Keller to stay calm. Stefan and Dr. Maddy were both here, but the presence Keller felt was not theirs.

Keller winced at that and settled deeper into the shadows, knowing that he couldn't do much if Tandy were really in any psychic danger. That was what she was mostly afraid of. Him too. They had fears that nobody could stop whatever the hell was going on in Tandy's world or in the twins' world.

Keller considered all the times she'd woken up at night, unsure if she was alone or not alone, wondering if she'd even been raped. How did she survive that hell?

He hoped for her sake there wasn't any of that level of physical abuse, but, if her mom had been selling her own body for sex, it made sense that Isabella would at least be trying to do the same thing with her daughter. Although Isabella was also very jealous, so that might have kept her from using her daughter that way. Yet Isabella was so emotionally unstable, even without all the drugs, so who the hell knew how far things could go with her? According to Tandy, Isabella had utilized everything in her book to attract men.

Maybe that's what this was all about. Maybe she literally couldn't let go of Tandy. With Isabella aging—as we all were—maybe Isabella would do a bait-and-switch con? Posting Tandy's pic online, taking prepayment, then Isabella showing up to meet the customer. Keller shook his head. No matter how hard he tried to get into Isabella's mind, he couldn't imagine the evil levels that Isabella operated on.

Keller moved his seat closer to Tandy and settled into the chair and waited and watched, gently grabbing her hand, combining their energies. He noted a weird shift in the energy of the room, but it wasn't for him to understand fully what was going on. He listened for Stefan to speak telepathically to him. Only as he recognized Stefan's and Dr. Maddy's energy moving around the room did he realize some sort of an energy war was going on. Not even a war. Hell, he didn't know what he would call it. If he could join them, he would, but he had promised Tandy that he would stay here by her side, and that's what he would do. Whatever the hell was going on, it was happening in that weird energy state.

Even as he watched all around him, almost a screech sounded throughout the room. Then suddenly silence came. He wasn't sure what had just happened, but the hairs had raised on the back of his neck, and all he could imagine was what Tandy had gone through all these years at the hands of her psychotic mother. Then Isabella's voice blasted through his brain.

*I'm not psychotic, you asshole. It's you. … It's men like you who made me like this.*

His eyes opened wide, and he quickly searched the room, but he found no sign of Isabella's ghost.

Stefan spoke to him then. *Keep her talking. Dr. Maddy and I are running scans on Tandy's body, finding Isabella's hooks. So keep her mother busy. It may take some time to find the anchors and to remove them.*

Isabella laughed. *You are all so simple, every one of you, but men especially*, she cried out. *Do you really think I'm here for fun and games?*

Keller snorted. *So, this isn't a game? It sure feels like it.*

*I need something from my daughter, and you're not going to stop me from getting it.*

*What do you need?* he asked.

She laughed. *It doesn't matter. None of this nonsense matters, and I'm not leaving until I get it.*

*Maybe if you tell me what it is*, he offered, *I can help you get it.*

*You won't help me. You're just like everybody else. You're trying to stop me.*

*Stop you from what?* he asked, trying to stay calm, when he was anything but. *You're already dead.*

She laughed. *Am I really?*

He froze, thinking about that. *Are you saying that you aren't dead?*

*I guess that's for you to figure out, isn't it?* she declared, a sense of triumph in her tone.

*Your body was cremated.*

*Was it?* she asked. *Was it even my body?*

*I don't know,* he admitted, staring around in shock. *I thought it was.*

*Besides, it's only a body,* she noted. *My soul will always live on, nothing else.*

*And how crazy are you to even think that?* he cried out. *You should leave your daughter alone and give her a chance to have a life of her own without you. You've tormented her all her life. Isn't that enough?*

*She was supposed to be me,* she shared, with a laugh. *My body was already drenched with drugs at that point, only to realize that Tandy was getting more beautiful every day. I couldn't allow that to happen, not unless I could take over and could be her. As soon as that idea was born, I was obsessed with it. I will be her,* she stated, laughing again, *and she will have no say in it. She's weak, where I am strong.*

*So, she gets no life then, only you?*

*Yes, … just me. I gave birth to her. I gave birth to the twins. They're all mine.*

*And what about the twins?* he snapped, staring around the room, his anger spilling over. *Why did you give them such a horrible life?*

*Who said I did?* she asked, once again laughing. *You know nothing.*

*No, I don't know anything, but I do hope that you don't get a second chance.*

*Too late*, she said, with a cackle, *I already have.*

*No, you're not getting her. You're not getting the twins. I love them all. I will protect them all from the likes of you.* Keller softly squeezed Tandy's hand, reassuring her that he was here for her, with her.

*You can't stop me. I put this in motion a long time ago, cultivating boyfriends, and our gifts, and adding blood transfusions, so all would keep me young, eternal.*

*What about the drug use? That aged you, hindered your gifts.*

*I needed the drugs to get there*, she cried out in frustration. *I tried all kinds of drugs, but her father finally managed to make it happen.*

At that, Keller snapped back sharply, *What are you talking about?*

She laughed. *See? You don't know anything. You think it's all about me, but it's not. Well, … it is, but it's not*, she said in complete satisfaction, confusing the hell out of him. *It is about me, but it's also about her and what I want to be as her.*

*You can't be Tandy. This is her life, her chance to live freely.*

*It's my life … and mine alone. He promised me that he would find a way for me to live forever.*

*Tandy's father? Good God, at the expense of his own daughter? That can't be.*

*Yes, it can*, she snapped. *I spent a lifetime sorting this out. He chose me over her.*

*But you didn't succeed, so there's nothing for you now, ex-*

*cept to give in and to cross over.*

*No*, she roared, *I will not give in.*

Suddenly Keller felt a *whoosh* of hard energy, and Isabella let out a cry, screaming bloody murder. *I'll be back.* And, with that, her energy swept through the room like a tornado, and she was gone.

Instantly a calm took over the room, but it was a fake calm because Keller knew that Isabella could come back at any time.

He whispered into the room, "Dr. Maddy, Stefan? Was that you expelling Isabella's ghost?" There was an immediate acknowledgment in his mind.

*Yes, took both of us this time. Now we're going in to help Tandy.*

Keller watched as Tandy's body shifted in some weird way, almost as if making room for the two of them. Keller swallowed hard, realizing that's probably exactly what was going on. Stefan and Dr. Maddy were in Tandy's body, slowly moving through it, through her soul, through the very essence of what made Tandy so special.

Keller only now realized how truly special Tandy really was, and it was heartbreaking to watch her suffer, heartbreaking to see the terror that she'd been through, the insecurity and the confusion. She really had no idea who she even was at this point in time.

But Stefan whispered in Keller's mind, *No, but we're on the cusp of finding out. Keep calm because she's responding to your energy. If you get upset, she will get upset. It's essential now that you stay calm and quiet, and stay connected to her, keep holding her hand,* Stefan said, *because she's responding to your energy and to your touch and to your words.*

Dr. Maddy forewarned Keller, saying, *If anything goes*

*wrong at this stage, I don't know what will happen. I just know it won't be good for her or possibly for us. Stand firm and stay strong, Keller. We'll be back.*

And, with that, Stefan and Dr. Maddy left Keller's mind, and the room went seriously quiet, too quiet—as if all sense of life had disappeared, including Tandy's. He felt the fear chase through his system, as he stared down at her.

Then he reset his thoughts, thinking only good thoughts, thinking of the life he and Tandy and the twins could have. He smiled and placed his free hand atop their joined hands, and almost instantly he heard a *buzz*, felt a calmness through him and maybe her. She seemed to relax into the bed more, and he felt a smile in his mind and recognized it as Stefan.

*Good, help her. This battle isn't over yet*, he murmured.

*I have no idea what I need to do.*

*Just be there for her. She needs help. I don't know whether we'll do it on that plane or this one*, Stefan muttered, *but she can't do it without us.* And, with that, once again Stefan disappeared from Keller's mind.

Keller remained sitting beside her, holding her hand, as he watched for ripples made by the most incredible healers he knew proceed to battle for possession of Tandy's soul. He had just met this woman, and yet now he couldn't imagine not having her and the twins beside him.

Whether that was based on the fact that he was here with her right now, where it seemed they would be here forever, he didn't know. Yet, in truth, the actual circumstances no longer mattered. Tandy was his—as were those twins—and, whenever this mess was over, he would find some way to prove it to her and to them. And he could only hope that she would forgive him for whatever these people were doing to her now because, God help him, he didn't know what he would do if she didn't.

STEFAN MOVED SILENTLY through the shadows of Tandy's mind. He felt Dr. Maddy moving swiftly, her energy silent and subtle, everybody quiet as they moved through what appeared to be almost a graveyard inside. Stefan couldn't believe what he saw, couldn't believe what he felt—or was not feeling. It's as if nobody was home, and yet he didn't know how that could possibly be. Somebody had to be here. If not, it just meant that Tandy was somehow restricted, had to be in a sectioned-off place, a compartmentalized place, like a child who'd been abused, hiding in the corner. As somebody who'd been taken over and was under possession, they tended to be walled in or something, but Stefan couldn't even see that.

Stefan had to keep his energy calm and quiet as he moved silently through this graveyard, trying to figure out what he was looking at. He felt Dr. Maddy's curiosity at the same time. They were looking for energy, they were looking for heat, they were looking for something that didn't belong. So far, he hadn't found anything that *did* belong, and that was so bizarre. He recalled everything, the conversations he'd had with Tandy, trying to figure out what this was.

She had shared how she never felt secure when she went to bed, and she always woke up, sore, stiff, sometimes her body feeling sexually violated, yet without any idea of what had gone on. And she knew that she had been drugged while she was younger. Some of it had continued, even when she was a little bit older. Even while living at her grandmother's, Tandy still suffered through those issues, although that didn't mean that her grandmother was involved by any means.

Once these entities had hooks in your system, they had permanent ways to enter—until the hooks were removed. Yet, with the hooks in place, these nefarious entities could take over your body, at least parts of your body, depending on the strength of their psychic energy, and it didn't matter where you were physically located. That's what some people tended to forget, and this case wasn't a simple one with an easy answer. It would be a whole lot more convoluted than that.

As Stefan walked through what seemed to be shadows upon shadows upon shadows, he felt Dr. Maddy touch him. He immediately turned in her direction, and there ahead was a glowing light. Finally that should be where Tandy was hiding, and, if they could coerce her out, they could help her see that she was in control of this body, that she was the one who did what she needed to do to get rid of her mother.

As they moved closer and closer, the light just kept getting farther away.

Stefan shifted energies, moving by thought alone, right to where the glow was. Only to have it once again be a long way away. He stopped, realizing it was an illusion, a mirage. Dr. Maddy, at his side, her form strong, clear, and pure, was just as confused as he was. They were in a world with dark trees, a world of dark shadows, with very little light, very little anything.

He felt Tandy's chest rise and fall with slumber. A forced slumber, which he wasn't even sure she realized wasn't of her making, but that of her mother's. He had no way to know for sure, but, from what he saw and felt on an energetic level, something was very unnatural about all this.

If Isabella was trying to take possession of Tandy's body, did Isabella have prior experience with this? Knowledge of how to do this? Stefan had never tried it. They'd been up against several cases with some similarities one way or another, but it had never gone like this. He didn't understand what *this* even was.

Once again, Dr. Maddy tapped his energy, blending with his, so there was more of a mind-meet.

*I've never seen anything like this,* she whispered.

He agreed, knowing they would never get to that glowing space because it just kept moving. *Think of illusions or mirrors,* he murmured.

*I have been, and I still don't see any common sense in this. I can't make heads nor tails of it.*

*No, but somebody somewhere has been playing with Tandy's system, probably since she was a child. Did we ever check for hooks or anchors or possessions in the twins' systems?*

*No,* Dr. Maddy replied. *I ran some basic checks to confirm they were physically healthy, and they are, but I never looked any deeper.*

*And yet we didn't intend to go this deep with Tandy either,* he pointed out.

*I'm not sure we're deep,* she noted. *I think we're back to this illusion, and we're only being shown what we're allowed to see.*

He thought about that for a moment and agreed. *But where does that leave us?*

*With somebody playing games,* she stated, feeling irritation to go along with her frustration. *Do you think it's her, Tandy herself, some protection element?*

*No,* Stefan replied. *I don't. I think she has allowed this, but only because she was a child trusting her mother, not having skills yet with her gifts. Her mother did this, long ago.*

*What about her father?*

*I don't know,* he admitted. *I don't understand exactly what we have here.*

*Neither do I,* she whispered. *I'm trying to run a scan on her actual physical body to confirm that it's all okay. That's a standard run for us, but I can't even get anything to work here.*

Surprised, Stefan shifted his view again, looking for the same thing she was—for actual energy centers and then the bones and muscles that made her physical body function, and he saw no sign of it. In a way he could admire the deception here, except it just pissed him off more.

*Don't be angry at her,* Dr. Maddy said.

*No, ... I won't. Just an awful lot of care and attention went into creating this,* he murmured, *and somebody wanted to ensure that nobody could ever navigate in here, not without their permission.*

*Their permission,* she asked, *or their control?*

Damn good question, and one he didn't have an answer for. He moved through the maze of darkness and shadows. Somebody had done a hell of a job, and he wasn't sure that he was providing any benefit by being in here. Dr. Maddy finally nudged him, and he turned to see still only sheer darkness, and she made a motion to leave. He closed his eyes and stepped out.

When he opened his eyes though, he found himself still in the shadows.

Startled, he looked around and saw Dr. Maddy staring at him, surprised, and he felt the beginnings of fear. He shook his head at that, and, with a wave of his hand, he made everything in front of them disappear, to bring them back to Tandy's room. Only things changed forms. Changed and shifted in a weird way, but it did not release them from the maze. He frowned as he looked around. How could that be? How could anybody have that level of control and, more so, even when Isabella wasn't here?

*A fail-safe*, Dr. Maddy whispered. *It is a fail-safe.*

*It's possible*, he conceded, and he had certainly set up similar things in other people in order to keep others out from where they were causing trouble. *It's fascinating.*

*Sure*, she noted in a light tone. *However, I would rather be fascinated outside of this bloody darkness.*

And he agreed. He looked around, then at her. *Somehow, we've been sucked into the same imagery.*

She nodded. *That's never happened before, and we've never been trapped like this.*

*What about the twins though?* he pointed out. *They do that all the time.*

Startled, she looked at him and then nodded. *True, they've created the world that we step in and out of.*

*But it's their world, and we're locked into their imagination. They created their world, and they allowed us to visit when they want. I would love to have their energy right now to combat this, but it's too dangerous for them.*

*True. And what we have here is Isabella's imagination at work*, Dr. Maddy suggested, her soft energy shifting and looking around.

*It's the same thing. The same bloody thing as Mark created*, Stefan noted. *It has to be.*

*Yet*, Dr. Maddy noted, *Mark was so strong, even at his young age, he built his own mirage to keep his mother out. Amazing.*

Stefan stared in wonder. *And Tandy? Does she have these amazing gifts too, just tamped down and hindered?*

Dr. Maddy nodded. *I'm betting she does. But do we dare tap into her energy?*

*No. Not yet. She's too fragile, as we can see the evidence of her mother's interference all around us. Okay, … so if we're locked into Isabella's image, that means …*

*We have believed something about it,* Dr. Maddy said, with a nod.

Stefan frowned. *That's another fascinating point because I didn't think we came in here with any preconceptions.*

*Of course we did,* Dr. Maddy stated, with a hearty laugh. *But we didn't think anybody else would have the ability to call us on them.*

He smiled at that. That was one thing about Dr. Maddy. She was always questioning, looking, and searching for answers, just like he was. He nodded and said, *So, we've been sucked into somebody else's psychosis, and now we're somehow connected, and it's not releasing us. So what do we do now?*

*Or we're thinking that it's not releasing us,* Dr. Maddy pointed out, *because we've given it that power.*

He nodded and gave a sweeping wave of his hand, as he normally would to dispel weaker energies. Yet it still didn't change the outlook. *It is fascinating,* he murmured.

*Yeah, it is,* Dr. Maddy conceded, as she turned slowly around and around in the space.

*What are you thinking?* he asked curiously.

*I'm wondering how this is related to the twins.*

*Do you think it is?*

*I don't see how it can't be,* she murmured. *Think about it. An incredible amount of energy is here, plus an incredible amount of ability in keeping—I won't say keeping us here because I don't think that's the intent. I think it's keeping this fabrication alive inside Tandy, to control her, a brainwashing on several levels.*

*But is Isabella the one fabricating this monster nightmare?*

*I don't know.* Dr. Maddy twisted to look at Stefan. *I'm not sure Isabella was that gifted. Maybe her husband was more powerful with his skills. Whoever it is may not even know either.*

*Meaning?*

*I just think it's very curious,* Dr. Maddy replied, *that so much talent is within the one family.*

*So, you're thinking it's Tandy again?*

*No, no,* Dr. Maddy clarified. *That isn't what I'm saying. I am wondering if her mother didn't put something in this and set it up when Tandy was a child to control her or to use her for something.*

*And yet Isabella used Tandy for visions and things all the time.*

*And that's also interesting because you would think that there wouldn't be any of that happening from looking around here. This is a graveyard. Did Isabella scare Tandy into submission by subjecting her daughter to this?*

He looked around at the shadows. *So maybe this was where Isabella had Tandy come to find the answers that she needed for the people who were paying.*

*Possibly,* Dr. Maddy conceded, *or this is where Tandy came to* not *give her mother the answers that these people were looking for.*

*Ooh,* Stefan replied, smiling at that. *I can almost see Tandy doing that.*

*Yes, I can definitely see her doing that,* Dr. Maddy agreed, with a big smile. *If you're trying to get away from somebody, and somebody else is trying to manipulate you into doing something you don't want to do, what response can you give them?*

*You do everything you can to get away,* Stefan suggested,

with a nod.

*My question is, why does it look like a graveyard?*

*Did Tandy construct this to scare away her mother?*

*Oh my,* muttered Dr. Maddy. *It fits with the level of skills I would think Tandy the child had, before her mother smothered them. Yet this trick certainly wouldn't have gotten her any food.*

He winced. *We have to consider Tandy in this situation at the age of eight or thereabouts. She had been a desperate child, looking for answers, looking for a way to control the craziness that her world had become, and, if you thought like a child, then maybe this was just a place for her to hide from her mother.*

*If this was her hiding spot,* Dr. Maddy noted, studying it, *it's pretty scary.*

*Or maybe it was her hiding spot* until *Isabella found it.* At that mention, the air started to lighten around them, and he nodded. *Now look at that,* he said softly.

*I'm liking her mother less and less.*

*I never liked her mother,* Stefan declared, staring at the world as it changed in front of them. *Definitely something is happening here but not enough for us to understand.*

*And I think that's why we aren't being allowed out yet,* she offered, *and I know that probably isn't what you want to hear, but I think we're not being allowed to leave because somebody wants us to understand something.*

He looked at her, startled, and then slowly nodded. *I can see that too,* he murmured. *So, what is it that they're trying to show us?*

*God only knows,* she muttered. *Everything here is just so messed up.*

*Yet messed up on purpose,* he stated. And, with that, he sent out a message to the space around them. *Show us what you want us to know.*

Almost immediately the air around them lightened even more, and, as he turned, he saw things glowing on the far side, a lot of something glowing. Moving with Dr. Maddy quietly at his side, he approached the area where the glow came from, stopping just short of it.

He didn't understand what he was looking at. *Dr. Maddy?*

*I have no idea.*

They moved silently forward and to what appeared to be—he didn't want to say eggs, but—eggs, huge eggs, maybe dinosaur eggs or something along that line, depending on the age of the child leading them in this direction. *Eggs.* He couldn't quite get that concept out of his mind.

*Think of them more as pods*, Dr. Maddy suggested.

Instantly he saw it. *Good God*, he muttered.

Together they approached the pods, searching for answers as to what exactly was going on here. As they approached the first one, he saw not necessarily the force of it but almost a supernatural futuristic setting for it. He frowned at it, then looked back toward Dr. Maddy, a question shimmering around him. But Dr. Maddy had no clue what they were looking at either.

He called out again. *We need more.*

Instantly the light spread out, and he saw so many more of these pods. Frowning, he went closer and closer, studying each one. It made no sense to him. What the devil were they? But as he stood in front of one, he noticed not a movement but water droplets gathering on the pod. It startled him. He tentatively reached out a hand and cleared the condensation off the surface. As he looked inside, his heart froze.

He gasped, seeing a body inside and a label on the pod: Chattanooga. He checked the two pods nearby and found one body inside each, but one labeled Joplin and the other Tuscaloosa. A little farther down, he reached some pods with names on them. *Gwen.* Tandy's grandmother. He saw other names, whether first or last, Stefan didn't know. But when he got to two pods labeled Mark and Matthew, he pointed. *We need to update Keller.* Then Stefan waved over Dr. Maddy, who appeared at his side.

Dr. Maddy went still, and she stared down into the darkness with him. *Good God,* she whispered. Instantly she disappeared.

No one was left here but Stefan. He called out, *Dr. Maddy, Dr. Maddy.*

There was nothing, not a sense of her, not a sense that she had ever even been here. He spun around, looking for her, but there was nothing. Yet beside him, one of the pods slowly opened. He reached over to take a look at what was in it, when something hard pushed him from behind, almost as if he were being forced into this pod. All of a sudden he was inside, and the top half slammed down tight over his head.

After that, he knew no more.

DR. MADDY SNAPPED back into the overnight room. She bolted to her feet and spun around in shock. Immediately Keller was at her side.

"What's the matter?" he asked quietly, frowning. "What happened?"

She looked at him, stunned, and then slowly turned to look around the room. "Good God," she muttered, rubbing her eyes.

"I didn't even see you come in here," he murmured, staring at her oddly.

"No, I don't remember coming in either," she whispered, wiping her face. "Christ, I don't know what's going on in there, but it's something we have never seen before."

"Which we already concluded before tonight," Keller stated, with a note of humor.

She shot him a dark look. "Yes, but the fact that Stefan didn't come back with me is a concern."

"Okay, what can I do to help?" he asked.

She blinked at him several times, turned to look at the sleeping woman, and muttered, "I'm not sure there's anything we can do."

"If he's hurt or in trouble, we have to help him."

She gave him a wry look. "You have no idea what that means."

"No, I don't," he whispered forcefully. "But Tandy's been making some very strange sounds, almost as if she was terrified."

"Interesting." She turned to Tandy. "She's obviously reacting to something."

"And she's not happy about it."

"No, neither are we," she declared. "I'm not sure exactly what is going on." Dr. Maddy ran her fingers through her hair. "I need to go back in."

"Is it that easy?"

"I hope so." She walked to the door and frowned, as she looked around the room again. "I'll go back in, and I'll see you in a little bit."

"But wait," Keller said. "What if you and Stefan *both* don't come back? How long do I wait for you? Who do I call next?"

Dr. Maddy grimaced. "No one."

Keller frowned, totally speechless.

She added, "If at least one of us is not back in an hour or so, the only help I suggest is that you and Tandy and the twins link energies. It would entail Tandy walking in the ethers, like she did to contact Stefan. She could follow his energy trail and probably find him in the maze that is her mind. However, …"

"However?" Keller repeated.

"Tandy and the twins are too fragile to attempt this, and you can't go in alone." And, with that, she exited the bedroom.

Obviously something really bad was going on. He rejoined Tandy, sitting beside her, grabbing her hand gently, and began to whisper to her, just trying to amp up their connection. "It's okay, sweetheart. It's okay. Whatever this is, we can handle it." He watched as she almost battled, struggled against some restraint of some kind. He had no idea what was going on, and, because of that, it scared him even more. He wanted to call Dr. Maddy back here and ask her what he should do, but he knew she had more important issues on her hands at the moment.

And the fact that Stefan was somewhere in there, without a connection to Dr. Maddy, was mind-boggling in itself. As far as most people were concerned, Stefan was the expert in this. But then again, everybody was an expert—until they came up against something they didn't know how to handle. Right now it seemed that none of them knew how to handle any of this. It terrified him to think that Tandy was in there fighting, waging some battle all on her own. And yet was it a battle of her making, or was she fighting off someone?

He moved closer to her and whispered encouragement to her, "Please keep fighting, honey, but don't fight against them, fight for you and for the twins."

He had no idea why he was even saying that, but he felt he needed to say something. Then he felt the urge to hug her gently, just being closer to her. "Take it easy, sweetie. I don't know what's going on, but Stefan and Dr. Maddy are there to help you, so remember that."

She whimpered in her sleep once again.

He kept repeating it, over and over again, reminding her that they were there to help and that she should let them. "We don't know what's happening, but they can help you," he murmured again. "They can help you and the twins."

Suddenly came this weird exhale, as if all the air was coming out of Tandy, not just from her lungs but from her body, as if ejecting something massive from her system. He wasn't at all sure what to think, but, when she took another deep breath and settled within herself, into almost a peaceful sleep, he realized that it was a good thing.

A few minutes later, Dr. Maddy walked back into the room, checking out Tandy.

Keller pointed, smiling. "She seems to be calm now. I'm not sure what you did, but …"

"I didn't do anything," she murmured, her tone harsher than he'd expected.

"What's happened?" Keller asked. "Where's Stefan?"

"Stefan, … Stefan is not back."

Keller frowned. "But didn't you go in to help, whatever that means?"

"Yes, I did," she confirmed, as she took a deep breath. "I went looking, but I couldn't find him."

"How is that possible?" he asked, staring at her in shock.

She shook her head. "I'm not sure. I couldn't even find the same space again," she admitted. "I do have other techniques. I'll return to see if I can find the last place where

I saw Stefan. I just wanted to check how Tandy was doing."

"I think she's fine right now. She had this absolutely massive exhale, as if every bone in her body was just letting go, as if she had released something major from her psyche."

Dr. Maddy stared at him funny. "I wonder if it was *released* or *ingested*," she said in an odd tone. He stared at her, wondering what the hell that meant, when she turned and walked right back out again.

"Wait," he called out, when she was just about to close the door. "Is there anything I can do?"

She looked at him for a long moment and then shook her head. "Maybe, but I don't know what. I just need to get Stefan back."

"Is it possible that he's on the ethers?" he asked her. "That is his home, isn't it? So surely he's not lost."

She stared at him for a long moment and nodded. "Yes, but we always come up against things that we've never seen before, and occasionally we come up against something that's dangerous to everyone. It appears as if that's what we've found in this case." She stared at the woman in the bed. "If she wakes up, let me know."

"Yeah, and how do you want me to do that?"

She smiled at him. "You probably have as much telepathic ability and energy-working gifts for this as we do."

"No, I don't," he argued. "I don't walk in the shadows like you guys do."

"No, but she does." Dr. Maddy turned to look at Tandy. "If she wakes up, tell me, because right now, up is down, and down is up. I might need her help. I'm going back in to find Stefan—if I can."

And, with that, she was gone again.

# CHAPTER 19

T ANDY FIDGETED RESTLESSLY in her sleep. Images of her childhood, images of nightmares, all wafted through her brain, even as she tried hard to stay asleep. Yet it seemed to be never-ending nightmares instead of the peaceful sleep and the rest that she needed rather desperately. She felt herself surfacing, with something slamming into her with a roar. Someone screamed, *No!* Startled, she succumbed again to the nightmares but didn't know why or what was happening. Yet she felt this odd sense of familiarity to it. As she lay here in a dream state, she saw images of her childhood long gone, images of her childhood that she didn't even want to recognize as being real. Nothing good for her was in these memories.

She sensed something familiar out there though, and something wrong too. Wrong that she also recognized as being unfamiliar. She'd had enough wrongs in her world to last her a lifetime. But this felt different.

*That's because it is different*, said someone close to her.

She blinked, and there was Dr. Maddy. She studied her for a moment and then smiled. *Hi, are we in the twins' room?*

*No*, Dr. Maddy replied, *we're in your world.*

*Oh.* She frowned. *Not a good place to be.*

*I can see that*, she replied, with a note of humor. *But you appear to be … I don't want to say comfortable, yet comfortable.*

*Definitely not comfortable*, Tandy clarified, *but I do know this place.*

*And do you know what goes on in this place?*

*It's my space, so I should*, she stated, staring at her.

*Yes, yes you should*, Dr. Maddy agreed, with a nod. *Did you know that Stefan was in here too?*

*Oh good*, she said, *maybe he can help me with a few things.*

*I'm sure he would be happy to help you, but he appears to have found a corner of your world that needed investigating.*

*Oh, that's not good*, Tandy muttered, feeling dread deep inside. *There are some places here that nobody should see.*

Dr. Maddy nodded. *Maybe you could show me where those places are.*

*No, no, no, no*, Tandy cried out. *You don't understand. They are dangerous places.*

*Yet they are your places.*

*They* were *my places, but then … they became Isabella's, and she's always lurking in the shadows.*

*How often does your mother come in here and see these places?*

*All the time. Lately … she's always in there*, she muttered. *It's one of the reasons why I had to lock everything down.*

*Is this what you meant about going to extreme measures to keep her out?*

She pondered that, not remembering when she had said such a thing. *If I said it, then maybe*, she muttered self-consciously. *I'm really not comfortable talking about my mother in here.*

*I understand. That's okay too*, Dr. Maddy stated. *It would help if I knew where Stefan was though.*

*Was he in here doing something? God only knows what you guys think you can do.*

*You tell us what you think we can do.*

*If you could stop everybody from coming in here, that would be lovely.*

*Ah, what do you mean by everybody coming in here?* Dr. Maddy asked curiously.

She stared at her. *I'm sure you've seen how many people just seem to come and go into my space,* she muttered. *Every time I see one, I have to lock it down. I just can't handle the people constantly trampling around down there.*

*When you say,* people?

*Men,* she stated.

After a moment of comprehension, Dr. Maddy smiled. *Of course, and I understand that completely.*

*Right,* Tandy replied, *but my mother never did.*

*Why is that?*

*Because men were to be used, information was to be gotten, and money or anything else that you needed came from men, but you could never really give them control. Because if you gave them control, they took it and ran with it. She told me that women were more powerful, but they had to learn those lessons first.*

*So, is it only men who come to visit you in here?*

She frowned, thought about it, and shook her head. *No, not only men, but mostly men.*

*Okay, and can you tell me where you locked all them down, so they couldn't do any harm?*

*Ha,* she muttered. *I wish I could. But that would mean going in and seeing them, and I don't like doing that.*

*You might not, but I want to see them,* Dr. Maddy said.

Tandy stared at her. *It's not very pretty,* she noted cautiously.

*Right,* Dr. Maddy nodded. *I can't imagine that it is. At*

*the same time, I don't think that they should stay there. Surely you want to get rid of all that?*

*I would love to, but it's not possible*, Tandy declared, with a headshake. *My mother made very sure of that.*

*Ah, we're back to that mother again. The all-seeing mother*, Dr. Maddy said, with a half-smile. *You know what I think though? I think that you are far stronger than your mother.*

*I want to be, but she's scary.*

Immediately Tandy tensed, as if that little girl was once again terrified. Dr. Maddy seemed to understand, and a warm hug came Tandy's way, which settled her down immediately. *You're not like her.*

*No, I'm not*, she agreed. *I would never do something like that to you.*

*Good*, she muttered. *It seems everybody just wants to hurt everybody else, and that's not the way it should be.*

*No, it shouldn't*, Tandy murmured.

*But I want to see where you have put in all your little security bits and pieces.*

*But it makes me feel uncomfortable*, Tandy shared, *and I don't think I want to show you.*

Dr. Maddy nodded. *Of course. I guess if you were to show me, you would feel as if you were losing control.*

Tandy had to think about that and then shrugged. *I don't know. But any time you mention going there, it makes me want to throw up.*

*Okay*, she agreed. *I can see that would be rough. How much does your mother have to deal with any of this part of your world?*

*I don't let my mother in there at all*, she stated.

*Is she in here now?*

*No.* Tandy's tone was adamant and instant. *This is not a*

*good place for her.*

*No, I would imagine it's not,* Dr. Maddy replied. *Can you tell me who else has been in here?*

Tandy waved her hand, and she felt the miles between the adult Tandy and the child Tandy disappearing rapidly, as she aged younger and younger.

Dr. Maddy whispered, *It's all right, just stay calm.*

*I'm calm, but I feel threatened.*

*Yes, I can see that,* she said. *Remember that I'm not here to hurt you.*

*And yet,* she muttered, her face taking on a pensive look, *I don't feel as if you're here to save me either.*

A startled note of surprise came from Dr. Maddy, who then smiled. *That's because I think you're perfectly capable of saving yourself.*

Tandy stared at her for a long moment. *I want to believe you, but I don't know if that is true.*

*Of course,* Dr. Maddy noted, with a gentle smile on her face. *Yet, when we come from a position of love, everything is possible.*

Tandy frowned at her, feeling as if the years were going by—now younger men and a younger her, long buried inside—with conversations, flashing pain, anger, fury, all of it coming together. Yet it didn't seem to affect Dr. Maddy at all.

It was almost like watching a movie beside her. *Let it go,* Dr. Maddy urged. *If you have more of these, bring them out, and let's get them gone.*

*Get them gone?* Tandy asked, startled. *Is that even a thing?*

*It absolutely is a thing,* she murmured. *We can release all this, and you won't have to live with it anymore.*

*I don't want to live with any of them,* Tandy wailed, tears forming in her eyes. *The memories, they hurt.*

*Of course they do.*

Such gentleness filled the woman's soft tone that Tandy felt more tears forming.

*And, when there are tears, let those go too,* Dr. Maddy murmured.

*It's not that easy.*

*It's also not that hard, not once you start,* Dr. Maddy suggested.

Tandy stared at her, feeling a wish to fight, a wish to snap back at her comment, as if Dr. Maddy couldn't possibly understand.

*You're right. I can't possibly know what you're going through or what you've been through.*

It seemed as if Dr. Maddy was reading Tandy's mind.

Dr. Maddy nodded. *What I do know is that you don't have to continue going through it. We can put away all these memories, and we can lock them up so they don't hurt you. If that is what you want, it is definitely something we can do.*

*But then I would forget,* she said, *and, if I do, what if all this happens over and over again?*

*It won't,* Dr. Maddy declared. *None of this has to happen ever again. Your mother controlled so much of your world back then, but she doesn't now.*

*But she does,* Tandy argued, *she's constantly trying to get back into my world.*

Dr. Maddy smiled. *Trying is not the same thing as* succeeding. *You have the right to say yes or no.*

*And yet what I say doesn't seem to matter to her. She's there. She's in my mind constantly.*

*But not for long, not when we purge all the scary memories she planted here, just to manipulate you,* Dr. Maddy murmured. *You have a lot here that we need to deal with, but, as soon as we do, Isabella can't get into your space anymore.*

Tandy desperately wanted to believe Dr. Maddy, she really did, but it just seemed too far-fetched.

Dr. Maddy nodded. *You've been lied to by one of the biggest con artists going. She's programmed your world to be what she wanted it to be, but only for her own sake, not for your sake, not for the twins.*

Tandy stared at Dr. Maddy. *She would say the opposite. She would say it was to keep us safe.*

*But did she keep you and the twins safe?* Dr. Maddy asked. *Aren't you the little girl who couldn't sleep at night because you didn't know who would try to get into your room? You didn't know who would get into your room or your mind. All invited by your mother.*

Tandy felt waves and waves of energy coming at her, memories hitting her of hiding in closets and crawling outside her bedroom window, all to avoid her mother coming home with strangers. Sleeping outside in the dog house so that nobody would know she was there, all of it.

Dr. Maddy just nodded. *I don't want to make you feel bad, or sad, or frightened. I just want you to remember. No judgment, just a sense of you. You don't have to keep criticizing anything you did to save yourself from a drug-addled parent, not anymore.*

*But I'm really scared she'll come back, she'll bring the bad men back with her.*

*Isabella is gone. She is dead. She is gone.*

*You keep telling me that, but she's not gone.*

*Then maybe you should lock her up,* Dr. Maddy suggested. *Lock her up just like you did all those men.*

Tandy paused and looked at her, the idea never once

having crossed her mind.

Dr. Maddy nodded. *Isabella has no right to do anything to you now, so, if she's infringing on your space or doing something that you consider harmful, you can lock her up.*

Tandy brightened up with a big smile. *Do you think that would work?*

*Why not? Hasn't it worked on the men?*

*Yes, it has.*

*Good, so I don't know how often your mother comes to you, but the next time she does, all you have to do is lock her up.*

Tandy stared at her in wonder. *Could it really be that simple?*

*Yes, it can be that simple,* she acknowledged. *You do not have to be a victim all your life.*

*I wonder,* she murmured.

*You don't need to wonder anymore. You have the proof, and you have the knowledge, and you have incredible abilities.*

*My mother would say I was stupid and I was ugly, and she would never make any money off me.* She almost missed Dr. Maddy's wince. *I know. She wasn't a good mother, was she?*

*No, she really wasn't. It wasn't her job or her right to make money off you either,* Dr. Maddy shared. *That is not what good mothers do. Can you think of why it mattered to her? Of why she did that?*

*I don't think it was the money as much as the control. That's why she showed me how to lock up the men.*

*She showed you that?*

*Yes,* she said, looking at her. *She showed me lots of things. I don't think I ever did them quite right, and she was never really happy with the job I did. But, once she showed me, then I did the best I could. But she always used to get mad at me too.*

*Mad at you? Why?*

*Sometimes she would say that I would go too far, or I was supposed to leave them alone. I don't know,* Tandy muttered, *but I couldn't stop locking them up at that point. If they came into the house, and they looked at me oddly or they did something strange, I just knew that they would be a predator.*

*So, you locked them up when they threatened you?*

*I couldn't lock them up until they approached, could I?* she asked. *I couldn't go around locking everybody up, and, if I did, … it was only those who were a threat. I don't want people around me, but I only locked up the predators.*

*Of course,* Dr. Maddy noted, with a smile. *And those were the ones you needed to watch out for.*

*Exactly.* She smiled and then waved her hands. *I haven't had to lock up anyone for a very long time now.*

*Good, who was the last one?*

She frowned, then looked around. *I don't know.*

*What do you mean, you don't know?* Dr. Maddy asked, her tone a little harsher.

*Some people come, and some people go, and I have these safeguards in here. So, once in a while they get triggered, and I don't know if they're getting locked up or not,* she muttered. *And I haven't looked.*

*You might have to. Stefan came in to help you, and your safeguards locked him up.*

She stared at her. *I wouldn't have done that unless he was being a predator,* she stated, narrowing her gaze at her.

*I guess it depends on what you consider being a predator. He came here to help, and he was here to help you because you were struggling so much.*

*But maybe he didn't ask to come in,* she said in a harsh tone. It was as if the child in Tandy was fighting with the adult, and even the child Tandy could sense the horror at the thought of having locked Stefan up. Surely that couldn't happen. Stefan had been good to her. And yet she also knew that she had made safeguards upon safeguards to confirm she was protected, and, should anybody get back into that space of hers, she really had no option.

Dr. Maddy suggested, *Maybe you need to check, and then we'll know whether it's him or not, and you can let him out.*

*I don't know how to let him out*, she said, with fear in her face. *I can't let him out because, if I do, I will have to let out everybody.*

*No*, Dr. Maddy said, a wave of love coming across her. *That's fear talking.*

Tandy shook her head. *If it's fear, it's fear for a reason*, she cried out. *I can't just let everybody go. They'll come back after me again.*

Now she felt the child inside screaming for protection, screaming for help. Dr. Maddy's warm comforting embrace wrapped her up. *You'll be fine. We'll both be just fine. I'm here to protect you.*

*You might think you can protect me*, Tandy said, with such sadness, *but it's not possible. No, I won't let anybody out. I can't.*

And, with that, she made a motion with her hand, and the room completely disappeared.

# CHAPTER 20

T ANDY WOKE UP with a start, almost jumping out of the bed, searching for the problem, only to find Keller there with his arms out, holding her and easing her under the covers again.

"Are you okay?" he asked.

She blinked several times and then stared at him. "I don't know. I'm not sure that I am." He frowned, and she nodded. "But I think, … I think it's worse than we thought. Oh God," she muttered, as the panic started to settle.

The door opened, and Dr. Maddy walked in.

"I'm sorry," Tandy cried out, "I'm so, so sorry. I didn't mean to."

Dr. Maddy nodded. "It's okay," she whispered, walking closer and wrapping her arms around Tandy. "We'll get there."

"Are you sure? I'm terrified."

"I get that. It would help a lot though if I could have gotten through to you the first time. I didn't think it would be that simple, but I was hoping." She smiled over at Keller. "Tandy has a reflex in place that she has utilized for probably most of her growing years, and it's something that she forgot to take down, or maybe doesn't want to take down because, in her mind, she's still not safe. And something, maybe even the death of her mother, but something has triggered that security system, for want of a better word."

"I don't think her death triggered it," Tandy replied. "I just think that at the moment I'm fighting something."

"What you're fighting is a lot of things, and one of those things is the fact that your mother has been trying to communicate with you. I'm not sure why or what it is that she's trying to do, if anything," Dr. Maddy added.

"Of course she is up to something," Tandy muttered. "You know she always is up to something."

"I know something is going on, but what I don't know is whether you potentially have locked up your mother into that system, and she's just trying to get loose, or is she already loose and haunting you now?"

Tandy sagged back onto the bed and stared at her in shock. "Good God."

"That's the thing. Your security system is really powerful, and I'm not sure how many people you have utilized it on in this way, but I'm pretty sure it's not good for you. It would explain your fatigue and the blackouts that you tend to ignore."

Tandy winced at that. "How did you even know about that?"

"I know about it because I have seen something close to this before, and I have experienced it as well."

"But what has this got to do with the twins?"

"That I'm not sure of yet," Dr. Maddy replied, "but I do need to go back and have another talk with little Tandy."

"She's not really interested in talking," Tandy shared.

"No, she might not be, but you have been allowing your inner child to control your adult world. Is that what you want for her and for you?"

Tandy stared at her for a long moment and then slowly

shook her head. "I guess I can't, can I?"

"No, you can't," Dr. Maddy agreed. "That's not healthy for either of you. We often have an inner child who likes to dominate, but giving them that kind of power when you grow up is a whole different story. Other things in life are probably far more important."

"Yet that inner child is terrified," Tandy whispered.

"Of course she is. She's been hurt, and she found a way to make it all go away, and that in itself is pretty magical. So, now we need to help her realize that there are other ways to live where you aren't completely under the control of just fear, and then you can relax and can let her go."

"Let her go? How do I let myself go?" Tandy asked.

"I'm not saying get rid of her. She is who you are, and she is who you were," Dr. Maddy corrected. "And we all know that inner child has a power that most of us don't recognize, and, in your case, your inner child created something pretty amazing."

"So why can't we just leave it alone?"

"Because I think you're hurting other people."

"But I'm sure they deserve to be hurt."

"Not everybody," Dr. Maddy suggested.

"So, why can't it just stay as it is, as a safeguard against those who deserve to be hurt?" she asked hesitantly. She could tell Keller was listening intently and still trying to figure out what all this meant. She just looked at him and explained, "It's really a bit of a mess. I told you before that you're probably better off without me."

"And I told you before it's not that easy to forget about you, to not see you every day," Keller countered. "Would it help to understand you better if you shared this with me? Yes." He looked over at Dr. Maddy to see her give an ever-so-slight shake of her head, so he sat back and smiled. "However, you don't have to tell me anything. I'll be here for you and the twins, regardless."

She groaned. "I should probably just leave all this alone," she muttered. "It would be the best answer."

"No, it wouldn't," Dr. Maddy corrected, with a gentle smile. "What we want for you is to be healthy, fully functioning, and hopefully having a relationship with the twins."

"That would be great," Tandy said, then frowned. "Yet I don't understand why the twins are hiding away in their playroom."

"Likely for the same reason you hide away in your secret place," Dr. Maddy shared, "because of danger. They feel threatened. Probably because your mother wasn't exactly the easiest to deal with, and I imagine that they had some pretty rough days themselves."

"They did," Tandy agreed. "And they're scared."

"Sure, they are," Dr. Maddy confirmed. "They're scared and running. The question is, who are they scared of?"

"Not me," Tandy said. "I don't even know them."

"I think you remember them. And I think, when you triggered your own security system, because they're family, Mark might have reached out and realized that you had a stronger system or a better warning, so he's gone into hiding too."

She sagged back onto the bed, frowning again. "But that would mean we're connected."

"You already know you're connected," Dr. Maddy said. "They are your siblings, and you have already communicated with them in Mark's world. And now, because Mark knows that something is wrong and is scary out there, it seems that he's quite prepared to stay in the new world he's created. It's up to you to tell him that it's okay to come out."

With that, Tandy's breath gushed out in a big *whoosh.* "But that would mean I would have to believe it myself."

"Exactly," Dr. Maddy said, "and, in order for you to do that, you have to deal with your own history."

Tandy clenched her fists, only to realize she was hanging tightly onto Keller's hands. She stared down at his fingers, then back up at Dr. Maddy. "I'm not sure I can do that."

"I need you to try," Dr. Maddy said, "for the sake of Mark and Matthew if nobody else."

"And if I fail?"

"We'll give it a fair chance, and then we'll try it again," Dr. Maddy murmured. "Because some things in life are worth struggling for, until you meet with success."

"It doesn't feel like this is a success. Yet my little girl, the young me, is happy inside with our safeguards."

"No, she's not. She's living in fear, terrorized, and locking up everything in her world, even people who are trying to help her, like Stefan. And that is no way to live. That little girl will expire from stress sooner rather than later, without ever having had a chance to really live. She's never had a chance to truly enjoy a sunrise because she's too afraid of what the day might bring. She's never had a chance to enjoy a sunset because she's too afraid of the night. She deserves better."

Tandy felt her stomach heave with the truth of those words. "It was terrible growing up," she whispered. "There were so many monsters in my world."

"There were monsters because your mother allowed those monsters inside," Dr. Maddy declared, "and now your mother is gone."

Tandy frowned at that. "But she keeps coming back."

"To a certain extent it seems she keeps coming back, but it very well may be because she thinks that she has control of you or because she's a remnant of the childhood monster you keep believing is there."

"Maybe she keeps coming back," Tandy pointed out, "because she knows about my system and wants very much to get control."

"What would she gain by having control of your system?" Dr. Maddy asked.

"Everything," Tandy said, "absolutely everything. She is all about control. So, let me see if I have this right. You're saying that, because of my reflexes and my fears, the twins are affected by what happened to me?"

"Yes, quite possibly because they've experienced a lot of the same traumas, plus the fact that you've already been trying to protect them—once you realized they had similar problems."

"But how did I know that?" she asked.

"You learned it from them."

"But I've hardly had anything to do with them."

Dr. Maddy shook her head. "No, that's not true. You've hardly had anything to do with them in person, but on an energy level, you've been there for them the whole time. You know that. You know when you walked in, there was absolutely no need for a greeting, there was no need for an introduction. Mark knew who you were, and you knew who he was, as did Matthew. And they trusted you implicitly because you've been protecting them all this time."

Tandy sagged back onto the bed, tears in her eyes, and whispered, "I couldn't let anything happen to them."

"Of course not, and that's what's so special about this. You did it on a level that nobody could know, and you did it successfully."

"But how successful was it, if they won't come out now?"

"They won't come out because you taught them how dangerous it is to come out. So, it's up to you to teach them that it's safer now and that they can come back to their lives."

"But I would be lying," she said, looking at her.

"No, you wouldn't be lying. You would be telling them that the danger is gone and that your mother and all her boyfriends are gone."

When Tandy obviously wanted to cry out to the contrary, Dr. Maddy smiled. "I hear you loud and clear. You're about to tell me that they're not gone at all because Isabella's still around. So, what is it that you have to do?"

"I have to get rid of her," she muttered.

"And yet you can't, and why is that?" Dr. Maddy studied her closely, as her features settled into a pensive expression. "You can't get rid of her because you already have Isabella locked up too."

KELLER QUICKLY RACED out behind Dr. Maddy as she exited the room. He caught her in the hallway, as she stood here, her hands on her head, deep in thought. "What about Stefan?" he asked her urgently.

She turned, looked at him, then smiled. "He's locked inside too." When he blinked at her several times, she nodded. "The thing is, … he could get himself out but would need to do it in a way that won't hurt her, and that's where the challenge comes in. The best thing would be if she would release him." He turned, looked back at the room, and she nodded. "Something she doesn't seem anxious to do."

"But I don't think she understands what's happened," he noted.

"She, … the adult Tandy, might not understand, but the child Tandy certainly does."

"I am very confused right now," he admitted, staring at her.

"The good news is, I'm not so confused now," Dr. Maddy declared, "but a part of me is in awe, and I'm trying very hard to figure out a solution."

"What was that about her mother?"

"I'm not exactly sure. Maybe it was a shot in the dark. Maybe it was the truth. I don't really know," she murmured. "It is something that I believe though."

"You think Tandy's imprisoned her mother?"

"Her mother is a threat, and anybody who has been or who appeared to be a threat in her world, she imprisoned."

"Yeah, but we're not talking physically imprisoned?"

"God no, she imprisoned a part of them. A piece of their soul, a piece of their energy, whatever, it was her way of manifesting some sense of control."

"Would it have any effect on these people?"

"Potentially it could have made some go crazy. Some may have become deficient in some way. Some might not have understood what was going on, while others might have understood on an energy level but not truly realizing what was happening or why."

"And yet, maybe we shouldn't feel too sorry for them because they were a threat?" Keller suggested.

Her smile tilted as she looked at him. "And yet there is Stefan."

"Right, because he was trying to help."

"Right, and our visit triggered her defense mechanism," she added, "and believe me when I say, I do not blame her at all. She's done whatever she needed to do in order to survive."

"Christ," he muttered, staring at her. "What was her life like before if *this* was surviving?"

"Exactly," she said, nodding at him. "We have to consider the child."

"But I still don't understand the twins."

"And that is something I'm not sure about either." Dr. Maddy stared at him, her gaze turning toward the room where the twins were sleeping as always.

"You're saying that she may have had something to do with their current lockdown?"

"No, I'm saying that I think because of her fears, she contacted Mark and showed him how to protect himself and his brother."

"Crap," Keller muttered, as he stared from one room to the other. "So, how do we get them to decide that they're safe?"

"That will be one of the challenges," Dr. Maddy admitted, shaking her head. "I've never seen anything like it or anybody who could do anything like this."

"When you say *this*, … what do you mean?"

"She seems to just bounce into people's space and do what she needs to do, all because she's trying to keep herself and the twins safe, so anybody who poses a threat will get locked up in her graveyard of pods in her mind." She frowned at him and added, "Yet you appear to be safe from that bias, even though you are a man, which she sees as all predators mostly."

"I'm not sure I'm safe at all," Keller muttered. "Is anybody safe? Is she killing people?"

"No, no, no, not at all."

He felt something inside him simmer back down again. "Okay, well thank God for that," he muttered.

She smiled. "What she's doing is a hell of a job."

"Maybe, but you're also making it sound as if it's something she shouldn't be doing."

"It's something I just wish she didn't feel that she needed to do—a big difference there."

"Pardon me if I'm not really seeing it," he shared, staring at her.

"Are you scared of her?"

"No, I'm not scared of her at all. I just wish I understood what was going on, so I could help her."

"The fact that you want to help is perfect, but it might require your going back in that room and talking to her."

"Talking? Would that help?" he asked. "I feel as if she's been talked to enough. The men in the world out there have talked to her and have shown the deficits in the world."

"Meaning?"

"Meaning that men probably talked to her," Keller explained, with a wave of his hand, "as they tried to get closer. Or didn't talk at all and just did whatever they wanted."

"And it's likely," Dr. Maddy noted, "that something did happen, and that's what started it. It could be that Isabella triggered this because it's obvious she's been a predator all her life."

He didn't even know what to say to that. "Isabella wants to take over Tandy's life, doesn't she?"

"I'd think so, but that won't happen." Dr. Maddy smiled at him. "Nothing is easy about the work we do.

Everybody who comes here to me and to see Stefan is hindered in some way, and what we try to do is empower them to free themselves of the underlying cause for all this stress and chaos, so they can move forward and can get free from it."

"Okay, I'm listening," Keller said, "and believe me that I love hearing it. I just don't quite understand how or what we're supposed to do now for Tandy."

"We need to convince her that she's safe."

"I don't know how to do that."

"No, and, at the moment, I don't either," she admitted. "I know that Stefan will be in there trying to figure it out himself as well."

"So, he's really trapped in there?"

"A part of him is in there," she pointed out. "Just a part, and, yes, I did panic in the beginning," she shared, and then she laughed. "Fear gripped me in there, and the fact that she could trigger my fear is pretty amazing." He looked at her, and she smiled with a nod. "Yes, the child Tandy's creation as a child is amazing. She's amazing. It's just a sign of how strong she is and how quickly she can take control. If anybody were to ever truly harm her, I can't imagine what the consequences would be."

"It wouldn't be good, that's for sure," Keller stated.

"No, it sure wouldn't." She pondered it. "Look. I'll take a breather, take a few minutes to stop and think. I want you to go back in the overnight room, spend time with her, and just be you. Be the you who is falling in love with her, in love with the twins, the you who wants her and the boys safe and sound and available to live a normal life out here," she suggested with a bright smile.

"That's not hard," he muttered. "I didn't really plan on

that, you know."

"I know," she said, "and that's what makes it all the more delicious. When we fall, we tend to fall hard, and the fact that you've fallen for somebody—for three somebodies—with this kind of energy is fascinating."

"No, no it's not," he muttered. "They deserve the best."

"But you are the best for them because it also means that your energy, your spiritual and emotional side, knows it can handle her and the twins." And, with that, she patted him on the shoulder and added, "Think about that, and I'll be back in a few minutes." And with that she headed to her office.

He wasn't even sure what she would do there, but it was left to him to go back in the overnight room and confirm that Tandy was doing okay.

As he walked back into the room, he saw her standing at the window, staring out. "Hey," he greeted her. "Should you be up?"

"I'm not an invalid," she murmured, as she turned to look back at him. "Is she planning on locking me up?" Her comment came out of the blue, and he stared at her in surprise, then watched her shoulders relax as she took in his reaction. "That's good to know," she muttered.

"Why would you even think that?"

She raised her hands. "Because that's what people do when they're scared."

"Did you mean to scare her?"

"No, of course I didn't mean to scare her," Tandy stated, turning to glare at him, "but apparently I scare people easily."

"If you're locking people up, that is kind of scary."

"What about you? Are you scared?"

"No, because I would never do anything to hurt you."

And, with that, her shoulders relaxed yet again. "I guess that's the difference, isn't it?" she muttered. "Anybody who has hurt me appears to be paying a penalty."

He just smiled, wrapping an arm around her. "I wouldn't worry about a penalty for those who have hurt you," he murmured. "Instead let's confirm that you're safe and sound and that we don't have to deal with any of this in the future."

She just nodded, but her gaze was ever watchful.

He didn't have a clue how to make her realize that he wasn't a threat. Even saying that he wasn't a threat wouldn't help because those were just words. "What would you really want to do?" he asked, suddenly studying her.

"I want to be free."

And, at that, he started to smile. "What if all that energy that you've been utilizing to keep all these predators locked up was burning through you, and effectively trapping you in the process, so that you could never be free, and there was nothing you could possibly do to get free?"

"That would imply that I did it to myself and that I don't have an exit strategy."

"Do you have an exit strategy?"

She stared at him and shook her head. "No, because I wasn't consciously aware that I was even doing this," she said. "The fact that I am supposedly doing something along this line is kind of terrifying."

"And yet you understand why."

"Sure, I was trying to stop the predators."

He nodded, giving her a gentle smile. "And it sounds as if you were looking after the twins at the same time."

"I can't have the same thing happen to them," she explained.

"So, if you were to look after them, would that be a help?"

"It would be a help," she declared, "but living the life that we live and the difficulties of raising them, financially for instance, would be quite a daunting undertaking."

"But it is possible?" he asked pointedly.

"Sure, it's possible, but Dr. Maddy would have to release them, and obviously they aren't capable yet of being out in the world."

"Yet maybe they could get to that point if they lived with somebody they trusted."

Silence followed for a moment, and then, in a small voice, she whispered, "I didn't mean to do it, you know?"

He tugged her closer to him. "I know that, and so do they."

She looked at him and shook her head. "I'm not sure about that."

He smiled. "I am. I've known Stefan and Dr. Maddy a long time, and I'm a really good judge of character. Believe me that they trust you."

"They couldn't possibly," she wailed, turning to him. "They wouldn't want me to lock up Stefan."

"I think, when it's over, they'll have more info and a pretty good idea of how to help others like you and the twins, and in a better way than before because Dr. Maddy and Stefan didn't know or understand all of it before. So, in that case, any information is important."

"So, I'm some sort of experiment then?" she asked, glaring at him.

He chuckled. "Oh no you don't. You won't pull me into a fight over that."

Her shoulders sagged. "Why are you even still here?"

"Because I want to be here, with you." He turned her fully around and just held her close. "You keep thinking you're a lost cause."

"I am. Look what I'm doing to people, good God."

"I think that's probably where your fear of killing somebody is coming from."

She looked up at him and frowned. "Do you think so?"

And he heard the hope in her tone. "Yes," he declared, "because actively you are only trying to stop them from hurting you. I just don't think you realize the power of what you're doing."

"Maybe not," she muttered. "I do remember being very tired of her friends."

"Do you want to tell me about it?"

"No," she snapped.

"That's fine," he said, looking at her. "You don't have to tell me anything." She frowned at him, and he smiled again.

"You can't be a nice guy all the time," she muttered, glaring at him again.

"Why not?" he asked, trying to smother the smile forcing its way out.

Her shoulders sagged. "Even if I was justified at one time, it's not something that I should still be doing."

"I agree with you," he replied cheerfully. "The thing is, you set that up when you were little, when you were eight probably, when you didn't know as much as you do now. You set it up so, even when you were sleeping, even when you were not there, nobody could take advantage of you," he explained. "I can't argue with that, and I would never fault you for looking after yourself. What you have to do is figure out how to go back in and shut it down."

"But if I shut it down—"

He smiled. "The little child inside you doesn't want to shut it down because she's hurting, and she's afraid. Do you really think you're still in the same position as you were back then?"

"No." Tandy frowned. "Of course not. I worked damn hard to get free of all that. I'm much better."

"Exactly, but you forgot to update the little girl inside."

"Yeah, but what you don't understand is that the little girl doesn't want to be updated. She's got it in her head that the world is a dangerous place."

"Of course she does. In her limited experience, it is a dangerous place."

"And," Tandy added, looking at him pointedly, "you can't tell me it's not."

"I would never tell you that," he said, raising his hands. "Absolutely not. Plenty of things go on in this world that we don't like, but that doesn't mean it will come get you. Besides, maybe you can leave something like that in place, but let go of everybody else, so that you're not using all that energy to hang on to them all the time."

She watched him closely as he went on.

"It's obviously draining you, particularly as you've put more and more people in there. Let them out and just leave it as some future safeguard."

As she contemplated his suggestion, Keller found her frown something to behold.

"I guess, as an adult, I won't make the same choices I made as a child."

"*You* won't be making any of those choices," Keller noted, "and that little girl didn't make those choices. They were made for her, ... by people who wanted to hurt her. She protected herself in the only way she knew how, and that's fine," he pointed out. "I am not against your having some safeguard in case somebody decides to attack you while you're alone in the car or with the kids or something."

She stared at him, nodded, then smiled. "Right, I guess it wouldn't hurt to have a safeguard for that."

"Exactly. I want you and the twins protected. So it wouldn't hurt to have a safeguard, but maybe not one that grabs them up and hangs on to them forever," he suggested, "because that's only exhausting you, and we're trying to let all these people go, so you'll be free."

She smiled. "How am I supposed to convince her of that?"

"What's her biggest fear?"

She frowned at him. "I don't know."

"Maybe you need to find that out," Keller suggested. "To me, … it seems to be a fear of being hurt."

"Sure, that would make sense, considering where she is and what she's been through."

"Of course it makes sense, and it doesn't matter if it doesn't make sense to anyone but her," Keller added, for emphasis. "Remember that this is about her, as this is her experience. However, now we want her to experience happy events in life, not just ones that hurt her."

"Then probably," Tandy shared, "like every little girl, she just wants to be loved."

"Right, and that is exactly what every little girl—and boy—wants, isn't it?"

"Sure," she agreed, "but who knew it was that hard to get."

"Yeah, not like the distorted sense of *love* that those other men were promising."

Tandy paled, her lips pinched together, but she nodded.

"Right." She looked over at him. "None of them knew the first thing about a normal relationship."

Keller sighed, grimacing. "Let's ensure the little girl inside is okay to take the steps required to get her out of that prison. Although she created it to imprison them, she locked herself up in the process."

"Right." Tandy frowned.

"And we don't want that for her."

"No, we don't," she whispered, then shuddered. "I can agree with that."

"Good, so can you go in and convince her that you can let it go now?"

She frowned as she thought about it.

Keller nodded. "I understand it has to be your decision, and, if you can't, then you can't."

"But I need to, don't I?"

He smiled. "Let's just say, it would be a really good thing, for you and for her, to free up all that energy by letting them go."

Her lips twitched, and she nodded. "I'm not even sure I need her permission."

"No, you don't," he agreed. "You absolutely do not, but I'm guessing that, if you *did* have her permission, she would appreciate it."

She pondered that for a long moment and then said, "Just a minute." Closing her eyes, she just seemed to disappear inside.

Keller was amazed as he watched Tandy. He'd never had a child relationship like that and had never felt the need to do something so crafty. As he waited, he thought about moving her somewhere more comfortable, but then she opened her eyes.

"Okay."

"Okay? Okay what?" he asked, smiling.

"She agrees, as long as we can keep some safeguards in place. She has agreed to let me do it."

"I would feel better if you had safeguards."

She stared at him for a moment, and then a smile crossed her face. "You really mean that, don't you?"

"Of course I do. I don't want you or the twins to get hurt, and, if an assailant happens to be out there, with an idea of harming any of you three, you can absolutely torch the guy." When she burst out laughing, he grinned. "It's all about making the decisions that are right for you and for those around you," he said. "But, for now, you need to go in there and release all those people."

"I don't know if I can."

"Will you at least give it a try? Remember that Stefan is in there too."

STEFAN STARED AROUND at his prison. He had respect, as in a mad respect for the person who had done this. Yet also had a certain amount of fury at himself, for having walked right into this trap. He knew he could get out of it, but it would cause a certain amount of damage to the host, and that was not something he was prepared to do.

He searched the area, looking for any cracks in the energy, but she had it locked down tight, and that in itself made him wonder how she even knew how to do that. Yet he shouldn't be surprised. She had been a child at the time after all, so to come up with an idea of what to do, then to implement the plan, had been truly remarkable.

He studied his prison, fascinated at how locked tight in

her mind she had made it. And even as he thought about that, more layers were added. He smiled and sent out waves and waves of love. If he could reach her with love, he would do it in a heartbeat, but, so far, every time he tried that, she immediately built the pod higher and deeper.

With sorrow swelling in his heart, he realized that could only mean that other people had used love as a weapon, both the words of love and the actions of what should have been love. So ultimately something had been just so wrong about the people in her world that she couldn't separate it. So anybody who posed a threat—himself included—had been imprisoned.

The fact that she created such an incredible prison filled him with awe, and, with that, he could almost feel the entity behind that energy stop and consider him. He sent out a pleasant greeting, telling her that she was incredibly talented and that he meant her no harm. A half laugh came, and he realized how many other people had probably said the same things to her.

"Do the people held in these pods talk to you?" he asked. "It must take an enormous amount of energy just to maintain this system."

Once again, an odd shrug came from within her psyche, and he realized just what a terrible drain this must have been for Tandy. Yet she wouldn't speak about or address the matter. No way that she would ever acknowledge such a thing. She couldn't because it would mean she needed to find another answer, to find another way to make this happen that didn't take so much energy from her. Yet she wasn't there yet. She might not ever get there, but he needed to help her realize that this prison system wasn't even necessarily for her anymore.

*I have to be safe*, came the whisper. *I have to be safe.*

"Yes, you do," he agreed, "and I can help you."

But that wave of disbelief came immediately, revealing how much energy she had expended over the years just dealing with all the energy she had imprisoned in each of these pods.

*Not energy*, she whispered. *People, bad people.*

He contemplated that for a long moment, wondering if she had killed somebody over this. When the answer came back as *Yes*, he winced, not knowing if it was the real truth, or the truth as she knew it, or something completely different. It was a harsh lesson for anybody who dealt in energy to realize that something like this could be out there.

She started to rattle his cage, quite literally.

"It's fine," he replied. "I understand. They were hurting you."

*Or they would have hurt me*, she clarified triumphantly, *but I didn't let them.*

"Okay, and what about your mother?"

*What about her?* she asked, the doubt and fear of a little girl adding almost a repulsiveness to her tone.

"It's hard to love somebody who hurts you, isn't it?" He almost felt the tears at the edge of her psyche as she tried desperately to hold them in, yet wanting to release the flood at the same time. "I'm so sorry," he murmured. "I still don't understand anything that explains why Isabella was like that."

*She showed me how to do this*, the little girl pointed out. *She showed me that this is what I needed to do.*

He stared around at his cage. "Why?"

*To stay safe.*

He frowned. "Did she tell you that this would keep the

bad people away from you, would keep you safe?"

*Yes, and it worked, didn't it?*

"Yes," he conceded. "You're very talented, aren't you? That's what she always told you."

*Yes,* she agreed, *and she kept telling me that this would be what I needed to do, that this would be the answer, and that nobody could hurt me.*

"Did she create any of this herself?"

*No.*

"Did she help you create all this?"

*No.*

"So this prison that Isabella told you that you needed, did Isabella create one just for herself somewhere else?"

*No.*

"Did Isabella ever hurt you?"

There was a moment of silence, and then she said, *Yes.*

"Did she have plans for these energies?"

*Yes.*

He frowned as he thought about that. "Is there any chance that she's the one who brought these mean people into your world?"

*Yes,* came the same simple answer.

"Right, and that's what you don't understand because why would Isabella do that?"

*There's no reason for her to do that,* she whispered. *She's just bad.*

"I won't argue with you there," he muttered. "I think you've been through enough."

*Enough lies, no more lies,* she cried out.

"No, of course not."

He still didn't know exactly what was going on here, whether Isabella had told the eight-year-old-child Tandy to trap the bad men by building this prison or not, whether Isabella had suggested that this might be a good way for Tandy to escape the bad men. He reminded himself that the Tandy who built this had been a child. Stefan knew adults had a hard enough time communicating well with each other, but what about when dealing with a child? "Did Isabella tell you to just *go inside?*"

*Yes,* she replied. *She told me to just let them do what they wanted and just go inside and ignore them.*

He winced and saw how a child might interpret that ever-so-slightly differently than the mother may have intended. "Did she do it often?"

*Yes,* she stated in the same childish tone.

"And did you tell her what you were doing?"

*No,* she murmured. *She told me to build a place where I felt safe, and I could just stay there and could let them do whatever.*

He felt the anger build inside him at the mother's callousness, realizing just what had gone on in this poor child's life because of a mother who just didn't care and who had actively pursued this type of abuse on her child. "So, she told you that you would be safe in here, while these men did whatever they wanted, right?"

*Yes.*

"When did it stop?"

*It never stopped. It's still going on. People are still out there who aren't safe.*

"Yes, bad people are still out in the world," he agreed, "but they aren't coming after you anymore, are they?"

*Yes, they still are.*

He pondered that information, wondering just what *safe* meant to her. He suspected that it was all tied up in a maze of other misinformation that went along with the craziness in her life. Stefan only had a couple ways to help her realize that those things didn't have to happen anymore.

But for her to *understand either one* was a whole different story, and he suspected she wouldn't take the news as truth just because he told her so.

*HELLO*, A VOICE broke through.

He stared around his prison, wondering who this was. "Hello?" he asked cautiously. And the voice that came back was Tandy.

*Hi, Stefan. Apparently you got caught up in one of my traps.*

Amazed that he was now speaking with adult Tandy, he replied, "Yes, that's quite true. Any chance you could let me out?" he asked politely.

There was a moment of hesitation. *I'm okay to let you out, but she's not.*

"Of course," he noted, understanding perfectly. "The child is still afraid."

*Yes, she is*, adult Tandy confirmed, *and with good reason.*

"Understood, but she need not fear me."

*No, maybe not you*, adult Tandy conceded, *but she, ... we have heard that many times before.*

"Of course." Stefan sighed. "How long do you keep them here?" When no answer came, his heart sank. "Are you really expending all that energy to keep them here forever?"

*Yes*, Tandy admitted, *and Keller just mentioned that too. He suggested that's why I'm so tired and that's why I can't function on so many levels because of my fatigue.*

"Which makes sense," Stefan murmured. "It takes an

incredible amount of energy to maintain all this."

*Of course, but, if I don't maintain it,* she explained, her tone breaking a bit, *bad things happen.*

He winced. "Bad things could happen, but bad things don't have to happen."

*Keller mentioned something similar, but we can't just trust that on your say-so.*

"How much of this was triggered by your mother?"

*I don't know,* she muttered.

"I thought you escaped from her."

*Apparently you never escape,* she muttered, *because I'm still doing this. How the hell could I escape if we are both here?*

"And yet you set it up as a child, then walked away, right?"

*Yes,* she replied, surprise in her tone.

Stefan smiled. "So, this is really a remnant of a world that you left behind, but you left it still functioning."

*I guess,* she noted cautiously. *Yes, that's true.*

"In that case, all you need to do is reassess whether it's still required, whether a scaled-back version now that you're an adult could be an adequate substitute."

*Maybe,* she muttered. *I'm still not clear on all the details.*

"Of course not," Stefan said. "Things that we set up as a child won't necessarily make any sense when we are adults."

*But they should,* she declared, *or why else would we do it?*

"Sometimes we do these things," he explained, "because we're prompted by other people."

*You're back to my mother again, aren't you?*

"Not necessarily. She wanted you to find a safe place, and you did. Answer me this. Did you tell the twins that too?" At her startled gasp, he realized that's exactly what had gone on there too. "So, what was it that triggered them going back inside?"

She whispered, *Me, I guess.*

"You or your mother?"

*I don't know,* she said. Then she stopped, thinking about it. *Yes, I do know. I think it would have been my mother.*

"So, when you recognized that your mother was hounding you again, did you tell the twins to stay inside?"

*I guess,* she whispered, but doubt filled her tone.

Stefan realized that he wasn't quite there yet with her. "Would your mother have wanted this?"

*Oh yes, absolutely she did. She hated men.*

He hesitated, frowning. "Even the men she let into the house?"

*Yes, she hated them.*

"And why is that?" he asked curiously.

*Because she didn't want them, she didn't want to need them. She didn't want to use them.*

"Ah, but she had to, and, therefore, she didn't like the fact that she was forced to use them."

*Yes.*

"What do you know about all the rituals?"

*I think she—I don't know.* The tone turned childlike again.

"Can I talk to the adult Tandy, please?" Stefan asked.

*No,* the child declared, *you can't.*

"I see," he said in an understanding tone. "And what about your mother? Do you talk to Isabella?"

*No,* she said.

"And why is that?"

*Because she's scary.*

"Yeah, you're not kidding," he agreed. "She is scary, isn't she? And not very nice at all."

*No, but she wants things from us.*

"What does Isabella want?" he asked curiously.

The child went silent, and, before Stefan could speak further, another tone stepped in.

*Just shut up. You're not supposed to talk about this to anybody.*

Surprised, he opened his mouth, hoping to communicate with this new entity, when the pod that he was in made a loud *click* and another layer was added. He felt his whole life force being sucked away. Startled, he began to fight, only to realize almost instantly that fighting was not the answer. So, with as much peace, joy, and love in his heart that he could muster, he sank back into the oblivion he'd come from.

# CHAPTER 21

TANDY STARED AT the scene in front of her. It was so well-known, like a part of her, and yet so foreign, like a part of her that she'd never dealt with. She glanced around, surprised at the complexity of everything she saw. She shook her head. "Wow, you've done an incredible job," she murmured.

"Right."

At that, Tandy turned to see her younger self sitting there, looking quite comfortable. "You do realize what a drain it is on us, right?"

Child Tandy shrugged. "That's okay. We can do this."

"Maybe we can do this, but maybe we shouldn't."

Her younger self looked at her. "Is the danger gone?" she asked in excitement.

Tandy hesitated, and then, not giving herself a chance to doubt it, she nodded. "Yes, it's a completely different world out there."

Her younger self chewed on her bottom lip. "Are you sure? Because we don't want to go out there and get hurt."

"Right, but I think we can do a modified version of this now. It would help us save our energy too."

Her younger self looked around and muttered, "Maybe." Doubt filled her tone.

"Or do you think we should just let it all go instead?"

Tandy asked, turning to face her younger self. "Then we wouldn't have to maintain any of it."

"No, no, no, we can't do that," younger Tandy exclaimed.

"In which case we need a modified version," adult Tandy suggested, with a smile.

Younger Tandy nodded at that. "Okay. … I *am* tired."

"Of course you are, sweetheart." Tandy walked closer and wrapped her arms around her inner child. "It's been a long hard job, but you have done really well." She just held her inner child close. Tears were in her own eyes as she realized just how disconnected she had been from this situation, from her childhood. All the many safeguards put in place had just taken over and had become an entity all on their own.

"We had to," her inner child muttered. "It's so bad out there. We had to be safe. We needed this."

"I know," Tandy whispered, "and we will be safe now."

A woman in a mocking tone shouted at her, "You fool, don't you believe that."

Holding her younger self, Tandy turned to see Isabella glaring at her. "You again," adult Tandy noted in disgust. "You are such a bitch. Can't you just die already?"

The little child in her arms went from sheer fear to surprise at Tandy's response. With that, adult Tandy realized just how much she had grown up and had moved away from her childhood trauma, but adult Tandy had forgotten about this little one. She'd completely forgotten that she had left younger Tandy on duty. And now here she was, younger Tandy, the one dealing with her mother all this time. God, that was terrible.

"It's her," her inner child whispered.

"I can deal with this and can put a stop to it now," adult Tandy declared. "We don't need to deal with Isabella anymore."

"Are you sure?" her inner child asked.

"I am sure," adult Tandy stated, "and I'm just so sorry I left you here."

Her mother sneered. "You're not sorry at all. You're just like all the rest."

Adult Tandy asked, "What are you even doing here?"

"What do you mean, what am I doing here? Do you think I didn't help you set up all this? Do you think you were smart enough to do all this on your own?"

"Yes," adult Tandy snapped. "I absolutely know we are smart enough to do this all on our own."

Her mother stared at her in surprise, but the sneer came back almost immediately. "What? You think you're an adult now? You think that since you've got a man in your life that this will all just be fine and dandy?" Isabella laughed. "Did you tell *her* that you've got a man in your life?"

At that, her inner self frowned up at her in surprise.

Tandy smiled at her reassuringly. "It's okay for her to know because life is different. It's not the same as when you were there, with your transient men."

"Oh, sure it is," Isabella muttered. "Men only want to use you."

"Or *you* only want to use them," Tandy pointed out. "It's not as if you ever gave. You only took."

"Oh, I gave," she muttered. "I gave and I gave and I gave, but all they ever did was take, take, and take."

Tandy winced. "When you *gave*, you gave with strings, and you hurt people. You gave them drugs, even if they didn't want them. You stole from them, even if they gave you what you wanted, and you hurt them in so many ways," she clarified. "We are not that person."

"No, you're not that person," Isabella grumbled, "which is too damn bad because you're weak. If you were that person, you wouldn't be in this situation." She laughed. "You know that your mother is right."

"No," Tandy argued. "You're not right. You've never been right, and I can't imagine you ever being right. Nothing is right about you."

Her mother stared at her in shock.

Tandy nodded, feeling the little girl trembling in her arms. "All you've done is hurt us. You never acknowledged that we were smarter, stronger, and better than you. You used our abilities all these years to make money for yourself. Then, when we wouldn't do it anymore, you tried to make us do it, and we fought back. You bullied us into setting this up to punish people, even if they weren't necessarily out to hurt us. Yet you made it seem as if they were."

Isabella laughed. "Anybody who wouldn't pay got the same treatment. I told you guys about people who owed me money, and you immediately took care of them." She cackled loudly.

At that revelation, Tandy's inner child jumped, startled, and she shifted to look up at her.

Tandy nodded. "Yes, she's been playing us the whole time. Definitely some people were out to hurt us," she added, her hand gently stroking the child's back, "but not as many as Isabella would have us believe. She would just send them our way, hoping that we would punish them because it was our instinctive, natural response to protect ourselves."

The child in her arms gasped in shock, spinning to look at her mother.

Isabella just laughed and laughed. "God, you're a fool."

"No," Tandy snapped. "I'm not a fool, and neither is she. We are still in some ways children, but that is no longer your problem. You are dead, remember?"

"Yes, but I'm here too, and I get to live with all these other people you have hurt over the years. It's great."

"In what way have *we* hurt them?" Tandy asked cautiously.

Isabella smirked. "By keeping some essence of them here, … their life on Earth is paying a price because you're draining their life force constantly, and they can't quite function the way that they should. They have lived on, yet sometimes with poor mental capacities, sometimes with poor physical capacities. Sometimes we even hurt them directly." She laughed and laughed. "Of course, the best part is, the ones we hurt directly were your grandmother and your father. I get to live forever. And one day you'll be tired, and I'll take over and be you—just as I always intended."

At that, Tandy stiffened and stared at her. "You killed our grandmother?"

"No, I did not, sweetheart. You did." Her mother giggled. "Even after everything she did for you, you are the one who killed her."

"I don't understand," Tandy said in shock.

"You imprisoned her. I told you that she would hurt you, and it took a bit to convince you of that. You fought that one much longer and harder than I would have liked," Isabella snapped. "Still, I knew that we could slowly kill her off. The trouble is, once we finally managed to kill her, you wouldn't even share the money or the house with me. You still haven't even sold the damn thing. And I couldn't control what you did with it, which really, really pissed me off."

"You're saying that you triggered a response, making us think Grandma would hurt us, and, by keeping her encapsulated or whatever, we ended her life?"

"Yeah, exactly. Entrapped in these pods causes all kinds of things. Cancer, heart attacks, suicide, all manner of things are possible," Isabella replied, with a smirk. "The beauty of this system is that the cause of death is never linked to me."

Tandy asked, "Are some of the people who we have locked up in these pods still alive?"

"They eventually die if you've got them here, but they can't cross over because you've stopped that from happening too."

Tandy began to feel seriously ill, just from hearing what she had heard—all triggered because of her mother, a mother who was even now dead. The pods explained the fear and the horror her mother had used to manipulate them.

Her mother laughed. "Gwen was not a very happy camper."

"Of course not," Tandy agreed faintly. "I would never have done that to her."

"Oh, she knows. She knows it's me, don't you worry. She took you away from me, and I made sure she suffered," Isabella snapped. "But I think it's even better that she suffered at your hands."

"No," the child cried out. "We were only trying to protect ourselves."

"And you did that, but, once we had such a great system set up, I could also use it for anybody who did me wrong too," Isabella explained. "It gives me immense pleasure to know that some of the people I detested the most are locked up here. Even though you didn't know or didn't care to know, this system was perfect for me."

Isabella smirked as she continued. "This is my twenty-first-century upgrade of a voodoo doll. If a replica of these people is locked up here, or some of their energy, I can influence their systems so they never quite function properly in the real world. They end up dealing with all kinds of diseases. And then they die."

"Good God," Tandy exclaimed, staring at her. "You murdered these people."

"Not in any way that can be proven." Isabella laughed hysterically.

"And you used us to do this."

"I've always had to be resourceful."

Tandy asked, "Is there no end to the evil in you?"

"No, probably not," she replied, with mocking laughter.

"And yet you still are able to run around and talk to people?"

"Of course. Where do you think you got your abilities from? I tried so hard to develop them, but, when drugs were free and everywhere for people to use, that's how we explored our ultra-consciousness," she shared, with a laugh. "So, I took more and more drugs, trying to get better and better results. But eventually it had its own way with me, and the drugs caused me all kinds of pain and problems," she muttered. "And I couldn't get off them. I'd become so addicted that I couldn't figure out how to get free of them. I needed energy, more energy. So, whenever I needed it, … I used yours. It was perfect."

"My energy?" Tandy asked.

"Yes, you kept me alive for a long time, and, once I realized my time would still come, I made sure that I got locked up here too, so I can access the energy from all your prisoners—and from you, as our host."

"Good Christ," Tandy muttered, staring at the woman who had tormented her for the bulk of her life.

"Yeah, isn't that great?" Isabella said. "I always loved to manipulate people, and this is my crowning glory."

"No," Tandy countered, "this is terribly wrong."

"Maybe wrong"—Isabella shrugged—"or maybe so right that you have no idea of what you can do."

"No matter what I can do," Tandy noted, "rest assured that I won't do it with you."

"I wouldn't count on that," Isabella said, with a snicker. "I'm here, and you can't get rid of me now that I'm already dead and gone. You burned my corpse," she stated ruefully. "I'm just energy now, and I'm here on a permanent basis." She just laughed and laughed.

"What about the twins?" Tandy asked.

Isabella's expression turned ugly. "Yeah, well, … the twins. I was trying to set them up to help me out too, but you wouldn't let me. You can be such a bitch. You kept protecting them, showing them how to protect themselves, and I couldn't get anywhere. You ruined that for me."

"I'm glad we did something right," she snarled at her mother. "And you're wrong. You're in my space, using my energy, so I don't have to deal with you at all."

"Oh, I think you do. You must, unless you want to see somebody else die."

"What are you talking about? You said I wasn't killing people."

"Some people you didn't, and some people you absolutely did. Now we'll kill one who is right here. What do you think about Stefan? Isn't he the latest guest in your house?"

"I won't kill him," Tandy declared, raising her tone. "He wasn't trying to hurt me at all."

"No, but he was trying to hurt me, so same difference," Isabella stated, with a wave of her hand. "And now that I'm here, this is all about me, not you."

The child inside trembled, and Tandy held her close, rubbed her back, and whispered, "It will be okay."

But younger Tandy kept shaking her head. "I didn't know. … I didn't know."

"I know you didn't, sweetheart, but it's okay. He'll be fine."

She looked up at adult Tandy and continued to shake her head. "I don't know," she muttered. "I don't think so. I really don't think so."

Tandy frowned down at her. "I *do* think so. Stefan is a good guy, and he's very capable."

"He's not that capable." Isabella laughed. "And you, my dear, are just a fool. He'll never get free."

Just as Isabella went to open her mouth one more time, Tandy couldn't control her reaction and just shut her mother's mouth with a flick of her hand. Funny, it had the effect of completely shutting off Isabella's energy too.

Tandy stared at the frozen specter of her mother in front of her and almost laughed. "That looks good on her." The child in her arms spun to face Isabella, looked back up at adult Tandy, her eyes wide, and she nodded. "We don't have to listen to her now," inner child Tandy exclaimed, "and we do not *want* to listen to her. She's bad. She hurt us, and she hurt other people. And she used us to hurt other people." Tears formed in the little girl's eyes. "I don't like her. She's scary."

"She is very scary," adult Tandy whispered, "but we are stronger than her."

Holding hands with her inner child, adult Tandy walked

closer to the ice specter of their mother that stood in front of them. With a hard kick, Tandy shattered it to the ground, letting the crystals collapse all around them. The child looked at the crystals, kicked a few herself, and shuddered. "Is she gone?"

"Yes, she's gone. And, if she isn't, we will lock her in a pod—but first let's unlock all this energy and release everything else," she suggested. "We do not want her back out loose again for sure."

And, with that, the two of them walked over to all the glowing pods. With their two energies entwined together, they released every one of them. A gush of energy flowed all around Tandy, as energies and spirits surged forth. Some angry, some grateful, some exhausted, and some not even seemingly there anymore, until only one remained.

Stefan stood in front of her, a beaming smile on his face. "Now that was well done."

She faced him, tears in her eyes.

He opened his arms, and she ran into them, the child still tucked up close. He held both of them and muttered, "Nice job, really nice job."

Whispering only loud enough for herself to hear, and not the child in her arms, adult Tandy asked, "Is Isabella gone?"

"Yes," Stefan confirmed. "She's finally gone."

# CHAPTER 22

T ANDY OPENED HER eyes to find herself on the floor of the overnight room, wrapped up tightly in Keller's arms. She shifted, then looked up at him and smiled. "Sorry about that."

He swore under his breath. "That was damn scary."

"It was scary," she agreed, "but your energy was inside me, wasn't it? I felt a different presence but almost one that was part of me." His big grin brought out the dimples on his cheeks that she'd never seen before.

"I wasn't about to let you go off and face the demons alone. Neither could I be perceived as a threat. So I just stayed in the background, offering my energy to anyone who needed it."

She smiled, stretched up, and gave him a gentle kiss. Surprised, he returned the kiss with a little more enthusiasm. She pulled back and smiled up at him. "Thank you."

"You are very welcome," he said, giving her another kiss. "I'm not at all sure what I just witnessed, but I'm hoping everything is all okay now. Is it?" he asked cautiously.

Just then the door opened to the overnight room, and in walked Stefan and Dr. Maddy. Tandy felt Stefan's relief. Slowly she made her way to her feet and walked over to him. He opened his arms and this time, physical body and all, he wrapped her up and held her tight. Tears ran from her eyes, and she finally lifted her head. "Thank you so much."

He shrugged. "Occasionally we see something we've never seen before, and it blows us away. That can happen, but your mother was definitely something else."

"I'm so grateful that you are using the past tense," she noted.

Stefan added, with a knowing smile, "We do have a couple other things that we need to do."

She nodded, then looked back at Keller, who was slowly getting to his feet. "You want to come?"

"I do, I just don't know where I'm coming to."

"We'll go see the twins," she announced, with a smile, "to let them know it's safe to come back out." She reached out a hand and laughed at Keller's surprise. Then the two of them raced to the observation room, with Stefan and Dr. Maddy following. Tandy stepped inside, took one look at the window, then nodded and headed back into the hallway, next to the twins' room. She pulled Keller with her.

Dr. Maddy stayed with Stefan in the observation room. When Tandy looked back at them curiously, Dr. Maddy just waved her on. "Go help them. After all, it will be you from here on out."

Tandy smiled at her and turned to Keller. "Are you okay with that?"

He didn't hesitate for a moment. "Of course I am. Haven't they been through enough?"

"They have, but they will still be kids," she warned.

He chuckled. "If you mean, regular kids, who will be screaming, yelling, laughing, and running in the hallways? I'll take that any day."

As she entered the kids' room, the twins were still curled up in bed, safe and secure in their fake world. She walked over and tapped her brother on the shoulder.

Mark opened his eyes, looked up, stretched, and asked, "Is it safe now?"

"Yes, it is definitely safe," she whispered. "Come on out, honey."

And, with that, Mark got up, still in their imaginary world, then looked around and reached down to pat his twin brother.

Matthew opened his eyes and bounced up to his feet, a big grin on his face and asked, "Is it playtime?"

"It is and it isn't," Tandy replied, with a knowing smile. "How about we play in the real world now?"

He looked at her in awe. "Does that mean it's safe?"

"Yes, it's safe." Then she held out a hand and pulled Keller closer. "This is Keller. He will be with us too."

Matthew asked, "Was he hiding too?"

She laughed. "I guess I was the one hiding, and he helped set me free. And now I'm helping to set you free again."

"Only if it's safe," Mark repeated, already looking at the door in the imaginary playroom. "I really want it to be safe," he whispered.

"It's safe," she repeated. "Come on. Let's go take a look."

Holding hands, the four of them raced to the door. As she opened it and stepped out of the imaginary world, the children in the bed in the real world rose up.

DR. MADDY SMILED as she now witnessed the real world of the twins from the observation room.

The two children in the beds opened their eyes and sat up to find Tandy and Keller, sitting on the bed with them.

Tandy opened her arms, and Mark fell into them in tears. Matthew wasn't far behind. The four of them were tucked up together, sharing hugs all around, the twins chattering nonstop, full of questions.

Dr. Maddy turned to Stefan, tears in her eyes. "Wow."

"I know," he replied, patting her on her shoulder. "This is one for the books."

"I never, ever could have imagined Mark's world—or Tandy's," Dr. Maddy muttered.

"That's why the absolute strength of humanity continues to push the boundaries," Stefan noted.

"And, boy, did they get pushed on this one." Dr. Maddy smiled. "We may have to write a book one day," she teased.

Stefan laughed. "The world is not ready for our book," he replied.

Dr. Maddy nodded. "Maybe later."

"Maybe we'll talk about writing a book in a few years," he said, chuckling. "Maybe the world will be ready for us then."

Dr. Maddy shook her head. "I don't think it will be ready, but today has been a very good day."

"It has, indeed. Are you ready to go in?"

"Absolutely."

They walked out of the observation room and into the twins' bedroom. As they opened the door and stepped inside, the twins stopped, froze, and then both of them smiled.

"Hi," Matthew greeted them. "I'm Matthew."

"Hi, Matthew," Dr. Maddy replied. "We're Stefan and Dr. Maddy."

He nodded. "I know. I recognize you from our world."

She smiled at him. "And now you should feel comfortable in our world."

He grinned. "It's all our world."

"Both sides are," Stefan agreed, with a smile.

"We're safe now," Mark declared, with a bright smile, "so we don't have to go there anymore."

Stefan laughed. "You are so right." He looked over at Keller and Tandy, who had their arms wrapped around each other and the kids. Stefan nodded to both of them. "Nice job, guys."

Keller shook his head, not sure what to say.

Dr. Maddy smiled. "You have no idea how much of an impetus you were for this, Keller. So don't even bother to deny that you did anything here."

He took a moment before speaking. "Let's just say that I didn't know what I was doing."

"And that's fine too," Stefan agreed, "but sometimes there is only one thing to do."

"And what's that?" Tandy asked, turning to him.

"Love," he replied. "To love who we are in all our forms—beautiful, ugly, and everything in between. And to remember that nothing stays dark when you shine the light of love on it."

# CHAPTER 23

*Several Months Later ...*

TANDY LOOKED UP as Keller walked in the door. The twins raced over, bouncing to get into his arms, and he picked them both up and twirled them around, laughing.

"Wow, it looks as if you guys must have had a great day," Keller noted, settling both boys in his arms now.

"We started school today," Matthew announced, "and I made a friend." Then he plunged into a dialogue on the little friend he had made at school.

Mark listened patiently, waiting for Matthew to finish speaking. When he took too long, Mark reached over, tapped him on the cheek, and said, "It's my turn now."

Tandy laughed because, if there was one thing that she had seen over the last few months, it was the return of normal children, herself included. Her own inner child was content, happy, and thankfully silent on the inside for the most part. They were all working with Dr. Maddy to help in lieu of therapy, since so many issues still remained for everyone to deal with, but they were coming along nicely.

Tandy added, "Let him get in the door now. Come on, guys."

With that, Keller set the twins on the floor, then walked over to Tandy, picking her up and swooping her into a big hug, kissing her on the cheek. "And how is Tandy doing today?"

"Tandy is doing just fine," she replied, with a smile.

"Are you ready to go back to work?"

"I am," she said, nodding at him. "I'm really looking forward to it."

"Good. Since we've managed to get moved into our house, and the kids are started in school, we're doing pretty well right now."

Tandy added, "And now that the paperwork for the twins is all taken care of, we're officially a family."

He smiled and nodded, then pulled her close and whispered something in her ear that made her blush.

Immediately Mark screeched out, "That's disgusting." Then he ran away, laughing, Matthew right behind him.

Tandy chuckled. "They are definitely normal children at this point in time," she murmured, "and I couldn't be happier."

"Good," Keller muttered, "and, if you're happy, I'm happy." She rolled her eyes at that, and he said, "I'm serious."

She smirked. "I don't know about that."

"I do," he declared. "You've come a long way."

"Doesn't mean I'll ever get to that point."

He laughed. "You're already at that point," he stated, "but I won't push. When you're ready, you can make that move." She frowned, bit on her bottom lip, and then he frowned, tapped it, and whispered, "None of that, no pressure."

"I did have another session with Dr. Maddy today, while the kids were at school."

"Good," he noted. "Any resolution?"

"Not necessarily a resolution," she clarified, "but definitely progress in that direction."

He looked up, his eyes twinkling. "That sounds good."

She rolled her eyes at him. "You would say that."

"Of course I would, but let's keep it for later, *huh?*"

"Yes," she agreed, with a laugh. "But just so you know, … there *will* be a later."

"I have no doubt about it," he said, with a smile. "You're the one telling me not to put any pressure on you."

"I wanted to surprise you when I get there."

"And it's not an issue," he said. "Honestly … it's not."

"How can you be so nice?" she asked, staring at him. "No matter what I do, no matter what I say, it's always okay."

He nodded. "Because it is okay. Just because you had some crappy years in the first part of your life doesn't mean the rest of it has to be bad."

"I hope not," she murmured, "because I'm really looking forward to whatever you've got coming."

He smirked. "I'm looking forward to all of it, and I mean *all of it*. You hear me?" he asked, giving her a kiss. "And that includes later tonight." With a twinkle in his eyes, he called out to the twins, "Ready or not, here I come."

Then he took off after them in a race they had started weeks ago when they had first moved into their house together. Her grandmother's house. The house had taken Tandy a bit of time to come to terms with, but it was their home now. She stepped off to the side, smiling as the twins squealed and ran ahead of Keller. And he, in very typical fashion, stayed just enough behind them to make them think they were winning. But then, at the last minute, when they were almost begging to be picked up, he scooped them both up and carried them back into the kitchen.

She smiled. "You're really good with them."

"I'm not really good with anybody," he replied, chuckling. "I'm just me. And one of these days you'll realize that *just being you* is exactly good enough."

And later that night, when he finally sagged down on the bed beside her, she realized he was right. Being her was good enough. She snuggled in closer, tears in her eyes, and he held her close.

"Are you okay?" he asked.

She nodded. "I'm okay. I'm better than okay."

He added, "Your pace at all times."

She shook her head. "I think I'm fine," she murmured. "It's taken me a long time to get here, but, now that I am, it's all good."

He leaned in to kiss her. "Better than good," he murmured, followed by a chuckle. "It's great." Then he gave such a ridiculous imitation tiger growl that she burst out laughing. He held up a hand and whispered, "Watch it. You'll get the twins in here."

Sure enough, five seconds later the door opened, and both boys barreled inside to jump onto the bed.

She laughed, grateful that their intimacy had a chance to get that far before the twins had arrived. Now they were tucked up beside her in bed, demanding a story.

She looked over at Keller and asked, "What kind of a story do you want?"

"A princess, a princess who fought her demons and who came out on the other side."

Matthew asked, "A princess? Don't you want a prince?"

"No," Mark stated, "because the prince will be the one who's waiting for her."

"Oh, I like that," Keller added. "I can't wait to hear this story." He settled back on the bed, looked over at her, and nodded. "Start at your convenience."

She laughed. "In that case, once upon a time …"

This concludes Book 27 of Psychic Visions: Endgame.
Read a sneak peek A Mother's Love: Psychic Visions,
Book 28

# A Mother's Love: Psychic Visions (Book #28)

When Eden and her best friend embarked on a 3-day retreat for some much-needed relaxation, she never anticipated the whirlwind romance that would ignite between Debbie and Richard, the leader of the retreat. Nor did she foresee her best friend's sudden personality change and subsequent betrayal, shattering a fifteen-year bond in mere hours.

Even more shocking was the discovery that, before the weekend concluded, Debbie would be found dead under mysterious circumstances.

Detective Eric Kent, a man with keen intuition and a knack for unraveling the unseen, was assigned to the case. While waiting for the autopsy results, he dove in and quickly found himself entangled in a web of questions. Eden's account of events was riddled with emotional pain and confusion, yet something deeper seemed to pulse beneath the surface—something much darker…

This was no ordinary case; it required a perspective that

transcended the obvious, a journey into the unknown where love and danger intertwined.

Please continue reading for a sneak peek…

"**G**OOD RIDDANCE," DEBBIE called out, as Eden stormed from the hotel.

It was the final straw as far as Eden was concerned. She threw her bag into the front of her car, determined to leave the retreat.

She snorted. *Retreat.* A three-day meditation retreat, supposedly *to get you back to normal, to break up the stress in your life, to just take a breather, to find time for yourself.* She and Debbie had both come, with the intention of taking time for that little bit of self-care that they needed, but then something went wrong right off the bat. Somehow Debbie's gaze had landed on the leader of the retreat—somebody who had organized it, somebody who had a decent name in the meditation industry.

And his gaze had fallen on Debbie.

Eden wasn't the jealous type, wasn't the kind to begrudge her friends getting good things in life. However, her bestie was already a little too loose and fancy-free with her affections, as least as far as Eden was concerned. Anyone looking from the outside in might call it jealousy, but it was not. Eden just preferred to actually know the name of the person she was sleeping with, whereas Debbie had a *life is for the living* attitude. Thus, while you were living, you should enjoy everything about it.

Eden turned and took one final look at the hotel and prepped for the two-hour drive back. Her friend stood just inside the front door of the lobby, staring at her. Debbie's expression, almost a mocking look, left Eden unsure of who the hell Debbie had become or how quickly her friend had switched into this other person who Eden didn't recognize.

Eden was about to lift a hand and wave, then thought, *Screw it.* Absolutely no reason to. Besides, Debbie would probably give her the finger in return, so Eden steeled herself and tried to avoid one last glance back.

Without success.

She looked up, and there was her supposed friend, literally giving her the finger. Shaking her head, and mad at herself for looking back against her better judgment, Eden got in her car, started the engine, and pulled away. It had been one of the craziest situations, and she still didn't quite understand how it had happened.

Friday night had been awkward, since Eden was unexpectedly alone, but they were both on their best behavior at that point. Then somehow the next day, it had become all about Debbie and *him.* He still conducted the planned meditations and everything else as scheduled, but Debbie had been right by his side, for every damn moment.

He flaunted Debbie right in front of everybody, and it had been unbelievable, but Eden couldn't do anything about it. At first, it had been fine, whatever—do whatever you want to do. She believed in free will and all. Her friend was apparently just having one of those lovely little moments with the meditation guru, but then Debbie quickly changed. A point came when she no longer appeared to be the Debbie who Eden knew.

Instead of joining Eden for a meal or just laughing and giggling about the relationship in the ladies' room, Debbie had been all in.

"I'm his favorite girl, and I'm going to stay here and to be with him forever."

Eden was surprised, but she really started to worry when Debbie added, "I already quit my job via text, and I gave notice on my lease as well. I'll be out of my apartment by the end of the month."

Eden had stared at Debbie in shock. The end of the month was in four days. "You did what? Debbie, this is way too fast. No, no, no, you can't just up and do that. Think about this before you go jumping into a relationship on a whim."

"I can do anything I want," Debbie declared, with a smirk in Eden's direction. "You're just jealous."

Eden hadn't been jealous. She had been stunned, never having seen her friend make such a snap decision, not liking the way she had gone about it. Eden had been without a clue as to how to make Debbie see the folly of her actions, see things with clear eyes and common sense.

Debbie had been adamant about Eden taking a hike, while Debbie declared she would spend the whole weekend with *him* anyway. Debbie added how their boss had insisted that she come back in for the standard two weeks' notice, or there would be issues.

Eden wasn't sure what those issues were, but they both worked at the same place. Eden worried this would affect her own work relationships.

Debbie was being so ridiculous about the whole thing. In addition to resolving things at work to their boss's satisfaction, Debbie also had to get rid of her stuff in her apartment, pack it all and move it. Debbie needed to take care of these things. Surely she couldn't get it all done in the next four days.

Eden didn't know what to think, she really didn't. But, as she drove away, fuming mad, she wasn't sure she cared anymore.

Fifteen years of a friendship down the tube, all because of some man. A man Debbie had barely just met. Like, what the hell?

Debbie had done this before, but that was minor compared to whatever this was. Usually she would get a boyfriend, and you wouldn't see her for the first month, and everything was *him, him, him, and him.* She had never been a moderate personality type. It was all or nothing, and she dove in headfirst, usually to come right back out again, bawling her eyes out because her most recent Prince Charming had turned out to be a frog not the Mr. Right she was looking for.

When Eden had tried to talk to her friend this time, Debbie had been beyond insulting about the whole damn thing, something that, for Eden, would never fly.

She shook her head, tears in her eyes, as she drove home, wondering what the hell had just happened. She was mad the whole time she drove, but, by the time she got home, she was just sad and more or less disgusted to realize how quickly her friend had morphed into this new personality and had ditched their long-term friendship they had shared up to this time. It was heartbreaking and absolutely devastating.

Eden pulled into her garage, parked, grabbed her gear, then headed into her home. She had bought her small bungalow a couple years ago, when the owners, an older couple, had decided it was time for them to move into a senior facility. The house had to be updated, inside and out, but she was happy to do all that, since she'd gotten it dirt cheap, and, for that, she would be forever grateful to them.

There was just something about having your own space, knowing you didn't ever have to leave or to deal with something unexpected, like a problem with a landlord, roommates, whatever. She walked into the main part of her house, dropped her bag at the foot of the stairs to take whenever she went up, then opened some windows to get some fresh air in—maybe to soothe her own soul too. She felt very much like she'd taken a beating, which was shocking, since she hadn't even realized she was on the docket to get one.

Shaking her head, she went to her kitchen, put on the teakettle, and prepared to wait for the water to boil, stepping out into the backyard, taking several deep calming breaths.

Here was the one place she had put a lot of time into. Most of the inside was done, so she was finishing up the backyard. The old pergola had a couple rotten beams, which she had replaced, then finally refinished the whole thing, as it had weathered badly.

She had gone whole hog on digging up the grass and learning to level off a mixture of sand and gravel to put down patio blocks, something that she had done slowly, over time. Now she had this beautiful pergola patio area, with great big gardens all around that were still pretty new, but they were growing beautifully. In the not-too-distant future, these garden beds would give her an even better oasis out here.

It was the one place of hers that Debbie absolutely loved, and she and Eden used to sit out here all the time, just relaxing. It was exactly what Eden needed for herself on a daily basis. Most people didn't understand the need for a peaceful space, or maybe everyone just didn't need it the way she did.

Every day when she came home from work, it was all

about finding that Zen space, a chance to just sit back and relax. Their work had been even more frustrating and stressful than usual, with a new manager who was making everybody's life miserable. The plan for a weekend away had seemed perfect to Eden. She intended to go alone and to focus on herself, but Debbie decided she would go too. She was a force to be reckoned with at times. The retreat had been for Friday, all day Saturday, and the better part of Sunday, ending around 2:00 p.m. However, the problems with Debbie had literally started on Friday night, when they had attended the initial meet-and-greet event.

Eden found it unbelievable to watch Debbie and *him.* While Eden was all for love at first sight, she was not one for becoming a different person who nobody could even recognize within hours of a relationship beginning. Even now, Eden was completely struck by how disastrous that whole event had been. To add to the insult, Eden had actually paid good money for the weekend that resulted in an early boot in the ass.

Groaning, she returned to the kitchen to pick up her tea, which had now steeped, then wandered around the garden for a little bit, trying to shake off the horrible feeling in her gut. She worried about returning to work tomorrow, knowing everybody would pester her with questions— questions she couldn't even begin to answer. *If Debbie quit, would she show up or not show up for her required notice period?* Eden didn't know.

And, if Debbie didn't show, it would put even more pressure on the rest of them to get the job done, until Debbie was replaced. That was just one more thing Eden was having a hard time coming to terms with about this whole mess. Was Debbie this selfish? Would she care, when she came out of the trance of it all?

Maybe.

How far would she take it?

That's debatable.

Until right now, Eden hadn't realized just how little Debbie would care, how she was completely willing to let everybody else pay the piper, just so she could do whatever in this new relationship.

Eden shook her head. It had all just been too much, too damn fast.

She cried out, "Why? Why so fast?"

"Why not take a moment and savor the growing relationship?"

"Why jump like a crazy woman into this chaotic mess?"

Eden didn't know.

There just didn't seem to be any rhyme or reason to it, and that, as much as anything, scared her. She wanted to pull out her phone to see if Debbie had texted her, but no way she would, not after all that craziness. Debbie was dug in and good.

Honest to God, Eden wouldn't even know what to say to Debbie now anyway. What her friend had done seemed to be such a foreign concept, including the way she had treated Eden. She wasn't entirely sure that she could ever go back to the way they were.

So many things had been said—awful things, nasty things, insulting to the core. How did one move past all that? I mean, it was easy for people to say, *Oh, she wasn't in her right mind,* but, if Debbie wasn't in her right mind, whose mind was she in? Because it was an unbelievable display of meanness. Some of the stuff Debbie had said was downright cruel. Sipping her tea, Eden felt the tears collecting in the corner of her eyes.

When her phone rang, she looked at it and snorted because, of course, it was Debbie. Eden shook her head at that and didn't answer. She was still too hurt, still in far-too-much pain from all Debbie had said. At this point, the call seemed like adding salt to the wound. It was impossible for Eden to even imagine exposing herself to such an irrational and unpredictable person right now.

Debbie phoned one more time a few hours later, but Eden didn't answer. She'd done her laundry and gotten ready for work the next day but hadn't done anything related to this horrid weekend or to her misguided friend. Eden was still very, very upset. She crawled into bed and, after a very difficult time, eventually crashed.

She woke up early in the morning to a phone call. Groggy, she answered it without thinking. "Hello?" A crackle came first on the phone, followed by man who said, "Hello, is this Eden Landon?"

"Yes," she said, shifting into a more upright position, trying to wipe the sleep out of her eyes as she gazed at her phone, not understanding the time, even as it glared right back at her.

"My name is Detective Eric Kent. We have your number from a friend of yours, a Debbie Kingston."

"Yes," Eden replied, her tone hardening. "What about her?"

Then came an odd silence, before he said, "Are you two friends?"

"Well, we were until this weekend," she stated, "but yes." She pinched the bridge of her nose. "Why? What's the matter?"

"I need some information before I can say anything."

She stared down at the phone, not comprehending.

Who was this person, and why was he asking questions about Debbie?

"I need to know what happened this weekend."

"Well, that's nice," she said. "I would like to know what happened too."

After a moment's hesitation, he added, "I need to come speak with you."

She groaned. "It's six o'clock in the morning."

"I know. My apologies."

"You want to tell me what this is about?"

He read off her address over the phone, and she confirmed, "Yes, that's me."

"I'll be there in ten minutes," he noted and hung up.

She stared down at her phone in shock. Would this mess ever be over with? She had to be at work all too soon, without an unexpected visitor to tend with.

She didn't even want to think about work, but she got up and managed a very quick shower, as much to wake herself up as anything, and had just got the coffee on when her doorbell rang.

Glaring, she walked over and opened the door to the detective standing in front of her. He held up his badge, and she looked at it and said, "Eric Kent? Police?"

"Yes. I'm a detective," he clarified, with a nod.

She frowned, not sure what this was all about. "What can I do for you, Detective Kent?"

He motioned at the door. "May I come in?"

She hesitated and then shrugged. "I guess." She let him in and added, "I just made some coffee. Would you like some?"

"I would love a cup," he said quietly.

She tossed a glance back in his direction, not exactly sure

if he was being facetious or not. Such an odd tone filled his voice. He followed her into the kitchen, but his gaze was searching, looking around constantly. "Look. I'm not sure why you're here," she said. "Maybe you could explain that first."

He hesitated, looked over at her, and asked, "How long have you known Deborah?"

She frowned, thinking it over. "Known her? Probably close to twenty years. Been friends with her for fifteen, and that just ended."

He was in the process of lifting his cup, when he looked at her in surprise. "Can you tell me what happened yesterday?"

Eden shrugged. "I mean, for a lot of people, it would probably be very normal," she said, "but, for me, it wasn't normal at all."

He stared at her and just waited.

She sighed. "We went to this retreat to take a break from all the chaos. Work has been extremely stressful lately, and I was feeling overwhelmed and just needed to get away."

"So, this retreat, what was it about?"

"A pretty standard off-grid kind of thing. Not unplugged but limited slots. The leader was a well-known meditation expert, a kind of self-help guru," she said, trying hard to hide her distaste. "I just needed a break."

He remained silent, letting her vent.

"I was going alone. Then Debbie decided to come with me, and now I wish to God she hadn't."

He stared at her, one eyebrow raised.

She shrugged, frowned, and added, "She fell for him … really badly."

"Him, being—"

"The meditation guru and, from one minute to the next, he was her whole life. He was everything to her. Nothing else would be in her world but him—way over the top. I couldn't believe it. She gave notice on her lease and quit her job via text, without proper notice apparently," she shared, raising her hands, "even though she knows we're completely swamped."

"Are you saying you two work together?"

"Yes, different jobs but at the same place," she said, groaning. "Anyway, yesterday, when I heard all that, I was trying to get her to slow down a bit, but she completely went off on me, saying a lot of horrible things. I ended up leaving early."

"Alone?"

"Yes, I left her there, even though we drove together, and it was …" She frowned as she stared down at her coffee. Then she sniffled. She looked up at him in horror because the threat of tears was coming again. "I will not cry. Just … gimme a minute."

He nodded but again his gaze was odd.

Rubbing the tears from her eyes, she continued. "Anyway, she was being so ugly and so mean that I just came home. And I don't really know what happened to make her act that way, but apparently we're no longer friends," she said. "There it is, the whole story. Does that answer your questions?"

He frowned.

She frowned back at him and nodded. "Clearly it doesn't, but that's okay because none of this makes any sense to me either."

"You mean, her relationship with the new man?"

"Yeah, her relationship with *him* for one thing," she said, taking a sip. "Honestly, she's always had a tendency to go crazy over men, especially whenever her relationship is new, but not like this. Usually when she meets a new guy, she gets overly excited about it, but she's never been like this, never turned … mean," she added quietly.

"So, she plays it kind of loose?"

"Always, as long as I have known her. She meets a guy and is immediately smitten, over the moon, but usually, within a short time, like one month to six weeks, she's back to herself, acting as if nothing ever happened, except that her heart has been broken all over again," she explained. "So, I don't know what to tell you, and I really don't know why you care."

When he looked directly at her, something churned in her gut.

"Because she's dead."

Find Book 28 here!

To find out more visit Dale Mayer's website.

https://geni.us/DMSAMothersLove

# Simon Says... Hide: Kate Morgan (Book #1)

**Welcome to a new thriller series from *USA Today* Best-Selling Author Dale Mayer. Set in Vancouver, BC, the team of Detective Kate Morgan and Simon St. Laurant, an unwilling psychic, marries all the elements of Dale's work that you've come to love, plus so much more.**

Detective Kate Morgan, newly promoted to the Vancouver PD Homicide Department, stands for the victims in her world. She was once a victim herself, just as her mother had been a victim, and then her brother—an unsolved missing child's case—was yet another victim. She can't stand those who take advantage of others, and the worst ones are those who prey on the hopes of desperate people to line their own pockets.

So, when she finds a connection between more than a half-dozen cold cases to a current case, where a child's life hangs in the balance, Kate would make a deal with the devil himself to find the culprit and to save the child.

Simon St. Laurant's grandmother had the Sight and had warned him that, once he used it, he could never walk away. Until now, her caution had made it easy to avoid that first step. But, when nightmares of his own past are triggered, Simon can't stand back and watch child after child be abused. Not without offering his help to those chasing the monsters.

Even if it means dealing with the cranky and critical Detective Kate Morgan …

Find Simon Says… Hide here!
To find out more visit Dale Mayer's website.
https://geni.us/DMSSHideUniversal

# Author's Note

Thank you for reading Endgame: Psychic Visions, Book 27!
If you enjoyed the book, please take a moment and leave a
short review.

Dear reader,

I love to hear from readers, and you can contact me at my
website: www.dalemayer.com or at my Facebook author
page. To be informed of new releases and special offers, sign
up for my newsletter or follow me on BookBub. And if you
are interested in joining Dale Mayer's Reader Group, here is
the Facebook sign up page.
http://geni.us/DaleMayerFBGroup

Cheers,
Dale Mayer

# About the Author

Dale Mayer is a *USA Today* best-selling author, best known for her SEALs military romances, her Psychic Visions series, and her Lovely Lethal Garden cozy series. Her contemporary romances are raw and full of passion and emotion (Broken But … Mending, Hathaway House series). Her thrillers will keep you guessing (Kate Morgan, By Death series), and her romantic comedies will keep you giggling (*It's a Dog's Life*, a stand-alone novella; and the Broken Protocols series, starring Charming Marvin, the cat).

Dale honors the stories that come to her—and some of them are crazy, break all the rules and cross multiple genres!

To go with her fiction, she also writes nonfiction in many different fields, with books available on résumé writing, companion gardening, and the US mortgage system. All her books are available in print and ebook format.

## Connect with Dale Mayer Online

*Dale's Website – www.dalemayer.com*
*Twitter – @DaleMayer*
*Facebook Page – geni.us/DaleMayerFBFanPage*
*Facebook Group – geni.us/DaleMayerFBGroup*
*BookBub – geni.us/DaleMayerBookbub*
*Instagram – geni.us/DaleMayerInstagram*
*Goodreads – geni.us/DaleMayerGoodreads*
*Newsletter – geni.us/DaleNews*